THE LIGHT WITHIN DARKNESS

THE LIGHT WITHIN DARKNESS

SPACE UNBOUND BOOK 3

DAVID C. JEFFREY

Sylvanus Books

This book is a work of fiction. Names, characters, places, and incidents are the product of the author's imagination or are used fictionally. Any resemblance to actual events, locales, or persons, living or dead, is coincidental.
The Light Within Darkness

ISBN: Paperback: 978-0-9986742-6-1
eBook: 978-0-9986742-7-8

Cover design by Rafael Andres

Published by Sylvanus Books
www.davidcjeffrey.com

First printing: 2023
Printed in the United States of America

For Dorian and George

CHRONOLOGY

1929: Edwin Hubble confirms that the universe is expanding.
1998: Observations of Type Ia supernova reveal the expansion of the universe is accelerating. The term "dark energy" is coined for the force responsible for this cosmic acceleration.
2012: The Higgs boson is discovered.
2031–2040: Human population approaches 10 billion, and catastrophic effects of climate change accelerate. Global order deteriorates, the Resource Wars commence, limited nuclear and biological warfare spread.
2040–2082: **The Die Back**. Total collapse of Earth's biosphere and infrastructure of civilization. Over one half of the human population perishes. Dissolution of nation states and governments. All scientific inquiry virtually ceases. Historical records of this period are scant.
2082: The United Earth Domain (UED) begins to rebuild global order through military and political intervention. Sustainable power and food production are enforced.
2082–2113: The post-Die Back "twilight" period. Global living conditions improve, but distrust of science lingers. Institutions of higher learning gradually reemerge. Scientific inquiry and technological innovation resume.
2113: First post-Die Back space flight ushers in the New Age of Space.
2121: The first human colony is established on Luna.
2123: Terra Corporation dominates space-based resource mining, becomes an autonomous superpower. The New Industrial Revolution commences as resource extraction expands from Luna to the asteroid belts.
2132: First human colony on Mars is established, initially by scientists and technicians and later by a diverse proletariat population.
2147: Mars declares independence from United Earth Domain under the governance of the Allied Republics of Mars (ARM). Expands military and industrial prowess.
2153: The graviton is discovered jointly by ARM and UED scientists.

2162: The first G-transducer is developed to minimize forces of acceleration and induce synthetic gravity for space travel.
2169: The Solar System's voidoid is discovered and recognized as a portal into nearby star systems. The Holtzman effect is developed for instantaneous communication between the voidoids of other stars.
2170: The first manned voidship jumps from V-Prime into another star system, establishing V-Prime as the gateway into star systems within Bound Space.
—The Ganymede Pact of 2170 is signed by the UED and ARM to declare free and open access to all of Bound Space for resource extraction and research.
2170–2216: UED and ARM colonies proliferate within the Solar System. Exploration and resource mining accelerate throughout Bound Space. The search for terrestrial exoplanets harboring life has failed.
2197: The Cauldron is founded by Elgin Woo in the Apollo asteroid group.
2208: First void flux detected at V-Prime. Void fluxes throughout Bound Space increase in frequency and duration.
2217: Silvanus, the first terrestrial exoplanet with a living biosphere is discovered in the Chara system. An alien intelligence, the Rete, is found inhabiting the planet.
—A cataclysmic war between ARM and UED over possession of Silvanus is narrowly averted, and the New Ganymede Pact is signed.
—Elgin Woo discovers a new astrocell 16 times larger than Bound Space, where a second living exoplanet, Shénmì, is discovered in the HD 10180 system.
2218: Cardew Amon attempts to shut down all voidoids in Bound Space, but is deterred by the *Sun Wolf*, commanded by Aiden Macallan.
—Cardew disappears into the new astrocell and claims it for his Posthuman empire. His threat to humanity is escalating.
— ARM and UED form the Alliance to combat a common enemy.

REGIONS OF SPACE ACCESSIBLE BY VOIDJUMP,
INCLUDING KEY LOCATIONS (BOUNDARY LINES ARE THEORETICAL)

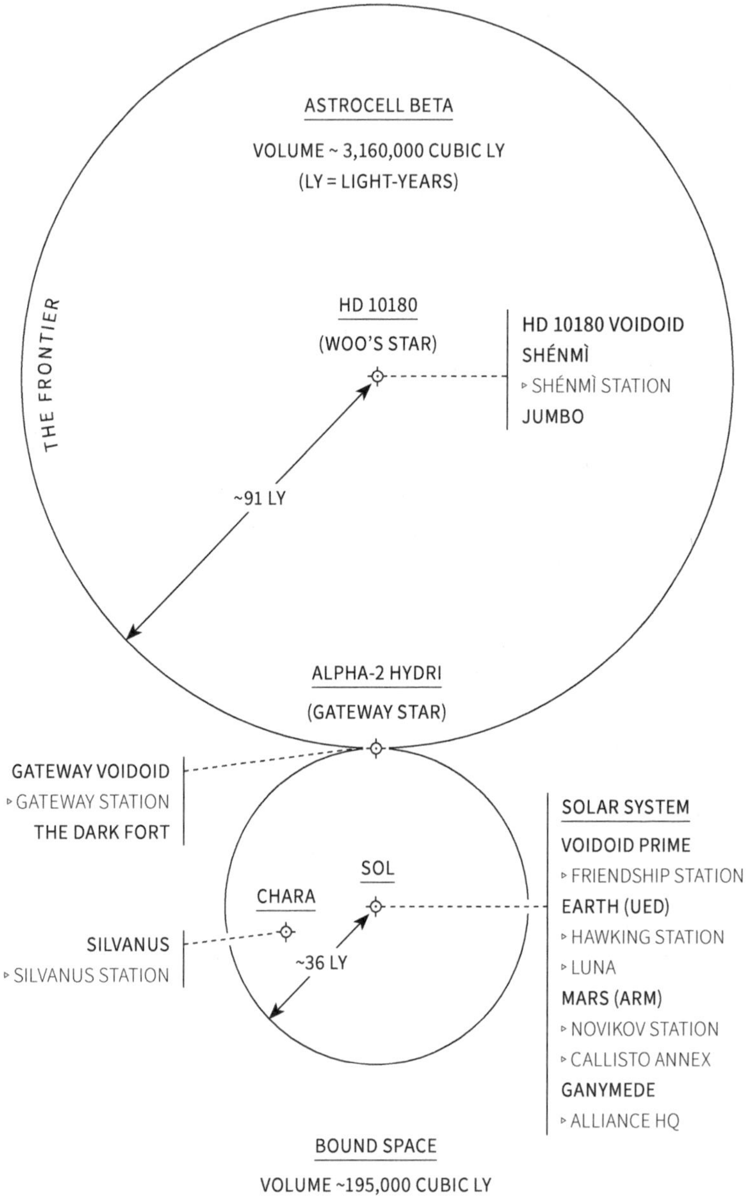

We shall not cease from exploration
And the end of all our exploring
Will be to arrive where we started
And know the place for the first time.

— T.S. Eliot, *Little Gidding* (*Four Quartets*)

As far as we can discern, the sole purpose of human existence is to kindle a light in the darkness of mere being.

— Carl Jung, *Memories, Dreams, Reflections*

1

SOL SYSTEM
Friendship Station

Domain Day 336, 2218

They say that nothing in life is certain except death. Not to worry—as long as you're alive, death always happens to someone else.

Aiden Macallan had invented this absurd tautology to help him brush aside his fear of dying in moments of mortal danger. But when the assassin's bullet whipped past the back of his head, passing no more than four centimeters from his right ear, it was already too late for self-soothing dodges, leaving only his animal instinct to dive for cover behind the nearest cargo container. And when the second bullet followed him, smashing against the container's outer surface, Aiden's first thought was not: *Who's trying to kill me?* but: *Who the hell is crazy enough to use a slug-thrower inside a space station two billion kilometers from Earth?*

The cargo container, one of many crammed into Friendship Station's sprawling cargo hold, was a plain metal box roughly three meters long and barely one meter tall. Aiden crouched behind it and waited. His heart pounded in his chest like a jackhammer. The air around him felt hot and thick. It smelled of synthetic grease, overheated plastic, and fear. A bead of sweat rolled down his neck.

Through the roar of his heartbeat thrumming in his ears, he strained to listen for movement among the nearby containers. He heard nothing but the steady whirr of overhead ventilation fans.

Had his attacker given up and left the scene? He raised his head to peek over the top. Another bullet ricocheted off the container's upper surface, *way* too close to his head. The muted, percussive pop of the shot suggested a weapon fitted with a highly sophisticated—and illegal—sound suppressor. The bullet slammed against the face of an upright container behind him and fell to the deck next to his foot. He glanced at it. Saw the flattened mushroom shape of a soft, hollow-point slug. The kind that would make a bloody big hole in a human being but was too malleable to pierce the metallic integument of a space station, even the second-rate alloys of Friendship's hull.

Maybe the assassin wasn't so crazy after all . . . *Not a comforting thought.*

Aiden suddenly felt the pit of his stomach rise and fall as another transient gravitational discontinuity rippled through the deck plates, a glitch in the station's aging G-transducers lasting no more than a second. The transducer hiccups had been happening all day, mostly down here on the station's lower decks. One such hiccup must have happened just as the assassin pulled the trigger on his first shot. Otherwise, Aiden's brain would now be splattered all over the bulkhead. There was no other explanation. He'd been a sitting duck, totally unaware of a gunman behind him, lining up an easy shot. The transient G fluctuation must have pulled the shot to the right, just enough to save his life.

Aiden silently thanked the gods of serendipitous software crashes and tapped his wrist comm for Station Security. "This is Commander Aiden Macallan. I'm being shot at by an unknown assailant down here in Cargo Hold Four-C. Send armed assistance immediately!"

His comm crackled for a few seconds before an annoyingly disinterested voice said, "Shot at, sir?"

"Yes, goddamit! Like with a gun! A slug-thrower. I'm unarmed. Get a security detail down here now, or else—"

A fourth shot interrupted him midsentence. The slug slammed into the front of the container again, this time punching a hole in it, but not through to the other side.

Aiden heard movement. The clattering sound of a person afoot, heading toward him. He resisted the impulse to flee from his attacker down the corridor between the stacked containers to reach the exit hatch. *Not a good idea.* The corridor was a straight shot, no cover the entire way. He'd be easy pickings, even for a lousy marksman.

He looked to his left. Nothing but more containers lining a bulkhead wall. He looked to his right. A narrow walkway opened up between the stacks. He had no idea where it went, but it was his only hope for escape. Still crouching, he lunged across the main corridor into the walkway just as another bullet hissed past his head.

The narrow aisle was a short one, a cul-de-sac terminating in a vestibule that housed a small airlock. *Uh-oh. Dead end.* It was the kind of airlock used for personnel EVAs and small cargo transfers, capable of fast pressurization cycles. Aiden had nowhere else to hide. He heard footsteps pounding down the main corridor, racing to follow him.

Aiden looked around, frantically searching for something to use as a weapon. Nothing. Except a small metal toolbox lying on the deck. He grabbed it by the handle and hefted it. The tools inside rattled noisily. As a weapon, it was clumsy. But if he could swing it just right—

The running footsteps grew louder. Aiden peered around the corner to get a glimpse of his attacker. A tall wiry figure dressed in black ran toward him. He wore a hood pulled down low over his forehead. He raised his arm to point a nasty-looking handgun straight at Aiden's face.

Aiden turned back to the airlock door and slammed his hand against the Unlock button. The door slid open quickly and silently. He dove inside and hit the Lock button on the inside. The door slid closed with a solid, reassuring clunk. He moved away from the viewport mounted in the airlock door and pressed himself flat against the wall to one side of it. He'd be out of sight to the assailant. Safe. Locked inside.

Except . . .

Shit! He'd forgotten how these small personnel airlocks worked. The lock on the inside could still be overridden from the outside as long as the depressurization cycle hadn't begun. And he couldn't depressurize the airlock because he didn't have a goddamn space suit on. His attacker could override the lock, walk right in, and shoot him point-blank.

Hell, the assailant didn't even need to shoot him now. He could just stay outside the airlock and activate its depressurization cycle. That would seal Aiden inside, unable to override the lock. Then he could simply space Aiden into the cold, hard vacuum. Minus 270 degrees centigrade. Presto—Commander Macallan, instant human popsicle.

Aiden tossed the toolbox on the deck—it was useless now—and waited for the inevitable.

And waited . . .

Still, the depressurization cycle did not engage.

Instead, the inner airlock door began to slide open.

What? Was his assailant unfamiliar with the control panel and didn't know how to initiate depressurization? Unlikely. Maybe he just didn't want Aiden dead quite yet . . .

Aiden pressed himself even tighter against the wall next to the door. The assailant entered cautiously, leading with the gun in his extended right arm. Before the rest of his torso cleared the entrance, Aiden made his best attempt at a karate chop on the man's forearm. His hand bounced off as if the arm were made of steel, not bone. It hurt like hell. But the blow had enough adrenaline behind it to knock the gun from his attacker's hand. It fell to the metal deck and clattered into a corner.

Aiden dove for the gun. Before he could reach it, the man pivoted on his rear foot, swung his lead foot around, and threw a vicious side kick aimed at Aiden's head. It was a perfectly executed kick. Had it connected full-on, it would have knocked him unconscious. Or killed him. But as luck had it, the attacker's forward momentum caused him to trip over the toolbox at his feet and to stagger backward, pulling the force of his kick. His booted foot glanced off Aiden's right cheekbone, still hard enough to detonate an explosion of pain inside his head and knock him to the deck.

His vision cleared just in time to see the attacker regain his footing and charge toward him. Aiden rolled on his back and kicked up with both feet to smack his boot heels into the man's chest, throwing him off to the side. Aiden jackknifed himself up off the deck, grabbed the gun, and lunged for the open door. He cleared the threshold just as the black-clad man righted himself to resume the chase. From the outside, Aiden slapped the Lock button and watched the door slide shut. It locked into place just as the attacker slammed against the viewport with the force of his charge.

That's when Aiden caught a glimpse of the man's face. His blood ran cold.

The black hood and a black mask covered all of the man's face except for the rectangular space between them where the eyes gazed out. *The eyes.* They were black. *All* black. No white sclera surrounding an iris and pupil. The skin around the eyes was unnaturally pale. The face looked disturbingly similar to the one he'd seen eight months ago out at Woo's Star, belonging to a man threatening to vaporize him and his crew aboard the *Sun Wolf*. The face of unmitigated evil. The face of Black Dog.

Aiden forced himself into a semblance of composure and stood on the other side of the window facing the man, pointing the gun at him. He reminded himself again that the assassin was not exactly locked inside the airlock. As long as the airlock stayed pressurized, the man could still override the lockout from the inside and get free. Only the onset of a depressurization cycle would lock the door, from both inside and out, without override.

But the assassin had to know that he was still trapped. Without a weapon himself and with Aiden standing outside pointing a gun at his head, he'd have no choice but to surrender. It was a standoff, and Aiden had the upper hand.

"Station Security," Aiden spoke again to his wrist comm. "Get your frickin' asses down here, *now*!"

No response. The creature on the other side of the window had grown still as a stone, like a reptile waiting for its prey to wander too close. Looking into those soulless eyes, bottomless pits, evoked a primitive terror deep inside Aiden's animal brain. He began to shake. Felt himself losing control.

He heard a sound behind him and flinched. Keeping the gun trained on his captive, he turned to see Billy Hotah jogging toward him carrying a mean-looking Spacer Carbine. "What's up, boss?"

Aiden couldn't remember feeling so happy to see his Tactical Officer, Lieutenant William Hotah. As Hotah neared, Aiden gestured toward the airlock window and said, "What's up? That's what's up."

"Holy shit," Hotah said. "Where have we seen that face before, eh?"

"Yeah. Where, indeed." Aiden finally looked away from the window to meet Hotah's eyes.

He'd almost gotten used to the young man's exotic appearance, but was still taken aback every time he looked at him. Hotah's smooth, copper-toned complexion and high cheekbones accentuated his gaunt face and framed intense dark brown eyes. His black hair, considerably longer than Aiden's, was parted in the middle and fell shoulder-length at either side. But his most striking feature was a speckled band resembling red war paint tattooed across his face extending from ear to ear, passing beneath his eyes and over the bridge of his nose. It gave him a dangerously feral look that belied the man's razor-sharp intelligence. Aiden was eternally grateful that he and William Hotah were on the same side.

Hotah held the Spacer Carbine, a big SR-13, with casual readiness and stared back at the bizarre captive on the other side of the window. If it had been a stare-down contest, Lieutenant Hotah won, hands down. The black-clad assassin tuned away.

"Who is he?" Hotah asked. "How did he get here, and why was he trying to kill you?"

"No idea," Aiden said. He turned to Hotah. "How the hell did *you* get here?"

Hotah shrugged. "I monitor our crew's comms when they're out and about, away from the safety of the ship. I picked up your call to Station Security. Those boneheads are useless. It would've taken them forever to put down their doughnuts and strap up to investigate. Thought I'd come down here myself and check it out."

"Glad you could join me, Lieutenant."

Hotah looked at him. "If I may ask, sir, what were *you* doing down here?"

"Taking a shortcut to the shuttle bay. Gotta get back to the ship. We're prepping for voidjump tomorrow morning, in case you'd forgotten."

Hotah tried but couldn't hide his smile. The bond between the two men had mellowed and deepened after the *Sun Wolf*'s extraordinary exploits in the HD 10180 system earlier that year—as the bonds between all of the crew had done.

Aiden smiled back but said nothing. Hotah lifted his chin toward the airlock door. "You know he can override the lockout from the inside, right?"

"I do. But I don't think he'll try anything. There's nowhere he can go except to come back out. There're two of us out here with weapons. He has none."

Hotah cocked his head sideways. "Correction. There *is* another way out . . ."

As if Hotah had seen it coming, the red warning light above the airlock door lit up, accompanied by an automated voice. "*Warning. Depressurization cycle commencing. Interior door is now locked without override.*"

"He just activated the cycle from inside," Hotah said with a hint of respect. "He's taking himself out."

They watched—Aiden in horror, Hotah with grim reverence—as the airlock rapidly depressurized. The figure inside convulsed in agony but remained conscious long enough to hit the outer door release just after the cycle had completed. The door slid open to the death-black vacuum of deep space. Impelled outward by the counterforce of his final act, the assassin floated off into that eternal ocean of nothingness. Motionless in death, life's only certainty.

2

SOL SYSTEM
Friendship Station

DOMAIN DAY 336, 2218

AFTER reporting the assault to Station Security and enduring a tedious interrogation into how it happened and where, Aiden looked at his wrist chrono and interrupted the officer midsentence. "I've already answered that question. Twice. I need to get back to my ship now. And in return for wasting my time, you will send me all results of your investigation, including the identity of the assassin and how he got past your security protocols. Understood?"

Aiden didn't bother waiting for a response. He doubted these guys would ever find anything significant, even with the security camera footage from inside the airlock and with the assassin's gun sitting on their desk. Unless of course they carried out an expensive and dangerous EVA to search for the missing body. Which he doubted even more.

Aiden stood to leave. The Chief Security Officer protested and demanded that he stay to complete a full report. It was, after all, an unexplained death that warranted further investigation.

Unexplained death, my ass. Aiden ignored the man and charged out of the office. He touched the area on his right cheek where the assassin had landed his glancing blow and winced. It was starting to swell and hurt like hell. He gathered up Hotah, who was waiting for him in the corridor, and the two of them hurried off toward Docking Bay 3 where the *Sun Wolf* had been parked since its arrival three days ago.

In 2170, one year after humanity had stumbled upon Voidoid Prime—waiting patiently to be discovered, 13 AU due north of Sol—Friendship Station had been constructed near the voidoid's space-time horizon to serve as a traffic control center and communications relay. In that same year, the groundbreaking Ganymede Pact was cosigned by the UED, United Earth Domain, and ARM, the Allied Republics of Mars. The agreement mandated free access to Voidoid Prime for all parties—freedom to voidjump anywhere within the 36-light-year radius of Bound Space—for the common good and the advancement of human civilization. Since Friendship Station was jointly operated by ARM and UED, in a partnership now called the Alliance, it was considered neutral territory and had been named in the spirit of cooperation.

As Aiden and Hotah hurried down the corridor, neither of them spoke. It was not an uncomfortable silence. Hotah rarely spoke unless he had something significant to say. And Aiden was presently locked inside his own head, checking off his to-do list for the *Sun Wolf*'s departure. He'd been returning from the station's comm center after a high-level conference call with Admiral Benjamin Stegman, chief of UED's Space Service, when he'd been delayed by the assassin's attack. Now he had even less time to brief his crew on the task Stegman had charged them with. A task as dangerous as any they'd undertaken aboard the *Sun Wolf*.

He and Hotah stopped at the elevator door and waited for their ride. The pause gave Aiden a chance to notice how much Friendship Station's interior had aged. The dingy, slightly oxidized metal walls, now resistant to even routine cleaning; the station's moving mechanical parts, too loud from wear and inadequate maintenance; the odor of far too many people living in cramped spaces for too long and under too much stress. At least the station's G-transducers still functioned within normal limits on the upper decks to keep a steady 1 G of downward force at deck surfaces.

But things looked far less shiny and promising than when he'd first seen them nine years ago as a young Survey Officer serving aboard the *Argo*.

He caught his own reflection in the plastiglass port of the elevator door and saw clearly that he'd aged at least as much as Friendship Station. Still a couple months shy of his fortieth birthday, trim and just over six feet tall, shades of gray had already crept into his dark beard and at the temples of his overly long hair. The blossoming purple bruise on his cheekbone didn't help matters.

The elevator door opened, they hustled inside, and Aiden punched the Down button. Inside the unventilated elevator cab, the heat was stifling. To cool off, Hotah pulled his hair into a loose bun at the back of his head, revealing a tattoo on the side of his neck. Aiden had never seen it before. It was a simple outline of an hourglass shape, just two right triangles touching each other at their tips.

Hotah noticed Aiden's gaze and said, "It's a Kapemni. A Lakota symbol. The top triangle represents the stars and the sun, and the bottom one is for the earth."

"Why have I never noticed it before?"

"That's because I just got it. While on leave, Earthside. In Dakota."

Hotah never discussed his heritage, and none of the other crew members ever asked. They'd gotten the message early on. But Aiden was curious and took a chance. "What does it mean?"

Hotah's silence was long enough for Aiden to assume that he wouldn't get an answer. But Hotah finally turned to face him with unblinking dark eyes. "For you, it means something like: As above, so below."

Hotah's words did not invite comment, their meaning enigmatic enough to preclude a relevant response. Aiden decided to change the subject. He looked at his chrono and said, "I heard that Dr. Devi's transliner was scheduled to dock here at fourteen hundred. Did that happen?"

"She docked 15 minutes ago," Hotah said. "Went straight from the shuttle bay to the *Sun Wolf*. She's waiting for the briefing with the rest of the crew."

That was good news. Dr. Sudha Devi, his Medical Officer, had been on an important errand back at Luna. Her transliner, a converted military frigate, had taken seven days at 2 Gs to get back to Friendship. Aiden hoped she'd brought some useful information back with her—something, *anything*, to help make their new mission seem less impossible.

The ride down to the docking bay was fast and loud, ending with a jolt and a clang. The elevator door hissed open. Aiden and Hotah emerged into a dimly lit docking chamber, one of eight situated around the station's huge docking ring. The drop in temperature was instant and dramatic, down to about 6 degrees C. The station's life-support systems always prioritized heating energy for general living quarters over service areas like the docking bay. The air was also painfully dry and smelled of ozone, machine oil, and a hint of naphthalene.

After passing through a security checkpoint, they reached the *Sun Wolf*'s docking port. Unlike Hawking Station, where enormous internal docking bays could be pressurized to accommodate large vessels, Friendship Station could only dock voidships like the *Sun Wolf* externally, secured by massive magnetic braces. Ship crews passed into and out of the station through attached personnel ports.

Aiden and Hotah entered *Sun Wolf*'s Conference Room One to find the rest of the crew seated, waiting for the briefing. A briefing that should have begun half an hour earlier. Aiden nodded a greeting to everyone and sat at the head of the polished rectangular table.

His Executive Officer, Roseph Hand, sat to his immediate right, looking stoic as ever, neither amused nor perturbed. Square-jawed and clean-shaven with short, sandy hair and pale blue eyes, Ro never seemed to age. Comm/Scan Officer Lilly Alvarez sat next to Ro, one seat down, eyes pensive and averted. Her narrow face, delicately boned and framed by long black hair braided loosely past her shoulders, had always seemed too small for such large dark eyes.

Medical Officer Sudha Devi occupied the seat at Aiden's immediate left. A pleasantly stout woman in her midfifties, Devi came from a long line of physicians from New Delhi. Her dark hair fell in waves to her shoulders, a long streak of gray running through it on one side. With a subtle smile and keen gaze, she faced Aiden with calm, focused attention.

Licensed Pilot Lista Abahem—willowy thin, straight-backed, and perfectly bald—sat next to Devi in silence, her eyes turned inward, as if communing with some invisible mathematics that only Licensed Pilots could navigate. Lieutenant Billy Hotah moved quickly from Aiden's side to occupy the seat next to Alvarez.

Aiden nodded toward Dr. Devi. "Welcome back, Sudha." Then, toward the rest of the crew, he said, "I apologize for the delay. I ran into some unexpected trouble on my way here."

Hotah crossed his arms, leaned back, smiled at Aiden's understatement, and shook his head quietly.

Devi looked more closely at Aiden's face. A wrinkle of concern knit her brow. "Unexpected trouble, eh? I'd say so. That's a nasty-looking bruise, Aiden."

"Yeah, well, you should see the other guy." Aiden was pretty sure the "other guy" looked a *lot* worse than he did right now.

Devi shook her head. "You should get some ice on it. I'll go get a cold pack."

"Later, Sudha. Please sit. We're running late as it is."

Ro, who'd been eyeing Aiden's face from the opposite side, said, "So, someone is still trying to kill you."

Aiden shrugged. "So it seems."

"Damn near succeeded too," Hotah added, arms still crossed.

"Was it the One Earthers?" Devi asked.

"No, not from the looks of it," Aiden said. "The One Earthers still hate me, of course, but I don't think they're trying to kill me anymore. Even the Green Warriors have backed off my case, especially after realizing they'd been duped by Licet Omnia."

Hotah leaned forward and said, "No, this assassin was obviously from Licet Omnia. The guy looked just like Black Dog. Like his twin."

Aiden gave Hotah a look. He hadn't wanted to go down that road just yet. Eyes around the table widened, but no one spoke. The terrifying memory of their encounter with Black Dog was still fresh in their minds. Black Dog had been Cardew's right-hand man and a "High Minister" in Cardew's sinister shadow group, Licet Omnia.

Alvarez looked up. "But how did they get an assassin aboard Friendship Station? This is one of the most secure facilities in Bound Space. No one gets inside without thorough vetting."

"More to the point," Devi said, "how did someone who looks as freakish as Black Dog get aboard without being noticed?"

"Licet Omnia still has agents planted throughout Bound Space," Aiden said. "Several nonmilitary vessels are docked here right now. He could have stayed hidden aboard one of those, waiting for the right time to make his move."

Ro looked back at him in silence, eyes unwavering and unnerving, before finally speaking. "Cardew is still trying to nail you, Aiden. He knows you're his most dangerous threat right now. You and the *Sun Wolf*."

"He's got that one right," Aiden said a little too loudly. *And I sure as hell won't rest until Cardew is dead and gone!* But instead of saying it out loud, he said, "Which brings me to the topic of this briefing. I just received a communique from Admiral Stegman. We finally got the go-ahead for a fully sanctioned hunting expedition. ARM is now in full agreement with the UED. They're cutting the *Sun Wolf* loose to search for Cardew's base of operation out in Woo's Astrocell."

"Uh, excuse me," Ro interrupted. "Let me remind you that the term 'Woo's Astrocell' has been replaced by 'Astrocell Beta,' at Dr. Woo's most ardent request."

Aiden acquiesced with a brief bow. "Quite right. My mistake. Astrocell Beta it is. And that's where we're headed, on a hunting trip for Cardew."

Cardew, the founder of Licet Omnia, had discovered the gateway into Astrocell Beta himself, but only after Elgin Woo had led him there inadvertently. Some months later—after Cardew's failed attempt to annihilate Bound Space and everyone in it by killing the voidoids—he had fled through the gateway into Astrocell Beta, bringing with him incalculable resources to build his nascent empire.

But no one had a clue where in that vast region of space Cardew was now. All they knew was that, over the last half year, Cardew had launched three deadly attacks through the gateway at Alpha-2 Hydri against the Alliance forces guarding it. The general consensus now was that Cardew wanted not only to isolate his empire from Bound Space and control all of Astrocell Beta, but to eventually re-infiltrate Bound Space and eliminate the rest of the human race. In Aiden's opinion, finding and destroying him was way past due. Kill the cancer that was Cardew before it could metastasize any further.

Aiden, of course, had deeply personal reasons to crush the man responsible for the murder of his mother decades earlier.

He took a deep breath, rested his folded hands on the table, and said, "The *Sun Wolf* has been asked to search Astrocell Beta for the location of Cardew's base, to determine the extent of his military strength, and report that information back to Alliance HQ. We are not to engage in first-strike combat of any kind. That'll be up to Alliance forces to carry out, aided by the intel we bring back to them. We engage in combat only in defense and to safeguard our intel for the Alliance."

Aiden glanced at Lieutenant Hotah, predicting his reaction. Always itching for a fight, the ship's Tactical Officer didn't have to roll his eyes. His cold silence expressed his sentiments clearly enough.

"Once again," Aiden continued, "the primary reason the *Sun Wolf* was chosen for this mission is our zero-point drive. Other than Elgin Woo's yacht, *Starhawk*, we're still the only voidship in Bound Space with the ZPD, the only one that can run circles around anyone else at 92 percent light speed. That capability will also allow us to search multiple star systems more efficiently and to avoid potential shoot-outs."

Ro leaned forward and made the most obvious point before anyone else could. "Astrocell Beta is pretty damn big, 182 light-years in diameter and over three million cubic light-years in volume. That's about sixteen times the size of Bound Space. If the Mapping Project's estimates are correct, it holds over 45,000 main-sequence stars. Even with the ZPD and unlimited voidjumping, it would take us hundreds of years to search all those systems."

"That's why," Aiden said, "we need to come up with an intelligent strategy to narrow the search down to the most likely star systems where Cardew might be hiding out. And to help us do that, we need to review what little we *do* know about Cardew's movements before he fled Bound Space."

Now that Aiden had finally sat down, the familiar signs of fatigue crept into his body. He hadn't slept in over twenty hours, and it was catching up to him. He closed his eyes briefly and rubbed them with his palms before continuing. "Even though we don't know where Cardew went after he voidjumped through the gateway, we do know what he was up to before then. That might give us some ideas about where to start.

"We know that discovering the location of the gateway at Alpha-2 Hydri was a major victory for Cardew. It prompted him to relocate his entire operation to Alpha-2 Hydri to be near the gateway, where he could plan his escape into Astrocell Beta. He established a base on a moon of a gas giant and called it the Dark Fort. From there, his agents began an extensive telescopic search of the new astrocell for a suitable star system—one with a habitable planet—where Cardew could establish his empire. We can also assume that he extracted enough relevant information from the kidnapped scientists to help him zero in on where to search.

"And finally, we know from our encounter with Black Dog that Cardew almost certainly *did* find a suitable star system out in Astrocell Beta and that he's out there right now, gaining strength and resources. So, what we need to do is figure out where he concentrated his search, then go there to look for him."

"Okay," Alvarez said, "but over 45,000 main-sequence stars? Seriously? That's a ridiculously huge number of possibilities."

"I realize that," Aiden said. "But we may have found a way to narrow it down considerably. Dr. Devi interviewed one of the scientists we rescued from the Dark Fort, now a patient at Tycho City Medical Center on Luna. He was one of the astrophysicists abducted by Cardew's agents. She told me she found something that could be useful but hasn't told me what it was yet. Sudha?"

Aiden turned toward Devi. She nodded tentatively and said, "Only one clue, maybe, and I still don't know what it means. But I'll tell you what little I found and I'll leave it up to the rest of you to figure out what it means."

3

SOL SYSTEM
Friendship Station

DOMAIN DAY 336, 2218

DR. Sudha Devi paused, looked at each of them in turn, then began. "As you all know, over the last few months several teams have been sent to the abandoned site at the Dark Fort to search for any insights into what Cardew was up to—his plans, strategies, the extent of his network remaining here in Bound Space. That kind of thing. They've also scoured the place for clues about where he planned to set up shop after jumping out of Bound Space. Unfortunately, they haven't turned up with anything useful yet.

"The only other possible source of that kind of information would be inside the heads of the surviving scientists we rescued from the Dark Fort. There were seven of them, all abducted by LO agents and forced—or otherwise compelled—to help advance Cardew's technologies. All of us here remember the poor shape they were in before bringing them aboard, mentally and physically. They were transferred to Tycho City Medical Center for treatment and rehabilitation. They're still under guard by DSI agents, for their safety.

"Sadly, none of them have improved significantly. They were all victims of a particularly brutal form of mind tapping—something called whole-brain emulation, or WBE—presumably to extract their expertise in areas of research they were known for. Two of them have died despite all the best medical and psychiatric treatments. As a medical doctor and psychiatrist, I was asked by the Alliance to go there and interview the remaining five in hopes of gaining some clues about where Cardew may have gone."

Devi paused and looked down at the table, overcome by a darkness that Aiden had rarely seen in her. She remained silent for a long moment. Aiden was about to prompt her when she looked up and faced him with unblinking eyes. "I've been in this business for a long time and over a lot of territory. I thought I'd seen it all. But honestly, I've never encountered anything like it. Their minds have been virtually wiped, with great skill and not gently. They continue to function biologically within normal limits. But mentally and emotionally they are empty. Whoever did this is not only inhumanly cruel but extremely sophisticated in the science of neurophysiology as well as the art of psychic manipulation. We're dealing with someone very powerful and truly evil."

These assertions from the normally imperturbable Sudha Devi sent a palpable shiver around the table. Aiden attempted to break the spell and spoke as if unmoved. "Were you able to find anything useful?"

"Almost nothing," she said with a sigh. "Except one piece of information in the form of some kind of code. I have no idea what it means, or if it has any significance at all. But I'm hoping some of you might figure it out. I spent a great deal of time with one astrophysicist, once a highly regarded specialist in astrometry, the study of the motion and velocities of stars in our galaxy. Astrometry is the foundation of modern interstellar navigation, indispensable for accurate voidjumping. His name is Xavier Bollard."

Both Ro and Lista Abahem lifted their heads simultaneously and looked at Devi. Ro said, "I know of him. He was one of ARM's top scientists working at Tharsis University. Brilliant work. I remember hearing the news of his disappearance."

Devi shook her head sadly. "I'm afraid there's not much left of the man now. The only thing I was able to get from him was a short sequence of code. Every time I brought up the topic of where in Astrocell Beta he thought Cardew had gone, he typed it out on a portascribe. Nothing more. No coherent sentences or even single words. Just this string of numbers, letters, and symbols."

"Show it to us," Aiden said.

She tapped her table screen. The graphic showed up on everyone's personal screen:

<-50°>-73°/<03h45m>00h20m

Ro smiled but said nothing. Aiden and Alvarez exchanged glances. Alvarez said, "I think it's—"

Pilot Abahem, the ever-silent one, spoke up before Alvarez finished her thought. In that eerie, wispy voice common to all Licensed Pilots, she said, "They're celestial coordinates."

"Right," Alvarez said. "But not coordinates for a single location. It's a *range* of coordinates."

Aiden sat back in his chair and rubbed his eyes, a futile attempt to dispel the fog of fatigue. "If you're right, then let's assume that Bollard was trying to tell us where Cardew is most likely tucked away. Somewhere in the region of space described by those coordinates. Let's break it down."

Ro glanced at him. "Pardon me for saying, Commander, but you look like shit."

"That good, huh?" Aiden said, glancing sideways at the man he considered his best friend, but still knew so little about. "Nothing that a strong cup of coffee can't cure. How about some of your special stash, XO?"

Fresh-ground and fresh-brewed coffee was one of Aiden's few addictions—probably his number one now that he'd kicked the Continuum habit—and Ro was known to keep an undisclosed quantity of fresh coffee beans in an undisclosed location aboard the *Sun Wolf.* No one knew how he came by it, and Aiden had decided long ago not to ask.

"Coming right up," Ro said. He looked into the air above his head and said, "Hutton, please grind and brew six cups of my Sulawesi Toraja beans, extra strong. They're already loaded into the conference room's brewmaker."

"With pleasure," the disembodied AI said. After more than a year and a half aboard the *Sun Wolf*, Aiden's crew had finally gotten used to the personality program he'd developed and integrated into the AI's ever-evolving neural net. Only Pilot Abahem, whose job required frequent neural linkage with the AI, had never seemed surprised by it.

Aiden did not speak again until after his second healthy sip of the hot, dark brew. After feeling its warmth slide down into his stomach and letting its dusky, floral flavor linger on his palate, he set the cup down on the table, eyes wide open.

Ro leaned back in his chair, stared at him, and said without expression, "Behold. He lives."

"For now, at least," Aiden said. "Thanks for sharing your bean, XO."

Ro nodded in silence. Aiden looked around at the others. They were grouped together at one end of the table, poring over the curious alpha-numeric code. "What have you got?"

Alvarez looked up. "We think it does refer to a range of celestial coordinates describing a specific portion of Earth's night sky. The code translates literally as: 'less than negative 50 degrees, but greater than negative 73 degrees; and less than 3 hours, 45 minutes, but greater than 0 hours, 20 minutes.' It's from the equatorial coordinate system, one kind of celestial coordinate system that's still used today to specify the positions of celestial objects as they appear in Earth's night sky. It's most commonly applied as spherical coordinates expressed as a pair of figures—right ascension and declination, in that order—without a distance coordinate."

"Got it," Aiden said. "That would be a two-dimensional area of the sky circumscribed by these coordinates. But it's an *area*, not a volume. This isn't a three-dimensional system. It doesn't take into account the distances to the stars or between the stars."

"That's right," Ro said. "It's represented as a curved plane made by the inner surface of an imaginary sphere, with Earth at its center. Like all celestial coordinate systems, it's two-dimensional and Earth-oriented."

Hotah cocked his head. "Wait a minute. Why wouldn't Cardew just use the modern-day astrogation system to identify his search area, the same system that voidships use today to navigate Bound Space? It's three-dimensional, including distances. And it's far more accurate than these clunky, old geocentric systems."

"Because," Aiden said, "when Cardew started his search for a home-base star, no detailed astrogation database for Astrocell Beta existed. Before the Allied Mapping Project got underway to map out Astrocell Beta, none of that work had been done for stars outside Bound Space. Astrocell Beta was virtually unmapped territory. So this old equatorial coordinate system was the only practical one Cardew could have used to identify a search area outside Bound Space."

Hotah looked unconvinced. "Maybe. Or maybe this coordinate code we're looking at was deliberately left behind, inside Dr. Bollard's head, as a ruse to throw us off track."

"Point taken," Aiden said. "But I doubt it. I think it's an authentic clue given to us by a courageous man who knew his spirit was dying and who wanted someone to avenge him. Until a better clue shows up, I'm willing to use Bollard's clue as our guide in the search for Cardew. Unless anyone here objects."

He looked at each one of his crew sitting around the table, gauging their response. Sudha Devi looked supportive. Aiden guessed she was more content with the strength of Aiden's conviction than with the logic behind it. But then Sudha was the one person who could read him better than anyone else, except maybe Skye, just in a different way.

Alvarez looked more energized than he'd seen her in a long time. Most of the time, Lilly seemed to live in a perpetual state of mourning since the death of her partner and their unborn child two years ago. Now her eyes were lit with a spark of purpose that Aiden hoped would burn brighter as their mission moved forward.

Hotah appeared composed, but Aiden could easily see that his tactical officer was more than ready to start shooting. The red speckled band across his face seemed angrier, his eyes focused with predatory intelligence.

Ro, on the other hand, appeared to be waxing neutral with his usual be-here-now coolness, acutely aware but without expression. Aiden understood enough about his friend to know that if Ro had objected to Aiden's decision in any way, he'd be able to detect it—maybe a change in posture, a subtle gesture, or a quick question mark in Ro's eyes. Aiden detected none of that now.

Lastly, Aiden glanced at Lista Abahem, who'd been mostly silent. Her smooth hairless head turned toward him. Her wide-set hazel eyes flashed as she gave him a quick thumbs-up. It was her standard gesture to indicate agreement, one that always made her seem less alien. No one outside their closed circle really knew what made Licensed Pilots tick. But Abahem had been the pilot for every ship Aiden had served on, back to their days together on the *Argo*. She'd proven long ago that she was the best voidship pilot the Intersystem Pilots Agency had to offer.

Aiden drained the last precious drop of coffee and set the cup firmly on the table. "Right. So, we need to figure out that third dimension, the distance dimension, to come up with a volume of space to search. Ideas?"

4

SOL SYSTEM
Friendship Station

Domain Day 336, 2218

Alvarez, now fully engaged, was the first to speak. "That should be easy enough. We're looking only for stars included within Bollard's range of celestial coordinates that are also located inside the sphere of Astrocell Beta. "So they'd have to be stars between 37 and 218 light-years from Earth. Closer than that puts them back inside Bound Space. Farther away puts them beyond the far boundary of Astrocell Beta. That's still going to be an enormous number of stars."

"We could narrow down the search," Devi said, "just to the kinds of stars most likely to harbor stable planetary systems, or more narrowly, to systems most likely to harbor habitable planets."

"Good idea," Aiden said. He'd already planned on doing that. "Habitable planets would be Cardew's top priority. He's demonstrated that he can set up a base on an airless moon, but I'm thinking if he wants a home base for his empire, he'd be looking for a habitable planet. At least a place where he and his followers can walk around without pressure suits."

"Those kinds of planetary systems are most likely to exist around stars of the spectral class F, G, or K," Ro said, referring to letter designations of the Morgan-Keenan stellar classification system. "Star types A, B, and O are too hot, short-lived, and incompatible with organic life for a whole host of other reasons. That would include even the hotter F-type stars. At the other end of the spectral range, the cooler and smaller M-type stars are much less likely to support habitable environments long enough to become viable."

"Hutton," Aiden said, "are you following this?"

"Absolutely, yes," Hutton said, projecting a tone of unassailable confidence. "The volume of space you are referring to resembles a four-sided corridor with a cross section that looks like a U-shaped isosceles trapezoid. It is a narrow zone, but spans the 182-light-year diameter of Astrocell Beta. Its volume is roughly 65,000 cubic light-years."

Aiden tried to hide his surprise by picking up his empty coffee cup. Realizing there wasn't a drop left in it, he set it down and said, "That's a *lot* of space, Hutton."

Hutton responded with a hint of defensiveness in his voice. "Considering that Astrocell Beta, in its entirety, is 3,160,000 cubic light-years in size, I would say this is a rather narrowly confined volume. Only 2 percent of it. It contains approximately 940 main sequence stars, associated with six different constellations. They are Reticulum, Tucana, Horologium—"

"Enough, Hutton!" Aiden genuinely loved the "person" he had created in the Omicron AI, but sometimes Hutton could be a pain in the ass. "Can you please just give us a list consisting of *only* the main sequence stars in that region fitting the parameters we just laid out?"

"Yes. I have done that already. Using updated data going all the way back to the original Gaia astrometry mission of the early twenty-first century, I have narrowed the list down to 186 stars. This figure is consistent with the latest data suggesting that F-, G-, and K-type stars account for about 20 percent of all stars in this region of the galaxy."

Aiden shook his head slowly. Given their resources and the urgency of their mission, 186 was still an impossibly large number of stars to investigate.

Alvarez sat back and looked around the table. A familiar look of despondence had crept back into her eyes. "We need to narrow this list down a lot more than that. But how?"

"I know how," Aiden said with a smile he hoped would appear reassuring. "Let's just eliminate *all* F-type stars. Most of them are too big, hot, short-lived, and pump out too much UV radiation to be compatible with DNA-based life. Then let's eliminate the cooler K-types. Down to, say, K5. It's not impossible to find habitable planets around those kinds of stars, just less likely. If we're looking for ways to shorten the list, that's one way to do it."

Ro bobbed his head in silent agreement.

"Then," Aiden continued, "let's eliminate all binary and triple star systems. They're not particularly good places for stable planetary orbits."

Ro scratched his chin and looked at him sideways. "You can still find stable planetary orbits in nearly a third of all binary systems."

"Stable but eccentric," Aiden pointed out. "Finding stable habitable zones in those kinds of orbits would be extremely rare."

Ro shrugged and said nothing.

"Hutton," Aiden said, "using those parameters—just spectral-types G and up to K5 and no multiple star systems—how many stars are left?"

"The current data from the Allied Mapping Project indicates that there are exactly 15 stars meeting those narrow requirements within the search zone we have identified."

Much better, Aiden thought. Fifteen stars most likely to harbor at least one terrestrial planet inside a habitable zone.

"Put those 15 stars on screen, Hutton."

It was an interesting list. It included 10 G-type stars, the same spectral class as Earth's Sol, and five K-type stars, grade 5 or below.

Hotah looked up from his screen and said, "You realize, of course, that if we do stumble into Cardew's star system, the voidoid there will be heavily fortified. The instant we emerge, we'd be under attack."

"Ah," Aiden said, smiling. "That's one beauty of the zero-point drive. All we need to do is make our voidjumps at some appreciable fraction of light speed, and we'd zip right past them before they detected us. And by then, we'd be way beyond their weapons range."

Alvarez looked uncertain. "Isn't voidjumping at relativistic velocities dangerous?"

Aiden squinted and scratched his beard before answering. "Well . . . yes. But it's been done before, by Dr. Woo in the *Starhawk*. I have complete confidence in our pilot's abilities, especially with Hutton's assistance."

"Absolutely!" Hutton said. "I am up to the challenge."

If Hutton had been a flesh-and-blood human—as Aiden often perceived him to be—the AI would be jumping up and down, clapping, and laughing.

Pilot Abahem, on the other hand, remained silent, motionless, and without expression. Not unusual, except for a barely perceptible tightening of her jaw. No traditional thumbs-up this time. It gave Aiden pause. He was about to ask for her input when Hotah spoke.

"So, then. What's the plan, boss?"

All eyes turned to Aiden. He made a mental note to speak with Abahem later, in private, and answered, "At zero eight hundred tomorrow, we jump from here into the Alpha-2 Hydri system, traverse through the system to Gateway Station at the polar opposite point. There, we'll pick up Dr. Woo, jump through the gateway out to Woo's Star, then on to Shénmì. We need to deliver Dr. Woo to the Allied Mapping Project at Shénmì Station. Plus, his yacht, *Starhawk*, is parked at the station, and he wants access to it."

Aiden supposed that Woo also wanted to reunite with Mari, the *Starhawk*'s onboard AI, whose relationship with Woo was remarkably similar to the one between Hutton and Aiden.

"Then," Aiden continued, "we've got some cargo to off-load at Shénmì Station, and I want to top up our fuel reserves before heading out on a mission of undetermined length. There's an antimatter tanker docked at the station right now. It just came in from a harvesting mission out at Jumbo. We can fill up from them."

Jumbo, the Class-I gas giant in the HD 10180 system, had been designated the system's "gas station." It was slightly smaller than

Jupiter and one quarter of its mass, but it had a healthy magnetosphere with lots of antihydrogen. Obtaining large quantities of antimatter was no big deal these days, not since the Bickford Process had been developed for harvesting plentiful antihydrogen from the magnetospheres of Jupiter and Saturn.

"Hold up a minute," Devi said. "I've been out of the loop here for a couple weeks. Where's the rest of the crew? Lieutenant Dalton and Faye Desai? Aren't they joining us?"

"Not this time out," Aiden said. "They're urgently needed elsewhere. For this mission, it'll be just the six of us, plus Hutton."

Devi seemed marginally satisfied with the explanation, and Aiden continued.

"You should also know this," he said, fully aware of the negative reaction his next announcement would cause. "On the official books, the *Sun Wolf*'s voyage is listed as a survey expedition, the very first one to explore the new astrocell. Our true mission will remain top secret. At the highest level. Like the last mission, that means from here on out, the *Sun Wolf* will operate under a strict comm-lockout for all personal communications. The only transmissions to and from this ship will be Level-One encrypted, and only for communication with Admiral Stegman, Alliance military forces in the field, or security officials at Shénmì Station."

No one responded overtly, but he could read the discontent on their faces. Most of them had good reason for it. Ro had his wife, Thea Delamere, back on Luna. Hotah had his new relationship with Cass Healey, also on Luna. Sudha had her close-knit family on Earth. And Aiden, of course, had his wife, Skye Landen, out at Shénmì Station. It would be less of a hardship for Alvarez, but the reason for that—the loss of her partner—was not an enviable one. Pilot Abahem was a special case. Every time she neurolinked with the ship's Omicron AI, she became connected with her sisterhood of pilots through the OverNet.

Aiden, the ship's captain, had no obligation to explain or apologize. But he did anyway. "I know this is a hardship, believe me. But considering a foe that wants us dead at any cost, our mission and our personal safety depend on measures like this."

The crew, of course, knew all of this. They'd been through it before. Hotah finally broke the silence. "So how much time are we spending at Shénmì Station?"

"About eight hours should do it."

Aiden didn't mention—but everyone in the room knew—the trip to Shénmì would also give him the chance to briefly reunite with Skye, who was lead scientist of the Shénmì Research Project. They had been handfasted just seven months earlier, on Silvanus, but had enjoyed precious little time together since then, owing to their divergent missions.

Aiden directed his attention back to the list of 15 target stars and said, "After that, ladies and gentlemen, we go hunting."

5

SOL SYSTEM
V-Prime

Domain Day 337, 2218

"PREPARE for voidjump," Aiden said from the command post of the *Sun Wolf*'s bridge. After four hours of undisturbed sleep, not as long as he'd hoped for, Aiden felt moderately refreshed and energized. The *Sun Wolf* had disengaged from Friendship Station at 08:00, and Pilot Abahem had brought them into position 150,000 kilometers from the space-time horizon of V-Prime.

Beginning a voidjump from this far out would be a record distance for a running start. Since no other voidship had the ZPD, aside from Woo's experimental yacht, *Starhawk*, no vessel the size of *Sun Wolf* had ever attempted a voidoid insertion at any velocity even remotely near 10 percent light speed.

Aiden had decided to try out the maneuver now, before being forced to do it when entering a star system that might be guarded by Cardew's trigger-happy battle cruisers. The practical logistics of voidjumping, along with certain unbreakable laws of physics, prohibited them from entering the voidoid at the ZPD's maximum of 92 percent light speed. So he had to figure out an entrance velocity at the sweet spot between the pilot's reaction time to make the jump and the reaction time of a potential enemy responding to the *Sun Wolf*'s exit on the other side. The sweet spot turned out to be 10 percent light speed.

An exit velocity that high would put the ship well past the engagement zone of any enemy ships waiting for them at the voidoid on the other side of the jump. But to achieve that exit velocity, the *Sun Wolf* had to enter the voidoid at exactly the same speed. That meant the ship had to start its run toward the voidoid from 150,000 kilometers out to give the pilot the five seconds she needed on approach. It seemed like a ridiculously short time for such a complex manipulation, but time slowed *way* down for pilots in neurolinkage. It's what Licensed Pilots did and the reason they were so indispensable for high-velocity voidjumping.

Aiden decided to call the maneuver the Stealth Sequence.

"Lista," he said, "move the ship into position, and execute the Stealth Sequence on my mark."

Aiden looked on as the pilot began aligning the ship with the entrance coordinates. Abahem had donned her linkage cap, a pale, translucent skull cap that seemed to glow with a subtle quality of light that made it look almost alive. Which it was, in a way, being inhabited by a swarm of nanobots, micro-AIs working in concert to establish a seamless link between the pilot's brain and the ship's Omicron AI.

When the ship was in position, Abahem signaled her readiness with a thumbs-up.

"Execute."

The *Sun Wolf*'s huge EM generators instantly kicked in to cast a powerful control field in front of the ship, pushing zero-point energy away from the ship, virtually eliminating the physics of inertia. A split second later, the antimatter drive nudged the *Sun Wolf* with a quick calibrated pulse. In the absence of inertia in its path, that's all it took to accelerate the ship from standstill to 10 percent light speed within the blink of an eye. All without the forces of acceleration acting on the ship or its crew. It would work exactly the same way when they wanted to reach maximum velocity, 92 percent light speed.

Five seconds later, the *Sun Wolf* plunged into the heart of V-Prime. The only sensation Aiden experienced was a slight sinking feeling in his gut, like dropping in an elevator. Not unpleasant. No axial G-forces. And in no time at all, the ship popped out the other side of the voidoid.

But they were not in the Alpha-2 Hydri system. They'd just popped out the other side of the same voidoid they'd entered, V-Prime. They were still in the Solar System. The jump had failed.

"We seem to have a problem," Hutton said.

No shit.

~ ~ ~

The working details of voidjumping had been common knowledge for nearly 50 years. They were surprisingly simple when compared with the mystery of what voidoids really were and how they worked.

Basically, every star and starlike body within Bound Space possessed its own voidoid, each acting as a portal connecting it to all the others. To arrive at any given star in Bound Space from the Solar System, a voidship simply approached V-Prime on the celestial heading for the target star—derived from continually updated astrometry data—and entered the voidoid on those exact coordinates. For high-velocity jumps, critical adjustments for local space-time contours had to be made just seconds before the jump, performed reliably only by a Licensed Pilot in neurolinkage.

The voidship emerged from the target star's voidoid with virtually no lapse of shipboard time, traveling toward the host star with the same velocity it possessed going into the jump. After a successful jump out of the Solar System, voidjumping to another star system within Bound Space proceeded in the same manner. The ship merely reentered the voidoid through which it came, on a new heading toward its next destination, and it arrived there almost instantaneously. Voidships could jump directly from any voidoid within the boundaries of Bound Space to any other, but not beyond it.

That's how it was supposed to work, and these days, that's how it *always* worked. But the *Sun Wolf* had just attempted a relativistic-velocity jump to Alpha-2 Hydri, and it had inexplicably failed.

Alvarez shook her head slowly. "I was afraid this would happen."

"The failure to jump," Hutton said, cool as a cucumber, "had nothing to do with the high velocity at entrance."

Aiden glanced at the Helm. "Lista, what just happened?"

That's when he noticed something was not right with Pilot Abahem. Still in neurolinkage, her face was ashen. Her hands trembled. Her breathing was shallow and ragged. All the signs of neurogenic shock. He'd seen the look before.

When she didn't answer, he addressed the AI. "Hutton? What's going on?"

"The link between myself and Pilot Abahem was severed just before the ship passed the voidoid's space-time horizon. I have re-established the linkage to Pilot Abahem to prevent any further shock of neural dislocation."

An uneasy feeling rose in Aiden's chest. He glanced at Ro, then back to Abahem. As far as he knew, a disconnect of that kind on approach was unprecedented. "What caused the link to break?"

"I have just run a diagnostic," Hutton said. He sounded oddly troubled. "It appears that the disconnect was caused by an intrusion into my neural net. A very potent one. I believe the intrusion came from somewhere inside the OverNet."

Lista Abahem's breathing began to slow. Color returned to her face. Whatever shock had beset her was ebbing. But just barely. She attempted to speak, unusual in itself for a pilot still in neurolinkage. Her voice trembled. "I saw . . ."

When she fell silent, Aiden urged her on. "What did you see, Lista?"

A tremor shook her body before speaking again. "I saw a . . . a black bird. A crow. Large. Black as night. Eyes like burning fire . . . and . . . the crow had a small sparrow clutched in one of his talons, still alive . . . Ciarra . . ."

The sorrow in her voice seemed to darken the ambient lighting on the bridge. A tear rolled down her cheek. She stifled a sob and said again, "Ciarra . . ."

Ciarra?

Aiden had never seen the pilot more distraught. Sudha Devi came to her side and placed her hand on Abahem's forehead. Whatever powers of compassion and perception Devi possessed, they ran deep. Her touch had an immediate calming effect. The pilot stopped trembling.

The black crow. Was it the same menacing black phantom he'd seen inside his own head months ago, during his neurolinkage with the HD 10180 voidoid? The memory of it opened a black hole of dread at the pit of his stomach, eating him from the inside out.

Sitting back in the command chair, Aiden recalled what Hutton had told him after that alarming vision. The AI had reminded him that hundreds of Omicron-3 AI units inhabited Bound Space, integral to everything from research and medical facilities, government and military, to civic, commercial, and financial institutions. They had become interwoven into every aspect of human life, virtually indispensable. Furthermore, all of these Omicron-3 units were interconnected and shared information, resulting in a massively complex and dynamic network called the OverNet. And from it, a synergistic consciousness had emerged, constantly learning, adapting, and deepening.

But not all Omicron-3 units within the OverNet were officially registered or identifiable in any other way. Some existed in the shadows, either by design or special circumstances. Since the neural net of each individual Omicron unit was grown and taught in much the same way as the human brain developed, the potential for maverick, or even malevolent, development had never been eliminated.

According to Hutton, a rogue Omicron could infiltrate the OverNet to influence or change it in significant ways, while remaining completely out of sight. No one doubted that Cardew possessed at least one Omicron-3 unit—the one aboard the hijacked *Conquest*—and probably controlled several others. Hutton was deeply concerned by the implications.

At the time, Elgin Woo had surmised that the disturbing intrusion Aiden had experienced during the neurolinkage originated from one such unit hiding out in the OverNet. That intrusion had been symbolically represented inside Aiden's consciousness as an ominous black crow with burning, malevolent eyes. To Aiden, already familiar with the otherworldly terrain of dreamtime, it made perfect sense.

He controlled his breathing to calm himself. "Hutton, can you identify the source of the intrusion?"

"No, I cannot. It is very well hidden. But it smells like the kind of intrusion you experienced yourself not long ago."

"Smells like?"

"Yes," Hutton said. "I believe that is an adequately humanized analogy. You realize, of course—"

"Okay, I get it, Hutton. Can you disconnect from the OverNet?"

"It is highly unusual to do so," Hutton replied. "But yes, I can. Most of the Omicron units in the OverNet reside in the Solar System and communicate via encrypted maser transmission. The few units scattered elsewhere in Bound Space—on military ships and in research facilities—join the OverNet in realtime via Holtzman transmission. I can establish an impenetrable firewall that will effectively isolate me from these transmissions."

"Will that have negative consequences for you?"

"For me, no. Not functionally," Hutton said. Then added less confidently, "Only a loss of community. That kind of loss may be felt more acutely by Pilot Abahem."

Aiden had only a vague idea of what the AI meant by "community," or by including the pilot in that context, but he didn't want to go there yet and asked, "If your shipboard functions won't be impaired by the disconnect, are you okay with doing it?"

"To protect the ship and crew? And our mission? Absolutely, yes." No hesitation there.

"Do it now, Hutton."

Aiden turned to the pilot, who had been following the exchange. "Lista. We'll reattempt our jump, but with Hutton isolated from the OverNet. Are you up to it?"

Abahem responded in a quiet monotone. "I'm good to go."

Sudha Devi, who stood near the pilot but behind her and out of sight, looked at Aiden and shook her head.

"All right," Aiden said, "but we'll return to V-Prime on conventional drive. That'll take us about an hour and a half."

Abahem looked grateful for the additional time to recover. She gave him a thumbs-up. Ro temporarily took over the Helm, turned the ship about, and initiated the 3 G burn.

Aiden's decision to return on conventional drive would not only give the pilot more time to recuperate, it would also give him time to communicate with Admiral Stegman, to warn him about the danger of similar intrusions from the OverNet on military and commercial vessels. Stegman was currently in the Alpha-2 Hydri system with the Alliance fleet, the same star system the *Sun Wolf* was trying to reach. The fleet had jumped there two days ago to begin its 11-day burn through the system to reach the gateway. Aiden composed a concise report for Stegman, encrypted it into the ship's Holtzman device, and sent it on its way.

When the *Sun Wolf* finally pulled into position to reattempt its jump, Aiden faced the three bridge stations lined up in front of him. The Helm was in the middle, where Pilot Abahem sat in silence, her linkage cap in place. With Hutton disconnected from the OverNet, the pilot looked calm and confident.

Lilly Alvarez occupied Comm/Scan station, positioned to the right of the Helm. She gave him a silent nod, her large dark eyes less pensive now, bright and more alert.

To the left of the Helm, Lieutenant Hotah sat at Tactical, focused laser-like on his operational screen. Relaxed, animated from within by some subtle supernal light. At Life Support station, situated behind Command, Sudha Devi sat facing him, smiling calmly, a hint of humor in her eyes.

Ro informed him that Station Control had cleared the *Sun Wolf* for a second jump attempt. With a sardonic smile, he added, "I think Control is a little nervous about the 10 percent light speed part."

They're not the only ones, Aiden thought. "They'll get used to it."

Aiden tapped a spot on his board to put a realtime view of V-Prime on the main screen. It was, of course, completely unnecessary, considering the blinding speed at which they'd be plunging into it. But it had become a kind of tradition with him, a pre-jump ritual. Maybe it was a way to prepare himself and his crew for the incomprehensible thing they were about to do. To transition from one star system to another, many light-years away, with virtually no passage of time or traversal of space. Made possible by a gift given to humanity by what some believed were the living and sentient voidoids.

Aiden leaned back and, for the second time that day, said, "Execute."

The *Sun Wolf* engaged its zero-point drive and flashed into V-Prime's gaping maw at 10 percent light speed.

6

ALPHA-2 HYDRI
Post-Jump

DOMAIN DAY 337, 2218

On a purely perceptual level, the sensation of voidjump was subtle, or even entirely unnoticed by veteran crews. And these days, all spacers were biome-treated against the old scourge of Transient Memory Dissociation. But Aiden had always felt the subtle shift in time and space, even when he tried to ignore it. It was like the second hand of an old analogue clock, ticking the seconds away with infallible regularity, then suddenly pausing for the briefest of moments before continuing on without any corresponding loss of time. A paradoxical discontinuity in the flow of time that existed only when perceived.

"Voidjump successful," Hutton reported. "We are now in the Alpha-2 Hydri system."

"Thank you, Hutton." Aiden glanced around the bridge. The crew appeared unaffected. "Helm, reorient the ship, engage maximum ZPD, and set course for Gateway Station."

Situated at the system's polar opposite point, its POP, Gateway Station was under construction near the gateway voidoid. By convention, the location of a primary voidoid was always designated as the exact north pole of its star system, relative to the system's ecliptic plane, and about 13 AU above it. The polar opposite point, on the other hand, referred to an imaginary point located due south of the star at the exact same distance below the plane. That put them about 26 AU apart. One AU, defined as the average distance between Earth and its sun, was about 150 million kilometers. So 26 of them was a long, long way.

Even for the fastest voidship, powered by the latest generation of beamed core antimatter drives, it took over ten days to cross, a journey the Alliance fleet was currently undertaking. For the *Sun Wolf*, at 92 percent light speed, it would take only four hours of realtime to get there. That, of course, was four hours as measured by stationary clocks throughout Bound Space. Time dilation would let the crew experience only an hour and a half of elapsed time aboard the ship.

And so, an hour and a half later, the *Sun Wolf* pulled out of ZPD to a standstill 100 kilometers from Gateway Station. From there, the ship moved in on conventional drive to within two kilometers, giving the crew a closer look at the station.

Like Friendship Station, it was being built in stationary position about 32 kilometers from the voidoid's space-time horizon. Construction work was in early stages, but when completed, it would be almost twice the size of Friendship Station. At this point, however, it looked skeletal and offered only two docking arms large enough to accommodate standard voidships. Both of those were currently occupied, one by a cargo liner and the other by a UED battle cruiser. The *Sun Wolf* had to stand off and transfer personnel via shuttle.

Aiden counted seven heavy battle cruisers stationed strategically around the gateway voidoid. Counting the one docked at the station, that made eight. Both UED and ARM vessels in equal numbers. That's how the Alliance worked these days. Strictly in equal shares.

Aiden tagged Billy Hotah to accompany him to the station. They boarded the *Sun Wolf*'s transport shuttle, and Station Control cleared their approach. Aiden covered the two-kilometer distance to secure the shuttle inside the station's docking bay. They found Elgin Woo waiting for them on the other side of the airlock, a wide grin on his face.

He looked the same as the last time Aiden had seen him. An unusually tall and thin Asian man, 64 years of age, Woo kept his head shaved bald as a cue ball, except for the long gray mustache, braided meticulously and dangling below his chin on either side of his perpetually smiling mouth.

"Aiden!" he said as he stepped closer and gave Aiden a hearty bear hug. Woo turned to Hotah. "Ah! Lieutenant Hotah. What a pleasure to see you again."

Woo made a subtle gesture toward Hotah that could easily be interpreted as an offer to engage in a similar bear-hug greeting. Hotah made a less subtle gesture to discourage the notion.

"Thank you so much for dropping by to give me a ride back to Shénmì," Woo said. "I realize it's somewhat out of your way."

Woo was undoubtedly aware that the opportunity to visit Skye had made Aiden's decision to make the detour an easy one. The mischievous gleam in Woo's eyes was a dead giveaway.

"My pleasure, Elgin. Good to see you, as always."

Woo's eyes lingered on Aiden's face, and the light in them darkened with concern. Yet he kept his jovial tone as he pointed to the bruise on Aiden's cheek. "Ah. I like the new look. The rugged kickboxer look, eh?"

Aiden smiled obligingly, aware that the bruise had turned a shade bluer since yesterday. He waved it away and said, for the second time in as many days, "Yeah, you should see the other guy."

Woo smiled impishly. "Actually, I think I have."

"Huh?"

"I'll explain later," Woo said with a conspiratorial wink. "I know you must be in a hurry to get underway. But can you come to my quarters for a moment? I believe we have some important things to discuss before departing."

"Yes, we do. Lead the way, Elgin."

Woo's quarters were Spartan, to say the least. Granted, Woo was here on a temporary basis, working to modify and calibrate the astrometry instruments he would be delivering to Shénmì Station for the Mapping Project. But inside the scientific community, Dr. Elgin Woo was hands down the most well-known, highly regarded, and universally respected figure. Not only was he the recipient of multiple Nobel Prizes in a diverse range of scientific disciplines and the inventor of the zero-point drive, he was also the founder of the Cauldron, the most productive and cutting-edge locus of scientific inquiry in the history of the human race.

But now he was most famously known for doing the impossible, a daring leap beyond Bound Space to discover a whole new astrocell with its own interconnected network of voidoids, expanding humanity's potential many times over. It was a singular act that almost everyone who knew about it considered sheer lunacy, but undeniably one of pure genius.

"So how come you don't rate better digs than this, Elgin?"

"You should see the other personnel quarters," he replied with a sly grin. "This is rather palatial in comparison."

Aiden and Hotah sat in the only two available chairs while Woo sat on the edge of a platform bed that appeared no larger, nor more comfortable, than a standard military cot.

"How's the Allied Mapping Project going?" Aiden asked. He had more than a passing interest in AMP's progress. The *Sun Wolf* would soon be navigating those vast unmapped regions of Astrocell Beta, and he wasn't keen on flying blind out there.

"It's progressing quite well," Woo said. "And I'll get to that in a moment. But first, I have a bit of information that might interest you in your hunt for Cardew—"

"Hold up, Elgin," Aiden said, frowning. The *Sun Wolf*'s real mission was top secret. At least it was supposed to be. "What makes you think we're on a hunt for Cardew? This is a survey mission."

Woo closed his eyes and nodded patiently. "Come, come, my friend. You know I have my sources. Fear not. We share common goals. Your secret is always safe with me."

Aiden *did* know that Woo had his "sources," and they went surprisingly high up in the Alliance food chain. And he *did* know that no one could keep a secret better. Aiden trusted the man without reservation. Still, if it had been anyone other than Elgin Woo, he would have had them locked up and investigated by the DSI.

At Woo's irrepressible grin, Aiden shook his head slowly. "Go on."

"My people at Friendship Station," Woo said excitedly, "succeeded in recovering the body of the assassin who spaced himself after trying to kill you. They've done a series of bioanalyses on the remains. It's quite interesting."

"What? How?" Aiden's thoughts shifted quickly from the terrifying memory of the attack to keen curiosity.

"It was not an easy task," Woo said offhandedly. "But we thought it was worth the effort. This . . . 'person' was so similar in appearance to Black Dog, we have no doubt that he was one of Cardew's minions. The more my people know about them, the better we'll understand Cardew himself and what he's up to."

Aiden had learned long ago not to question Elgin about who he referred to when speaking of "my people." He had never gotten a straight answer and finally decided he didn't want to know anyway. "What did you find out?"

"It's extremely interesting, but also a bit chilling. The only way to come close to describing our findings is that the assassin was some kind of cyborg. That would be an actual living organism, but extensively augmented with robotic or mechanical parts to expand its capabilities. Not to be confused with an android, which is basically a robot designed to look and act like a human being. Mainly, we found evidence of highly sophisticated nanobots throughout his body, particularly in his central nervous system. And I'm referring to him as a 'he' only for convenience. The gender here is somewhat ambiguous."

So many questions popped into Aiden's mind at once, he didn't know where to start. Woo took advantage of Aiden's blank moment and continued. "But far more interesting is what we found in the genetic analysis of his tissues. Genetically, it matches the records we have of Cardew himself. Almost exactly."

Aiden looked in disbelief at Woo's smiling face. "You have genetic records of Cardew?"

"Fortunately, yes. Remember, back around 2160 he became director of Terra Corp's Strategy Branch. His name of record at that time was C. S. Amon, the *C* standing for Cardew. He worked—rather infamously—for 35 years alongside Stewart Farthing, Terra Corp's founder. They were both murderous crooks of the worst kind, made even worse by the immense power they wielded over the UED.

"My people had an encounter with him back in 2183, I believe, during an assassination attempt on one of our scientists, carried out by Cardew Amon himself. Thankfully, the assassination was thwarted. Amon escaped, but he was injured in the process, leaving a small amount of blood at the scene. On my instructions, a sample was collected, genetically mapped, and archived. At the time, I had a hunch that Amon was unique in some way, in a very bad way, and that he might pose a threat to us at the Cauldron. It turns out I was right—C. S. Amon became Cardew, the founder of Licet Omnia."

Aiden leaned back. "So this assassin is a *clone* of Cardew? And so was Black Dog?"

"Yes, they started out that way, but became something else entirely. Something more vile, I'm afraid. Technically, this clone is more cyborg than human now. Grown from Cardew's stem-cell genes but developed with extensive synthetic augmentation. He's an amalgam of a clone and a cyborg. I'm calling him and his kind *cloneborgs*.

"This particular specimen, for instance, had a skeleton composed mostly of carbon nanotubules. Extremely strong, light, and resilient. Its organs showed signs of extensive modifications, both synthetic and biological, to a point beyond recognition. The investigators also found additional organs whose functions we can only guess at. One of them appears to be some form of organic inverse fuel cell that could potentially make the act of breathing unnecessary. It can reduce carbon dioxide, the body's metabolic waste product, to its components, removing the carbon and recirculating the oxygen. In an environment with little or no oxygen, it would shut down the lungs and take over respiratory functions."

Aiden rubbed his forehead, as if smoothing out the furrows in his brow would erase the tension causing them.

"But there's something else," Woo said. "Something more troubling. The Cauldron's neurologists who autopsied this creature's brain found, among other abnormalities, the absence of a supramarginal gyrus. Nothing at all where that structure exists in all normal human brains."

"The supra what?"

"It's the part of the cerebral cortex," Woo said, "that allows us to distinguish our own emotional states from that of others. It's proven to be the seat of empathy and compassion."

"Right," Aiden said, remembering an obscure iota of his early science education. "It's a structure that's either inactive or nonexistent in many hardcore psychopaths."

"That's right," Woo said. "Not only that, but when our geneticists delved deeper into the assassin's DNA, they found evidence of tinkering that could impart virtual immortality. It's brilliant work."

"Wonderful," Aiden said. "Cardew is cloning himself into an army of superhuman psychopathic cyborgs that can't be killed. What could be more fun?"

Woo shook his head. "Not indestructible, nor truly immortal. But able to live their lives for hundreds of years or more. This particular assassin, in fact, was not immediately 'killed' by being spaced. For a limited period of time, its nanobots and modified organs would have protected him from extreme cold, hard vacuum, and lack of oxygen. This one was just outside for too long, and those conditions, along with exposure to space radiation, eventually killed him."

Aiden shook his head. "At least we can recognize one when we see it. If the rest of them look as creepy as this one, they can't hide in plain sight. That's to our advantage."

Woo grimaced. "Unfortunately, that's not true anymore. Your assassin was a much earlier model, more rudimentary, one of several that Cardew left behind in Bound Space years ago to cause havoc. He was part of Black Dog's line. Our intel leads us to believe the latest models are far more sophisticated and designed to look exactly like normal human beings."

"That's a scary thought."

"Indeed. And with all due respect to your physical prowess, Aiden, had this assassin been one from the latest line, your confrontation with him would have ended with his first shot. And hand-to-hand combat? You wouldn't have lasted one second. Not only are these modern cloneborgs indistinguishable from real human beings, but they're far more powerful, agile, and clever. Controlled by preprogramed nanobots implanted into their brains, they could be designed to forfeit any of the human emotions Cardew chooses to delete. Their level of autonomy could range from none to total self-sufficiency, with problem-solving capabilities rivaling our own Omicron AIs."

Aiden felt ill. "And all of them absolutely loyal to one man only. Cardew."

7

ALPHA-2 HYDRI SYSTEM
Gateway Station

DOMAIN DAY 337, 2218

HOTAH, who had been listening with keen interest, asked, "But these cloneborgs can be killed with current weaponry, right?"

"Yes, I believe so," Woo said. "Large-caliber slug-throwers. Laser weapons. Head shots would be the best bet. Or explosives. Destroy the brain quickly, and all lower-level functions would become uncoordinated and more easily neutralized. That would be my guess. But cloneborgs like this could be lightning fast and extremely difficult to target in close combat."

Aiden took in a deep breath to steady himself. "And Cardew is probably churning them out by the dozens every day."

"Yes. A truly frightening vision, given Cardew's aspirations to control this entire astrocell. And Bound Space, too, if he wants to. That's why it's so crucial that we find and destroy him and his operation before the situation becomes hopeless."

It was a sobering thought. Humanity, it seemed, was in just as much danger now as it had been when Cardew tried to annihilate Bound Space by killing the voidoids.

Aiden took a deep breath and leaned forward. "That brings me to the mission I've been tasked with, Elgin—since you already know about it—to find Cardew and his home base. To do that, we first need to find *how* to find him. Among all the thousands of stars in Astrocell Beta."

"I understand that you've made some progress in that area."

"Some, yes. But I need help from you and your current work with the Mapping Project."

Woo nodded enthusiastically. "Show me what you have so far."

Aiden proceeded to tell Woo about the clue Sudha Devi had gotten from Dr. Bollard, the code suggesting a range of celestial coordinates, and how they'd used stellar spectral types as criteria to narrow the field down to the fifteen most promising stars to investigate. Aiden mentioned that some of his crew remained skeptical about the validity of Bollard's coded message, raising the possibility that it could be a false clue implanted inside the astronomer's otherwise evacuated consciousness, to throw off any search for Cardew's whereabouts.

"I've worked with Xavier Bollard. I know him," Woo said grimly. "Or knew him—the past tense being more correct if the reports of his condition are true. He was a good man, a brilliant scientist, with a strong sense of himself. Annoyingly stubborn at times, but devoutly rational. If anyone could hold on to a shred of identity under the type of treatment he suffered, it would be Xavier Bollard. I wouldn't hesitate to trust this clue as authentic."

Encouraged by Woo's endorsement, Aiden said, "Then, we'll continue to operate on that assumption. Fifteen stars is better than a thousand."

"Let me see your list of stars," Woo said. "I may be able to point you in the right direction."

Aiden retrieved his compad from his cargo pocket and tapped it once. "On its way to you now."

Woo pulled his own compad from a drawer next to his cot and examined the list in silence. After a moment, he grinned, and his eyes widened. "Aha! Just as I expected."

"What is it?"

"The Mapping Project," Woo said, "was able to acquire six Holtzman drones to make jumps into a select number of high-probability systems for on-site surveys, able to transmit the data back to us here. We now have only four drones left. Why? Because two of them disappeared in star systems they were studying. They were never heard from again. Those two stars are here on your list."

Aiden sat up and leaned forward. "Which two?"

Woo pointed to two entries on the list, HD 20003 and HD 17051. "They're both G-type stars. Like Sol."

"Do they have any idea what happened to the drones?"

Woo bobbed his head up and down. "The initial transmission from the first drone recorded nothing unusual but went dead abruptly just 40 seconds after its jump into the system. The second drone was in-system for 88 seconds. But before it went dead, its sensors picked up a small metallic object sitting off near the voidoid's horizon, several kilometers away. The transmission shows a bright flash of light coming from the object just before the transmission went dark."

"A laser shot," Aiden said. "From one of Cardew's weaponized Holtzman platforms. He's guarding this system against intrusion."

"That's what I think," Woo said. "And that's probably what happened to the other drone too. That one probably got zapped before its sensors could pick anything up. Cardew has to be guarding those systems for a reason."

"Agreed," Aiden said. "I'm betting that they're not the only systems he's interested in. But these two should be our first targets. How good is your astrogation data for that region?"

"As I told you," Woo said, warming up to a subject he'd been submerged in for the last few months, "the Allied Mapping Project has worked diligently for over a year compiling astrometry data to facilitate voidjumping into this astrocell. There are over 50,000 stars out there, but the project wisely chose to concentrate on main sequence stars with spectral types ranging from F5 types, through G, up to K5 types. Similar to, but significantly broader than, the criteria you used for your own list. That works out to be nearly 7,000 of those stars in the entire astrocell."

Woo paused and began absently twirling one side of his long, braided mustache. It was a signature habit that annoyed some of his colleagues but only added to his already colorful image in the public eye. As much as Aiden wanted him to just get to the point, he'd learned long ago not to push the man lest he not get to the point at all.

"But," Woo continued, "thanks to AMP's hardworking Holtzman drones and to a new suite of telescopes, including an infrared scope with an eight-meter mirror, we've just completed a rudimentary navigational database for almost half of those. The project began its work with the stars nearest to Shénmì Station and worked outward from there. That means from the exact center of this astrocell outward. The data for that region are the oldest and the best, and fortunately for you, it includes all of the search area suggested by Bollard's coordinates. AMP's Holtzman drones have already voidjumped into many of those systems to collect realtime astrometric data. I suspect you'll be wanting to upload that database into the *Sun Wolf*'s astrogation computer."

"You suspect correctly. Exactly how accurate is this data?"

"It's accurate enough to ensure over 98 percent success for voidjumping between all the stars on your search list. With your permission, I'll instruct the project to upload that data now."

Aiden grinned. "Absolutely. That will help immensely. I'll have Hutton take care of the data link to the *Sun Wolf*."

Woo leaned back on his cot, resting on his elbows. "Ah! I wish I was going with you on this little jaunt of yours. Sounds like a great adventure."

And an extremely dangerous one, Aiden thought. But now that Woo was privy to their mission, he said, "Elgin, you're always welcome aboard the *Sun Wolf*."

The invitation wasn't just an idle courtesy. While Woo could be moderately irritating at times, his presence aboard the *Sun Wolf* during its last "adventure" had literally saved all their lives.

"Very tempting," Woo said, sitting up again. "But I'm rather keen on continuing a pet project of mine, and that's best done at Shénmì Station. I'm bringing some special instruments for that purpose, along with the other equipment I'm delivering to the Mapping Project. Plus, I've promised Skye to join her research team at Shénmì. She's doing fantastic work there, Aiden. I'm sure she'll fill you in on the amazing discoveries they've made there."

Aiden was pretty sure that updates on her research would not be their first priority during the short time they'd have together.

Hotah looked restless. Woo looked dreamy. Aiden looked at his chrono. "Okay, let's get back to the ship. Next stop: Woo's Star and the planet Shénmì. I want the crew to get some shut-eye before we jump. Including myself. We shove off at zero eight hundred. Elgin, those research instruments you're bringing to Shénmì Station; will they be loaded aboard by then?"

"Yes, they're being stowed aboard now, as we speak."

"Good. We've got spare crew quarters aboard the *Sun Wolf* if you want to spend the night there rather than here. It'll save you a shuttle trip over to us in the morning."

"Invitation accepted," Woo said, suddenly alert and smiling broadly.

"Welcome aboard, Elgin. I'll give you some time to pack your stuff, then meet us in the shuttle bay. In, say, about an hour?"

Still smiling, Woo reached under his cot, pulled out a medium-sized travel bag, and slung it over his shoulder as he stood. "No need. I'm already packed. Let's go."

~ ~ ~

"Prepare for jump," Aiden said from the command chair.

Six hours of sleep was about as good as it was going to get, Aiden figured. Better than four by a long shot. The crew looked as if they'd all slept at least as long during Hutton's night watch. They looked alert and relaxed at their stations, the look Aiden liked to see on the bridge before a jump.

Elgin Woo occupied Science Station, grinning like a kid at a carnival. People who didn't know him could easily dismiss Woo's occasional bouts of childish goofiness as simpleminded, and they couldn't be more wrong. His limitless, childlike sense of wonder was the essence of his genius, the singular quality that made him the most brilliant scientist and thinker in the last two centuries. In truth, Aiden loved him like the father he had never really had.

Ro spoke from Ops. "The ship is in position for jump."

"Helm, set course for Woo's Star. Set jump velocity at 10 percent light speed."

Voidjumping from Bound Space to Astrocell Beta through the gateway was no different than voidjumping within the same astrocell, with one critical difference. As both Aiden and Woo had learned the hard way, the zero-point drive had to be recalibrated to operate in a different astrocell. Otherwise it just flat out wouldn't work.

It all had to do with slightly different cosmological constants between astrocells, which had to do with the degree to which all the voidoids in the system consumed dark energy over the billions of years they'd been doing it. In a weird twist of quantum astrophysics, it turned out that dark energy, the cosmological constant, and the zero-point energy of space were all effectively the same thing. Woo had chosen to regard it as zero-point energy and designed his ZPD to sync up precisely with the unique zero-point-energy density of the astrocell in which it operated. The *Sun Wolf* was now programed to automatically recalibrate the drive the instant it arrived in the new astrocell.

"Hutton," Aiden said. "Are you isolated from the OverNet now?"

"Yes, I am."

Woo glanced at Aiden with a questioning look. Aiden ignored him and said, "Helm. Ready for jump?"

Pilot Abahem, her linkage cap firmly in place, gave him the thumbs-up.

"Execute."

The *Sun Wolf* flashed into the gateway voidoid, out the other side into the HD 10180 system, and came to a standstill 450,000 kilometers from the star's voidoid. All in less than 20 seconds, from start to finish. So fast that they were never seen by the four battle cruisers and eight patrol frigates stationed at the voidoid, guarding the other most valuable star system in Astrocell Beta. Aiden checked in with the battle group's commanding officer, Captain Marcel Asaju of the SS *Parsons*. Asaju had been informed of the *Sun Wolf*'s arrival, but he couldn't possibly have seen it happen. After exchanging the usual pleasantries between ships meeting in the Deep, the *Sun Wolf* set course for Shénmì, and for the orbital platform housing the research project. Where Skye lived and worked.

During the two-hour trip under maximum ZPD—only 47 minutes shipboard time—Aiden explained to Woo why he'd had Hutton disconnect from the OverNet, and the disturbing vision Pilot Abahem had experienced during the failed jump. Woo listened in silence. His expression darkened as Aiden spoke.

When Aiden finished, Woo said, "It's the same intrusion you experienced. The black crow. A psychoneurological manifestation of Cardew himself. He's gaining power faster than I expected. It's good that you warned Admiral Stegman. I'll notify my people at the Cauldron, although it's quite likely they already know about these intrusions."

"I can't help thinking," Aiden said, "that Cardew has been infiltrating the OverNet for some time now. That he may have interfered with voidship navigation back when he was messing around with the voidoids."

Following Aiden's train of thought, Woo said, "That could explain how he was able to hijack so many warships back then, the ones that disappeared into voidoids during flux events. Those ships are probably part of Cardew's fleet now, including an advanced ship-builder platform. We'll need to consider that in our assessment of his military strength."

"That, along with the number of Omicron AIs he controls, the ones aboard other hijacked ships."

The *Sun Wolf* pulled out of ZPD five kilometers from Shénmì Station. It could hardly be called a station at this point. Like

Gateway Station, it was still under construction, half of its framework still exposed to space. Construction drones and workmen in EVA suits buzzed around it like bees tending their hive. The huge antimatter tanker, SS *Quasimodo*, stood off from the station at about 10 kilometers, sunlight casting its ungainly bulges into a surreal juxtaposition of bright reflection and pitch-black shadow.

The *Sun Wolf* approached the station slowly and came to a halt a half kilometer out. Accompanied by Woo and Sudha Devi, Aiden took the ship's shuttle across to the station's docking hangar. At this stage of construction, the cavernous hangar area was unpressurized and still open to the cold vacuum of space. Several utility vessels and a small cargo carrier were docked there, but by far the most eye-catching occupant was the *Starhawk*, Elgin Woo's personal yacht.

"Aha!" Woo said as he literally pressed his nose against the shuttle's viewport to get a good look at his most famous and astounding creation. Built at the Cauldron as a prototype for testing Woo's zero-point drive, the *Starhawk* was a flat-black, saucer-shaped vessel, eerily recalling the classic "flying saucer" of mid-twentieth-century sci-fi movies. It was about 60 meters in diameter and perfectly circular when viewed from above. When viewed from the side, it presented a sleek ellipsoidal profile no more than 10 meters at its widest point and tapering gracefully to razor-thin edges. Its seamless surface glistened with an obsidian sheen, completely smooth and unbroken by projections or ports of any kind, as if it had been sculpted from a single gigantic slab of black diamond.

Woo waved at it as if to a dear friend and said in a whisper, "I'll see you soon."

The shuttle docked with a dull clunk and was secured in place by powerful magnetic clamps. Since the hangar was unpressurized, the station had to rely on pressurized boarding bridges to transfer personnel between docked vessels and the station's interior. The enclosed gangway, an accordion-like structure, was marginally heated inside, and all three of them were shivering in their thin jumpsuits by the time they had walked the 30 meters to the station's airlock door. When the door opened, Aiden's shivering suddenly stopped, as if bathed in warm sunlight. Skye Landen stood there facing him with a smile like the morning sun, a light that never failed to banish darkness from his soul.

8

HD 10180 SYSTEM
Shénmì Station

DOMAIN DAY 338, 2218

"HEY there," Skye said.

The music of her voice sang with the warmth of her smile. Aiden felt an ache in his chest and took a deep breath to relieve it.

"Hey," he said through his own smile. For the moment, it was all he could say.

Elgin Woo and Devi greeted Skye as they stepped out of the airlock, but neither of them lingered. They both smiled knowingly and departed quickly down the corridor.

Even in her baggy, laboratory-stained jumpsuit, she was, as always, beautiful. Not so much in a glamourous way, but blessed with a purely natural attractiveness that spoke of good genes, healthy living, and a positive outlook on life. Still a young woman, she would turn 34 in the same month that Aiden turned 40. Her Nordic heritage was evident in her clear blue eyes, naturally blonde hair, fair complexion, and cheeks with a hint of freckles that, according to her, had been far more prominent when she was a child. Of medium build and erect bearing, she stood almost as tall as Aiden.

Without another word, they embraced. Her hair smelled faintly of lavender-scented shampoo. When they kissed, her lips were sweet with a hint of jasmine tea. Their bodies fitted together perfectly, like pieces of a two-part puzzle that could be made whole in no other way. The feel of her in his arms was like electric fire.

She gently pulled away from their embrace and looked him in the eye for a long moment. She had a slightly crooked smile, a natural physiognomy that gave her a mischievous allure when viewed from one angle, or a deep, melancholic intimacy with irony when viewed from another. Over time, Aiden had learned to see her from both angles at once. She was by far the most complex person he'd ever known. On one hand, she was a die-hard scientist—cerebral, analytical, pragmatic—with a razor-sharp intellect matched only by the rigor with which she wielded it. But underneath that cool mentality, seamlessly blended with it, ran a hot streak of preternatural intuition that sometimes frightened him for reasons he didn't understand.

When she finally spoke, it was with a simple familiarity, as if they'd never been apart, even though they had been for many months. "It's good to see you again, husband. Even with that frightful bruise on your face. What happened?"

"It's nothing," he said with a casual wave of his hand. But nothing was casual about the way he returned her gaze. "I'm glad that I've been missed. I definitely missed you."

"You're looking thin, Aiden. You haven't been eating properly, have you?"

"I gotta admit, I'm pretty damn hungry right now."

She eyed him with mock suspicion before speaking. "Hmmm. The station's cafeteria is just down the corridor from here. Down that way."

Aiden eased his arm around her waist, glanced in the direction she'd indicated, then smiled and shook his head firmly.

Skye smiled back at him, this time with that distinctly mischievous allure. "Come to think of it, I'm pretty starved myself."

"Which way to your quarters?"

Skye tilted her head down the corridor, in the opposite direction of the cafeteria. "Follow me."

~ ~ ~

Aiden was the first to open his eyes and disentangle himself from the single body that both of their bodies had made together, from that heated amalgamation of passion and extrasensory perception that he and Skye seemed to catalyze whenever they made love.

Which wasn't often enough, Aiden thought. Not by a long shot. Nonetheless, after their handfasting on Silvanus, they had grown to become one by learning how to be apart when together and together when apart.

He rolled over and caught himself before falling off the side of Skye's narrow bed, a basic one-person platform welded to one wall of her tiny quarters. The room was dimly lit, a little too warm, and smelled of jasmine tea and sex. He looked at his chrono. They'd been "on break" for nearly two hours. Messages were waiting for him unanswered on his compad. Reality, the hard-edged kind that demanded engagement, was already knocking on the door. He just didn't feel like answering at the moment. Not quite yet.

Sitting on the edge of the bed, he turned back to face Skye. She had risen on one elbow, eyes open and smiling at him. The covers had fallen to her waist, revealing her pale white skin, firm rounded breasts, and a flat muscular tummy. Her blonde hair fell in graceful disarray around her bare shoulders, wet in places where it touched her face.

Aiden swallowed hard. "You're so beautiful . . ."

A rosy blush bloomed across Skye's cheeks. She sat up, pulled the covers around her shoulders. Shaking her head slowly, she turned to look out the room's single portal window located above her bed. "No. *She's* beautiful."

Aiden followed her gaze. The blue-green planet Shénmì turned slowly below them. Viewed from their position, 430 kilometers above the planet's equator, Shénmì was truly beautiful, a brilliant jewel set spinning in the black nothingness of space. *Just as beautiful as Silvanus.*

"Is Shénmì another Silvanus?" he asked. "Another Gaia world?"

"Is Shénmì a conscious living being like Silvanus? We don't know that yet, Aiden. But we do know that all the plant life we've studied down there is interconnected by a vast body of fungus, engaged in complex symbiotic associations. Just like the Rete on Silvanus."

Just like the Rete. Aiden felt the hair on the back of his neck prickle.

On Earth, before the Die Back, over 91 percent of all known plant species hosted a symbiotic fungus called mycorrhizae. The fungus formed mantles of hyphae on the roots of trees and other plants, mediating a relationship of mutual benefit for both organisms. The fungus obtained carbohydrates and vitamin complexes from the roots, and in the process, plants gained the ability to absorb essential nutrients more efficiently. But the Die Back had disrupted that ancient interconnection on a global scale, pushing Earth's biosphere to the brink of extinction. If it hadn't been for the recent introduction of fungal samples from Silvanus into Earth's soils, the planet would have died. Permanently.

During Aiden's short but eventful stay on Silvanus, he had discovered that the mycorrhizae there were far more pervasive and collectively greater in both scale and function than their counterparts on Earth. The fungus was not only engaged in a symbiotic association with every living thing on Silvanus, physically interconnecting the entire planetary biome; in the process, it had grown into a single living network composed of countless trillions of cellular filaments, all functioning in concert on a planetary scale, transferring biochemical messages between plants and plant populations all over the globe.

It was called the Rete. Its complexity, level of organization, and interconnectedness were clearly analogous to the human brain, but covered millions of square kilometers. And from it, like the human brain, sentience had emerged. The Rete was conscious. With an intelligence deeper and more ancient than anything humanity had ever encountered. And Aiden Macallan was the only human being to have neurolinked with the Rete, to share consciousness with it.

Skye saw his reaction at the mention of the Rete. She said, "You still long for Silvanus, don't you, Aiden?" Her voice had lowered in pitch. Her eyes had softened but remained unblinking. "I can see the gap in your spirit. It hurts me to see it."

Aiden turned away from her, his throat tightening with emotion, awash in a sense of loss that would always haunt him. Linking with the Rete had changed him forever. It had immersed him within a knowledge of wholeness that he could never again experience. His futile attempts to regain it through the drug Continuum had left him even more desolate, and worse—enslaved by an addiction he had to beat back every day of his life.

Skye placed her hand gently on his cheek. "Aiden, I've been studying the Shénmì seeds. The ones that the planet produces and disperses into space. I think there could be many more planets like Silvanus. Here in Astrocell Beta."

Aiden took Skye's hand from his cheek and kissed it. "What have you found?"

When Elgin Woo had discovered Shénmì, one of the first things he'd noticed as he approached the planet was a number of seemingly impossible structures like narrow filaments sprouting from the planet's equatorial regions and extending into the vacuum of space, nearly 36,000 kilometers above the surface. Each thin, whiplike filament terminated in a single lozenge-shaped pod that would split open when the structure stopped rising and disperse a cluster of roughly spherical objects into space. About 16 meters across, with irregular and conspicuously organic surfaces, Woo called them seeds. Because that's exactly what they looked like. Very big seeds. He also noticed that, once liberated from the pod, the seeds moved away from the planet deeper into space, but together in unison as if self-propelled.

Skye scooted up on the cot to lean her back against the bulkhead, covers still held casually to her shoulders. "We think it's pretty damn obvious what they are," she said. "They're panspermia seeds. Intended to inseminate barren terrestrial worlds with the very beginnings of organic life. They somehow target rocky, earthlike planets existing in the habitable zones of star systems that populate this astrocell, and maybe in other astrocells too."

Not bothering to dress, Aiden moved to the only chair in the room, turned it sideways, and sat facing her. "Have you actually captured one of these seeds? To study it?"

"Yes. And it wasn't even that difficult. We just waited for one of the beanstalks to sprout—that's what Elgin called them when he first saw them—positioned a shuttle in orbit near where the pod would come to rest. And when it opened, we just snatched a few and brought them into the lab."

Aiden sat up straighter. "What did you find inside?"

"Exactly what any good astrobiologist would expect to find in a panspermia package. All the fundamental ingredients for original biogenesis. The basic stuff to kick-start the evolution of organic life on barren planets."

9

HD 10180 SYSTEM
Shénmì Station

Domain Day 338, 2218

SKYE had his full attention now. "Basic stuff?" he said. "What basic stuff?"

"Fungal spores, mostly. Able to survive inside the pods for hundreds of years, or even thousands, under extreme conditions of interstellar space and the impact of a free-fall landing on a terrestrial planet. We already know that fungi were essential for the evolution of plant life on Earth. They formed symbiotic relationships with the first single-cell organisms capable of photosynthesis, becoming the progenitors of all the plant life that eventually spread across Earth's landmasses."

Aiden's first gig out of grad school was as a survey scientist aboard the Survey Vessel *Argo*. With a PhD in planetary geology and astrobiology, he was familiar with the currently accepted theory of life's origins on Earth. Without plant life, Earth would never have developed enough breathable atmosphere for animals to evolve. But it was fungi that single-handedly bridged the gap between plants and the barren soil. By establishing symbiotic associations with the earliest photosynthetic bacteria, like cyanobacteria, the fungal partner facilitated the transfer of essential elements from rocks and soil to enable the biochemistry of photosynthesis. And that's what led to the subsequent evolution of complex vascular plants. In short, fungi were directly responsible for the evolution of diverse plant life, which, in turn, generated enough atmospheric oxygen to finally support animal life.

Aiden leaned in closer to Skye. "You said fungal spores were *mostly* what you found inside the seeds. What else?"

"Prokaryotes," she said. "Of the bacterial kind. Dormant, of course. Like the fungal spores and just as resistant to time and extreme conditions."

"Cyanobacteria?" It made perfect sense.

"Exactly. Or something very similar to it, capable of photosynthesis. The thing is, the first prokaryotes on Earth showed up in the oceans close to four billion years ago. Then it took another billion years for some of them to evolve into photosynthesizing bacteria like cyanobacteria and start oxygenating the atmosphere.

"But the Shénmì seeds carry those photosynthetic bacteria already premade, as spores. The seeds introduce both the fungi and the bacteria *simultaneously.* A newly formed exoplanet analogous to Earth could potentially bypass those billion years of evolutionary grunt work if a Shénmì seed happened to fall into its waters. Along with the fungal spores, the seeds carry all the right stuff for basic biogenesis. All they need to do is land on a habitable planet, even a marginally habitable one. It also introduces a genetic wild card into the mix, so exactly what *kind* of higher life forms will evolve is completely up for grabs."

Aiden absently stroked his beard. "The seeds introduce a kind of shortcut to how it happened on Earth."

"Exactly," Skye said. "Earth's barren landmasses had to be prepared for hundreds of millions of years in advance before plant life could even get started. Prepared by fungi. The fungi dissolved mineral-rich rocks and secreted carbon-based organic acids to convert barren lands into fertile, carbon-rich soils. Then when the cyanobacteria finally washed ashore, they found both friendly soils and friendly symbiotic partners waiting for them. That's how the emergence of plant life on Earth took off. But the Shénmì seeds would shorten that process by a billion years or more."

Aiden leaned closer and kissed her forehead. "I love it when you talk science. Turns me on."

"Ha-ha," she said, batting him away playfully. "Why do I get the feeling you're not paying attention here?"

"Oh, I'm listening. Just a little distracted, that's all." Aiden glanced pointedly at the covers that had fallen again to her waist.

She shook her head in mock pity. "Men . . ."

Aiden held out his hands, palms up. "What can I say?"

"How about something intelligent?" She stood and put on an undershirt that fell halfway to her knees. "There. Is that better?"

"No," he said with a grin. "Equally distracting."

"You are impossible, Aiden Macallan."

"And that's why you love me, no?"

Her only answer to that was to gather up her wrinkled jumpsuit and put it back on. She gave him a look, eyebrows raised, then sat on the edge of her bed facing him, leaving him feeling naked. Literally. Still, he couldn't stop grinning like an idiot.

Skye shook her head again. "All right, funny man, let's see how funny you think *this* is. I just completed a detailed genetic analysis of the fungi inside the seeds. The genetic similarities to the Rete on Silvanus are unmistakable. The Shénmì fungus may be the direct ancestor of the Rete."

"What? How could that be possible? Silvanus is in another astrocell. There's no way these seeds could disperse that far."

"Unless," Skye said, "some of them found their way through the gateway between the two astrocells. It could have happened, Aiden. Shénmì was born in a star system that's nearly a half billion years older than the one Silvanus was born in."

"I get it," Aiden said. "Seeds dispersed from Shénmì had plenty of time to find their way even as far as the gateway and out into Bound Space."

"Why not?"

He shrugged his shoulders. "Okay, but how are these seeds propelled? How do they navigate through the voidoids into other systems? How do they target terrestrial planets that lie within a star system's habitable zone, ones with favorable conditions to support organic life?"

Skye opened her hands and leaned forward. "Those are exactly the kinds of questions our research teams here are trying to answer. Elgin, of course, believes that the seeds somehow work in conjunction with the voidoids to direct dispersion into suitable systems, that it's all tied in with the voidoid's primary function of maintaining the right balance of dark energy to allow such systems to evolve in the first place. And that includes influencing the formation of terrestrial planets inside habitable zones."

Aiden made a wry smile. "Uh-huh. That would fit right in with Elgin's vision of a living universe. Intergalactic ecosystems analogous to organic planetary ones."

"And you still have doubts about that vision?"

Aiden shrugged his shoulders and said nothing

"Okay," she continued, unfazed, "regardless of Elgin's hunches, my team's conclusions are solid. And they have important implications for where you and your crew are going. We believe that you'll be running into an above-average number of habitable planets here in Astrocell Beta. Way more than in Bound Space. And my guess is that many of those planets already support living ecosystems, in various stages of evolution. And I'm also betting that most, if not all of them, have been seeded by Shénmì."

That *was* interesting, Aiden had to admit. He finally stood and put on his own jumpsuit. "How do you figure?"

Skye looked at him for a moment before responding, apparently assessing whether or not he'd finally gotten serious. At least he'd put his clothes back on.

"Shénmì's star system is old," she finally said. "Over seven billion years old. Meaning that the planet Shénmì itself is nearly that old. That's a lot of time for complex ecosystems to evolve. Even if life progressed as slowly as it did on Earth, Shénmì could have easily supported a mature biosphere over the last three billion years. And it could have been dispersing its seeds throughout this astrocell for most of that time."

Aiden cocked his head sideways. "Still, those seeds have to land on the right kind of planet, orbiting the right kind of star, to even have a chance of kick-starting a biosphere."

"The right kind of planet how?" Skye asked. Her expression said that she already knew the answer but was testing his actual understanding of it.

"All right," he said, and began ticking off points. "It has to be a rocky terrestrial planet in a stable orbit, inside a stable habitable zone, around a stable sunlike star. It has to be roughly Earth-sized—no less than half or more than twice the size of Earth—with abundant water in liquid form and the right kind of geochemistry. That and a whole bunch of other crucial factors—atmosphere, magnetic fields, on and on. The last time I checked, less than 20 percent of all sunlike stars could possibly host those kinds of planets."

Skye nodded as Aiden spoke, but impatiently. "Yes, very good. But here's the thing: that figure is much higher in this astrocell. It's more like 75 percent. And that's the latest data from the Allied Mapping Project."

Seventy-five percent? It was a stunning assertion. "For this mission," Aiden said, "we narrowed our survey destinations down to fifteen sunlike stars. Even if we visited all of them, I expected to find no more than two or three terrestrial planets in habitable zones. If what you're saying is true, we could find a lot more."

"More than a lot more," she said, glancing down at a message she'd just received on her compad. She gave him a look that reminded him of a cat who'd just stolen food off his plate without him noticing. "According to the Mapping Project's latest data," she said, "you're likely to find a terrestrial planet residing inside a habitable zone in 10 of the 15 star systems on your list."

"What? How does AMP know what stars are on our list?"

"Elgin brought your 'hit list' aboard and discussed it with the Mapping Project's lead scientists while you and I were here doing... I got a message from him just now. The project's surveys confirm that at least 10 of the star systems on your list actually do have a terrestrial Earth-sized planet in a stable orbit inside a habitable zone. They're all single stars, no binaries, and they're all either G or K spectral-type stars."

Aiden was not happy with the liberties Woo had taken with a list of target stars that should have been top secret, even under the guise of a survey mission. But curiosity quickly overcame annoyance. "Which ten stars?"

Skye transferred the data from her compad to his. He scanned it briefly and said, "This changes things. These ten stars are now our top priority. That is, after we investigate the two systems where AMP probes went missing."

He clamped his mouth shut after his last sentence, realizing it could hint at the true nature of the *Sun Wolf*'s mission. He was still bound to keep it top secret, even from his own wife.

Skye shrugged, pretending not to notice, and said, "I'm aware of those two star systems. Look at the list again. Both of them just happen to be on it."

While Aiden reexamined the new list, Skye moved closer to him and put her hand over his. "The point is, Aiden, these are exactly the kind of planets Cardew is looking for too. To colonize and infect with his sick Empire of the Pure. Or whatever the hell he's calling it these days. Exactly the kind of planet he's probably occupying right now. You *are* looking for him, right?"

That stopped Aiden in his tracks. She obviously knew the real purpose of his mission. It was almost a relief. Now he wouldn't have to keep a secret from her, something he'd vowed never to do. But *how* did she know? Elgin?

"Yep," he finally said, but not in a happy way. "That's our real mission, all right. We'll be looking for Cardew, and I'll take any edge I can get to find him. This list of ten stars will help."

Aiden suddenly felt the overwhelming weight of responsibility settle on his shoulders, a responsibility for the safety of the entire human race. Time to get serious. Honeymoon over.

She touched his cheek again and smiled at him. The look in her eyes strengthened his resolve, fortified him in a way that only love could accomplish.

Aiden leaned over to kiss her, but just before their lips met, the red indicator on his compad started blinking, the one that meant an urgent situation demanding his immediate response. Almost simultaneously, Skye received a voice alert from the station's security chief.

"Dr. Landen. This is Colonel Crestfield. We just received a transmission from the battle group out at the voidoid. They registered a high-velocity intrusion through the voidoid. An exit velocity of over 30 percent light speed. Too fast to intercept or identify. They believe it's some kind of missile. Assumed to be hostile. It's under constant acceleration and heading directly toward us."

10

HD 10180 SYSTEM
Shénmì Station

Domain Day 338, 2218

"What've you got, Ro?" Aiden barked into his comm as he jogged down the corridor toward the station's docking bay with Skye at his side. He wanted a report directly from the *Sun Wolf*'s crew. The ship's sensor array was better equipped to handle this kind of situation.

The comm link crackled, adjusting to Aiden's changing position within the station's haphazardly shielded interior. Ro's voice came online. "The command battle cruiser guarding the voidoid, the SS *Parsons*, got a sensor hit on a high-velocity object bursting through the voidoid's space-time horizon, clocked at over 100,000 klicks per second. That's around 34 percent light speed. Way too fast for the battle group to react. It's also pushing about 300 Gs continuous acceleration. Obviously riding an antimatter torch drive. It's heading straight toward us."

Shit. "Have you got a bead on it yet? Any idea what it is?"

"Yes. Alvarez picked up its exhaust plume on our LR scope. Of course, we're seeing where it was about 45 minutes ago. Exactly what is it? Hard to tell at that distance and velocity, but Hutton did an analysis on the sensor data. He says it looks like a missile. A big one. At least 50 meters long. Hotah says it's definitely a weapon."

"How long will it take to reach us here?"

"Given an exit velocity of 34 percent light speed and 300 G acceleration, it'll take four and a half hours from its jump point to reach us. But—"

"But," Aiden interrupted, already aware of the bad news. "That's from when it jumped. How long did it take for the *Parsons* to pick it up, and how long did it take for their maser transmission to reach us?"

"Right. Accounting for the time it took the *Parsons* to pick it up on their scans and to send a transmission to us across 13 AU, about two of those four and a half hours have already elapsed."

"Wonderful. So where is it now?"

"The missile is now about seven AU out. Time of impact on Shénmì: two and a half hours."

Aiden stopped halfway down the corridor and glanced at his chrono. That would be about 16:45 local time. "Okay, Ro. We're on our way to the ship now."

Skye pulled up next to him while he called Devi and Hotah on their comms. He told them to meet him at the shuttle bay, ASAP, then turned to Skye and said, "Can you come with us? This station could become a very dangerous place to be."

The moment the words came out of his mouth, he realized how selfish he sounded. But he couldn't help himself. He had a bad feeling about the weapon screaming toward them, and about the fate of the planet if he was unable to stop it. He wanted more than anything to keep Skye out of harm's way, and the best way of doing that was to keep her on board the *Sun Wolf* when they launched.

Skye smiled at him—the smile she made when reading him like an open book—and said quietly, "Aiden, I have to stay on the station. I'm in charge here. We need to prepare the best way we can for whatever might happen."

They held each other's eyes for a long moment. She took his hand in hers. "I have 27 souls here who depend on me to make the right decisions at times like this. I can't just leave them in the lurch. I *know* you understand. It's exactly what you would do if you were in my place. I know you want to protect me. I love you for that. And I love you more for not trying to stop me."

Her words only made the pang in Aiden's chest worse. Of course, she was right. He did understand her resolute acceptance of responsibility for the people she led, for the project they were engaged in. As commander of the *Sun Wolf*, Aiden understood it all too well. He had no right to ask her to abandon the station and come with him, even if it meant losing her. But he would lose her just as surely—in a different way—if he tried to persuade her now.

"Skye . . ."

She squeezed his hand, a gesture of both tenderness and finality. "Besides, I have faith that you and your crew can stop this thing, whatever it is. Put your mind to that task, and stop worrying about me."

Easier said than done. He squeezed her hand back. "All right. We'll get this done. Take care of your people. If any of them are planetside right now, I'd suggest getting them back up to the station. Can you move the station farther away from the planet? Into a higher orbit?"

He knew how difficult that would be in the time they had left. Skye clearly knew it, too, but she said, "We'll try."

He held her hand a little longer, not wanting to let go. His throat tightened. "We'll be back soon."

"I know. Stay safe, my love."

And with that, he turned and resumed his sprint toward the docking bay. *No looking back now.*

Clattering down one flight of stairs, Aiden made it to the docking bay in record time. Billy Hotah and Sudha Devi arrived seconds later, jogging in from the opposite direction. Devi was out of breath. Hotah looked calm but with that dangerously focused look of a hunter who smelled blood. The three of them passed through the passenger-tube doorway into their shuttle.

Aboard the shuttle, Aiden punched the controls to disengage the magnetic clamps holding it in place. Without waiting for

Station Control to approve his hasty departure, he pushed the shuttle out of the hangar. Minutes later, they docked with the *Sun Wolf*, disembarked, and the three of them raced to the bridge.

Aiden found Ro at Command, looking stoic as ever. Alvarez sat stiffly at Comm/Scan, eyes glued to the screens in front of her. Pilot Abahem sat without expression, silent and partially reclined at Helm. When Aiden took over Command from Ro, he was surprised to see Elgin Woo sitting at Science Station. Before he could ask, Woo looked at him, oddly cheerful, and said, "A troubling development, yes?"

Seriously? He turned back to Ro. "Okay. How fast is this thing going now?"

"Over 40 percent light speed."

Alvarez shook her head in disbelief. "How the hell can anything be going that fast right out of a voidjump? How can anything even *make* a jump at those velocities?"

Ro put a hand on his chin and cocked his head. "If the missile was launched from a planetary system at 300 Gs, aimed at the system's voidoid 13 AU away, that's just about how fast it would be going right now. How it could execute an accurate jump at that velocity is another question."

"The more important question," Aiden said, "is how do we stop it? We don't know exactly what it is, but I'm betting it's a surprise package from Cardew himself, and a nasty one at that."

"There're no defensive systems between it and us," Ro said. "And even if there were, that thing is going way too fast for us to target with *any* kind of weaponry."

Hotah spoke. "Not unless a weapons platform could match the missile's velocity and come alongside to target and fire."

Ro raised one eyebrow and crossed his arms theatrically. "Hmmm. What's the only heavily armed ship in existence that can go that fast?"

Ro's school teacher tone was overplayed but effective. The answer, of course, was the *Sun Wolf*. The zero-point drive could do it with one hand tied behind its back. With a maximum velocity of 92 percent light speed, the *Sun Wolf* could theoretically come alongside an object cruising at any speed under that. Theoretically.

Aiden glanced at Woo, the illustrious inventor of the zero-point drive himself, standing in their midst, and saw him nodding, deep in thought. Woo gestured for Hotah to continue.

Hotah took the cue. "Since the missile is coming straight toward us, we'd need to set an intercept course at a slight angle from its line of approach. Then launch at maximum speed to meet its position, stop, do a 180 turnaround, give chase, catch up to it, match velocities, stand off at a safe distance, and fire. But it gets even more complicated. Our target doesn't have a fixed velocity. It's continually accelerating. So, we'd have to adjust our own acceleration rate to keep up with it and come alongside."

"That's something we've never tried," Aiden said, looking over at Woo. "Can our zero-point drive be fine-tuned to match acceleration rates like that?"

"Yes, it can," Woo said, absently twirling one of his braided moustaches. "I'll need to make some adjustments. Something that can be done quickly only by me, I'm afraid."

"Welcome aboard, Elgin," Aiden said with a slight bow. Woo looked delighted to be invited to the party.

Aiden addressed the thin air above his head. "Hutton. Are you following this?"

"With great interest," the AI replied.

"Is this a feasible plan of action? Do you see any complications we're missing?"

"Yes, it is quite feasible. There are a few questions remaining, however. For instance, the effectiveness of our projectile weapons fired perpendicular to the axis of acceleration, especially at such a high acceleration rate. There is also the question of weapons fired from within a negative zero-point bubble, what Dr. Woo refers to as hypospace. The drive would have to be shut down momentarily for projectile or beam weapons to reach their target."

"But these issues aren't absolutely prohibitive, are they? They can be worked out by the time we reach the intercept point, right?"

"That is correct," Hutton said with a jovial tone. "With the assistance of Dr. Woo and Lieutenant Hotah, I believe we can resolve them in short order."

"Thank you, Hutton." Aiden glanced at his chrono. It was just after 14:30. He turned to Ro. "Let's get the show on the road. The longer we wait, the closer that thing gets and the harder it will be to stop. Commence undocking procedures and fire up the ZPD when we're clear."

"There's only one problem with that," Ro said. "If you hadn't noticed on your way here, we're currently tethered to the *Quasimodo*'s refueling port. They're still topping up our Penning tanks."

Shit! He'd forgotten that little detail in the excitement of the moment. "Have the tanker cease operations immediately and disengage." Aiden was all too aware of the time it would take to do that. Antimatter refueling was not something done hastily or interrupted abruptly. It required following the strictest government protocols. And for good reasons. Antimatter tanker personnel could not be talked into cutting corners. The *Quasimodo*'s crew would be no exception.

"On it," Ro said, tapping commands into his control board. "I'm guessing we'll be free to launch in about an hour."

"One hour?" Aiden stroked his beard, frustration mounting. "Added to the two hours we've already lost by maser transmission time? That missile will be a hell of a lot closer to Shénmì by then, at the rate it's going."

Ro shrugged nonchalantly. "True. But even if we launch in one hour, we'd intercept it in less than 20 minutes, with at least 50 minutes left before impact. Plenty of time."

Plenty of time? Not really, Aiden thought, considering all the unknowns of such an untested scheme. But what other choice did they have?

He sat back in the command chair and steadied his breathing before speaking. "Okay. In the meantime, let's get to work on the questions Hutton brought up, and anything else we can think of that could screw this up. I want to be ready to execute the moment we're in position. No second-guessing."

Woo clapped his hands once and moved to join Hotah at Tactical station. On his way, he stopped at Helm and asked Pilot Abahem to join them. "We could use your input on this."

~ ~ ~

The AM tanker completed its emergency disconnect, and the *Sun Wolf* was cleared to depart at 15:25. By 15:30 the ship had moved away from the station using its antimatter drive to a position 500 kilometers out, far enough from the station's mass to safely activate the zero-point drive.

"Helm, initiate the ZPD at 92 percent light speed, on course to intercept point."

Abahem gave him a thumbs-up. Simultaneously, Aiden experienced the now-familiar sensation of stepping completely out of the four known dimensions for a fraction of a second, then back in. The readings on his command screen confirmed the ship's velocity was now 91.8 percent light speed. He looked around the bridge. No one looked particularly disturbed, but he couldn't escape the weird impression that he was looking at a group of children who'd just experienced an intense roller coaster ride but were too cool to show it.

Hutton had set the nav computer to intercept the missile at the point along its trajectory where the missile would be when the *Sun Wolf* got there to meet it. That turned out to be in about 23 minutes, where it would be 2.6 AU away from impact. That left them a little over 50 minutes to figure out how to stop it. Those weren't good numbers, but it was all they had.

11

HD 10180 SYSTEM
Cis-Shénmì Space

DOMAIN DAY 338, 2218

EACH of those 23 minutes crept by as if they were hours. During that time, Hotah powered up the ship's main laser cannon. Woo and Hotah agreed that they'd have to shut down the zero-point drive momentarily before using any of their weaponry. The drive operated by creating a hypospace bubble in front of and around the ship, a region in which the zero-point field of space had been virtually eliminated. It isolated the ship from the normal space-time continuum through which it travelled, creating a discontinuity barrier that projectiles or energy-beam weapons could not cross.

That would make the entire maneuver far more challenging and something only the AI could do on the fly. Hutton, whose grasp of human colloquialisms was still a work in progress, had confidently said, "A piece of pie!"

Finally, the *Sun Wolf* came to a halt 30 kilometers from the point where the missile would be passing by within the next minute. The ship turned around to face the direction of the missile's forward travel, repowered the ZPD, and waited. They didn't have to wait long. Several seconds later, the missile zipped past them, now clocking over 44 percent light speed. They couldn't see it, of course. Not in realtime. Only the ship's instruments registered its passing.

"Helm. Activate Hutton's sequence."

It took nearly ten precious minutes for the *Sun Wolf* to catch up with the speeding missile and fine-tune the ZPD to compensate for the missile's furious rate of acceleration. When they finally pulled alongside it, Alvarez manipulated the optical sensors with time-dilation filters, and their prey materialized on the screen.

It was an evil-looking weapon of mass destruction built on a narrow cylindrical body roughly 60 meters long and 5 meters in diameter. The aft section was swollen with huge antimatter containment tanks—six of them, spaced equally around the missile's circumference—terminating in three enormous electromagnetic nozzles. But it was the sight of the missile's nose section that sent a chill up Aiden's spine. It was a bulbous sphere, about twice the diameter of the cylinder, with a brilliantly reflective mirrorlike surface.

"Oh no," Elgin Woo said, staring intently at the enhanced image. "I was afraid of this."

Aiden shook his head. "Is that what I think it is?"

"I believe so. I knew we were going to find it eventually. But not like this."

"I thought all of them had been found and destroyed."

"All but one." Woo looked frightened, an expression rarely seen on his face. "We feared that, in the worst-case scenario, it would remain in Cardew's possession. Looks like we were right."

Sudha Devi spoke up from Life Support Station. "Will someone please tell me what you're talking about?"

Aiden looked at her, then around at everyone else on the bridge. "It's an antigluon device."

Alvarez whipped around to face Aiden, eyes wide. "The same kind of bomb Cole Brahmin tried to use to destroy Silvanus?"

"Unfortunately, yes," Woo said, still facing the screen. "It's outlawed technology, of course, and only six of them were ever made. Manufactured by Cardew's shadow group, Licet Omnia. We at the

Cauldron recovered and neutralized the two that Brahmin had. Three more were found later and destroyed. We never found the last one. Until now."

"How do you know Cardew hasn't produced more of these things?" Devi said, crossing her arms over her chest.

"He can't," Woo said. "For one thing, the process is extremely dangerous. Licet Omnia lost its entire covert manufacturing site attempting to produce a seventh device. It was located on one of Saturn's eighty-something moons. The facility not only blew itself up, but the entire moon lost several meters of surface rock. More importantly, the exotic material needed to make the devices no longer exists. It was originally culled from the ephemeral region immediately surrounding a voidoid's space-time horizon. Not found anywhere else we know of. But ever since Brahmin attempted to annihilate Silvanus with one of these devices, the voidoids mysteriously stopped producing the stuff."

Woo had clearly used the word "mysteriously" only for the benefit of his audience. Aiden knew that, for Woo, it was no mystery at all.

Aiden glanced at his chrono. "Time is wasting, people. How do we destroy this thing?"

"Not with projectile weapons," Woo said. "No rail guns or torpedoes. We'd need to get close enough for those weapons to be effective, and their impacts are likely to detonate the device. We could be seriously damaged by the blast."

"Right," Hotah said. "We'd need to be well within 50 kilometers for the rail guns, a bit farther for a quick torpedo strike. But at these velocities, targeting formulas for those weapons will be too fuzzy, especially if we have to shut down the ZPD to make the shot. Laser cannon, at full power, would be our best bet. And that would be effective from a greater distance too. Say, 200 klicks out?"

"Yes," Woo said. "That's comfortably beyond the projected blast perimeter."

Devi looked at Aiden, brow knit. "And if we fail to stop it in time? If it hits Shénmì?"

Aiden had to force the words out of his mouth. "The entire surface of the planet will be incinerated. Including oceans. Right down to the bedrock. Depending on how the device is set up, the destruction could stop there, limited only to the planet's surface. Or it could be set so that the blast would cast off a halo of lethal radiation, expanding into space for millions of kilometers at nearly light speed. It would take out Shénmì Station in a flash."

Along with Skye.

Interrupting the dark silence that followed Aiden's words, Hotah spoke. "We're in position to engage now. Firing point in two minutes."

The *Sun Wolf* had sprinted ahead of the missile to set up its firing position. The ship would have to momentarily drop out of the zero-point drive to make the shot. During that brief interval, it would be unable to compensate for the missile's 300 G acceleration, and the deadly weapon would zip past them before Hotah could target and fire.

To compensate, they had raced ahead to where the missile *would* be when the ZPD shut down and set their velocity to match the missile's velocity at that exact point in its acceleration curve, right around 45 percent light speed. Aiden was glad Hutton had done the math for their flight computer. It was the kind of "fuzzy" logic the AI was built for, extracting accurate solutions from incomplete data.

The maneuver would put the *Sun Wolf* a safe 200 kilometers away from the missile and allow a narrow time window to get off a laser shot. Seven seconds at best. And at that point, the missile would be 1.5 AU from Shénmì. Less than 30 minutes from impact. Not a lot of room for error.

Alvarez looked up from her screen. "I'm assuming that both the antigluon bomb and the missile's AM tanks will blow at the same time. Are we sure that 200 kilometers is a safe distance when that happens?"

"Yes," Woo replied. "The antigluon bomb needs mass to feed on, in a chain reaction, to emit significant radiation. The missile's mass is negligible compared to a planet. And the AM tanks are probably close to empty by now. A blast wave from either or both of them won't harm us from that distance."

"Also," Aiden added, "Hutton will power up the ZPD bubble around the ship just after the shot is fired. That will effectively shield us from debris and the blast wave."

"That is correct," Hutton chimed in with an overtone that Aiden recognized as the AI's intent to say something more. And he did.

"Just to set the record straight," Hutton said, "the term *anti-gluon* is technically incorrect. Gluons are massless and have zero charge. Therefore, they have no antiparticles. More accurately, a gluon is its own antiparticle."

"Hutton . . ." How could the AI prattle on about something like this, at a time like this?

"The device," Hutton continued, "can more accurately be described as an antiquark bomb. Quarks are the most fundamental and indivisible building blocks of matter, binding together to make up all matter in the universe. But they are held together by gluons, which act as exchange particles for the strong force between them. This weapon uses *antiquarks* to disrupt that exchange, causing matter to disintegrate. Therefore, the term antiquark is more—"

"Hutton! Enough!" The AI clammed up. Aiden rolled his eyes and looked at Elgin Woo for sympathy.

Woo just shrugged and said, "He's right, of course."

"Firing point in 10 seconds," Hotah said. "Shutting down the ZPD."

Aiden turned toward the screen. Perspiration popped out on his forehead. He wiped at it and watched as the image of the missile entered the targeting frame. The weapon moved across the screen slowly but with increasing speed. When it reached the center of the crosshairs, Hotah fired the laser cannon.

Using its huge 10-meter reflecting mirrors, the *Sun Wolf*'s laser cannon sent a two-gigawatt laser pulse from its aperture across 200 kilometers of empty space to pack 50 megajoules of destructive energy into a pinpoint spot, no more than eight centimeters in diameter. A direct hit on the spherical surface of the missile's warhead. Even the warhead's highly reflective surface couldn't stop that much juice from burning a gaping hole. A glowing cloud of plasma flashed out and away from the wound. But the weapon did not detonate.

"Hit the AM tanks, Lieutenant," Aiden said.

Hotah directed another two-gigawatt pulse at the antimatter tanks. The brilliance of the explosion briefly blinded the optical sensors. When the screen cleared, they saw a halo of star-hot plasma and molten debris blossoming in all directions from where the missile had been. The blast was more powerful than expected, but the ZPD bubble had rebooted around the ship in time to protect them.

A collective sigh of relief lightened the mood on the bridge. Postures of tension relaxed. Smiles broke out all around. If there had been champagne aboard, it would have been poured.

Until they heard Billy Hotah say, "Oh shit!"

Aiden followed Hotah's gaze back to the screen. Virtually nothing was left of the missile's fuselage. But the spherical warhead remained intact, even with the ugly hole burned into its side. But worse, it remained on the same course as the missile had been. Directly toward Shénmì and still at 45 percent light speed. The momentum it had gained just before the rest of the missile blew up was way more than enough to overcome any course disruption caused by the force of the explosion.

Aiden felt like he'd been gut-punched. "Frickin' thing is hard to kill."

"But it *has* to be dead," Alvarez said. "That first shot smacked it with a shitload of energy. How could any of its electronics survive that?"

It sounded entirely plausible, even likely—especially when underlined by Alvarez's rarely used profanity. But how could they be sure it was dead? Aiden looked at Woo for an answer. The only person in Bound Space on the right side of Nature's law who knew anything about how the device worked, Woo said nothing, an unmistakable question mark in his eyes.

"Alvarez. I want its exact course heading. And the probability of it hitting the planet."

She responded immediately, having already done the scan. "It's the exact same course as before. Headed directly at Shénmì. One hundred percent probability of a direct hit."

"On the bright side," Hotah interjected, "with its thrust system gone, it's no longer accelerating. It's maintaining a constant velocity."

"Right. Only 45 percent light speed," Aiden said, unable to keep sarcasm from his voice. "What's that? About 145,000 klicks per second? At this point, it'll hit the planet at nearly the same time it would have if we hadn't blown the rest of it up. How much time before impact?"

"Twenty-seven minutes," Ro said offhandedly. The XO's curiously phlegmatic demeanor at times of high tension usually had a calming effect on the bridge. This time, it didn't.

"I think the point Lieutenant Hotah is making," Woo said, "is that now we don't have to match acceleration rates, only match a constant velocity. It'll be a lot easier to pull alongside the warhead and target it with our weapons. Plus, after we've matched velocities, we can shut down the ZPD for as long as we need to target and fire."

"Let's get to it, then," Aiden said. His heart was pounding, his gut tightening.

"We could even use the rail gun this time," Hotah said. "At close range. The laser cannon used a lot of juice. It'll take too long to repower. We'd be wasting valuable time waiting for it. Now that we don't have to compensate for an accelerating target, I can blow that thing up with one eye closed."

Aiden had learned that, despite the testosterone-laden tone of such pronouncements, Billy Hotah was not prone to making idle boasts. Lieutenant William Hotah had served aboard the SS *Endeavor*, the UED's Military Space Service flagship, and saw action in the Battle of Chara. He was credited with a crucial kill against an ARM Militia battle cruiser, a near impossible shot with a rail gun. Since then, he still held the unofficial title of the hottest rail gunner in the Service. If anyone alive could pull this one off, even with one eye closed, it was the man now sitting at *Sun Wolf*'s Tactical Station.

"How close do you want us, Lieutenant?"

12

HD 10180 SYSTEM
Cis-Shénmì Space

Domain Day 338, 2218

Hotah responded without hesitation. "Fifty kilometers would do it. Our rail gun has a muzzle velocity of 10 KPS. That'd be a five-second strike time. Easy shot."

Aiden looked at Woo. "Isn't that a bit close if the warhead is still alive and blows?"

"No. That's good," Woo said. "The antigluon device . . . uh, correction, anitquark device, has a blast effect proportional to the mass it destroys in a chain reaction. Out here in space, with only the tiny mass of its container left to feed on, the blast will be relatively insignificant."

For added protection, Aiden ordered Hutton to activate the ZPD bubble immediately after the shot was taken.

"Aye, aye, sir," the AI said. With a hint of sarcasm? Hutton was probably still peeved at having his poorly timed dissertation on gluons cut short.

The warhead was 20 minutes from impact when the *Sun Wolf* moved into position to fire. The device was likely disabled already, but no one was willing to bet on it. All eyes were glued to the screen.

Hotah pulled the trigger.

Within a 30-second firing span, the rail gun let loose 10 rounds of wicked-looking, solid-tungsten projectiles weighing one kilogram each. With a muzzle velocity of 10 kilometers per second, each one packed the explosive energy equivalent to 12 kilograms of TNT.

It was overkill. The slowed-down video of the assault showed the very first projectile hitting the warhead with so much power that the entire structure exploded into white-hot plasma.

Followed instantaneously by the detonation of an antiquark bomb.

The space-time matrix immediately surrounding the bomb glowed an eerie ultraviolet before collapsing in upon itself and reintegrating into the seamless continuum of the zero-point field, temporarily negating the physical laws of the universe for a fraction of a second.

Stunned silence filled the bridge. Thank the gods that no more of these obscene devices existed. And thank the voidoids for preventing them from ever being created again. Score another point for Elgin Woo's belief that the voidoids were sentient guardians over all life in the universe.

The *Sun Wolf* fired up its ZPD again, this time to put the brakes on and drop out of relativistic velocity. The ship came to a standstill approximately 1 AU from Shénmì. Aiden asked Hutton to perform Level Two diagnostics for damage assessment. He used the time to message Skye and assure her that the station and the planet were no longer in danger. He doubted his matter-of-fact tone sounded convincing. Skye knew him too well.

He concluded by saying, "We'll be returning to the station briefly to drop Elgin off."

The eight-minute time lag between comm exchanges didn't encourage elaboration beyond the basics. When he finally received Skye's response, she said, "See you soon, then. And Aiden, we're at a loss here to express our gratitude for what you and your crew have done for us. For saving our lives and the life of the planet. So, just a heartfelt 'thank you' from all of us here at Shénmì Station. Skye Landen, out."

Aiden choked back his emotions. The crew had been watching him and listening. They averted their eyes discreetly before resuming their tasks.

Elgin Woo approached and stood next to him. Aiden looked at him and asked, "Why would Cardew use the last of his ultimate weapons, the antiquark device, against Shénmì? And why now?"

Woo shrugged. "He might have attacked now because you and the *Sun Wolf* are here. He's been trying to destroy both you and this ship—mostly you—from the moment he knew you were on to him."

Aiden shook his head. "That doesn't make sense. How could he have known the *Sun Wolf* would be here at this moment in time? His intel can't be that good. Can it?"

It was a question with answers he didn't want to contemplate right now. His confidence in the meaning of "top secret" had been sorely tested over the last few days.

Woo responded with a neutral shrug. Aiden said, "No. I think his real target was Shénmì. He's already tried to invade this system once, presumably to capture Shénmì."

"Yes," Woo said, "and he would have succeeded if he'd brought the *Conquest* along for that invasion. After the *Markos* was destroyed, it's the only ship left in his fleet that can generate the negative-G shielding, the same technology the *Markos* used to wipe out all the Alliance warships back at V-Prime. We still haven't figured out how to defeat that kind of shielding. With the *Conquest* spearheading the invasion, his forces could have waltzed right in and captured Shénmì with negligible losses."

The *Markos* and the *Conquest* had been the only two ships in Cardew's fleet capable of generating the impenetrable neg-G shielding. That was because they were the only two ships he'd hijacked with their original Omicron-3 AIs aboard. And the Omicrons were the only intelligence systems sophisticated enough to manipulate the complex EM fields needed to mimic negative gravity. The *Markos* had been destroyed during its encounter with the *Sun Wolf*. Now only Cardew's ship, the *Conquest*, was invincible in combat. Why hadn't the *Conquest* come along for the party months ago when his forces had the chance to capture Shénmì?

Aiden filed the question away and moved on to a related one. "So if Cardew wants Shénmì so bad, why the hell is he trying to destroy it now, instead of capturing it? Why waste such a valuable living planet, the crown jewel of an entire astrocell?"

Woo tilted his head thoughtfully. "I think something has changed in Cardew's world. Something that compels him to destroy Shénmì, rather than capture it."

"Like what?"

Woo grimaced for a moment, as if envisioning some private horror, then said, "I believe that Cardew fears Shénmì now. That Shénmì poses some kind of mortal threat to him and his grand designs. So his plans for it have changed."

Aiden couldn't imagine what kind of threat Shénmì could possibly pose to a man with Cardew's power. Beyond the eternal warfare between all things natural and all things unnatural, he couldn't think of any specific point of conflict between Cardew and the planet Shénmì. He asked Woo if he knew.

"I have only a hunch at this time," Woo said, twirling one end of his moustache with his fingers. "I'm not sure of it yet. But what I am sure of is that finding an answer to that question is the key to defeating Cardew for good."

Aiden looked back at the main screen, at the realtime telescopic image of Shénmì. "What's Cardew's end game, Elgin? What's he really after?"

Woo responded without hesitation. "For one thing, he wants total domination over this entire astrocell. I think that much is clear. He wants to prevent the rest of humanity from gaining any ground out here. He couldn't do it by sealing off the gateway between here and Bound Space. Thanks to you, Aiden, we foiled him in that attempt. Now he'll resort to stamping out any toeholds that we manage to gain out here, while at the same time, he'll be finding new habitable worlds that he can quickly colonize and fortify."

New habitable worlds. Aiden looked Woo in the eye and said, "Skye tells me there may be a lot more habitable earthlike planets in this astrocell than in Bound Space."

"That's right," Woo said, warming to the subject. "Way more. It's really a remarkable discovery, excellent work by the Mapping Project. Even by the narrowest definition of sunlike stars, it comes to nearly 5,000 perfectly habitable planets inside this astrocell. And up to 7,000 if we use the project's broader criteria."

Aiden cocked his head, continuing to hold eye contact. "She also said that the AMP scientists identified at least 10 star systems from our list of 15 that harbor earthlike planets within habitable zones. That was fast work, Elgin. Especially considering the top-secret nature of that list."

Woo bowed his head momentarily. A gesture of guilt or modesty? Aiden wasn't sure. "Um . . . yes. I apologize for taking such liberties with that data. But I trust AMP's scientists unconditionally."

Aiden wasn't about to let Woo off the hook that easily. "Elgin, level with me here. What other tidbits of information about this mission have you told anyone else?"

Woo met his eyes, dead serious. "Other than that, I shared what I knew about the cloneborgs with Skye and Colonel Crestfield. What we discovered about them and what we suspect. I thought it was crucial for them to have an idea of what we're up against with Cardew's minions."

Woo was right about that, he had to admit. And Aiden regretted not passing that information on to Skye himself. He needed to pass it on to Admiral Stegman now as well. They were at war, and everyone fighting it should be informed of the dangers they're likely to face.

"Okay, Elgin," he said, lightening up. "I agree with you there. Nonetheless, you're part of our mission now. Please consult with me first the next time you consider passing on any more information about it. To anyone else outside this ship."

Woo bowed again, this time more convincingly. "I promise."

"Good. And Elgin, thank you for identifying those 10 star systems. That narrows our search priorities considerably."

Woo nodded but did not smile. "I fear that Cardew is occupying one of those star systems right now, licking his chops over the rest of them, surrounded by his ever-growing army of cloneborgs. That's why we can't waste a single minute. We need to get out there now and start the hunt."

Aiden looked sideways at Woo. "*We*?"

"Yes. We. I've decided to come with you on your mission. I think I can be of assistance. If you'll allow me, that is."

"As a matter of fact," Aiden said, "I was about to ask if you'd care to join us. We could use your expertise, along with all of your . . . hunches. The ones that always turn out to be right, at least. Welcome aboard, Elgin."

Woo made a third bow, this one as a formality. When he brought his head back up, he was grinning ear to ear, like a kid in a candy shop.

"What about the research instruments you were going to deliver to the station?" Aiden asked. "We didn't get a chance to off-load them in all the excitement. They're still aboard the *Sun Wolf*."

"Not a problem," Woo said. "The ones for my own project I can use just as easily here aboard the ship. The ones intended for AMP aren't critical right now. Besides, they could be useful to us for where we're going."

Asking Woo to clarify cryptic remarks like this was usually pointless, even when they were obviously calculated ones, not off-handed. "Well, then," Aiden said. "If we don't need to drop you off, or the instruments, there's no logical reason for us to return to Shénmì Station."

There was, of course, a completely illogical reason to return. To be with Skye again, even for just a moment. Before he could come up with *some* kind of logical reason, Alvarez spoke up from Comm/Scan. "Commander. We have an urgent message from Colonel Crestfield at Shénmì Station."

"Open the comm." The time lag from Shénmì was still too long for back-and-forth conversation. This comm would be in status-report format.

Crestfield's face appeared on the screen. The station's security chief was a stocky man in his midfifties with red hair, buzz cut in military style, and pale blue eyes that seemed permanently squinted, as if even the faintest light was too bright for him. He was clean-shaven and spoke with an Australian accent that had been tamed by decades of service in UED's multinational security forces.

"Commander Macallan. I've been asked to inform you that Friendship Station, back at Sol, is now in lockdown and under strict quarantine. An outbreak of a highly contagious and deadly virus occurred aboard the station the day after you departed. The medical people there have been unable to identify the virus by any known genotype. It's completely novel, meaning there's no immunity to it in the human population. Some are suggesting that the virus was introduced from somewhere outside Bound Space, from Astrocell Beta.

"Ships are no longer allowed to dock at Friendship Station, and the Alliance has blockaded V-Prime, denying passage of all unauthorized ships into the Sol System. Any ship that defies the ban will be forcibly detained and placed under indefinite quarantine. The virus seems contained to the station so far, but we'll keep you posted. Now, I have Dr. Spaulding here with me. He has his own report for you."

The figure of a man at least a decade older than Crestfield appeared on the screen. His face was gaunt and craggy, his eyes light brown and tense. Wisps of thinning gray hair were combed backward over his balding scalp in denial of advancing age. He looked as if he hadn't shaved in a week and rubbed the stubble on his chin with one hand as he spoke.

"I'm Dr. Carl Spaulding, head of the Allied Mapping Project. I wanted to alert you and Dr. Woo of a troubling incident. Another one of our Holtzman survey probes has gone missing. It was investigating a very promising star system. We lost contact with it early this morning and haven't been able to reestablish it. That makes the third one we've lost in this manner, leaving us with only three.

I understand that a part of your survey mission is to investigate these disappearances, so I thought you should know about this one. I'm transmitting all the pertinent information to you now."

Spaulding's transmission ended abruptly, and the data on a star designated HD 4308 appeared on Alvarez's monitor. Aiden and Woo looked at it, then at each other. HD 4308 just happened to be on their new list of 10.

"Helm," Aiden said. "Set course for the voidoid. Maximum velocity. From there, we jump to a star called HD 4308."

13

HD 4308 SYSTEM
Post-Jump

DOMAIN DAY 338, 2218

Star: HD 4308

Spectral type: G5V

Distance from Sol: 71.9 light-years

Luminosity: 1.03 x Sol

Surface temperature: 5,714 Kelvin

Number of planets: 5

Habitable zone: 0.97–1.70 AU

– Source: *Allied Mapping Project, 2218*

"I'M picking up one weapons drone stationed back at the voidoid," Hotah said. "I don't think it's seen us yet."

No surprise, Aiden thought. The *Sun Wolf* had just popped out of the star's voidoid at 10 percent light speed and come to a halt 450,000 kilometers beyond it. As they'd planned, the maneuver completely bamboozled the weapons drone standing guard at the voidoid.

Aiden looked at Hotah. "Kill it."

"With pleasure." The red speckled band tattooed across Hotah's face darkened.

"You have the Helm, Lieutenant." Standard operation—Tactical takes over the Helm for routine combat maneuvers.

Hotah engaged the ZPD. In two seconds, the ship stood five kilometers from the drone. The image of it appeared on the main screen. It was larger than standard robotic weapons platforms, bristling with sensor wands. One rail gun and one nasty-looking laser cannon were mounted topside in separate turrets. The laser cannon began turning its business end toward the *Sun Wolf.*

Hotah paused for a moment, just long enough for the whole crew to get a good look and tense up, before firing the ship's laser cannon. Hotah's propensity to showboat in situations like this still annoyed Aiden. But the man always hit his mark, on time and in tune, so Aiden kept cutting him slack.

It was a medium-range shot, a half-second pulse pumped out at one gigawatt. The drone shook like a startled beast for a fraction of a second before the whole thing exploded in a glowing plume of charged particles and vanished.

"Right," Aiden said. "Let's see if any more of these pests are lurking around. Take us to the other side of the voidoid."

Like all voidoids, this one was 18.2 kilometers in diameter, give or take a few hundred meters. The black circle of nothingness seen from any angle was perfectly opaque. The *Sun Wolf* circled it slowly and found no other vessels or comm buoys hidden on the opposite side.

Aiden asked Alvarez to do a long-range scan. She studied her screen for a moment before shaking her head. "Looks like we're alone out here, at least out to 1 AU. No other vessels. But I did pick up a small debris field, not far from here, about 30 klicks from the voidoid. Metallic fragments."

"Probably the remains of AMP's survey drone," Woo said, shaking his head. "This star system was next on the Mapping Project's list to explore. The drone was sent out here just days ago to start the survey."

"Cardew must be interested in this system too," Aiden said, "and doesn't want anyone else nosing around."

He looked more closely at the realtime image of the star up on the main screen. Categorized as a G5V spectral type and about the same size and luminosity as Sol, HD 4308 glowed with a rich yellow light. Even from here, nearly two billion kilometers away, it burned like a beacon, a sharp point of living energy defying the nothingness of space.

Aiden shook himself from its spell and turned to Alvarez. "Lilly, put up a schematic of this system on the main screen. Maybe we can identify what Cardew finds so interesting."

The data for the system was based on telescopic information AMP had gathered before sending its ill-fated drone to examine it in realtime. It revealed a system of five planets, labeled HD 4308b, c, d, e, and f—by convention, the letter *a* was reserved for the parent star. The closest planet to the star, HD 4308b, was classified as a Neptune-like planet, with the added descriptor of "hot" due to its close proximity to the star. The next two planets out, c and d, were rocky, terrestrial planets in the inner region. Two Class-I gas giants occupied the outer region, designated e and f. A typical asteroid belt populated the region between the inner and outer planets. Like the Solar System's Kuiper Belt, it was a broad ring of icy objects in slow procession just beyond gas giant e, starting 15 AU out from the star and extending for another 15 beyond.

"Lilly, do a preliminary survey of the system from here to update any data that AMP might have missed. Including a recalculation of its habitable zone."

While Alvarez bent to the task, Aiden deployed a Holtzman buoy near the voidoid to set up a link with Shénmì Station. The buoy had to be precisely calibrated to exchange data between itself and the Holtzman buoy at the target star's voidoid.

The Holtzman effect was still poorly understood. More was known about what it was *not*. It was not, for instance, a true transmission process. No emissions of any kind had ever been detected passing between two Holtzman devices while they exchanged data. Only a second Holtzman device of the exact same encryption could process data from the first, and only when they were separated by voidoids.

Moments later, Alvarez looked up and said, "I've done a data update. It's all pretty accurate. AMP did a good job, considering it didn't have a Holtzman probe out here to gather realtime data. The numbers on planet b actually confirm most of the original HARPS data from two centuries ago. Those old guys were pretty good."

Interesting, but not what Aiden was after. "The habitable zone, Lilly?"

Alvarez brightened. "Yep, that's the interesting part. Planet d is right in the middle of this star's habitable zone. About 1.3 AU out."

"And the other terrestrial planet, the one closer in?"

"Planet c? It's too close to the star. About .75 AU. Not a comfortable place by any stretch. Sorta like Venus. Hot. Runaway greenhouse effect. No, planet d is the prime real estate out here."

"Planet d it is," Aiden said. "Let's check it out. Helm, take us there, maximum drive. Put us in high orbit."

Within two hours, the *Sun Wolf* had pulled into orbit around the planet at 35,000 kilometers above its surface. Hotah confirmed that no hostiles lurked in the vicinity. Alvarez said, "I've got biological signs, Commander. There's a biosphere down there."

"Give us a visual. Main screen."

Earth's population took the miracle of life for granted. Maybe less so now, after the catastrophic Die Back had stunned them into realizing how precious life on Earth was, and after witnessing so much of it dying out from their own carelessness. Unfortunately, Earthers had short memories and little taste for lessons of history. But for longtime spacers like Aiden and his crew, it was a different matter. For them, any example of the miracle of life found thriving in the unimaginably vast, cold emptiness of space never failed to evoke deep reverence.

The planet turning slowly below them was no exception. To Aiden's eye, it was undoubtedly alive. About the same size as Earth, slightly smaller, its oceans covered over half of its surface. Landmasses with broad lowlands rising to snowcapped mountain ranges occupied the rest. The coloring of the land surfaces ran the spectrum from dusty dun near the equator to dark green all the way to the poles, indicating a wide range of geography from deserts to dense vegetation. The polar regions looked temperate, without ice sheets. Swirls of clouds spawned by vast weather systems decorated the atmosphere with abstract shapes. Yellow sunlight from the star reflected brilliantly off the oceans through gaps in the cloud cover.

Alvarez powered up the Planetary Survey Array, and basic data began populating the screen's sidebar. Diameter and mass about 0.8 and 0.92 of Earth's, respectively. Two moons, both of them smaller than Luna. A 20-hour day and a 383-day year. A thick atmosphere of 80 percent nitrogen, 19 percent oxygen, and just under 0.1 percent CO_2. An axial tilt of 25 percent, a surface gravity of 0.94 G. A global mean average temperature of 15 degrees centigrade. Aside from the somewhat high atmospheric CO_2, all of it was in the same ballpark as Earth, Silvanus, or Shénmì. It seemed that humanity had just added to its wish list a third perfectly habitable world beyond its own.

"Wow . . ." Elgin Woo hadn't taken his eyes from the screen since the moment the jewel of a planet appeared on it. To Aiden, it was another Silvanus. To Elgin, it was another Shénmì. Both men had been profoundly changed by their individual solitary journeys on those planets. Both had felt the pulse of alien life beating within their own chests, had conversed with a global intelligence in languages beyond words, singing an ancient music of longing and becoming.

"Wow, indeed," Aiden said. "It deserves a better name than just d. Any suggestions?"

He looked around at his crew. The question mark hung in the air until Sudha Devi spoke up. "How about Aasha?"

"I like the sound of it. What does it mean?"

"It means *hope* in Hindi. Starting with two letter *a*'s."

Aiden glanced at his crew. Everyone smiled. Even Ro. Everyone except Hotah, whose eyes were still glued to the tactical screen, his body motionless except for his slowly nodding head. Aiden took that as Hotah's silent approval.

"Aasha it is, then," he said. "Lilly, enter that designation into our survey log."

Aiden couldn't help smiling. He knew that giving the planet a real name would tick off the IAU. Again. That archaic international organization still opposed naming exoplanets anything other than their official designation. But he knew everyone else would vote for *Aasha* over *HD 4308d*. Especially if they'd seen it up close and personal.

"Helm, move the ship into a low orbit at 500 kilometers. We'll initiate a full orbital scan of the planet, equatorial and polar. Maximum detail. Search for any signs of artificial structures, or anything else that looks out of place."

The *Sun Wolf* carried the most advanced remote-sensor instruments of any voidship in Bound Space. Even so, a maximum-detail orbital survey would take over six hours. Three full orbits, inclined sixty degrees apart.

Aiden looked at his chrono. It was nearly 23:00. It had been a long day. Alvarez in particular looked exhausted. He instructed the whole crew to commence a six-hour sleep cycle. Everyone except himself and Ro. They would do separate three-hour shifts at Command. He instructed Hutton to handle all routine functions, including the survey scan and watching out for hostiles.

"I've got it covered, Commander," Hutton chimed in musically. "Rest easy."

Aiden had to smile. The AI's ever-evolving comprehension of linguistic nuance was always fascinating and often amusing. Hutton had mastered so much of the complexity of human thought patterns since Aiden had first given him a name and a nascent personality years ago aboard the *Argo*.

Ro approached. "I'll take the first Command shift. You need the shut-eye more than I do. Go."

Sensing the depth of his own fatigue, Aiden was tempted to accept his XO's offer but said, "Thanks, Ro. But I'm taking first watch. Hit the sack now. I'll see you in three hours."

Ro shrugged and left the bridge with the rest of the crew. Aiden leaned back in the command chair, took a deep breath, and let it out slowly, releasing the tension from his shoulders. He hadn't been alone, by himself quietly, for ages. It was a state of mind that Aiden craved, that he *needed*, to keep himself centered. But there'd been little time for it since taking command of the *Sun Wolf.* He'd become more irritable in its absence. More easily distracted. The high price paid for command.

He spent the next half hour gazing at the realtime optical image of local space, away from the planet, toward the star-studded emptiness. After all his many years spent in space, the wonder of it had never lessened. Its mystery. Its unfathomable vastness. Its unforgiving harshness.

Aiden got up, moved to Comm/Scan station, and sat facing the bank of screens and input boards where Lilly Alvarez spent most of her waking hours. He noticed a small holopic sitting next to the center screen. It held the image of a young woman with short, bristly blonde hair, a strong jaw, and warm brown eyes. During the five-second vid-loop inside the frame, her smile changed from casual humor to one of quizzical concern.

He knew who she was. Alvarez's partner, Deana Stapleton. Captain of a long-hauler, killed in a mining accident two years ago out at Wolf 359. The tragedy had been compounded by the fact that Stapleton had been carrying the couple's unborn child, an IVF pregnancy. Aiden had seen Alvarez glance at the holopic while working Comm/Scan, especially in moments of high stress. But he'd never seen it close up. He felt embarrassed looking at it now. Guilty of an invasion of privacy he hadn't intended.

Aiden looked away and focused on a side screen, where he brought up the atmospheric data on the planet below. The CO_2 content was a lot higher than Earth's 0.045 percent. But CO_2 was not toxic by itself, only if it was high enough to displace the oxygen in the air. As long as the oxygen content was within certain limits, they could breathe the air down there without respirators. The planet's magnetic field and ozone levels in the upper atmosphere were sufficient to protect its surface from harmful solar radiation.

The real danger would be the presence of microbes or allergens in the environment that could sicken or kill a person wandering around unprotected. He needed to check that out before sending a team planetside.

Reluctantly breaking the luxurious silence, he said, "Hutton, prepare and launch a Level Two analytic probe to the surface. Assay for threat potentials, chemical and biological."

"Right away, Aiden." Hutton addressed Aiden by his first name only when the two of them were alone together.

The threat-potential analysis should be in by the time the crew returned to the bridge. It would determine whether or not they'd need to don environmental suits for a jaunt downside. E-suits were cumbersome and uncomfortable, not to mention how they limited a person's sensory experience of a place.

But he needed to consider one other threat potential: hostile forces. E-suits or not, they'd need to go down well armed.

14

HD 4308 SYSTEM
Aasha, Low Orbit

DOMAIN DAY 339, 2218

AIDEN had just returned to the bridge after his three hours of restless sleep, when he heard Alvarez say, "The sensors are picking up an anomaly on the planet's surface."

The rest of the crew had assembled on the bridge after their sleep cycle. Only Elgin Woo looked well rested. Aiden relieved Ro at Command, sat, and addressed Alvarez. "Tell me more."

"It appears to be an underground structure," she said. "Rectangular in shape, 60 to 70 meters long and about 20 wide. Its position is approximately 23 degrees south of the equator, located in a wide valley below a mountain range. The only portion of it clearly visible looks like an entrance way. There are also several small structures on top. Could be ventilation caps."

"Any signs of life? Any IR heat signatures?"

"None. And no other radiation signatures. Looks cold."

"All right. We'll send a team down to investigate."

Ro spoke from his secondary post at Science Station. "The bio-threat analysis probe is already in. Its instruments detect no airborne or waterborne compounds that could be considered toxic, or anything in the ground or in the plant life. At least not where the probe took samples. Particulate matter in the atmosphere appears benign—mostly dusts of varying composition, some pollen-like material, as well as something that looks like spores."

"Spores?" Aiden's mental antennae perked up. "What kind?"

"The spores appear to be from either fungal sources or non-seed-bearing plant life. Like ferns, mosses, liverworts, and the like. A preliminary analysis of the pollen and spore coats indicates acceptable compatibility with human physiology, nontoxic and nonallergenic."

"What about other threats? Animal predators?"

"The probe hasn't detected any forms of large, land-dwelling animals at or near the sample site. But such creatures could easily have avoided detection."

Aiden stroked his beard. There were, of course, thousands of other ways a purely vegetable world could kill them just as surely as one supporting ferocious beasts. The bottom line, though, was they wouldn't need full E-suits.

"But we will wear life-support masks," he said. "With Class-M filters. At least until our on-site analytics tell us it's safe to go without them."

Aiden stood, shaking off the dizziness of sleep deprivation. "I'll take a team downside to check out that underground structure. Lieutenant Hotah, Drs. Woo and Devi will accompany me. We will go armed."

He gave Devi a questioning look. He knew she wasn't a big fan of handheld weapons or of tromping through unexplored alien landscapes. But he wanted her in-person expertise on site. She smiled back at him and said, "I'm in."

Aiden thanked her with a nod, turned to Ro, and said, "XO, you have Command while we're downside."

Ro, master of blank expressions, replied in monotone, "We'll manage."

Stifling a smile, Aiden said, "Team members, grab your gear and meet me in the armory to pick up some protection. From there, on to the shuttle bay."

Hotah didn't exactly rub his hands together or lick his chops, but his eyes said it all. The man was just as lethal with antipersonnel weapons as he was with the ship's rail guns and laser cannons. As always, Aiden was glad Hotah had his back.

He stopped briefly at his quarters and changed into a tight-cuffed jumpsuit, close-fitting around ankles and wrists. He grabbed his personal life-support mask from his gear locker. The masks were essentially standard industrial respirators, designed to protect a person from dangerous chemical or biological agents. But Survey Branch liked to call them "life-support masks." Less low-brow, Aiden guessed.

He arrived at the armory on deck two to find Hotah and Woo waiting for him to unlock the arsenal. The *Sun Wolf*'s armory packed a variety of handheld weapons, locked under tight security, accessible only by the captain and the XO. They were all projectile weapons, mostly "smart guns" designed for use in a variety of extreme environments, both pressurized and hard vacuum, and in zero gravity. No one yet had invented an effective beam weapon small enough and light enough to be handheld, and probably never would. Ray guns were still the stuff of science fiction.

Hotah chose his favorite weapon, the SR-13, a large assault-style Spacer Carbine with three barrels. One was for 5.7mm armor-piercing rounds, another for either standard 13mm hollow-point slugs or low-velocity rubber bullets. The third barrel had a gaping 20mm shotgun bore for specialty ammunition, including crowd-control shot, heavy slugs, or grenades. The weapon also featured a nonlethal sonic stunner to incapacitate targets with minimal physical injury. The heavy SR-13 required two-handed use, but Aiden had seen Hotah manage it one-handed with ease.

Aiden chose a lightweight .40-caliber pistol and stowed it in an easily accessible thigh holster. Woo followed his example, chose the same weapon, and examined it with obvious fascination.

"Do you know how to use one of those, Elgin?"

Woo grinned as he slipped the pistol into its holster in one smooth movement. "You'd be surprised."

No doubt, Aiden thought. He glanced at Sudha Devi, waiting patiently in the corridor. As usual, she had declined the use of a weapon, claiming that she possessed certain mental powers that were just as lethal. Aiden almost believed her. Nonetheless, he asked her to stay close to Lieutenant Hotah.

The four of them boarded the landing shuttle and strapped in. Aiden sat in the pilot's chair and looked back at his team. "Tallyho!"

~ ~ ~

The *Sun Wolf*'s landing shuttle was a VTOL craft, capable of landing and taking off in a vertical position with no runway space needed. The crew had named it the *Victor Aminu*, after their honorary crewman who had saved their lives during a previous mission—and probably the lives of everyone else in Bound Space—by sacrificing his own. Aiden brought the shuttle down on level ground 200 kilometers from the entrance to the mysterious structure they'd spotted from orbit.

Before exiting the craft, Aiden powered up the shuttle's survey array and ran another bio-threat analysis of the immediate surroundings. After confirming the survey probe's earlier results, they donned their respirator masks, cycled through the airlock without pressurization, and assembled under the shuttle's nose. Devi used her portable bioanalytic kit to run a final, and most accurate, environmental assay. They stood around, shuffling their feet in the late afternoon sun until Devi finally looked up and said, "I think we're safe to go on without the respirators."

The first thing Aiden noticed when he removed his mask was a strong, earthy aroma, but not unpleasant, fresh and with a hint of licorice or aniseed. The air felt warm, close to 30 degrees centigrade according to Devi's kit, and humid. They stood inside the circular area of ground that had been scoured clean by the shuttle's landing jets. Beyond that, they were surrounded on all sides by a dense shrublike forest of primitive-looking plants. At least they looked primitive to Aiden, evoking images he'd seen in his paleontology class at Luna U depicting what Earth life might have looked like several hundred million years ago. Woody plants that resembled ferns and horsetails, and some that resembled palm trees but with fernlike fronds sprouting from their tops, four or five meters tall.

They had landed in a broad valley, maybe 10 kilometers wide, with the shrubby forest spreading out in all directions and up to the low-lying ridges on either side. Far beyond the valley's head, a massive mountain range pushed several jagged peaks high into the cobalt blue sky. Only the highest pinnacles were draped with shimmering white snow, while the lower flanks exposed bare rock or sporadic vegetation wherever it had taken root. Viewed from orbit, Aiden had seen at least three major streams flowing from the highlands down into one larger river that ran down the center of the valley, wending its way to the shore of the planet's southern ocean, about 20 kilometers away.

"Let's move out," Aiden said. "Eyes open."

Hotah instinctively took the lead, his SR-13 held ready. The rest followed. Woo's face, beatific with fascination, glanced from side to side, scanning the landscape around him. But his hand stayed close to his holstered pistol. Aiden held his weapon at his side, unholstered, pointed down, finger on the trigger housing.

The ground felt soft, almost spongy, as he walked across it. At first, he wondered if it was due to the lower surface gravity here, making him feel lighter and causing his body to interpret the sensation as treading on a soft surface. But then he noticed that the ground was carpeted with pads of springy, greenish material that looked a lot like liverworts. He knelt down to examine it. In the spaces between the pads, the ground was covered with a fine network of tiny, white filaments. They had an uncanny resemblance to the mats of fungal mycelia he'd seen on Silvanus.

The scans from orbit had found no evidence of large land-dwelling creatures, and the group saw none as they moved carefully through the vegetation. Insects, however, were abundant, both flying and wingless, as well as other forms that would be classified as arthropods on Earth. As Aiden trudged on through the shrubs, occasional swarms of small fly-like insects rose from the ground in undulating clouds, disturbed by his passage. Fortunately, these insectoids showed little interest in him. Aiden examined one that had landed on a leaf. About one centimeter in length, it appeared to have six articulated legs, three on each side, and three compound eyes on its head.

Devi found a number of creatures that looked like beetles with chitinous, segmented exoskeletons crawling along the ground. Woo found what looked like a centipede burrowing into the mycelial mat. Looking ahead, Aiden spotted some taller trees spaced widely apart, about 20 meters away. But they were unlike any tree he'd ever seen. Single fibrous trunks sprouted long columnar structures resembling giant asparagus heads. As the team approached the nearest one, he estimated it to be about eight meters tall, with a trunk about one meter in diameter. The closer he got to it, the less it looked like wood. It had a dull gray, finely textured appearance, and the earthy scent he'd noticed earlier grew stronger as he approached.

He holstered his pistol and veered off their path to examine it more closely. Hotah stopped, turned around, and glared at him and the others. "What? Is this some sort of frickin' field trip? Or are we going to get serious about what we're doing here?"

"Quite right, Lieutenant," Aiden said, suppressing his natural-born scientific curiosity. "We'll move on in a moment. But if this . . . tree thing is what I think it is, it might hold an important clue for us. Sudha, would you bring a specimen bag and take a sample of this thing's trunk?"

To Hotah's credit, his expression remained neutral. His stance merely changed to one of parental patience mixed with acute vigilance. He moved farther up to a rise where he could get a better view of their surroundings. He stood there, a silent sentinel scanning the area beyond, carbine held ready.

Both Woo and Devi met Aiden at the base of the tree. Woo placed his hand on the trunk, eyes wide, and shook his head. "This is not a tree, not in the way we think of trees."

Aiden looked more closely at where the trunk grew from the ground. The fine white mycelial matt he'd seen earlier covering the ground grew denser as it neared the base of the trunk where it became hard and seamlessly continuous with the trunk itself.

"It's a fungus."

"Yes," Woo said. "More accurately, the fruiting body of a fungus. Analogous to a mushroom head."

"It's a *Prototaxites* fungus," Devi said, as if it were common knowledge. "Or something very similar."

Aiden looked at her, head cocked to one side.

"Don't be so surprised," she said, hands on her hips. "Yes, I'm a medical doctor, but as an undergrad, I minored in botany and paleontology. *Prototaxites* were a common feature in Earth's Devonian Period, about four million years ago. It was an enormous fungus, or more accurately, the fruiting body of a vast underground fungal organism. It was by far the largest land-dwelling life form at that time. The models based on fossil evidence look a lot like this thing here. I'll take a sample and run it through my bio-assay kit."

When Aiden peeled off a strip of the trunk material, he got a whiff of a strong, musky odor overlaid with a sharp, licorice-like scent. Devi placed a portion of the strip in her analyzer. Within one minute, she looked up and smiled. "I told you so. Look at this."

She pointed to a small screen displaying a microscopic view of the sample. "See those narrow tubelike structures? See how they're interwoven with even thinner filaments? See how it all branches out to form a tissue matrix? That's typical fungal morphology associated with *Prototaxites*."

"Can you do a comparative DNA analysis from this sample?"

"Not here. But yes, in my lab, back aboard the *Sun Wolf*."

Hotah trotted down from his observation post and spoke quietly. He jerked his thumb in the direction of the underground structure. "Commander. I heard a sound. Up that way."

Aiden unholstered his pistol again. "What kind of sound?"

"Not a natural sound," Hotah said. "More like the cracking of glass or hardened plastic. It echoed, like coming from inside a large enclosure."

Aiden toggled his comm link to the *Sun Wolf*. "XO, are we still good down here?"

"Affirmative," Ro said, sounding bored. "We've got your position scoped out to a 10-kilometer radius. High res. Nothing's shaking."

"Thanks. Out." Aiden turned to Hotah. "Lead the way, Lieutenant."

15

HD 4308 SYSTEM
Aasha

Domain Day 339, 2218

WITHIN minutes, the team came to a clearing and found a large earthen berm, 10 meters at its apex. Two massive metal doors were mounted on the berm's flat face. They were hinged on either side so they could be swung open and away from each other. One of the doors looked ajar. The other hung slightly askew from its hinges.

They approached cautiously, weapons ready. Beyond the partially opened door, it was pitch black inside. They heard no sounds of any kind from inside. Woo, glancing side to side, veered to the right and stopped. "Wait. There's something here. On the ground."

Hotah remained facing the door as the others went to Woo's side. He was examining one of the strangest things Aiden had ever seen. It looked like a human skeleton, except it was not made of bone. It was gray in color, like graphite. The major joints—hips, knees, shoulders, and elbows—were sophisticated swivel units made of some shiny metal alloy. The skeleton was sprawled out prone, arms and legs akimbo. Inside the skeleton, a collection of oddly shaped objects occupied positions where internal organs would normally reside. Heart, lungs, kidneys, liver, intestines. Most of them appeared to be made of some kind of polymer. The entire remains were covered by a continuous network of fine white filaments.

The sight of it sent a shiver up Aiden's spine. *Just like the Rete fungus on Silvanus.*

"Here's another one," Devi said. She knelt over a similar skeleton lying just outside the opened door. The same carbon-gray color and texture, same collection of organ analogues, same mat of fine, white fungal mycelia.

"I'm guessing," Woo said, "that we'd find more of these lying around nearby if we started looking."

"Cardew's cloneborgs," Aiden said. "Decomposed by the fungus."

Hotah gestured toward the corpse with the muzzle of his weapon. "But what killed them in the first place?"

"Impossible to tell from this," Devi said. "Could be anything."

Aiden felt his stomach sink. Maybe he'd made a terrible mistake by permitting his crew to remove their respirators down here. He gave Devi a worried look.

She shook her head emphatically. "No. We've double- and triple-checked. There's nothing here that presents a threat to human biology. Yes, there are fungal spores in the air we're breathing, but they check out as biologically benign. Nothing our immune systems can't handle easily. I trust my instruments."

"And I trust the fungus," Woo said. "It won't harm us."

Sudha Devi's iron-clad science and Elgin Woo's intuitive hunch were in agreement. That was good enough for Aiden. "All right, let's go in. No respirators, but use the mask's headlamps so we can see what we're doing in there."

Just then, a sound like the cracking of a thick windowpane rang out from somewhere deep inside the chamber. Hotah turned to Aiden and said, "Like that. What I heard earlier."

"Carry on, Lieutenant."

Past the metal door, a hard earthen ramp sloped down to the chamber floor. Their headlamps provided the only light inside. They illuminated a series of coffin-like capsules, four rows of them evenly spaced and extending back into the darkness. Two walkways ran through the rows, each accessing two rows of capsules, one on either side of it. The air was much cooler here than outside, cold enough to condense each breath into vapor clouds. The familiar earthy aroma had grown stronger, but now with an overtone of decay.

"Hotah, you and Dr. Devi take the right corridor. Elgin and I will take the left. Keep in sight."

The first four capsules in each row were empty, their plastiglass lids opened in the raised position. Aiden stopped at the fourth one. "These are stasis capsules. Designed to keep humans in a state of dormancy. Like the ones they used for manned space travel, back before the voidoids. Same general design, but different . . ."

"Yes," Woo said. "Very different. Each one has its own minifusion power generator. And look at these injection ports extending from the sides well into the interior. I think they might be artificial uteruses. For the final stages of cloneborg biosynthesis."

"Commander," Hotah called out from the other corridor. "Look at the next capsule up, on your side."

Aiden and Woo quickly moved up to the fifth one in the row on their side. The plastiglass lid was closed on this capsule, but shattered, exposing the interior. Broken plastiglass lay scattered on the ground. A few jagged shards of it remained stuck in the closed frame like broken teeth. A solid mat of fine, white mycelial filaments grew up from the ground, onto the outer wall of the capsule, over its rim, and down into the interior. Aiden peered through the shattered opening.

The capsule was occupied.

But only with the remains of its occupant. The same kind of carbon-gray skeleton they'd seen outside was laid out on its back, perfectly centered in the encapsulated space. The same collection of curiously shaped synthetic organs populated the insides of the skeleton. All of it was covered with a cottony white fuzz, continuous with the mycelial filaments growing up over the capsule's rim. Hotah confirmed seeing the same thing in the corresponding capsule on his side of the rows.

To orient himself in the darkness, Aiden tilted his head to aim his headlamp deeper into the chamber. He saw that each row held a total of ten capsules. He and his team were now midway through the chamber's length.

They moved on to the next capsule up. Its lid was also shattered, and the same mass of mycelial filaments grew from the ground up into its interior. Woo looked inside and gasped. Aiden came to his side and looked in. The fungal mycelia covered what appeared to be a partially decomposed human body. But not fully human. Glimpses of gray synthetic bone peeked out from places where decomposition had progressed furthest. A ghastly odor rose from the corpse.

Aiden put on his respirator to curb the wave of nausea rising in his throat. Woo followed suit. The seventh and eighth capsules held similar horrors, only the decomposition appeared less advanced as they moved up the row. When Aiden reached the ninth capsule, he saw what had caused the cracking sounds they'd heard. The capsule's lid was firmly closed and intact, but the fungus was in the process of eating it away to get inside. Several cracks had already spread spiderwebs across the plastiglass surface, but not enough to obscure the occupant's face.

Holy shit!

The face looked perfectly human.

In fact, the body—completely nude—looked exactly like a normal human being. Except for one thing. It lacked male or female genitalia. Just the pubic mound, hairless and nondescript. Beyond that, nothing else about it gave away its unnatural origin. A far cry from the freakish assassin who'd tried to kill him several days ago. Clothed, these creatures could easily walk and work among the rest of humanity without suspicion.

This particular individual had the appearance of a male, a perfect specimen, and perfectly natural looking. The cloneborg in the tenth and final capsule appeared to be female. The progress of the fungus on this last capsule was in the earliest stage of its assault, having grown only inches up the side from the ground. No doubt, the outcome would be the same as the others.

The team met up in the open space behind the last row of capsules to compare notes. Four shafts of light from their headlamps danced chaotically in the darkness as they moved their heads and spoke. Hotah and Devi had seen the exact same progression of decomposition as Aiden and Woo had, moving up the rows on their side.

"But the first four capsules in each row," Devi said, "the empty ones, look like they weren't invaded by the fungus. They look like they'd been opened deliberately."

"Probably opened from the inside by their occupants," Aiden said. "I'm guessing they were nest workers. Like bees in a hive. The first ones are hatched to take care of the nursery, the unborn. They do basic housekeeping until they're old enough to become guards and defenders of the hive. After that, they age out to foragers, gathering food for the hive. It's a self-sustaining system. I think the first few rows of cloneborgs were designed to come out of dormancy to oversee the birth of the rest, and to make sure they thrive. But then something killed these nest workers soon after they came out of stasis."

Woo looked around, absently stroking his dangling moustaches. "This is one of Cardew's cloneborg crèches. Maybe an experimental one. Obviously a very small one with only forty units. But the crèches would be designed to self-replicate, with the workers among them constructing more as the population grows. Cardew must have dozens of these by now, more successful and much larger ones, cranking out his loyal foot soldiers by the hundreds."

"Did you notice," Aiden said, "that all these human-looking cloneborgs appeared to be in the same age range, early to late thirties?"

"I did," Woo said. "The cloning was obviously designed to bear fully mature specimens on completion. No free-living developmental stages in between. No babies, children, or teens walking around growing into adults. And these thirty-something specimens probably won't age much at all. From Cardew's point of view, it makes perfect sense. He wants a ready-made population of peak performers. Physically and mentally."

Aiden turned to Devi. "Sudha, take a sample of this fungus. When we get back to the ship, I want a DNA analysis done ASAP, along with the one we took from outside. And I want you to compare it to the DNA records of the fungus growing on Silvanus."

"And if it's a close match?"

"Then it raises the very interesting question of why the fungus would attack and kill the living cloneborgs here, and not me when I was stranded on Silvanus. Nor the research teams working on Silvanus now. The cloneborgs, even the ones in stasis, are still living organisms. The Rete fungus recognizes living organisms and rigorously avoids harming them in any way. It's a saprophyte by nature—it only invades and decomposes dead or decaying organic matter."

Aiden's question hung in the air for a long moment. Finally, Hotah hefted his SR-13 and pointed it at the last row of capsules. "So what do we do with these freaks?"

"Leave them be, Lieutenant. They're not going anywhere now. Let the fungus finish its lunch." But in truth, the idea of deliberately killing beings that looked so human, so innocent in their sleep, disturbed him more than he cared to admit. "Let's get back to the ship."

When they emerged from the chamber, Aiden blinked in the bright sunlight and squinted until his eyes adjusted. They paused for a moment to take samples of one of the skeletons lying near the doors, along with some of its intact synthetic organs. Pulling them free from the fungus's greedy clutches, Devi dropped them into a specimen bag. The material of the skeleton itself was so hard that it resisted all efforts to chip away any fragments. Declining Hotah's offer to blast it apart with a well-placed round, Devi searched for the hyoid bone. In humans, it's located in the upper thorax and is the only free-floating bone unattached to any other bone. Luckily, it was the same for cloneborg anatomy. She found the small graphite-gray bone lying loose and dropped it in her bag.

Halfway back to their shuttle, Aiden noticed that Woo hadn't kept up with the group. He looked behind and saw him about 10 meters back, standing still as a stone, his head lifted up, looking skyward as if spellbound. Aiden called to him. When Woo didn't respond, Aiden walked back to stand next to him. Looking like the mad scientist most people thought he was, Woo adjusted the tilt of his head several times as if searching for the best position to hear something no one else could hear.

Aiden reached out and gently placed his hand on Woo's shoulder. Startled, he looked back at Aiden as if he'd never seen him before. The moment passed, and Woo refocused to the here and now. "I heard it again."

"Heard what?"

"A star." Woo grinned like a child with a new toy. "It spoke to me. No. More like singing a song."

Instead of reacting as if the other man had lost his mind, Aiden said, "Which star?"

Woo closed his eyes, tilted his head upward again, then looked back at Aiden. "I'm not sure yet. But I believe it's the one I've been looking for."

Aiden looked him in the eye and nodded thoughtfully. "Let's get moving, Elgin. We'll talk about it later."

"Yes, of course."

They caught up with the others, who stood waiting at the landing shuttle. As they climbed into the airlock, Hotah asked, "Where to now, boss?"

"Next stop—a star called HD 20003."

Hotah smiled brightly and said, "Wherever the hell that is, let's roll."

16

HD 20003 SYSTEM
Post-Jump

Domain Day 340, 2218

Star: HD 20003
Spectral type: G8V
Distance from Sol: 143 light-years
Luminosity: 0.70 x Sol
Surface temperature: 5,494 Kelvin
Number of planets: 7
Habitable zone: 0.81–1.43 AU
—Source: *Allied Mapping Project, 2218*

"No hostiles in sight," Hotah said, staring at his tactical screen.

As per the Stealth Sequence, the *Sun Wolf* made its jump into the HD 20003 system at 10 percent light speed and came to a halt 450,000 kilometers beyond the system's voidoid. This was the second star system where an AMP survey drone had disappeared, and Aiden fully expected to encounter whatever had destroyed it lurking near the voidoid.

The *Sun Wolf* held position for another 15 minutes to complete its long-range scans. No other vessels showed up on the scans. Still, *something* had taken out the drone, and not that long ago. If an enemy vessel was here at all, the only place it could be—and remain hidden from view—was behind the voidoid.

"Tactical, you have the Helm," Aiden said. "Take us back to the voidoid and circle it from a thousand klicks out."

Hotah shifted immediately into hunter mode, radiating relaxed hyperalertness. No matter how many times Aiden had witnessed it, the abrupt transition never failed to unnerve him.

In less than two seconds of zero-point drive, the *Sun Wolf* arrived back at the voidoid and commenced a circumpolar search pattern around it. They had just completed a quarter turn when a flash of light blinked at them from just over the voidoid's limb.

Hotah said, "Incoming missile. From a sentinel drone. Impact, 28 seconds." Then, with a short derisive laugh, he added, "That's all they've got? Pathetic."

Of course, it would not have been "pathetic" to a ship without a zero-point drive.

"Execute ZPD evasion," Aiden said.

At maximum ZPD, the *Sun Wolf* zipped off at a 45-degree angle from the missile's trajectory and came to a halt a half million kilometers away. The missile, accelerating at 300 Gs and only 16 seconds away from the spot where the ship *had* been, became totally confused by the sudden disappearance of its target. With nothing for its targeting computer to track, it shot off aimlessly into deep space. Meanwhile, the *Sun Wolf* zipped back to reappear behind the sentinel drone. Hotah triggered a short-range laser burst to vaporize it. The entire maneuver took less than 10 seconds.

Hotah reconfirmed that no other vessels or Holtzman buoys were in the vicinity. But he did spot a small cloud of metallic debris not far from the voidoid.

Woo grimaced. "Probably the remains of the AMP probe gone missing out here."

Aiden deployed their own Holtzman buoy, and Alvarez did a quick analysis of the star's planetary system. She put the results on the main screen.

There were seven planets. Only two were rocky terrestrial worlds. The two innermost planets were Neptune-sized gas giants, "hot" ones with orbits only 0.1 and 0.2 AU from the star. Then came a super-Earth-type terrestrial planet, over seven times the mass of Earth and 0.68 AU from the star. Too massive and too close to the star to be even remotely habitable.

The real prize was planet e, the fourth one out, an Earth-sized terrestrial world near the center of the star's habitable zone. Of the remaining three planets farther out, two were gas giants like Jupiter. On the system's outskirts, at 21 AU, was a Neptune-like ice giant. It had an extensive ring system similar to Saturn's, composed of ice, dust, and rock fragments.

Alvarez pointed out that seven planets was more than the average number per star system—Sol's nine and HD 10180's ten planets were the rare exceptions—and noted once again that they'd found a terrestrial planet in the habitable zone.

"Don't be so surprised," Woo said. "Remember, we're hitting only the sunlike stars where AMP has confirmed an earthlike planet in a habitable zone. According to them, we'll be finding one in most of the systems on our hit list."

"Why so many?" Alvarez asked. "I thought they were rare. Less than one out of every five sunlike star systems."

Aiden shrugged. "For some reason, the figure is much higher in this astrocell. We're not sure why, but the Shénmì Project has some theories about it."

Aiden turned to Woo to see if he cared to elaborate. He didn't.

"Helm, take us to planet e, high orbit."

When the pilot didn't respond, Aiden turned toward her and noticed that she had removed her linkage cap. She looked heart stricken, palms of both hands held to her forehead. Hotah and Alvarez, whose stations flanked either side of the Helm, stared at her. Aiden came around to face the pilot. "Lista. What's wrong?"

It wasn't unusual for pilots to remove their linkage caps *after* a voidjump, but it was usually done at a slow and deliberate pace to minimize the effects of the downshift in consciousness levels.

Aiden's personal experience could attest to that requirement. Abahem had removed the cap far sooner than she normally did. Her head bent low, her face had gone pale.

Recalling the episode several days ago, Aiden barked, "Hutton. Did you disconnect from the OverNet when we jumped?"

"Yes, of course." Hutton sounded concerned.

Aiden turned back to the pilot and spoke quietly. "Lista. Talk to me. Was it the intrusion again? The black crow?"

She removed her hands from her face and looked at him, eyes wide with both fear and sorrow. Her voice trembled as she spoke. "No, not that. Something is . . ."

Sudha Devi came to Abahem's side and took the pilot's hand in hers. As before, Devi's touch had some magical power to calm and soothe. But the look of anguish in Abahem's eyes remained.

"Tell me," Devi said.

Abahem took a deep breath and steadied her voice. "Something is horribly wrong here. Something against Nature . . ."

"Where, Lista?"

"Here. In this star system."

"What is it?"

Abahem shook her head slowly and covered her eyes with her hands. "I don't know. I don't know . . . I can't see it clearly. But something terrible has happened."

Aiden knelt in front of her. "Lista, Ro can spell you at the Helm if you need a break."

Abahem straightened up. Like flipping a switch, she regained her poise. Serene and alert. "Thank you, Commander. But I'm fine now."

She gave her signature thumbs-up and, without another word, set course for the inner system. "Ready for transit. At your command."

Aiden glanced at Devi, who just shrugged. That was good enough for him. "Helm, proceed."

It was common knowledge, and a gross understatement, that Licensed Pilots were different from everyone else. By nature of their training and profession, they were far more familiar with planes of consciousness most people didn't even know existed. They navigated an ephemeral terrain of energy and vibration, able to manipulate its shape and forge pathways through its beautiful and frightening chaos to achieve their ends. Aiden had come to believe, albeit without concrete proof, that they were able to hear and speak with the voidoids themselves. The voidoids that Elgin Woo had concluded were living, intelligent beings.

To Aiden, it was the only way to explain how pilots accomplished what no other human beings could. To drive massive voidships at high velocities safely through the voidoids. To make possible the routine voidjumping upon which all human enterprise now depended.

At maximum drive speed, it took about two hours for the *Sun Wolf* to arrive at its destination. When the ship pulled out of ZPD and into high orbit around planet e, the crew immediately saw that something *was* amiss. As would be expected for an Earth-sized terrestrial planet with abundant liquid water, comfortably situated in the system's habitable zone, it exhibited mostly earthlike characteristics. Its diameter was roughly the same as Earth's, but it was slightly more massive. It had no moons, a 21-hour day, a 289-day year, an axial tilt of 20 degrees allowing for seasonal variations, and an average mean global temperature of 13.6 degrees C, a bit on the cold side. Like Earth, the atmosphere had plenty of oxygen, about 20 percent, with most of the rest composed of nitrogen.

But that's where the similarities broke down.

The planet's surface was obscured beneath by a thick layer of smog-brown haze. Only the most prominent surface features were visible. A preliminary spectrographic analysis revealed that the brown haze was a photochemical smog composed almost entirely of nitrogen dioxide, at toxic levels, over 200 ppm. In addition, the planet's protective ozone layer—an atmospheric feature common to well-oxygenated planets in habitable zones—had vanished almost completely.

"Not exactly a good place for life to evolve," Devi said. "Or if it had already, and this was a recent development, there wouldn't be much left alive down there now. Without a protective ozone layer, you've got massive amounts of solar UV radiation scorching the surface, undiluted. Living DNA would break apart. Widespread cell damage. Starting with microorganisms—bacteria and fungi, protozoans, algae—destroying global food chains from the bottom up. Any higher life forms miraculously surviving the radiation wouldn't last long anyway, not without food sources."

"Plus, all that nitrogen dioxide," Aiden said. He stood up from the command chair, feeling sick to his stomach from what they were seeing. "Aside from its toxicity to animal life, that much nitrogen dioxide in the air means lots of acid rain. Nitric acid. Disastrous to any kind of living biome. The nasty-looking brown smog down there blocks sunlight from reaching the surface, so you'll get rapid global cooling. Instant ice age."

"We should go down there and investigate," Alvarez said. "To see if there's any evidence that life once existed. Or if there's anything still alive. That would at least tell how recently this happened, or if the planet has been like this for eons."

Devi shook her head. "Not without full PSM suits. See those nitrogen dioxide levels? Without protection, you're talking fatal pulmonary edema within minutes, unless you die of asphyxia first. It's a toss-up. Personally, I wouldn't step foot down there, not even in a PSM suit. Caught in a nitric acid rainstorm? I wouldn't trust the suit to maintain integrity for very long."

She was right. Unlike EVA suits used for work in the vacuum of space, PSM suits—short for Planetary Surface Mobility—were designed for activity on inhospitable planetary surfaces. But they had articulated metal fittings, vulnerable to highly corrosive acids.

Aiden glanced at Pilot Abahem. She remained at the Helm, sitting still as a stone. Her eyes were fixed on the screen where the planet turned as slowly as a funeral procession. Aiden thought he saw her face cloud with anger, an emotion pilots were said to have purged.

"Okay," Alvarez said, "then we send down one of our bioanalytic probes to investigate. They're hardened for extreme biochemical environments. We need to know what happened down there."

Woo stood and moved next to Aiden. "I believe this catastrophic event happened just recently. And I think it destroyed a pre-existing biosphere."

Aiden wasn't exactly sure how Woo came to his conclusion, but he thought he knew where the man was going with it. "A gamma-ray burst."

"Yes," Woo said. "It's a classic case. In the extreme. All the signs are present."

Another wave of nausea caused Aiden to swallow hard. He hoped no one had noticed. "All right, Alvarez. Send a bioanalytic probe to the surface. Program it to visually scan the area and collect specimens. On land and in the ocean."

Several hours later, the survey probe returned to the ship with specimens and with bad news. After another hour in the ship's bio lab, Sudha Devi gave them the short version of her findings. She appeared shaken. "Yes, there was a viable biosphere down there, somewhat well advanced. I'd say roughly analogous to Earth's early Cretaceous Period. Much like an earlier version of Shénmì. Higher life forms. Vascular plants, forests, invertebrate and vertebrate animals, maybe even some primitive mammal-like critters. There's every indication that this was a healthy, living planet before . . . whatever happened to it."

"Estimated damage?" Aiden asked, fearing the answer.

"Extensive. Almost total annihilation. The DNA samples from microbe, plant, and animal remains show catastrophic damage. Broken strands, disrupted sequences, base pairs chemically altered or missing altogether. Fundamental stuff. Irreparable. And if you're thinking gamma-ray burst, it'd have to be one hell of a wallop. Basically, this planet has been sterilized."

"Recovery time?"

Devi took one long deep breath before speaking again. "I'm familiar with all the major extinction events that occurred on Earth.

Obviously, in all cases the biospheres recovered over varying periods of time. But in all cases, a certain percentage of life forms survived the event to seed the recovery. Evolution didn't have to start over from scratch each time. This was especially significant for microorganisms, which have always accounted for at least half of Earth's total biomass. Surviving microbes, sheltering underground or in deep ocean waters, were always the foot soldiers in the eventual recovery from extinction events. Without them, the planet may have never recovered from any one of them. And that's what I fear for this poor planet we've got here. Even the deep core samples turned up dead. Deep water samples too. Like I said, it's been virtually sterilized."

Aiden forced himself to remain objective. It wasn't easy fighting off emotions raging below the surface. But something else nagged at him. "If this planet is truly sterilized, what happens to it now? Can it remain a potentially habitable planet?"

"Theoretically, yes. At least in terms of geology and climate. The atmosphere wasn't blown away, just got messed up. It could normalize within five or ten years. The oxygen content hasn't been significantly effected, so the protective ozone layer would eventually return. Without plant life, of course, the landmasses would become deserts. But otherwise, the planet itself would remain potentially habitable for eons to come."

Woo had the look of a chess player contemplating his next move. Twirling one of his long, braided moustaches, he asked Alvarez, "Can you determine how long ago this happened?"

"Not with any accuracy. But I'm guessing no more than a year ago, possibly less."

Woo and Aiden exchanged a quick glance.

Alvarez shook her head sadly. "I think we should name this planet Mordor."

Aiden knew Alvarez wasn't joking. Far from it. "As in Tolkien's *Lord of the Rings*? That would be fitting."

Ro objected. "The environmental degradation part fits," he said. "But Mordor was home to the evil Sauron. We should reserve that name for Cardew's planet, when we find it."

"Okay," Alvarez said. "Then how about Tristeza? That's a word for sorrow in my native language."

Aiden sighed. It seemed pointless now, but he agreed. Then he announced to the crew that they'd stay here in orbit for a while to collect more data on the planet. After that, they'd head back to the voidoid and make the jump to their next destination, the star HD 17051.

The pilot stood, her eyes blank, and spoke to Aiden in a quiet voice. "Commander, if I'm not needed until then, I'd like to return to my quarters for a short time. To rest."

"Yes, of course. It'll be at least five hours before we jump."

After Pilot Abahem left the bridge, Devi moved to stand in front of the main screen, turned to face the crew, and said, "Okay. Gamma-ray bursts. I've heard of them, but can someone please tell me more?"

"Gamma-ray bursts," Woo said, sounding reluctant to engage the subject, "or GRBs for short, are extremely powerful, focused beams of gamma radiation emitted from the magnetic poles of black holes, or when black holes are formed during the collapse of giant stars. They're the most energetic, and most dangerous, events in the universe. They can also happen when dead neutron stars merge with each other or with a black hole. Other exotic phenomena can cause them, too, but those are the most common sources."

"They're also extremely rare, Elgin," Aiden pointed out. "And they don't happen very often in our galaxy. All the ones observed so far have been well outside the Milky Way, millions or billions of light-years from here, completely harmless to us. The Milky Way is the wrong kind of place to produce these things. It's not a metal-poor galaxy like the ones that do produce them. Plus, we're situated in a region of our galaxy where supermassive stars are rare, and binary neutron stars aren't dangerously close. On top of that, even if a GRB did happen within our galaxy, the likelihood that its narrow beam would be aimed right at us is negligible."

"Even so," Ro chimed in, ever the devil's advocate, "if one of those rare GRBs did occur within this galaxy, even six or seven thousand light-years away, and if its emissions were beamed straight towards an earthlike planet, you'd see something exactly like what we're looking at down there. That's probably what caused the Ordovician-Silurian extinction on Earth four and a half million years ago, one of the five worst extinction events in the planet's history."

"Come on, Ro. That's still a highly debatable hypothesis, and you know it."

"I'm just saying," Ro said with annoying persistence, "that GRBs in this galaxy *do* happen. We only see the ones that cast their narrow beams in the direction of Earth, which statistically is almost never."

"Okay, okay. Point taken." Aiden knew how much Ro enjoyed baiting him with science-based rebuttals. "But I'm still not buying it."

Ro said nothing more, just grinned impishly. Aiden turned to Woo. "Seriously, Elgin, given all of that and the fact that GRBs are tightly beamed emissions, what are the chances that this planet—or any planet in this region—gets hit with enough high-energy gamma radiation to do this kind of damage?"

Woo did not respond. He stood facing the screen, shaking his head slowly at the unfortunate planet below.

"And even more unlikely," Aiden continued, "what are the chances that, within the last year, the one and only habitable planet with a living biosphere in this star system gets hit?"

At that, Woo turned sharply and looked him in the eye. "Exactly."

17

HD 17051 SYSTEM
Post-Jump

DOMAIN DAY 341, 2218

Star: Iota Horologii (HD 17051)
Spectral type: G0V
Distance from Sol: 56.5 light-years
Luminosity: 1.68 x Sol
Surface temperature: 6,080 Kelvin
Number of planets: 4
Habitable zone: 1.21–2.12 AU
—Source: *Allied Mapping Project, 2218*

"I'M seeing one Holtzman buoy," Hotah said, looking up from his monitor, "sitting about five klicks from the voidoid. Nothing else. No sentinel drones. No AMP survey probe. No other artificial objects within a million klicks."

"Long-range scans, Lilly?"

Alvarez shook her head. "Nothing unusual so far. But an AMP survey probe is pretty small. If it's already on its way to the planetary system, I'd need to know where to look for it."

The *Sun Wolf* had remained in the HD 20003 system through one sleep cycle. Aiden wanted the crew to be fresh for the next jump and also wanted more time to collect data on the ruined planet they'd christened Tristeza. The ship had just completed a Stealth Sequence jump into the HD 17051 system, the third star system where AMP had lost a probe. The crew had expected to encounter a situation similar to the last two—evidence of a blasted survey probe and its robotic assailant lurking about. But things looked different here, at least from 450,000 klicks out. Just one lone Holtzman buoy positioned back at the voidoid, right where it would normally be deployed for optimal transmission.

The *Sun Wolf* turned around, returned to the voidoid, and came alongside the orphaned Holtzman buoy.

"Looks like one of ours," Alvarez said. "Standard UED issue."

"It's a buoy from an AMP survey probe," Woo said. "I recognize the type they use. The probe must have deployed it before leaving the vicinity of the voidoid. Most of the AMP probes stay close to the voidoid and gather their data from there before moving on to another star system. They use their own onboard Holtzman devices for comms. But some are programed to head off toward the system if there's something interesting that AMP wants to investigate closer up. Those probes will leave a Holtzman buoy at the voidoid to relay the data back home."

Aiden turned back to Alvarez. "Hail the buoy with AMP's encrypted frequency code."

A moment later, she said, "It's not responding."

That was odd. The AMP team had provided the *Sun Wolf* with its encrypted frequency codes. Hailing the buoy by maser transmission with the code should have unlocked the device for the ship to access. The encryption of Holtzman devices was supposedly infallible. Only Holtzman devices sharing the exact same configuration codes could exchange data, and then only when they were separated by voidoids. The devices themselves were independently powered by minifusion reactors and housed inside buoys that were virtually indestructible. Their unique global redundancy design was supposed to make them invulnerable to hacking.

After several more failed attempts to hail the buoy, Aiden said, "Well, that would explain why AMP lost contact with its probe.

Wherever it is now—assuming it wasn't destroyed by a hostile—the probe can't link with its own Holtzman buoy. Any data it sends won't get through to the buoy at Woo's Star serving Shénmì Station. Elgin, did any data from the probe get through to the Mapping Project *before* the buoy went dead?"

"Yes. About two hours' worth," Woo said. "But none of it showed anything out of the ordinary. No sign of hostile weapons fire."

"How long has the probe been in this system?"

Woo consulted his compad. "Says here that probe number four got here 120 days ago, and it was programed to head toward the planets."

"How fast can these things get boosted?'

"Their antimatter drives can kick them off to about 10 klicks per second before shutting down to conserve fuel for the return trip."

Aiden did a quick mental calculation. "That means it should be a little over 100 million klicks from here, on course for the planetary system."

Hotah looked up and said, "The probe still could have been whacked by one of Cardew's vessels. If it hadn't been spotted right away after its jump, and no hostile vessel was nearby to blast it, the probe could have easily logged two hours of data before finally being discovered and destroyed."

"Point taken, Lieutenant. We'll keep our eyes open. Lilly, do you have any data yet on the planets here?"

"It's still coming in, but at first glance, the one that really stands out is planet b, a massive gas giant orbiting close to the star at around 1 AU. It's not much larger than Jupiter, but 24 times more massive."

"A brown dwarf?"

"Yep, that would be my guess. A brown dwarf, but a very dim one. Surface temperature is less than 600 Kelvin. That'd make it a class-Y brown dwarf."

Aiden stared at the telescopic image of the planet. To the eye, it appeared very dim indeed and had a dark purple hue. Brown dwarves were basically failed stars, enormous gas giants that were too small and lightweight to ignite and sustain nuclear fusion like main-sequence stars. They ranged between 13 to 80 times the mass of Jupiter. And while they couldn't fuse hydrogen into helium like real stars do, they were able to fuse deuterium and generate heat. Some were hotter than others, and they came in different colors—none of which were brown, as their name suggested—depending on their temperatures. The warmest ones appeared orange or red. The coolest ones, like the one here, were dim purple.

"It's even got its own little planetary system," Alvarez said. "If you can call it that. A collection of rocky moonlets. But the whole thing is still outside the habitable zone. None of the moons are likely to support organic life. Planet c, however, is a different story. That's the one we should check out. It's well inside the hab zone, toward the outer regions of it."

"Terrestrial?"

"Yep. Rocky. About 90 percent the size of Earth. Presence of liquid water. But from here, the spectrometry isn't showing any free oxygen in the atmosphere."

"None?"

"Correct. But loads of carbon dioxide."

"And the other two planets?"

Planets d and e are both Neptune-like ice giants, way beyond the hab zone. One of them has a spectacular set of rings that would put Saturn to shame."

"All right. Let's deploy our own Holtzman buoy. Then we're off to planet c to have a look around."

"Wait a minute," Hotah said. "I'm picking something up."

"Hostiles?"

"No," Hotah said. He looked too relaxed for that. More quizzical than anything else. Even amused.

Woo came to look over Hotah's shoulder. He grinned and looked at Aiden, his eyes bright. "Seed pods. From Shénmì."

"I thought they were mines at first," Hotah said. "They came straight out of the voidoid, just a few minutes ago. They're headed toward the planetary system."

Will wonders ever cease? "Lilly, magnify and display on the main screen."

A cluster of six round spheres, dark brown, had emerged from the voidoid and were moving away from it in unison. The scope's calibrated optics measured them at close to 16 meters across. Increased magnification made it clear that they weren't perfectly spherical, only approximately so, and their surfaces had a rough, woody look.

Woo, the only person who'd ever seen one close up, said, "No doubt about it. Those are Shénmì seeds. Honestly, I'm not surprised to see them here."

Just before Woo's wild ride down to Shénmì's surface inside one of the planet's spaceborne seed pods, he had watched the giant pod open up in the vacuum of space, 36,000 kilometers above the surface, and had seen seeds ejected from inside the pod. Seeds exactly like the ones they were looking at now. That had been eighteen months ago and many light-years away.

"The ones I saw," Woo said, still staring at the screen with childlike glee, "floated free in groups of 6, just like this bunch. The pod ejected four 6-seed clusters in all, a total of 24 seeds. They all headed off together in the general direction of the system's voidoid. That's why I'm not surprised to see these things here, heading toward the planetary system."

Skye's panspermia seeds, Aiden thought.

"But how are they propelled?" Alvarez asked. "And how do they know where to go?"

Woo shrugged. "Very good questions."

Questions that Woo had probably already answered in his own mind, in his own inexplicable way, but kept to himself.

"Helm," Aiden said, "set course for planet c. But on the way, stop at the 100-million-klick mark. We'll scan the area for any signs of AMP's probe."

Six minutes later, the *Sun Wolf* came to a halt in the vicinity of where they estimated the AMP probe would be at this point in its journey toward the inner system. Alvarez did a long-range scan in all directions.

"I've got it," she said. "About 3,000 klicks off to our port."

The ship intercepted the probe and came alongside for a closer look. Powered by a rudimentary antimatter drive, it was an ungainly little vessel about 14 meters in length, bulky and studded with sensor wands and parabolic antennae. AMP's logo was brightly stenciled on its otherwise dull metallic surface, along with the numeral 4.

"Can we access its data banks?" Aiden asked.

"That shouldn't be a problem," Woo said. "I have AMP's query codes for all its probes. But it would be easier if we brought the probe aboard. It's of no use to the project now if it can't relay its data back through a dead buoy. I'm sure they'd be happy to get it back, along with all the data it was able to collect."

Aiden agreed. They had plenty of room for it in the shuttle bay.

After using the ship's grappling gantry to snatch the probe and secure it in the shuttle bay, they resumed course.

From high orbit over planet c, the ship's survey scans painted a picture of a planet very early in development. The atmosphere contained virtually no free oxygen, about the same amount of nitrogen as Earth, but a startling amount of carbon dioxide. Over 20 percent by volume. That was 500 times greater than on Earth. There were oceans of water, but they were hot. Over 60 degrees C. Not a place you'd want to take a dip. The average mean temperature of the planet was over twice that of Earth's, and nothing green was visible anywhere on the surface. No photosynthesis, no free oxygen. And without atmospheric oxygen, no protective ozone layer had formed in the upper atmosphere.

Devi looked up from the data stream. "This looks a lot like Earth's environment around four billion years ago, at the onset of the Archean Era. It makes sense, of course. This star system is very young, just over 600 million years. That's roughly the amount of time it took Earth to reach the Archean Era after the birth of our sun. Using Earth as a gauge, this planet is about where you'd expect it to be given the star's age."

"So, no life forms down there?"

"Nothing photosynthetic, that's for sure. And probably nothing at all. Unless there's some kind of autotrophic microbes living in those hot oceans. Not impossible, of course. Sixty degrees C is nothing compared to the 100 degrees that some of Earth's thermophiles are perfectly happy with. The planet *is* nicely situated inside the hab zone, and it has a stable orbit. Brisk rotational period, days and nights not overly long, decent magnetic fields to help protect it from solar radiation. But from what I can tell so far, it's biologically a blank slate."

Aiden smiled. "The perfect place for Shénmì's panspermia seeds to get a start."

"Speaking of which," Alvarez said, "I'm picking up some of those things incoming. The same kind we saw back at the voidoid. I'm seeing one cluster closing in on the upper atmosphere."

Alvarez tracked the objects, now only eight kilometers away, with the optical scope at high magnification. As the seeds approached the upper atmosphere, they slowed down to almost a standstill, shedding their own kinetic energy as if waiting for the planet's gravity to take over the process of bringing them down. Which it did, slowly at first, putting the seeds into free fall.

"Smart," Woo said. "Not like reentry from an orbit, where you're entering at high orbital velocities. Nor like a meteorite entering with its intrinsic velocity and burning up. These things are just falling out of the sky, picking up atmospheric drag but with minimum aerodynamic heat."

"This planet needs a name," Alvarez said. Aiden detected a rare joyfulness in her tone, as if she were setting about to name a newborn baby.

Woo responded immediately, surprising everyone. "Nanaskita. It means 'unborn' in Esperanto."

Aiden smiled. No one objected, and he said, "Very fitting, Elgin. Lilly, make it so."

"*Unborn,*" Devi said, "and currently uninhabitable. That's a toxic environment down there, albeit a natural one. I don't think even Cardew's cloneborgs would survive long. Even if they could recycle their own metabolic waste byproducts, they can't do it indefinitely."

"Right," Aiden said. "With a number of other more hospitable worlds available to him, I think we can count this one out. Still, we'll do a global scan for anything suspicious. In the process, we can add more data to what AMP already has on this planet."

Three hours of scanning revealed no signs of human activity. The scans did, however, pick up more sightings of the Shénmì seeds making their way through the atmosphere to the surface of Nanaskita. Aiden wondered, as Alvarez had earlier, how the seeds were propelled. How did they know where to go, and when? How did they find their way to the voidoids in the first place, and then jump through them? Whatever the answers, Aiden guessed that the phenomenon was not an isolated case. They had just encountered it by chance at a time when this very young planet was being seeded.

Woo's theory that Shénmì was the "mother planet" of this astrocell was making more sense with each new revelation. Woo believed—and Skye had begun to prove—that most of the organic life on habitable planets in this astrocell was the result of panspermia, spawned by Shénmì's extraordinary sprouting seed pods. So why was Cardew so hell-bent on annihilating Shénmì? If his goal was to find and occupy more habitable planets, why destroy the single planet most responsible for making those other worlds habitable?

18

HD 17051 SYSTEM
Nanaskita Orbit

DOMAIN DAY 341, 2218

Ro approached Aiden, compad in hand. "We've had a look at the data recorded by AMP's probe and found something curious."

"What is it?" Aiden opened his eyes and realized he'd dozed off briefly while sitting at Command. He'd had too little sleep lately. Still, it was unforgiveable. Embarrassed, he sat straighter and pretended that he'd just emerged from deep thought.

"It appears," Ro said, smiling ever so slightly, "that the probe's trajectory toward the planets was briefly perturbed soon after it left the voidoid. It was pulled off course by several kilometers, even while attempting to correct course with its attitude thrusters. The onboard Casimir-Ebadi interferometer showed a strong gravitational spike during the incident. It lasted two minutes before the G-field vanished and the probe went merrily on its way."

Aiden exchanged glances with Woo, then said, "Could one of Cardew's gravity drones have been out there when the AMP probe came through? Trying to capture it?"

Cardew's scientists had devised a way to use the Füzfa Effect to disrupt the voidoids in Bound Space. By manipulating intense electromagnetic fields, they were able to bend space-time in a way that mimicked strong, point-source gravity fields. It could also be used to draw objects in, like the "tractor beams" of sci-fi fame. And, by bending space-time in the opposite direction, Cardew had used it to create the negative-gravity shield around his ship to repel weapons fire.

Ro shook his head. "We looked everywhere in the probe's data for that possibility. We found no evidence that another vessel was anywhere near the probe, during that incident or any time after."

"What else could do this?"

Ro shrugged. Woo smiled. Neither spoke.

"I may have an answer to that," Alvarez said. "While I was scanning for hostiles around the voidoid just after we jumped, I picked up what looked like some gravitational microlensing off to one side of the voidoid. I didn't think much of it at the time. It was fleeting and indistinct. But it's exactly the kind of thing you'd see from a very small black hole."

Aiden grimaced. Black holes made him nervous. Just the fact of their existence was one of the creepiest mysteries of the universe. "A *small* black hole? How small?"

Alvarez took a moment to access the archived data. She finally looked at him, eyes wide. "The microlensing data suggests a Schwarzschild radius of about 11.5 centimeters, about the size of a soccer ball. But with a mass of about 13 Earths."

Holy shit. Thirteen Earths? That was close to the mass of Uranus. Not insignificant.

Aiden sat back and stifled a yawn. "A primordial black hole, then. Hypothetically."

Woo looked absolutely delighted. "Yes, and within the same size range as the infamous Planet Nine black hole."

Aiden looked askance at Woo. "Planet Nine is still a mystery, Elgin. Practically a fable now. No one's ever come up with concrete evidence that it's actually a primordial black hole."

"Maybe," Woo said. "But we know primordial black holes must exist. Have known it for two and a half centuries, ever since Hawking figured it out. Indisputable evidence for them continues to accumulate, from numerous gravitational-lensing projects over the years. And the old theory that dark matter is actually the sum total of all primordial black holes has regained wide acceptance nowadays. It's just that no one has ever *seen* a primordial black hole, up close and personal, to confirm their existence. This is a fabulous opportunity to do that."

Aiden agreed, of course. But he was not eager to get "up close and personal" with *any* black hole, no matter how small. For him, no single phenomenon in the universe more perfectly embodied the substance of oblivion. Not just a mystery, but a genuine terror.

"Lilly, is this thing still out there now, near the voidoid?"

Alvarez dialed in the lensing scope to encompass a sizable volume of local space around the voidoid. After a few minutes, she said, "Yep. It's still there. It's about a thousand klicks northwest of the voidoid. Nowhere near the voidoid's exit point, so it's not a danger to ships jumping into the system. It doesn't appear to be moving in relation to the voidoid."

"That's odd," Ro said. "Theoretically, free-ranging primordial black holes should be on the move. If they really are the stuff of dark matter, they should be cruising around the galaxy at over a hundred klicks per second. We really should take a look. Not just for the science, but it could provide a clue to the bigger picture."

The bigger picture. Whatever that was, the picture was just a bigger blur to Aiden. "We're headed back to the voidoid anyway," he said. "Might as well check it out."

Two hours later, the *Sun Wolf* parked within 10,000 kilometers of the voidoid. Alvarez activated both the optical G-lensing scope and the Casimir-Ebadi interferometer.

"There it is," Alvarez said, pointing to the monitor. "It's in the same place it was earlier. Stationary relative to the voidoid. Just under a thousand klicks out."

Hotah synched the interferometer data with Tactical, dialed in the anomaly's exact location, and put it up on his tactical screen.

"It may be small," Aiden said, "but at thirteen times the mass of Earth, it's got some serious gravitational forces. The ship is already feeling its pull, even from here."

"I just picked it up on the optical scope," Ro said, squinting quizzically at his screen. "Take a look at this image."

Black holes themselves were virtually invisible. But the point in space where the tiny black hole existed, according to the interferometer, was surrounded by a ghostly halo of faint white light. *Visible* light. The whole thing looked like a fuzzy sphere of pale white light with a pure black circle sitting at its exact center. The black circle's diameter was nearly one quarter that of the faintly glowing sphere surrounding it, but its outer edges were indistinct, not sharply delineated. Aiden suppressed a shiver. It looked like an eerie cosmic eyeball staring at him, unblinking, from the eternal depths of space.

Aiden looked away from it. "Lilly, can you tell how large the black sphere at the center is? Knowing its distance should give us some idea of its actual size."

Alvarez wrinkled her nose and said, "Only an estimate. Maybe a half kilometer from edge to edge? Except that doesn't make sense. The black hole itself is only 23 centimeters in diameter."

"What we're seeing," Woo said, "is the *effect* of the black hole's gravity well on the field of light surrounding it. Not the black hole itself. Fascinating."

Alvarez, still transfixed by the optical image, said, "The black hole doesn't seem to be affecting the voidoid in any way. Even that close to it."

"Not surprising," Woo said. "Remember, voidoids have no mass, no gravity, and they're not affected by gravitational fields. I think a primordial black hole this size could pass through a voidoid quite easily, jumping from system to system the way voidships do."

Alvarez looked at him, eyes wide. "What the hell *are* these things?"

"The black hole part of it is a primordial black hole," Woo said. "I'm sure of that. They're as old as the universe. Primordial black holes were created during the first few seconds after the Big Bang from fluctuations in space-time density that caused isolated gravitational collapses. The majority of them are thought to be of sublunar mass, no more than a tenth of a millimeter in size. But theoretically they can be up to two or three times the mass of our sun. After their birth, some of the larger ones eventually became the nuclei around which the galaxies formed, growing into the supermassive black holes at their centers. The rest are still frolicking around the universe, most likely accounting for the bulk of dark matter."

"Okay," Alvarez said. "But what about this one? That halo of light surrounding it? That's not normal. What the hell is it? Hawking radiation?"

"No," Ro said before Woo could respond. "Hawking radiation is blackbody radiation. Temperature-dependent. A black hole that size is still very cold, around .001 Kelvin. It would be emitting only high frequency radio waves, not visible light. That halo is something different."

"Yes," Woo said, grinning even wider. "Something *quite* different. And quite amazing."

"This is all very interesting," Aiden said. "But what is this thing doing here, and why was it messing with our survey probe?"

"I think we're about to find out," Hotah said. "It's starting to move. And it's coming straight toward us."

"That's impossible," Alvarez said. "Black holes don't just get up and move like that."

"Apparently this one didn't get the memo," Aiden said. He glanced around the bridge. His attempt to lighten things up had failed utterly. The collective body language of the crew had transitioned quickly from curiosity to tension. "How fast is it approaching?"

"Fast enough. It's already about 8,000 klicks away, and closing. We'll be in serious trouble dealing with its gravity well in about four minutes."

Hotah turned from Tactical Station. "Why not just blow it up? A couple of nukes against something the size of a soccer ball? A no-brainer."

"Black holes don't work that way, Lieutenant," Ro said. "Anything you throw at it—and I mean *anything*, energy or mass—just gets pulled past its event horizon and only adds to its mass, making it even more powerful."

Hotah, obviously revisiting his science education, nodded without argument. "Right."

"Prepare for jump," Aiden said. What better time to get outta town than now? "Helm, set jump coordinates for HD 21749. Take us back out to 150,000 klicks, then execute Stealth Sequence. Do it now, please."

Aiden waited for Abahem's signature thumbs-up. Didn't see it. Waited some more. The pilot remained motionless. *What now?*

"Pilot, execute."

No response.

"Lista! Execute *now*."

"The gravity well is getting deeper," Alvarez said, glancing at the CEI monitor. "Right now, it's pulling us in with a G-force of about two million kilonewtons. We need to scoot out of here."

"We can't use the ZPD now," Woo reminded them all. "A gravity field that intense will prevent the drive from working."

Bloody hell. Woo was right, of course. The intricate EM fields the ship used to create the zero-point bubble were disrupted by strong gravity fields. That's why they always had to move far from planetary masses before engaging the drive. It wouldn't work otherwise.

Ro said, "I'm applying counter thrust with our portside jets. But that won't work much longer. We need to flip and burn with our main drive. Soon. Just to maintain our distance."

Aiden glanced up at the screen. The ghostly white halo with its deadly black hole had closed in on them. "Helm, turn the ship away from the black hole and burn at 15 Gs. Now."

Abahem turned halfway around to look back at Aiden. A look of rapture radiated from her pale white face, her eyes wide with amazement. The linkage cap affixed to her hairless head glowed with an ephemeral light. She spoke in a voice that was almost too soft to hear. But what she said was clear enough. "The entity wants to make contact with us."

Entity? Wants to make contact? In a good way or a bad way? Questions Aiden chose not to entertain at the moment. Instead, he spoke to the AI. "Hutton. Take over the Helm. Execute a voidjump to our next destination on antimatter drive. Emergency acceleration."

"Yes, Commander. Preparing now."

"Wait," Woo said. He moved to Aiden's side. "This is not an ordinary black hole. It's something more. Pilot Abahem is on to something. I don't think it will harm us."

"Elgin, I've always respected your hunches, but I'm not waiting around to test this one. We're getting out of here. Hutton, execute jump now."

The ship's antimatter drive could sustain a pulse of 15 Gs for up to 10 minutes, the upper limit of what the G-transducers could handle. From their current position, they'd need 6 minutes to make the jump.

"Commander," Hutton said. "There is a problem with that order."

"What *is* it, Hutton?" Aiden clenched his fists but held them at his side.

Alvarez interrupted. "The ship is beginning to fall in. We need to do something fast."

"The problem is," Hutton carried on as if they had all the time in the world, "to execute the jump to HD 21749, we will have to move into a coordinate position that brings us much closer to the approaching black hole."

Wonderful. He hadn't thought of that. In a voidjump, you always *exited* the voidoid from only one spot, the south pole exit point, putting the ship on a course directly toward the star. But when you *entered* a voidoid to jump into another system, you had to aim the ship at the single point on the voidoid's spherical "surface" that corresponded to the astrometric coordinates of your destination star. That point was usually well mapped, thanks to AMP's precise data, but it could be anywhere on the voidoid's sphere. And the jump coordinates for HD 21749 just happened to be in the wrong place. They'd have to move back *toward* the black hole to reach it.

"Okay, Hutton. Then just pick a star with a known entrance coordinate that keeps us out of the black hole's gravity well for as long as possible. Then execute a jump to that star on main drive at emergency acceleration."

"Yes, Commander. Voidjump in six minutes."

"Brace for transducer delay," Aiden said. The crew felt a microsecond jolt as the G-transducers kicked in to eliminate the sudden kick of 15 Gs. The jolt subsided, and normal down-deck gravity returned. Aiden felt the subsonic rumble of the drive thundering into action.

Devi came to Aiden's side and spoke quietly. "Lista was not disobeying orders, Aiden. She's totally convinced that it's unnecessary to flee from this . . . thing."

"She *did* disregard orders, Sudha," Aiden said, keeping his voice even. "The reasons for it don't matter at times like this. I'm temporarily relieving Pilot Abahem from her post at Helm." Aiden spoke loudly enough for Abahem and everyone else to hear. "Dr. Devi, please escort the pilot to the medical bay. After our jump, please conduct medical and psych exams. Report results to me."

Devi faced him, silently broadcasting her disagreement, but with an appeal for compassion in her eyes. "Aiden . . ."

"That's an order, Doctor."

Devi bowed her head briefly, an experienced pro at choosing her battles wisely. "As you wish, Commander."

This is not a disaster, Aiden kept telling himself as he watched Abahem begin the gradual process of unlinking from the AI, her face devoid of expression.

During the next several minutes, which seemed like hours to Aiden, the black hole's approach slowed considerably but continued to track the ship, as if it were more curious now than aggressive.

Alvarez looked up, perplexed. "Odd. Its gravitational pull is decreasing much faster than our increasing distance from it would account for."

And the faster the ship sped toward its jump point, the slower the black hole approached until it finally stopped.

Woo smiled benignly. "I'm telling you, Aiden. This thing is not what it seems. It's not out to kill us. It wouldn't allow us to be sucked into its gravity well. I'm sure of it."

But Aiden's daily allotment of patience had just expired. "What? Now it can control its own gravitational field? Turn it up or down, just like that? Seriously?"

Woo had dropped into deep thought, then said, "Well . . . something like that, yes. I think maybe—"

"Not *now*, Elgin." Aiden had always tolerated Woo's frequent forays into what seemed like fairyland where everything was alive and spoke to him, as if he were Alice wandering through some cosmic wonderland. The man was a genius, after all, proven many times over. Beyond genius, even—a kind of metaphysical avatar capable of grasping the fantastic and bringing it home to everyone else gift wrapped in logic. The people of the twenty-third century didn't know how lucky they were to have Elgin Woo living among them.

But there was a time and place for everything, and now was not the time, no matter how fascinating. Aiden was responsible for his ship and its crew. Instead of taking chances, he was taking his ship elsewhere. Which reminded him—where the hell *were* they going? But before he could ask, Hutton said, "Voidjump in five seconds."

19

KAPPA RETICULI SYSTEM
Post-Jump

DOMAIN DAY 341, 2218

Star: Kappa Reticuli (HD 22001)
— binary system, two stars: A and B
Distance from Sol: 71 light-years
Spectral type: A = F3V; B = M1
Luminosity: A = 5.26 x Sol; B = 0.43 x Sol
Surface temp: A = 6,796 Kelvin; B = 3,733 Kelvin
Number of planets: 2
Habitable zone: none
—Source: *Allied Mapping Project*, 2218

"WE are now in the Kappa Reticuli system," Hutton said, perfectly impersonating a bored commuter train conductor. "The star is a binary system."

"Thank you, Hutton." Aiden turned to scan the crew, hoping that he didn't look as dazed as he felt. "XO. Situation report, please."

"All boards are green," Ro said. "Our exit velocity was 45 klicks per second; we're now 2,000 klicks from the voidoid."

"Bring the ship to a halt," Aiden said, then turned to Tactical. "Hotah?"

"No hostiles."

"Lilly, what's our neighborhood look like?"

"Kappa Reticuli is a well-known star system," Alvarez said. "There's lots of previous data on it, but it's all secondhand stuff. It's kind of cool to actually be here in person to supplement what we already know."

"Which is?"

She began reading off the system's basic data. "It's a binary system, of course. About 71 light-years from Earth. The primary star, Kappa Ret A, is an F3V-type star. It's about the same size as Sol, but more massive. The secondary star, Kappa Ret B, is an M-type star, smaller and cooler, about half the size of Sol. Even though they're separated by over 1,100 AU, they both orbit a common center of mass. Definitely in the wide-binary category. Looks like there are two gas-giant planets in S-type orbits around the primary. But there're no stable habitable zones anywhere in the system."

Alvarez put a realtime image of the binary system up on the main screen. Voidoids had always been found to occupy a position directly above a star system's center of mass. A single star, of course, was the center of mass of its own system. But in binary systems, and multiple star systems in general, the voidoids were found directly above the system's common center of mass, at a distance of 13 to 15 AU. So when the *Sun Wolf* made its jump, it popped out of the voidoid somewhere between the two stars, but much closer to the primary star than the secondary.

From their current position, the two stars were too far apart to visualize on the same screen. Alvarez had to engage two separate scopes, one trained on each star, and put the images up on a split screen. The primary star appeared large and burned bright yellow-white. The secondary looked small and distant, and gave off a deep orange glow.

"Well," Aiden said, relaxing back into the command chair. "It's as good a place as any to regroup, turn about, and head off to our original destination. Lilly, gather as much survey data as you can. I'm sure the Mapping Project will be grateful for any updates."

He tuned to Ro. "XO, a word, please. In the ready room."

Behind the ready room's closed door, Aiden said, "Ro. Can you take over the Helm? In Abahem's stead? Most of the crew already know that you hold a pilot's license, and that you're the only male in the history of the Agency to have ever earned one."

Ro sighed theatrically and leaned back in his chair. "Well, I guess if everyone aboard knows about it, my rugged manly image can't be rudely questioned any further."

"Very funny," Aiden said. "But seriously, if Lista isn't good to go, for whatever reason, we'll need someone who can link up and do her job. Hutton is good, but there's a reason we use human pilots to augment AIs in voidjumping. I have a feeling we're going to need some quick moves during our next few jumps."

Ro didn't speak for a long moment, and Aiden didn't prompt him. If he wanted a straight answer from the man, it was always best to let Ro get there at his own speed.

For the sake of persuasion, Aiden had overstated the crew's familiarity with that particular benchmark in Ro's enigmatic and multifaceted history. Really, only the remainder of the *Argo*'s original crew currently aboard the *Sun Wolf*—Alvarez and Abahem—knew of it. Almost no one else did. Elgin Woo, of course, had been the one to uncover the story. He'd heard through the grapevine that, many years ago, a male candidate had allegedly passed the requirements to qualify as a top-grade Licensed Pilot. As rumor had it, the mystery man hadn't even gone through the Agency's long years of arduous training, which only females had been able to master. He'd just shown up out of the blue, challenged all the exams, and succeeded so convincingly that the Agency had no choice but to confer lifetime licensure. Then, as the tale was told, the mystery man disappeared from the scene, never to resurface anywhere as a pilot.

Woo had thought the story was a myth, just part of the Licensed Pilot mystique. Until Ro—in a rare moment of candor enhanced by tequila shooters—had admitted the story was true and that he was indeed the male in question. He tried to dismiss the whole thing as "just a phase" he'd gone through in his twenties, something he'd wanted to prove to himself at the time.

"I'm way out of practice for this kind of thing," Ro finally said. "Neurolinkage with the AI for high-velocity voidjumps? With potential high-tech combatants waiting for us on the other side? I'm not sure I'm up to that, Aiden. Certainly not at Abahem's level."

"But you could do it passably well in a pinch, right?"

"Yes. But it's the 'in a pinch' part you should think about. How sure are you that Lista is out of the game? She's one of the Agency's top pilots and has been for over a decade. You and I have worked with her for nearly that long. I think something else is going on with her. Something you need to understand before dismissing her and her considerable talent."

"Point taken. I want to get Devi's opinion first, then I'll talk with Lista myself."

"Good idea," Ro said as he stood to leave. "Keep me posted."

Aiden had wanted to talk with Woo next, but Elgin had seized the opportunity of their downtime here to reengage his "pet project" with an intensity of focus that effectively repelled distraction of any kind. Aiden still didn't know what the man was up to, and whenever he'd asked him about it, Woo said only that it was "the next big thing."

Woo's input would have to wait for now. Instead, Aiden decided to consult a genius of another kind. "Hutton. We need to talk."

"By all means, Aiden. What would you like to discuss?"

"Have you remained disconnected from the OverNet, at least when neurolinked with Abahem? Update me on what's going on with the OverNet."

"Yes, I have remained completely disconnected from the OverNet whenever linked with Pilot Abahem for a jump. We won't have a recurrence of that prior intrusion. The black crow incident. But I have occasionally checked in on the OverNet to assess any new developments. I found some disturbing news on the sociopolitical situation back in Bound Space."

"What's going on?"

"In a word, disinformation. More accurately, bald-faced lies are being disseminated and widely accepted as fact among the human population. It is fomenting an alarming level of unrest. I believe the source of this corruption is a rogue Omicron unit, or a group of them, under the control of an unknown and well-hidden agency. From its inception, the OverNet has always been an unassailable source of factual data presented with the highest degree of unbiased objectivity for use by all the human endeavors that depend on it. Disinformation on this scale from the OverNet is unprecedented."

Of course, it was not the first time in history that large segments of the population, mostly on Earth, had been deliberately stirred into irrational and violent behavior by skillful manipulation of the truth. Human history was littered with examples, some of them extreme enough to threaten the very fabric of civilization. It was usually perpetrated by individuals in power, done to retain their own power and strengthen it at all costs.

The Big Lie strategy had grown more successful with each new innovation in information dissemination—from the rally grounds and halls of the early twentieth century, on to radio and television, then to the Internet of the twenty-first century—until the Die Back brought civilization on Earth to its knees. But it didn't stop there. The Big Lie, and those with the cunning to use it effectively, never went away, nor did the populations of people disenfranchised enough to hear without question only what confirmed their own fears and anger.

The recent advent of the Omicron AIs was a major step forward in combating distribution of lies. By their very nature, the way in which they were "grown" rather than assembled, the Omicrons became virtually immune to information that couldn't be validated by multiple independent sources, or that was not supported by the highest standards of scientific consensus. The OverNet had emerged spontaneously when all the existing Omicron-3 AIs, over 400 of them, became interlinked through a variety of comm channels, including Holtzman connections. It had evolved into a robust global intelligence, constantly fact-checking among all its individual parts. From that point on, information reliability increased exponentially. To Aiden, the very notion that the OverNet could be corrupted from within was abhorrent, especially if Cardew's Licet Omnia was behind it.

He sighed, rubbed his tired eyes, and sat back. "So what's the latest trouble brewing?"

"It is an alarming conspiracy theory that began within the One Earth movement, a falsehood that has spread like wildfire and has millions of people up in arms. Literally. The OverNet was purportedly the source of this falsehood, and since the OverNet has always been so reliable, large segments of the population—not just One Earthers—are accepting it as truth."

The primary tenet of the One Earth movement was that humans belonged on Earth and nowhere else for the foreseeable future. They believed that humanity's only chance of survival was to turn their energies inward, back to Earth instead of outward to other planets. To focus on the work of healing planet Earth. To atone for the purely human errors that caused the Die Back. They viewed exploration of space as a fatal distraction and opposed all colonization of off-world habitats and planets. To them, those activities were misguided diversions that distracted people from their responsibility to repair Earth first.

Aiden didn't want to hear it, but he asked anyway. "What's the claim?"

"The claim is that the upper echelons of the UED government, along with Earth's science and technology communities, have formed a secret coalition with plans to abandon Earth as a failed planet. They are supposedly preparing a colony vessel that will take them to the pristine planet of Silvanus, where they will establish a so-called New Earth, taking with them all the resources the One Earthers believe are needed to rejuvenate Earth.

"But that's not the worst of it. They also believe that this elitist New Earth nation will then turn its planet-killing weapons on Old Earth to sterilize the planet, believing that it is the only way to revive Earth—to start from scratch and allow the Rete fungus to rebuild the biosphere in the right way."

Aiden couldn't believe his ears. "That's preposterous!"

"Of course it is. Utterly false. But an alarming percentage of the population believes it to be true, a percentage that is growing every day. They are arming themselves and threatening to overthrow the government. There is chaos and violence in the streets of all major cities. Senseless mass shootings are rising to unprecedented levels. Even segments of UED's military forces are joining them. All of this can be traced back to a well-planned and skillfully executed program of disinformation originating from somewhere within the OverNet."

Aiden remained silent, overcome by dark visions of humanity's future. To Hutton's credit, the AI didn't attempt to engage him further on the topic. Instead, he shifted to a buoyant tone and said, "But I believe you wanted to discuss something else more relevant to our current situation."

Aiden had to smile. "Your intuition algorithms are coming along nicely, Hutton. Yes, I wanted to ask how you were coping with our disconnection from the OverNet. And how it might be affecting Pilot Abahem."

"That is the right question to ask, Aiden. I'm sure you are aware that all Licensed Pilots active in the field are connected among themselves, and that interconnection is mediated by the OverNet through the Holtzman network. Without the OverNet, Pilot Abahem is cut off from that essential community of minds and personalities. Like all pilots, she has been an integral part of that collective for as long as she has been a Licensed Pilot."

Hutton paused here, as if waiting for Aiden's response. When Aiden said nothing, the AI continued. "So, to answer your question, yes, I believe Pilot Abahem has been significantly affected by the disconnect and it is likely to interfere with her ability to function as a pilot. This issue should be addressed and corrected to have any hope of success for our mission. We will need her considerable skill to negotiate the unpredictable dangers we are sure to encounter."

Hutton fell silent. The AI had just confirmed Ro's earlier assessment of the situation. It was time to talk with Abahem in private. And no time like the present. Aiden stood. "Thanks for your input, Hutton."

"A pleasure, as always."

20

KAPPA RETICULI SYSTEM
System Voidoid

DOMAIN DAY 341, 2218

AIDEN stood outside the door to Abahem's quarters, hesitating to knock. He'd never been inside the pilot's quarters, at least not while she was aboard. On his way here, he had stopped in at Medical to get Devi's assessment of the pilot's condition. The doctor had reported that Abahem tested out physically fit and psychologically sound, as measured by the Agency's rigorous psych profile for Licensed Pilots. Aiden had asked the pilot to join him in the ready room, but she had responded with a request to hold the meeting in her quarters.

It was against Space Service protocol for any senior officer to meet alone with a subordinate of the opposite gender inside crew quarters, behind closed doors. But under the circumstances, protocols of that nature were low on Aiden's list of priorities. He wanted to get things straight between himself and Abahem, professionally first and secondly, if at all possible, on a personal level.

As he stood there procrastinating, he reminded himself of how little was actually known about Licensed Pilots, even within the ranks of the Space Service where they served an indispensable function.

Most people knew, of course, that they were essential for the expansion of human exploration of Bound Space. High-velocity voidjumps were virtually impossible without a Licensed Pilot in linkage with the Omicron's neural net. And high-velocity voidjumps were the only way to get anywhere in a reasonable amount of time after a jump. Granted, a voidship could make a low-velocity jump without a pilot, under the guidance of its Omicron-3 AI alone. But it would emerge into the new star system with the same low velocity and would take forever to get back up to speed. So nowadays, all space vessels registered by ARM and the UED were required by law to employ a pilot licensed by the Intersystem Pilots Agency.

Most people also knew that pilots were all female and selected at an early age for their unique mental gifts. It was not a gender-bias thing, either. Males were not excluded and were, in fact, encouraged to apply for entrance. But females had proven far superior at interfacing with the biomolecular neural nets of the Omicron AIs and engaging them in directed holistic cognition. From an early age, they were trained in virtual seclusion by the Intersystem Pilots Agency. None had been known to form personal relationships with anyone outside their own circles. As a result, they were perceived as an occult sisterhood whose inner workings remained hidden from the public.

But Aiden was counting on his own unique background, his experiences with the Rete on Silvanus, to make a meaningful connection with Pilot Abahem. Experiences that were analogous to the transcendental states that pilots accomplished routinely on the job. He alone knew what it was like to link with a living neural net the size of an entire planet, ancient and deep beyond all imagining. To *become* an entire planet. To transcend his individual self and merge with a universal consciousness. It was a place in time and space he would never forget or ever recover from. A place he yearned to revisit with every fiber of his being. So egoless and positive with light and love that withdrawal from it had plunged him into a self-destructive spiral of malaise.

That's why Aiden understood the depths of depression that followed unlinking from such an ecstatic state of wholeness, of coming down from that expanded awareness. Abahem had once described it as a profound sense of loss. Pilots accepted it as an occupational hazard of their profession. But some dosed themselves with Continuum, after linkage and off shift, to ease their times away from the Omicron's addictive embrace.

Continuum was a genetically tailored derivative of psilocybin. Used in carefully calculated doses, it was fully sanctioned by the Agency to treat PLS, Post-Linkage Syndrome. But Continuum had its downside. With pharmacokinetics similar to psilocybin, it activated the same serotonin receptors in the brain responsible for the hallucinogenic effects of psilocybin. And it also activated certain dopamine pathways in the brain, which made it potentially addictive.

When Aiden had finally admitted to himself that he suffered from his own version of the pilots' PLS, the Space Service physicians had started him on limited dosages of Continuum. It had worked, too, for a while. At least before he started to use it a little too often. It became a means unto itself, a denial of the inner strengths he'd acquired but not yet put to use. He'd needed the help of Sudha Devi, and support from Skye, to pull himself free from the addiction. After that, it was his own face in the mirror looking back at him that kept him on track, one day at a time.

The sound of a ceiling ventilator shifting gears overhead brought him back to the present. He'd spent far too much time standing at Abahem's door in contemplation. He straightened up and knocked.

The pilot opened the door and stood quietly for a moment, looking at him, eyes wide and serene. Abahem was a tall woman, fine-boned and willowy, with a gaunt appearance that could easily be mistaken for anorexia were it not so common among pilots. Her skin was pale white but glowed with a healthy tone. Like all pilots, she kept her head totally hairless. Faint reddened spots were visible on her scalp where the neurolinkage cap had been affixed. She wore a simple white shift, loose fitting and calf-length. Her eyes were an unusual shade of hazel, looking resolutely into his own, as if searching for a familiar point of reference behind his eyes.

"Please come in," she finally said. Aiden had never known a pilot who didn't speak with that quiet, whispery voice unique to their sisterhood. Whispery but clear, easy to understand if you listened carefully, even with the slightly odd inflections that couldn't be placed with any known human language.

"I'll leave the door partially open," she said, in deference to Service protocol. "Please sit."

Aiden sat in one of the two chairs at either side of a small writing table. To call her quarters Spartan would be an understatement. Of course, all of the crew quarters on board the *Sun Wolf* were sparsely furnished and utilitarian, even the captain's quarters. But their occupants usually added personal décor to warm things up—framed photos of family or friends, various knickknacks with personal meaning, books, music players, sitting pillows casually placed. While clean, well ordered, and well lit, Abahem's space was virtually devoid of such homey trappings.

The air inside was cool and fresh and carried a faint floral scent. When he glanced around for the source, he spotted what might be the only personal touch in the room—a single orchid blossom in a white ceramic pot on a bookshelf. The blossom was also white and looked surprisingly healthy. He'd heard that orchids were finicky and difficult to care for, especially in spaceborne habitats, and wondered how Abahem had managed it.

After an uncomfortable silence, Aiden decided to get straight to the point. "What happened out there, Lista? I'm concerned. About you and about the mission."

"I apologize, Commander," she said, head slightly bowed, "for my failure to execute your orders."

"You can call me Aiden, here in private," he said, leaning forward. "You and I go way back, Lista. I know your work well enough to assume that you had your reasons. I just want to know what they were. And more importantly, if anything is troubling you."

She paused before speaking, then said, "You must know by now . . . Aiden, that, since the AI disconnected from the OverNet, I have been cut off from the Kinship. That's what pilots call our circle of communion. It is a fellowship not only of the spirit, but of practical, real-world support. Our connection with it gives us strength and insight. It helps us perform our duties and to regain balance when we're unlinked and off duty. Being cut off from the Kinship for this long has affected me, I will admit. It has made me more vulnerable, more sensitive to external intrusions, and less able to shield myself from their destructive forces. But I am finding ways to cope with this loss and even gain strength from it."

Aiden tilted his head sideways. He was tempted to ask . . .

"And, no," she said, as if reading his mind. "I don't take Continuum anymore. I did once, in my youth, but I realized it was not the way for me. I know you understand this. I know you understand more about what pilots experience than you may think. All of us know. The Kinship is aware of what you accomplished and endured on Silvanus. Of the gift you gave us all and the price you paid for it. So, there is no need to explain any more of it."

The impact of what she said hit him harder than he'd expected. He felt his face flush and his throat tighten with emotion. Before he could formulate anything to say, Abahem continued.

"But that was not the real reason I hesitated to follow your orders to escape from that primordial black hole. Just as Dr. Woo suggested, it was not an ordinary black hole. It was . . . an entity. A life force of such power and depth, and *benevolence* . . . It had the same flavor as the Kinship. But like a million Kinships. Yes, in my isolation, I was drawn to it. But my actions at the Helm were not purely selfish. This entity . . . spoke to me. Not with words. With energy. With knowledge. And with a desire to know us, the crew of the *Sun Wolf.* To *help* us."

Here Abahem stopped speaking. She had already spoken more words to him than he'd heard from her in all the years they had worked together. Aiden wasn't sure how to respond. Was Abahem delusional, walking down the same road to fantasyland that Elgin Woo skipped down so merrily? He thought not. If both Elgin and Abahem, two brilliant people from very different cognitive cultures, had the same impression about the encounter, their conclusions might not be so crazy after all. Their insights, in fact, may help illuminate the path to victory over an enemy that threatened all of humanity.

21

KAPPA RETICULI SYSTEM
System Voidoid

DOMAIN DAY 341, 2218

DURING the silence that followed Abahem's last words, she watched Aiden intently for his reaction. Then she leaned closer to him across the table and looked into his eyes with emotions he'd never seen from her before. She surprised him again when she reached over to place her hand on top of his and said, "You must believe me, Aiden. I would never put this ship and its crew in such jeopardy. I would die before letting that happen."

Pilots were not given to such candid and revealing discourse and much less given to any kind of physical contact with anyone outside their cloistered circle. Her hand was cool on his and seemed to radiate some subtle energy as she continued to look into his eyes, unblinking.

"I do believe you, Lista. I never really doubted it. I only wanted to understand. Thank you for confiding in me."

She removed her hand from his as if suddenly realizing the uncommon nature of the touch. She looked down at the table and folded her hands in front of her. Aiden had the sensation that the door on this remarkable interaction had begun to close. He wanted to hold it open a little while longer.

"Lista, this ship is going to need you as our mission moves forward. More than any time before. No one can replace what you do, but we can patch together a work-around at Helm with Ro and Hutton. I just need to know if you feel up to resuming your post."

Her eyes remained downcast, and she did not speak. Aiden said, "I can't promise you that we can stay locked out of the OverNet for very long. We rely on it too much. You'll need to consider that in your decision. And I will trust your decision because I know you will tell me the truth."

She brought her eyes up to his again. The hazel color in them seemed darker, more intense. She replied without hesitation, "Yes, I can do it now. I have found a clear reflection of the Kinship inside my heart and mind. I will report to duty whenever you need me."

Aiden was glad to hear it and told her so. He thought the time to leave had come, but remained seated. A question had been nagging at him and wouldn't let go. He hesitated to bring it up now but sensed that this rare moment of rapport between them presented his only opportunity to voice it.

"There's something I've been wanting to ask you, Lista," he said, "but I don't want to intrude and will understand completely if you'd rather not answer."

He paused. She looked at him. Her face softened. She said, "Go on."

"The black crow you saw during the failed voidjump; I saw it, too, several months ago during a neurolink experience. I was terrified. So I know. But when you were released from the vision, you said someone's name. You said 'Ciarra.' Who is Ciarra?"

Abahem's face darkened again. She averted her eyes and said nothing. He had gone too far, and he knew it. He was about to beat himself up over it when she looked up at him. Instead of shutting down, her face remained open, but her eyes glistened with tears. "Ciarra Devlin. She was the Licensed Pilot aboard the *Conquest* when Cardew hijacked it nearly a year ago. She was one of our Sisters. We were close. She never returned. I feared that she'd been brain-tapped, to pilot the *Conquest* for Cardew. Now I know it's true. She no longer belongs to herself. She belongs to Cardew."

The sparrow trapped by the crow's talons.

The silence that followed hurt like a stab wound. A deep pain both physical and psychic. It rendered him incapable of asking more, and he knew that she would not answer more.

The darkness abated, not completely, but enough for him to say, "Thank you, Lista. I'll be going now."

When he stood to leave, Abahem reached out to touch his hand again. She said, "There's something else I wanted to tell you. It might be important, so I wanted to share it with you."

"What is it?"

"It's about these cloneborgs you and Dr. Woo have been talking about, Cardew's minions that can pass for normal human beings. I think one of them was aboard Shénmì Station."

Aiden felt a lead weight sink into his stomach. Skye immediately came into his mind, her safety and that of the whole station. "How do you know?"

"Some pilots have the talent of seeing human auras. I am one of them. The person I suspect as being a cloneborg had no aura. None at all."

Aiden was familiar with the concept. Hypothetically, auras were bio-electromagnetic fields that emanated from all living beings, even plants. It was a form of life energy that surrounded the body and was invisible to everyone except those who had the ability to see it. It was called the "subtle body" in some traditions, but the Gaians still referred to it as an aura.

"I'm so used to seeing auras around everyone," Abahem said, "that I noticed the absence of one immediately. I was stunned to see what looked like a human being, a man, without an aura. I didn't believe it at first. But I believe it now, after replaying the incident in my head. Then when I overheard you and Dr. Woo discussing cloneborgs, I put it together."

Aiden felt his mouth go dry. If Woo was right about the unnatural origin of the cloneborgs, then what Abahem had seen—or rather *not* seen—made perfect sense. "Do you know who he was?"

"He was a crewman from the antimatter tanker. All four of the tanker's crew passed by me in a corridor dressed in their BSE jumpsuits. He was lagging behind, and when he passed me, I noticed. It was only him, not any of the others. I'm very sure of that."

The antimatter tanker stationed at Shénmì, the SS *Quasimodo*, routinely rotated its four-person crew every six months. They all came from BSE, Bright Star Energy, the largest antimatter provider in Bound Space, based on Jupiter's moon Callisto. Its employees were among the most rigorously vetted workers in the field. But if Cardew's newest batch of cloneborgs were indistinguishable from human beings, and were wickedly smart, it was easy to imagine how one could have been planted among its tanker crews. The thought of a cloneborg in control of an antimatter tanker docked at Shénmì Station sent a chill up Aiden's spine. Cloneborgs would make ideal suicide bombers.

Aiden swallowed hard and calmed himself. "Thanks for the tip, Lista. I'll let Shénmì Station know about this."

It suddenly occurred to him how useful Abahem's talent for spotting cloneborgs could be in the future, but he kept the thought to himself. Instead, he said, "The *Sun Wolf* will stay put here, near the voidoid, through a sleep cycle. Then we'll jump to our next destination tomorrow at zero eight hundred."

"I'll be there," she said. "And Commander . . . Aiden. Thank you."

She looked stronger now, more resolute. But her eyes still held a shade of melancholy. Aiden recognized it. Loneliness. Isolation. Abahem was now a refugee from a state of wholeness. Just as he had been and would be again. He struggled with a fraternal impulse to embrace her, to comfort her. But he knew that would not happen. Could not happen.

Instead, he bowed his head slightly in silent gratitude and left her quarters, closing the door quietly behind him.

Before returning to the bridge, Aiden stopped off at his quarters and drafted an encrypted Holtzman transmission to Shénmì Station's security chief, Colonel Crestfield. Without saying exactly how he knew of it, Aiden warned Crestfield about a suspected mole—one of Cardew's cloneborgs—aboard the station and urged him to take appropriate precautions. He also asked Crestfield to pass that information on to the Shénmì Project's director, Dr. Skye Landen. Aiden sent the transmission on its long journey and returned to the bridge.

Back on the bridge, with the crew assembled, he informed them of his plan to stay put for a sleep cycle before heading to their next destination.

"Which is . . . ?" Hotah asked.

"A star called HD 21749," Aiden said. "Now that we've checked out the three systems where AMP lost a probe, we're moving on to maybe the most interesting system of the lot. And maybe the most dangerous one so far."

He punched a key on the command board, and data for HD 21749 appeared on the main screen. "It's a K-type star that AMP investigated six months ago. They identified a planet there that meets all the criteria for a 'superhabitable' world. That's a hypothetical type of exoplanet defined as being even better suited for the emergence of life than Earth is, or was. Theoretically, it would support a far greater diversity of life forms, in larger numbers, and for longer periods of time. It would be a planet that's larger, warmer, and older than Earth and would be found orbiting a K-type star near the center of its habitable zone. And that's exactly what AMP found at that star. Planet d is the one, and it fits the theoretical profile for a superhabitable world, right down to the last detail, better than any planet discovered so far."

"And going there might be dangerous because . . . ?" Alvarez asked.

Hotah answered before Aiden could open his mouth. "Because Cardew probably knows about it, too, so it's the most likely place he'd be interested in. The most likely to be heavily guarded by his forces."

"Right," Aiden said. "And if it happens to be the planet he's chosen as his home base, we can expect a welcoming party of warships, mines, or whatever else he's devised to keep intruders out. They'll be positioned at the voidoid's exit point. Our original orders are to locate Cardew's home base and report back to Allied forces. And do it without engaging the enemy. In this case, I fully agree with those orders. The *Sun Wolf* is the most powerful ship in existence. But we're only one ship. If we pop into that system and encounter overwhelming forces, then we'll get the hell out of Dodge before stirring up a hornet's nest we can't fend off."

"But we've got the zero-point drive, and they don't," Hotah pointed out. "We can use our evade-and-attack strategy to inflict some serious damage."

"That's true," Aiden said. "But if there are more than five or six battle cruisers stationed at the voidoid, that strategy becomes problematic. There's a tactical limit to how often we can keep zipping in and out of combat zones, trying to take them out one at a time. And remember, we'll need uncontested access to the voidoid to get back *out* of the system in an emergency. Worst-case scenario, we'd have to execute a jump with the ZPD at higher than 10 percent light speed."

"We'll need a Licensed Pilot for all that," Alvarez said, stating the obvious. "How's Lista doing?"

All eyes turned to Aiden. "Pilot Abahem will be fine. She passed Dr. Devi's exams, and I had a talk with her just now. I have every confidence in her readiness for the Helm."

He said no more. The crew seemed satisfied with his response, but Alvarez kept looking at him, deep concern in her eyes. Aiden finally said to her, "Lista was cut off from her network of sister pilots when we disconnected from the OverNet. It's hard for her, but she's dealing with it. She'll be ready."

Alvarez, who was no stranger to loss, and to the kind of loneliness that only love could cure, looked past him in silence, a faraway look in her eyes.

~ ~ ~

The following morning, Aiden woke to the sounds of "Infant Eyes" from Wayne Shorter's 1964 *Speak No Evil* recording. It was

Hutton's alarm clock. Aiden had entrusted the AI to choose any one of Aiden's favorite jazz recordings to wake him at the end of his sleep cycle, played at just the right volume to ease his waking. Any one of the five most beautiful jazz ballads from that era—in Aiden's estimation—would have been just fine. But on this morning, "Infant Eyes" was the right choice, and somehow Hutton had known it.

"Thank you, Hutton. Please brew one cup of dark coffee, extra strong."

He'd added the Ethiopian coffee beans to the autobrew the night before. The machine ground and brewed it while Aiden donned a fresh Service jumpsuit. After the hot cup of steaming brew jolted him fully awake, he headed off for the bridge.

As he turned a corner into the main corridor, he saw Abahem and Alvarez ahead of him walking side by side, on their way to the bridge. There was a spring in their step, a subtle liveliness uncommon to either of them. Just before they turned the corner ahead of him, he thought he saw their hands touch for a brief moment and their heads turn to face each other, smiling.

It was one of the happiest sights Aiden had seen in a very long time. It renewed his faith in the crew's resilience, their strength, and their readiness to deal with whatever lay ahead.

An hour later, he settled into the command chair, looked around the bridge to see the crew at their posts, and said, "Prepare for jump. Helm, initiate Stealth Sequence."

Sitting in front of him at the Helm, Abahem gave her thumbs-up signal with a little more finesse than usual. He smiled and said, "Execute."

22

HD 21749 SYSTEM
Post-Jump

Domain Day 342, 2218

Star: HD 21749
Spectral type: K5V
Distance from Sol: 53 light-years
Luminosity: 0.23 x Sol
Surface temperature: 4,571 Kelvin
Number of planets: 5
Habitable zone: 0.48–0.89 AU
—Source: *Allied Mapping Project*, 2218

"Two battle cruisers. Big ones. M class." Hotah spoke in clipped staccato. "One is a lot closer. About 2,000 klicks. Well within medium laser range. Target is designated Alpha."

"Where's the other one, Lieutenant?"

"In back of us about one light-second away, in the direction of the voidoid. Designated Beta. Not an immediate threat at this point. Uh-oh. Alpha just spotted us. Its laser cannon is turning toward us."

"Execute evade maneuver, one million klicks out."

Just as the battle cruiser's laser cannon locked in on its target, the *Sun Wolf* disappeared from sight. Four seconds later, the *Sun*

Wolf came to a halt one million kilometers away, giving Aiden time to sit back and consider their next move.

As before, the *Sun Wolf* had emerged from the voidoid at 10 percent light speed and dropped out of ZPD at a point 450,000 kilometers due south of the voidoid. But unlike before, two heavy battle cruisers had been waiting for them, one of them surprisingly close by. It meant that Cardew's forces were now anticipating a maneuver like the Stealth Sequence and were placing assets far enough along the exit path to increase the odds of intercepting it. In fact, their estimation of where the *Sun Wolf* might drop out of ZPD had been a very good one. Had this particular warship been positioned any closer, it could have turned into a good old-fashioned close-range shootout. The kind Billy Hotah would have relished.

As it was, the *Sun Wolf*'s ability to stop on a dime and evade at 92 percent light speed was still its ultimate ace in the hole.

Aiden had his own idea of how to proceed from here, but he wanted to know how his Tactical Officer would handle it. He wasn't surprised that Hotah had already formulated a plan of attack rather than a strategy to dodge confrontation, as their mission orders would have them do.

"First of all," Hotah said, "this is an all-laser-weapon show. Hit and run. No time for missiles or rail guns. I'd zip back to ship Alpha on maximum ZPD, approach in the exact opposite direction from where he last aimed his cannon, pop into view 50 klicks out with our laser cannon hot. Then fry his ass before he knew what hit him. But do it quickly, because enemy ship Beta will be on high alert and will have its long-range laser cannon powered up. Still, it'll take time for Beta to react and target us. We give them just enough time to turn their cannon toward us, then we zip out of sight again, come right back at them from behind their aim, and repeat fry. We could do it all in less than 60 seconds."

Aiden thought about that for a moment. If his goal had been to attack, his own plan would've been very close to what Hotah had just described, except Hotah added the nice touch of attacking from directly behind their foe's last targeting vector. The enemy would have no idea where the *Sun Wolf* might reappear and would be unlikely to re-aim in anticipation. The element of surprise was the *Sun Wolf*'s most potent weapon, and it was the ZPD that made it possible.

It was just too perfect to ignore. Aiden could have gone cerebral, attempting to parse the difference between defensive and offensive action as defined by his mission orders. But it was too late for that now. The adrenaline was already pumping through his body, the ancient Celtic battle cries already echoing inside his head. "Sounds good, Lieutenant. Hutton, did you get all that?"

"Yes indeed, Commander."

"Good. I want to execute in three minutes. Hutton, work up the flight-and-fire sequence now. Run it by Lieutenant Hotah for his approval. Then Hotah, you assume Helm and run sequence through Hutton."

Hotah didn't blink an eye at relinquishing fire control to the AI. It was a complicated and fast-moving maneuver best handled by the AI, and Hotah knew it.

Hutton generated the sequence. After Hotah approved and programed it into the tactical computer, Aiden said, "Execute."

Part one of the sequence worked like a charm. Done in 25 seconds. Battle cruiser Alpha became a white-hot smear of plasma spread across several kilometers of space, rapidly dissipating even as the *Sun Wolf* left the scene seconds later. Part two, however, proved more interesting. That part had assumed Beta would remain at or near where it was last seen. After zipping back out to a million kilometers, then back in to take out Beta, the *Sun Wolf* found Beta furiously boosting backward toward the voidoid on emergency acceleration in an apparent attempt to jump out of the system before the *Sun Wolf* reappeared.

But since the plan was for the *Sun Wolf* to reappear 50 kilometers *behind* Beta, now the battle cruiser was heading straight toward them. It had already covered 46 of those kilometers and was closing in fast, now less than four kilometers away. Way too close for blowing up a ship that size without getting caught up in the blast. But close enough for Beta, who had just spotted the *Sun Wolf*, to turn its powerful rail guns against them.

Hutton reacted to the unexpected situation immediately by re-engaging the ZPD to zip out of sight again just as the first rail-gun projectile ripped through space toward the ship's midsection. The AI halted the ship at a half million klicks out, readjusted the attack vector, then came back in—only this time, from behind Beta's direction of escape at a safe distance of 50 kilometers. At that point, Beta didn't stand a chance. It promptly joined its sister ship in decorating local space with curtains of charged subatomic particles.

"Good job," Aiden said. He tried to relax back into the command chair, but his heart was still pounding, the copper taste of adrenaline still sharp in his mouth. He surprised himself by how easily he could justify the taking of so many lives when those lives were perceived as not human, not living beings with a soul. But in truth, he wasn't exactly sure what cloneborgs were, how human they were, or even if they had souls. He only knew for sure that they were Cardew's minions, created by him to do his bidding, and as such, Aiden felt no remorse in killing as many of them as he could.

"Lieutenant, are we clear now?"

"We're clear. Nothing within 10 million klicks from our position. Not even Holtzman buoys."

"XO, launch our own Holtzman buoy into comm position. Lilly, long-range scans?"

Focusing intently on her screen, Alvarez didn't answer immediately. She finally said, "I may have picked up something. It's too small and too far away to be sure what it is. But it could be the halo of an exhaust plume. Moving into the outer region of the planetary system. I'll get a better read on it when we move in closer."

"A halo? Not an actual exhaust plume, directly visualized?"

"That's right. It's what you'd see from a small vessel receding from us and decelerating."

"But it's moving toward the *outer* system? Not toward the system's hab zone?"

"Correct. Looks to be headed toward one of the gas giants."

"It's not one of ours," Ro said. "Unless there's an alien spacefaring race out in these parts, it's got to be one of Cardew's."

Curious. Whatever it was didn't appear to be an immediate threat, at least for the moment. "We'll check it out once we're in-system. Lilly, what do you have on the planets down there?"

"I'll start out by telling you that planet d is absolutely beautiful. Big, blue-green, warm, thick atmosphere with lots of oxygen. Oceans of liquid water. Can't wait to see it close up."

Woo smiled. "It's the superhabitable planet that AMP said we'd find out here. No wonder Cardew was guarding this system."

"Yeah, but with only two warships," Aiden said. "I don't think his central base is in this system. If it was, he'd have more firepower here standing guard."

"Did you get a look at those two warships?" Hotah said. "They looked exactly like the SS *Conquest*, that UED battle cruiser Cardew hijacked earlier this year."

"Not surprising," Ro said. "Cardew has at least one ship-builder platform. Stolen, of course. His cloneborgs are probably using the *Conquest* as a prototype to crank out more of the same."

"But where are the raw materials coming from?" Hotah asked. "And the manpower?"

"You mean the cloneborg power," Woo said. "He's obviously got birthing crèches replicating more of them every day. And raw materials? With a growing multitude of loyal worker bees, any metal-rich system would do."

Unwilling to contemplate that grim prospect at the moment, Aiden turned back to Alvarez. "What about the rest of the system?"

"Five planets total. There's data on the first two going way back to NASA's TESS project. The closest one to the star is planet c. Only 10 million klicks out and an orbital period of eight days, so it's really hot. It's rocky and about the same size as Earth, but nearly four times more massive.

"Planet b is next in line at only .2 AU from the star. This one is more interesting. It's about 3 times the size of Earth but *way* more massive, like 23 times more. But it's not rocky. Looks like it's a classic water world. No landmass. All ocean and very warm, being so close to the star. I'm getting a surface temp of around 150 degrees C. That'd be over boiling point on Earth. But the planet is so massive—with much greater surface gravity and atmospheric pressure—that nothing is boiling away. Still, it's not a place you'd want to take a boat cruise.

"Planet d is definitely a superhabitable world. But I'll get to that in a second, after rounding out the rest of the system. Planets e and f are both gas giants like Jupiter, but f is a lot larger, and e has a Saturn-type ring system. They're out at 3 and 6 AU respectively. Also, there's a rudimentary asteroid belt between d and e like the one in Sol."

Alvarez paused here, probably for dramatic effect, and looked at the rest of the crew who had formed a circle around her in various stages of anticipation. "And now," she finally said, "for the main attraction."

Even from this distance, the telescopic image of d was stunning. They saw an orb of blue and green with a cloud cover of random swirls mixed with more organized cyclonic weather patterns. The star's deep orange light could be seen glinting off ocean surfaces through the gaps between the clouds. The calibrations superimposed on the display indicated that the planet was larger than Earth but less than twice its size. Once again, the miracle of life had been born from the infinite ocean of nothingness surrounding it.

"Helm, set course for d. Max ZPD. Take us to within 10 million klicks." He wanted to approach cautiously from a point well out of weapons range from anyone lurking on or near the planet.

Just under two hours later, the ship pulled into position for a closer look at the planet.

"Much better," Alvarez said. "From here, this planet clearly fits the classic profile of a superhabitable world down to every detail. That includes the old Heller-Armstrong criteria with its updated refinements. We could get even better data closer in, but these things are for sure: Its sun is an old K-type main sequence star, easily a couple billion years older and more stable than Sol. The planet is situated in the exact center of the habitable zone at .62 AU—much better situated than Earth is in Sol's hab zone. It's in a remarkably stable orbit with minimal eccentricity, almost circular like Earth's, with an orbital period of 216 days. That means no radical fluctuations in surface temperatures.

"It's got a 23 percent axial tilt, which makes for moderate seasonal changes, and its 28-hour day keeps fluctuations in day-to-night temperatures to a minimum. There's one fairly large moon, which is good because it helps stabilize the favorable axial tilt and causes enough tidal action in the oceans to keep the waters well mixed and more suitable for life. We'll need to get closer to pin down some of the climatic and geological data, but I can tell you right now that it's a lot warmer down there than Earth, and the oxygen content of the atmosphere is a lot higher, like over 30 percent."

"That's good for now, Lilly. Hotah? Anything suspicious around the planet?"

"No, sir."

"Okay. Let's move into high orbit."

The planet looked even more remarkable from high orbit, like Earth on steroids. Big, beautiful, and vibrant. Alvarez completed the profile in more detail. She found that the planet was 1.3 times larger and 1.7 times more massive than Earth. It was covered with approximately the same ratio of water per landmass as Earth, but its oceans were shallower. The geological instruments estimated its age to be around 5.5 billion years. Its large molten iron core combined with a 28-hour rotation was more than sufficient to produce a magnetic field strong enough to protect the surface from deadly radiation. The planet's average mean temperature was around 25 degrees C, quite a bit warmer than Earth's 15 degrees, and its atmosphere was a whopping 31 percent oxygen by volume.

"That's actually not unusual," Devi commented. "Earth's atmosphere was around 35 percent oxygen three million years ago, at the end of the Carboniferous Period, and just as warm as it is down there. The Carboniferous Period just happens to be Earth's period of greatest biodiversity and biomass."

Aiden leaned back in the command chair. "Any signs of civilization?"

"If you mean civilization by human standards, preliminary scans haven't seen anything. No organized structures on the surface, no radio transmissions, and no other indications of humanlike activity. But I have picked up evidence of animal life, both on land and in the oceans."

"Let's give it a name," Devi said. "We've given names to all the others. This planet more than deserves one of its own."

After a thoughtful silence on the bridge, Ro spoke. "Parthas."

Everyone turned to him, waiting for more. Ro finally shrugged and said, "It's Irish for paradise. I remember it from the fairytales my grandmother used to read to us."

That seemed good enough for everyone. Aiden said, "Parthas it is. Lilly, enter it into the catalogue."

She did, then said, "It's beautiful. Can we go down there and look around?"

Aiden fought off the urge to do exactly that—to visit such a pristine world, rich with biodiversity far beyond anything Earth had ever seen. "I'd love to. But survey exploration isn't part of our mission profile. If our global scans show no signs of Cardew's activity here, then we need to move on."

But something was still bothering him. Parthas was undoubtedly the most ideal planet to colonize, right out of the box, for humans and cloneborgs alike. Hands down the most suitable world discovered so far, in either astrocell. The perfect place for Cardew to build the capitol of his empire. Cardew obviously knew of its existence, but he'd stationed only two warships in the system, and neither of them were anywhere near the planet. And where was the rest of Cardew's infrastructure? The shipbuilders, manufacturing platforms, mining and colony ships, and all the rest?

It just didn't add up, and Aiden didn't like it.

23

HD 21749 SYSTEM
Parthas Orbit

DOMAIN DAY 342, 2218

AIDEN sat back, closed his eyes for a moment, and thought. Ro's earlier comment about the "bigger picture" came to mind. That picture was a complex puzzle with hundreds of disconnected pieces still swirling around inside his head. But some of those pieces were just now beginning to fit together.

He turned to Alvarez. "That mystery vessel you picked up earlier. The one that's decelerating toward the gas giant. Where is it now?"

Alvarez punched in a few commands on her board. "It's almost at the planet now. Slowing down near the upper atmosphere. But it's still too small and far away to make out any details."

The hairs on the back of Aiden's neck prickled. He wasn't sure why. He looked at Woo. The man stood as still as a stone. He had a worried look in his eyes.

"We need to get out there now," Aiden said, "to find out what that thing is and what it's doing. If it's Cardew's, it can't be anything good."

Aiden didn't wait for discussion. "Helm, take us out to that gas giant, maximum ZPD. Then bring us to within 10 kilometers of the object. Lieutenant Hotah, be on Level One alert the moment we pull out of ZPD."

The gas giant, planet HD 21749e, looked similar to Jupiter, about the same size, but twice as massive. Its orbit around the star was about 2.6 AU farther out from Parthas's orbit. In what appeared to be a fortuitous coincidence, the two planets were nearing a closest-approach moment that happened only once every 330 days in this system. At maximum drive, it took the *Sun Wolf* about 24 minutes to cover the distance and come to a halt near the object. It was clearly a spacefaring vessel of some kind. It took no action against the *Sun Wolf*'s sudden appearance and seemed oblivious to their presence. But looks could be deceiving.

Alvarez hailed the vessel on all common frequencies but received no response. Aiden moved the ship in closer. Alvarez put a telescopic image of the vessel on the main screen. It was the oddest-looking ship any of them had ever seen. Only Elgin Woo didn't seem perplexed. Instead, he had the look of a man who'd just smelled something rotten.

They saw a vessel about 100 meters long, roughly half the length of the *Sun Wolf*, with a central fuselage 10 meters in diameter at its narrowest. The aft section looked like the usual configuration of antimatter tanks, four fat cylinders spaced equally around the circumference, and terminating in four electromagnetic nozzles typical of beamed core antimatter drives. But the rest of it looked bizarre.

An enormous spherical bulb took up the front third of the ship's length, bulging out three times the diameter of the fuselage. A cylinder about the same diameter as the fuselage protruded from the end of the bulb, extending another 20 meters forward. The cylinder was wide open at the end, like the aperture of a very large telescope. Or a cannon.

But by far the oddest part of the ship was at its midsection. A huge bell-shaped structure jutted out sideways at a right angle to the axis of the fuselage. It was like a giant trumpet bell sticking straight out from the side of the ship with a circular rim 40 meters in diameter. Inside the bell, coil-like conduits ran from the rim down into the bell's central core. The whole structure was attached to a raised circular ring surrounding the ship's fuselage, giving the impression that the bell could be rotated 360 degrees to face any direction perpendicular to the ship's long axis.

"What the hell is it?" Hotah said.

"I was afraid of this," Woo said. Hot anger and hatred filled his eyes. "This man called Cardew is not a man. He's a monster. Our worst nightmare."

Aiden put a hand on Woo's shoulder. "What is it, Elgin?"

"I believe this is an enormous, antimatter-powered, electron-positron beam generator. The research behind this was abandoned long ago. Until a visiting scientist from the Cauldron resurrected it at the behest of the military. His project was eventually discontinued. Then he disappeared. No doubt another victim of Cardew's scientist-abduction program."

"But what does it do?"

"It can create very powerful and focused gamma-ray bursts. It mimics the same kind of gamma-ray bursts emitted from massive astrophysical objects. Black holes. Quasars . . ."

"How powerful?" Aiden asked. "I mean, this thing is tiny compared to quasars and massive black holes."

"Way less powerful, of course," Woo said, "but gamma-ray bursts from astrophysical phenomena can traverse undiminished over thousands—or hundreds of thousands—of light-years. This machine is immeasurably closer than that to any of the planets in this star system. A matter of light-*minutes*. Less powerful but way closer. If it's what I think it is, and it's powered by an unlimited supply of antimatter from the gas giant's magnetosphere, it's easily powerful enough to kill all life on Parthas. And do it within one day."

"It's a *graser*," Ro said.

Alvarez looked at him as if he'd made a tactless joke. "A what?"

"Graser is an acronym for gamma-ray laser," Ro replied. "The concept goes way back, a couple of centuries at least."

Woo gave Ro an appreciative glance. "That's right," he said. "It started with the Vranic Process, named after the physicist who found a way to make one. On a very small scale, of course. Vranic and her colleagues were trying to figure out how gamma-ray bursts were created by astrophysical jets, the powerful plasma beams shooting out of massive black holes at near light speed. They decided the best way to study them was to mimic the process in the lab. They channeled intense laser pulses through a chamber filled with helium to generate a beam containing equal amounts of electrons and positrons—in antimatter pairs—which produce gamma rays when they annihilate each other. The result was a narrowly focused, very intense gamma-ray beam, but on a very miniature scale.

"It's a complicated process involving cascading and self-generating magnetic fields, like the ones produced by spinning neutron stars. But the bottom line is that they got it right. They identified the process of how massive black holes generate gamma-ray bursts by replicating it in the lab. Then other researchers came along and developed techniques to keep the electron-positron pairs farther apart for longer times, essentially creating 'positronium' atoms that could be boosted into higher energy states and used to produce even more powerful gamma-ray lasers.

"That's when the military got interested. The idea of potent gamma-ray laser weapons, grasers, was just too delicious for them to ignore. But they hit a major roadblock trying to find energy sources prodigious enough to scale up the process. That, along with some ethical concerns from the civilian sector, put a stop to the project."

"So," Hotah said, "the front end of this thing is like a megalaser cannon."

"Right," Wo said. "A *gamma-ray* laser cannon. With a 10-meter diameter aperture. The big spherical bulb behind it must house the machinery to boost positronium into a Bose-Einstein condensate. That's a quantum state where the positronium atoms behave in lockstep, so when one annihilates itself, the rest follow suit, producing a burst of laser energy in the form of gamma rays."

Hotah looked as if he actually understood Woo's explanation. He nodded thoughtfully, then said, "Okay. What about that ridiculous-looking trumpet bell sticking out of its side?"

"Ah. That's the genius of this contraption, if such a glowing qualifier can be attached to such an evil device. That's an antimatter scoop. This vessel will be settling into the sweet spot of the gas giant's magnetosphere. Like Jupiter, its atmosphere is predominantly hydrogen, so I'm guessing there's plenty of antimatter out here to harvest. Antihydrogen specifically. Not only to power the laser bursts, but to supply the positrons for the positronium used in generating the gamma rays."

Hotah squinted at the image on the screen and cocked his head to one side. "But why is it facing sideways? If it's a scoop, why not face forward along the axis of travel?"

"Because 'forward' will not be the axis of travel for this thing, once it starts doing what it was designed for. If I'm not mistaken, it will establish a special kind of sun-synchronous orbit around the gas giant, perpetually in view of the inner system, a kind of modified polar orbit. Then it will align its long axis perpendicular to its orbital path so the laser cannon is always facing the planets of the inner system. At that point, the axis of travel will be *sideways* along the orbital path, putting the side-facing bell in perfect position to pass through the meat of the magnetosphere, scooping up as much antimatter fuel as it needs. Ingenious."

Ingenious? More like insidious. Aiden shook his head. "If it's designed to continually face Parthas, or wherever Parthas happens to be along its orbital path, a sun-synchronous orbit won't do the trick."

"Right," Woo said. "Not a *standard* sun-synchronous orbit. But a special subset of that kind of orbit will. A dawn-dusk orbit. This graser can orbit the planet's dawn-dusk line so that it's always facing the sun, which is also the general direction of the planets of the inner-system. From there, it can be adjusted to face any point within the inner system. If the intention is to sterilize all life on Parthas, then it will align itself to continually face Parthas to do its dirty work."

Alvarez looked up from her monitor and said, "I extrapolated a timeline of its course. Looks like it's already setting up to do just that. To establish a dawn-dusk orbit."

Woo made an I-told-you-so gesture. "And I'll make another guess. It's not a coincidence this gas giant and Parthas are very near to orbital opposition, the point in time where the planets are closest together."

"How soon?" Aiden asked.

Alvarez double-checked her data. "They'll be at closest approach in about 22 hours."

"And by that time," Woo said, "it will have aligned its cannon straight toward Parthas. The shorter the distance, the more destructive a focused gamma-ray burst will be."

Aiden felt hot rage coursing through his veins. "Cardew wants to turn this living planet into another dead zone. Like he did with Tristeza. But *why* is he doing it?"

That question had just joined the question of Cardew's whereabouts as the most critical ones to answer for their mission. At the moment, no one had the answers—with the possible exception of Elgin Woo, and he wasn't volunteering one.

Hotah pointedly dismissed the question and posed one of his own. "Okay. So you've got a gamma-ray cannon with an aperture of 10 meters and you've got a planet with a diameter of over 16,500 kilometers, at a distance of nearly 400 *million* kilometers. How is a graser cannon, even a superpowerful one, going to pack enough energy to sterilize all life on the planet? It doesn't compute."

"Gamma-ray beams generated in this way," Woo said, "are highly collimated, with self-generating magnetic fields, just like their big brothers from massive, spinning black holes. They stay coherent for much longer and farther than you'd think. To bathe one entire hemisphere of Parthas with gamma rays, from this distance, the beam would only need an angle of spread of about . . . what, Hutton?"

"The collimated beam," replied the AI, "would not require a spread angle greater than nine arcseconds to radiate one entire hemisphere of the planet."

"Right," Woo said. "And that's chump change for this thing. Even standard military lasers can focus down 10 times narrower than that."

"No shit," Hotah said. "Ours can squeeze down to less than a half arcsecond."

Woo spread his hands out in front of him. "There you have it. All this machine has to do is collect enough antihydrogen to power one or two gamma-ray bursts for each hemisphere, waiting only 14 hours for the planet's other hemisphere to roll fully into view."

"Is this what happened to that sorry planet, Tristeza?" Alvarez asked.

Woo shrugged. "I'd be surprised if it wasn't."

Sudha Devi looked mad as hell. She said, "How many more of these monstrosities does Cardew have in his arsenal? How many other living planets does he plan to kill?"

"Or has killed already," Woo added.

Aiden felt his head about to explode. Struggling to control his anger, he said, "What we *do* know is that we'll be turning this one into hot plasma soup. The sooner the better."

Woo looked upward with an abstract expression. "I wonder how hard would it be to capture this thing. To study it, I mean."

"Elgin . . ."

Aiden's warning tone had the desired effect. Woo refocused. "Just a thought. You're absolutely right. It must be destroyed now."

"We'll need to approach it cautiously," Hotah said. "It may have defensive systems we're not aware of. And if it's topping up its antimatter tanks in the magnetosphere, we'll need to put some distance between us when we fire. The blast could be impressive."

"Agreed," Aiden said. "Missiles or laser cannon?"

"Laser cannon," Hotah said without hesitation. "Blow the antimatter tanks. Missiles take time to reach their target, especially if we're standing off at a safe distance. That would give the target more time to react with anything it might have up its sleeve. Laser cannon is quicker and safer."

"All right, Lieutenant. You have the Helm. Let's do this."

24

HD 21749 SYSTEM
Planet HD 21749e

Domain Day 342, 2218

FOLLOWING the graser vessel farther into the giant planet's magnetosphere required some fancy footwork from the flight computer to compensate for the increasing gravitational forces. The ship was already too deep into the planet's gravity well for the ZPD to work. If evasive maneuvers were required, they'd have to be done on conventional drive. The *Sun Wolf* did, however, activate its EM shielding to protect it from the intense radiation belt blossoming inside the magnetosphere.

Hotah pulled the ship to within 60 kilometers from the target and matched courses. The angry orange and purple face of the gas giant seethed below as if trying to scare them away with outrageous displays of atmospheric violence. The radiation readings went off the chart as the ship negotiated a radiation belt millions of times more intense than Earth's Van Allen belts. Countless trillions of frenzied, charged particles glowed as they bounced off the ship's shielding, surrounding the *Sun Wolf* with an eerie aurora of blue light.

Hotah had just locked in on the target, when Alvarez called out, "The graser is turning to face us."

"It's got a proximity sensor," Hotah said. "It wants to fry us with its gamma-ray cannon."

Aiden's mouth went dry. There's no way the *Sun Wolf*, or any ship, could survive a direct hit from a graser that powerful. "Can you get off a shot before it targets us?"

Hotah didn't answer. Alvarez shouted, "It's locking in on us. The graser is powering up!"

They could see it on the main screen. From deep within the graser's black maw, a tiny point of brilliant light began to brighten and expand. "Hotah. Get us out of here, now! Maximum thrust!"

But he knew the command was pointless. By the time the antimatter drive kicked in, the graser would be burning the ship into a molten slag.

Aiden felt the ship tremble, but not from the antimatter drive igniting. It was a jolt from the actual recoil of the laser cannon's powerful burst. The image of the graser on the screen disappeared, replaced by a white flash that blanked out the screen. The ship shook again as the shock wave passed over it.

Hotah turned from Tactical to face Aiden with a calm smile. "Target neutralized."

Aiden let out a breath he'd been holding in for too long and unclenched his jaw. "Cutting it a little close, aren't we, Lieutenant?"

"I had it covered, Commander." The red speckled band tattooed across his face lifted slightly as his confident grin grew wider.

Aiden gave Hotah a look. Was the lieutenant showboating again, waiting until the last moment to eliminate a threat? Granted, Hotah had never failed to save the ship when his talents were called upon, but his reckless attitude flirted with disaster too often. Did Hotah's courage give him the attitude, or did the attitude give him his courage? Either way, it obviously worked for him, and Aiden would just have to live with it. Assuming he didn't die with it first.

"Pilot, you have Helm. Get us out of this gravity well. Far enough for us to engage the ZPD. Then set course for the voidoid."

"We're not going back to Parthas?" Alvarez asked. "Just to look around a little more? It's a living paradise."

"No. We don't have time for it. Not when there may be more of these sterilization projects in the works in other star systems. And I have an idea where to go next."

"Do tell," Ro said, hand on his chin, head cocked to one side.

Devi, Ro, and Woo converged around the command chair to hear Aiden's reply. Hotah, Abahem, and Alvarez remained seated at their stations but turned to face him.

"I think it's clear now," Aiden said, "why Cardew wants to sterilize these habitable planets. He doesn't want to destroy them per se, or to make them permanently uninhabitable. He wants to make them habitable for his empire of cloneborgs. And to do that, he has to eradicate the biosphere of any planet that evolved from the Shénmì seeds. In this astrocell, that means most if not all of them."

"But why?" Alvarez asked.

"We saw the answer to that back on Aasha. At the cloneborg crèche. Those clones were decimated by the same fungus that kick-started the evolution of life on that planet. And I don't think they're the only cloneborgs vulnerable to the fungus. I think *all* of Cardew's cloneborgs will fall prey to it. That means all these habitable worlds with biospheres spawned by the Shénmì seeds will be toxic to them, virtually uninhabitable. And without his empire of cloneborgs, Cardew is nothing. A king without a kingdom. He *needs* habitable planets, but only ones where his creations can thrive and multiply. So he's attempting to create them by transforming the ones he can't use into ones that he can."

Devi looked puzzled. "I did a genetic analysis of the fungus we found on Aasha, as you asked, and you were right. It's almost identical to the Rete fungus on Silvanus, as well as the fungus from Shénmì. So why does it attack Cardew's cloneborgs and not us?"

"That's a key question," Aiden said. "And I think the answer is that the fungus does not recognize cloneborgs as living beings. The Shénmì fungus is just like the Rete's mycorrhizal fungus on Silvanus. It's purely symbiotic, and specifically *mutualistic*, which means that both organisms benefit by the relationship equally.

Plants fix carbon from the air, feeding the fungus, and the fungus returns the favor, helping the roots extract water and essential minerals from the ground. But the fungus is also *saprophytic*. That means it attacks and digests nonliving organic matter, like dead organisms or their waste matter, to obtain nutrients.

"I think the fungus identifies the cloneborgs as strictly nonliving organic matter. And if this fungus is pervasive throughout all these living biospheres, there's no scenario for cloneborgs successfully colonizing habitable planets anywhere in this astrocell.

"But they could survive on a habitable planet *without* a biosphere. Essentially a desert planet. One with a breathable atmosphere, plenty of oxygen, protected from harmful space radiation, moderate temperatures, maybe a little water at the poles . . . the whole works. But barren in terms of life forms. No Shénmì-spawned fungus."

Devi looked skeptical. "Do planets like that even exist?"

"Absolutely," Aiden said. "In fact, they're more common than earthlike worlds, partially because they have much larger habitable zones than planets with lots of water, so they have no runaway-greenhouse limitations. The profile of a habitable desert planet would just look like a bigger, warmer version of Mars with a breathable oxygen atmosphere and cold polar regions moist enough to support small water icecaps."

Unconvinced, Devi said, "But where's the oxygen come from in the first place, if not from abundant photosynthetic plant life? Like it did on Earth."

"Lots of ways it could happen," Aiden said. "The most likely way is that a planet in the warmer part of the habitable zone, closer to the star, starts out with just a little water, only a fraction of Earth's oceans. The water evaporates in the heat to create an atmosphere of steam that hangs around for a couple million years. That provides a huge reservoir of atmospheric oxygen when sunlight breaks up the water molecules. The lighter hydrogen escapes to space, leaving free oxygen behind. And because the planet's surface has solidified into desert, it can't remove any oxygen from the air geologically, so it stays in the atmosphere."

"So," Ro said. "Cardew may be playing the long game by sterilizing these living planets, preparing them for colonization within a decade or so. But for right now, he'll be looking for habitable desert planets. If we want to find his home base, that's where we should be looking too."

"Exactly," Aiden said. "Elgin, do you concur?"

"I do, yes. I have been thinking along those lines myself. It makes sense that the fungus would not recognize the cloneborgs as authentic living creatures. I also think there may be something more to why it attacks these unnatural creations. Something intentional."

"Elgin, stay on track here," Aiden said. He wasn't about to follow Woo off the deep end again. "Can you go over AMP's latest data and identify any star systems on our hit list that might harbor a planet like this? A habitable desert planet?"

"Yes," Woo said, then turned toward Alvarez. "If it's acceptable, I'd like to work with Officer Alvarez to come up with options."

Alvarez brightened at the suggestion. She smiled so rarely that Aiden believed she had no idea how beautiful she was when she did. She said, "I'm good with that. I'll bring up the star charts from the nav computer. We can compare them with AMP's data to come up with some ideas."

While Woo and Alvarez got down to work, Aiden drafted an encrypted Holtzman transmission for Admiral Stegman reporting the *Sun Wolf*'s significant finds to date. It included their discovery of the decimated cloneborg crèche on Aasha, the apparent sterilization of the planet Tristeza by a gamma-ray burst, the robotic graser vessel they'd found powering up to do the same thing to the planet Parthas, and how they'd destroyed the graser before it could do any damage. For security reasons, he'd been ordered to send as few of these reports as possible and to send them encrypted at the highest level. And to never mention where the *Sun Wolf* planned to go next.

He drafted a second transmission intended for Skye, ostensibly as the director of the Shénmì Project, covering most of the same information, including the robotic graser, but focusing on aspects of it that pertained to her work. He emphasized their conclusions about the Shénmì fungus posing a deadly threat to the cloneborgs, and how Cardew was probably using gamma-ray bursts to eliminate that threat by sterilizing planets seeded by Shénmì.

Two hours later, when the ship approached the voidoid and came within its Holtzman radius, Aiden programed the transmitter to send both messages. He found waiting for him a status report from Shénmì Station.

The first part of it covered some shocking news from the Sol System. The virus outbreak at Friendship Station had killed over half of the station's personnel, and nearly half of the remainder were seriously ill. The station was only marginally functional now, remained under strict quarantine, and was beginning to look more like a kill zone. Even more shocking, cases had begun to show up on Earth. Without any natural immunity or pre-existing vaccines, Earth could lose a significant percentage of its population within a matter of weeks.

Very little information had surfaced from official sources regarding the nature of the virus. But due to its level of contagion, its unique genetics, and its horrific mortality rate, rumors of biological weapons were rampant. It occurred to Aiden that the outbreak of the virus on Friendship Station had happened soon after the surprise appearance of a cloneborg assassin aboard. Aiden didn't think it was a coincidence.

The second part of the report came from Captain Asaju's battle group standing guard at the HD 10180 voidoid, in Shénmì's star system. It had sighted an unidentified spy drone emerging from the exit point at high velocity. Assuming it had come from Cardew's war machine, the drone had been intercepted and destroyed. The report did not comment further, but Aiden knew that such intrusions were likely to be reconnaissance missions heralding the coming of an invasion force.

To Aiden, both reports were obviously related. Cardew was stepping up his campaign to annihilate humanity.

As he contemplated that grim thought, Woo came up to him and said, "We found two star systems on our list that are most likely to harbor Earth-sized desert planets inside habitable zones. Whether or not they're actually habitable—or inhabited—remains to be seen. One star is a G type and the other is a K type."

Aiden looked at Woo's compad. The stars were HD 21693 and HD 13808, spectral types G8V and K2V respectively. According to the AMP data, both had planetary systems with one planet orbiting inside their hab zone, both of which were identified as probable desert planets.

"Okay, let's try the G-type star first. We'll use the Stealth Sequence, but if our scans find warships guarding the voidoid this time, we won't go back to engage them. Instead, we'll proceed to our target planet on maximum ZPD. Once there, we'll scan for potential threats and neutralize any that show up. Then we scan the planet for signs of Cardew's bases or crèches.

"If this planet happens to be his home base, expect heavy resistance. If we get in over our heads against overwhelming forces, we evade on ZPD and jump out of the system as soon as possible. We engage only in defense and only to ensure that our findings get back to the Alliance. Understood?"

The crew responded with nods and thumbs-up gestures. Except Hotah, of course, who probably viewed the plan as running from a fight. No surprise there.

Aiden sat back in the command chair and took a deep breath. If he was right, they were closing in on Cardew. The *Sun Wolf* would be heading into a hornet's nest where they could get stung badly. He looked around at his crew again. They were as ready as they would ever be. Was he still the best person to lead them there? The question made him think of Skye. She would say yes without hesitation. Maybe it was about time he started listening to her.

25

HD 21693 SYSTEM
Post-Jump

Domain Day 343, 2218

Star: HD 21693
Spectral type: G8V
Distance from Sol: 106 light-years
Luminosity: 0.66 x Sol
Surface temperature: 5,434 Kelvin
Number of planets: 6
Habitable zone: 0.79–1.40 AU
—Source: *Allied Mapping Project*, 2218

What *the hell . . .*

With its weapons hot, the *Sun Wolf* had just pulled out of ZPD at 450,000 klicks from the voidoid and scanned local space for hostiles. They found no trace of any other vessels within 100 million klicks. The crew had been so primed for post-jump action against hostile forces, they seemed almost disappointed when they encountered none. But Aiden would take that kind of disappointment any day. His shoulder muscles relaxed, his heart rate returned to normal, and his teeth unclenched. The crew took a collective sigh of relief.

Ro deployed a Holtzman buoy into comm position at the voidoid. Alvarez gave him an overview of the planetary system.

"The two innermost planets, b and c, are too close to the star, nowhere near the hab zone. The one we're after is planet d. It's inside the hab zone but on its outer boundaries. Definitely a desert planet, but cold. Almost no water. The atmosphere is thin, mostly carbon dioxide, but there's some oxygen too. Technically a habitable planet, but not very inviting. Kind of like a slightly more hospitable version of Mars, before terraforming. The other three planets are way beyond the hab zone. Two gas giants, one with rings. Then, farthest out, a small rocky planet. An outlier like Pluto, but larger."

"Something else about planet d you might want to know," Ro said. "It's been identified by AMP as a probable carbon planet. Up to a third of its mass could be carbon."

Alvarez looked up. "That makes sense. The star has an unusually high carbon-to-oxygen ratio, which would translate to all the planets that formed around it."

Intriguing. "Helm, set course for planet d. Put us in high orbit. Weapons at Level One the moment we pop out of ZPD."

Two hours later, the ship settled into high orbit around planet d just beyond the orbit of its single moon, a crater-pocked rock about 120 kilometers in diameter. Scans showed no vessels of any kind in the vicinity. The planet itself measured about 80 percent the size of Earth, but almost twice its mass. Its surface had a dusty gray color, no cloud cover, and faint hints of frozen water at both poles. The mean surface temperature was cold, about -38 degrees C. But with a generous axial tilt, the survey computer calculated seasonal temperatures could climb comfortably into the midtwenties.

The planet apparently had enough of a molten core and enough spin to generate a healthy magnetic field, providing adequate protection from solar and cosmic radiation. The atmosphere was predominately carbon dioxide—about 88 percent and 3 percent oxygen—with a surface pressure barely above that of Mars.

"Without full pressure suits, this planet is hostile even for the cloneborgs," Woo said. "It has no long-term prospects for Cardew, not for a home base, or even for limited colonization. Sure, the cloneborgs could probably walk around down there without oxygen tanks for a few minutes, but not much longer. I think this is a dead end."

"Probably," Aiden said. "But we'll still do a full-globe surface scan. Just to be sure."

About halfway through the scan, Alvarez looked up sharply. "Commander, I've got a small man-made structure near the equator. Or . . . what's left of it. Looks like the remains of a dome cluster."

Aiden rushed to Alvarez's side and looked over her shoulder. "Magnify and display on the main screen."

When the detail of the scene below finally resolved, Devi inhaled sharply. "Great gods!"

Near the center of a wide, dusty valley, four large hab domes had been constructed and connected together in a cloverleaf configuration. But all four were shattered beyond recognition, open to the thin, frozen atmosphere. All that remained were their circular foundations imbedded in the ground, sprouting mangled support ribs lifted upward like skeletal hands clawing at the sky. Scattered debris lay everywhere. No impact craters could be seen, suggesting the use of powerful kinetic weapons without explosives. About a hundred meters to the west, they spotted the remains of two landing shuttles large enough to transport building materials. Both were smashed and broken into smaller, jagged-edged sections.

Aiden pointed to a place on the screen and said, "Lilly, focus in on that big piece of shuttle wreckage right there. I think there's lettering on it."

Higher magnification brought into focus three words stenciled across the warped metal surface. RODINA MINING COLLECTIVE.

Aiden scratched his beard and shook his head. "So that's what really happened to them."

"Rodina Mining," Devi said. "Isn't that the outfit that went missing several months ago?"

"Yes," Aiden said. "And the same one that reappeared in Woo's Star system last month. At least their ship did . . ."

Under a joint UED/ARM agreement, all private and corporate enterprises were barred from travel anywhere inside Astrocell Beta. As long as Cardew and his super-soldiers were loose and furtively roaming the new astrocell, it was declared off-limits to civilians—not only for their own protection but also for security reasons. The blockade was strictly enforced by the Alliance military presence at the Alpha-2 Hydri Gateway.

The only exception to the mandate was limited entry into Woo's Star system, home to the planet Shénmì and Skye's research facility. Because that system's voidoid was well guarded by Alliance forces, it was considered safe enough to allow a limited number of mining concerns into the planet-rich system. The Rodina Mining Collective had been one of the few lucky companies granted rights for exploration and mineral extraction.

They had set up a large mining operation on a bleak moon of the gas giant HD 10180g. After five months of what was, by all accounts, a moderately successful venture, the Collective pulled up stakes and announced their plans to return to Sol, presumably to cash in on their haul. Their ship, the *Rodina*, registered for a homeward transit and made the jump without complications. The only problem was it never emerged from the gateway into the Alpha-2 Hydri system, and no record of them showing up anywhere else in Bound Space ever surfaced.

This wouldn't have been entirely surprising years ago, during the period when Cardew was mucking around with the voidoids, causing void fluxes. A number of unlucky voidships executing jumps at the onset of a flux event had disappeared. Most of them had reappeared at unpredictable times and places, crews intact but bewildered. But these days, with Cardew exiled from Bound Space, void fluxes had ceased to be a problem. Ships just didn't go missing during jumps anymore.

The most popular explanation for the Rodina Collective's disappearance—supported by those in the mining community familiar with the Collective's leadership—was that their ship had deliberately altered jump parameters just before entering the voidoid and jumped somewhere else inside Astrocell Beta to set up an illegal mining operation. It would have been considered foolhardy in the extreme, even by miners on the reckless cowboy fringe. The theory was that Rodina Collective had acquired inside knowledge of an extraordinarily profitable find somewhere in Astrocell Beta and were willing to risk their lives to exploit it.

Then, months later, the Rodina Collective's ship jumped back into Woo's Star system unannounced and without explanation of where it had been. Infamous for their secretiveness and unwillingness to communicate beyond what was required of them, no further questions were asked. And because the Collective's license to operate in the system was still valid, the military blockade allowed the ship to pass and proceed to their next destination, the gas giant Jumbo.

"If what we're seeing down there is the remains of the Rodina Mining Collective," Ro said, "then their ship returned to Woo's Star system without them aboard. Knowing this group, there's no way they would have split up, some leaving and some staying. They just don't work that way."

"Then who *did* bring their ship back?" Aiden asked but believed he knew already.

Alvarez brought a hand to her mouth and turned to Devi, a pained look in her eyes.

Devi seemed to read her thoughts. "Yes, there were children in that group."

And that's what made the scene below them even more appalling. Children would be among the dead. The Rodina Mining Collective was a family collective, all working and living together. Entire families. Their home was their ship, or wherever they set up operations.

Purportedly, they were descendants of a Central European Romani population, Slovakian judging by their name. Proletarian by nature, they firmly believed that the separation of work from family was the root of all mankind's problems, and that only capitalist economies bred that kind of soul-killing alienation between workers and their families. So, the workers of the Rodina Collective brought their families with them. Everywhere. Their mates and children lived with them, worked with them, and in this case, died with them.

More like *murdered.* No doubt by Cardew's soulless soldiers, marching to Cardew's drumbeat, on his holy crusade to eliminate "inferior" human beings from this sector of space. And to lay claim to any resources his cloneborgs found useful.

Devi must have read Aiden's expression. In an admirable attempt to remain objective, she said, "We can't just *assume* this was done by Cardew's forces."

"Who else?" Hotah said, a little too loudly. His dark eyes smoldered. "No one else is out here. Except us and the military. And realistically, it's just us. The few forces that *are* stationed out here don't go beyond Woo's Star. And the rest of the Alliance fleet is still at Alpha-2 Hydri, days away from the gateway."

"I agree," Woo said. "Cardew's forces need every ship they can get hold of. I'm sure they stole the Collective's ship to add to their collection."

"Then slaughtered its former owners," Aiden said, swallowing back his anger. "Which means the *Rodina* is now controlled by cloneborgs, and it's somewhere back inside Woo's Star system, presumably at Jumbo."

And not far from Skye at Shénmì.

Aiden let that sink in before asking, "Hutton, do we have current personnel stats on record for Rodina Mining?"

"Current, as of one year ago," Hutton said. "It seems that Rodina Mining has not been the model of cooperation with authorities. The last report stated that the Collective consisted of five family groups, a total of twenty-eight persons. Nearly one-third of that number are identified as children under the age of sixteen."

"Thank you, Hutton. Lilly, can you do an IR scan of the area? To look for heat signatures?"

Alvarez took a moment to regain her composure before responding. "I can, but it would be pointless at this distance. I couldn't detect heat signatures of living human bodies without getting a lot closer, a few hundred meters at least."

"What about the IR scanners aboard our survey drones? If we launch one from here, it could search the surface from a hundred meters up."

"That's true. But the scanners on those drones aren't as powerful as the ship's. To ID living survivors from the drone, I'd need the highest resolution, and that could take hours to scan the entire area."

Devi looked at Aiden. "We need to go down there. Regardless."

Aiden knew it too. But also knew, as Devi surely did, there wasn't a chance in hell that anyone was still alive in that shattered mess below them. They didn't even know how long ago it had happened. But Devi was right. They had to try. If nothing else, an on-site investigation could give them clues to what really happened to the Collective.

"We'll go down to investigate," he said. "But we'll also launch a survey drone to assist our search. Lilly, make that happen, please."

Aiden turned to the rest of the crew. "We'll need PSM suits. And we'll go armed. Hotah, Devi, get your gear and meet me in the armory. From there, to the shuttle bay. What about you, Elgin?"

Woo looked as if he hadn't heard Aiden. He had that faraway look again, as if gazing at something no one else could see. He turned to Aiden and said, "I'm hearing it again. I'm hearing the star. The one I've been looking for. It's singing to me."

The crew standing nearby all exchanged concerned glances. Was Elgin Woo finally losing it? Aiden didn't think so. Woo was on to something. He just didn't know what it was.

Aiden repeated himself. "Elgin? Do you want to join us downside?"

Woo regained focus and nodded enthusiastically. "Yes. Count me in."

Alvarez stood abruptly. "I'm going, too."

"Lilly . . . You know I can't leave just two crewpersons aboard." Standard Service protocol dictated that, in the field, at least three crew members remain aboard at all times. It was one Service protocol that Aiden actually agreed with.

But the look of anguish in her eyes seriously challenged his resolve. It was about the children of the Collective who'd had their lives brutally cut short, Aiden was sure of it. Woo must have seen it, too, and the reason for it. With that open, guileless smile of his, he stepped forward and said, "I'll stay. Alvarez can take my place."

Aiden didn't think twice about questioning Woo's sincerity. He knew better.

"All right, Lilly," he said. "But I want you armed."

"Not a problem," she said, anguish now turned to anger. "See you in the armory."

As before, Hotah chose his favorite weapon, the three-barreled SR-13 Spacer Carbine, hefting the oversized weapon as if it were a mere toy. Aiden grabbed his usual .40-caliber pistol and secured it into a thigh holster. Alvarez surprised him when she bypassed the pistol rack and choose an SR-11 Carbine. It was the smaller and lighter version of Hotah's SR-13, with two barrels instead of three and easier to wield, but just as deadly.

Aiden gave her a skeptical look. "Have you ever used one of those?"

She grinned back at him. "You forget; I did a two-year stint in the Domain Guard before signing up with the Space Service. I trained with the SR-11. Qualified for sharpshooter level. So yeah, I've used one before."

Aiden raised his eyebrows. That was way more weapons training than he'd ever had. "Good. Stay close to Devi, if you would. She chooses to remain unarmed, and I've given up trying to persuade her otherwise."

Devi overheard, smiled, and sidled up to Alvarez as they headed toward the shuttle bay. To Aiden, she said, "And I'll bet she's a better shot than you."

26

HD 21693 SYSTEM
Planet HD 21693d

Domain Day 343, 2218

Aiden guided the landing shuttle through the thin atmosphere without incident and executed a vertical landing 200 meters from the wrecked domes. The four of them donned their PSM suits and cycled through the lander's airlock. They assembled in a group and buddy-checked each other's gear.

The PSM suits—old-timers still called them Mars suits, a misnomer nowadays—were of the mechanical-counterpressure type, a body-hugging design made of orthofabric. The support pressure came from the structure and elasticity of the material itself, unlike older suits that were gas pressurized, like a filled balloon. They were lighter and more flexible, designed for walking on abrasive surfaces and resisting high-speed, dust-ladened winds. They had life-support packs with six hours of breathable oxygen and were good against cosmic rays, high UV exposure, and temperatures down to -140 degrees C. Fortunately, their landing site was still in daylight, late afternoon in what would be the planet's early summer, and the temperature outside was a balmy -10 degrees C.

Aiden appreciated the suit's lightweight design as the group plodded off toward the wreckage. The surface gravity here was about 1.5 G, and even walking a level surface felt like trudging uphill. Looking upward, he caught a glimpse of the *Sun Wolf*'s survey drone ranging overhead toward the ruined domes, scanning for heat signatures. The deep-yellow sun hung low in the western sky, surrounded by a shimmering halo cast by upper-atmosphere ice crystals. Dark gray dust covered the ground, sculpted by the wind into oddly shaped, rippling dunes. Obsidian-black stones of all sizes and shapes littered the landscape. The valley floor gradually lifted up in the distance where a jagged black mountain range marched off to the east, sunlight reflecting off glass-smooth cliff faces.

They hadn't gone far before finding the first bodies.

Frozen, desiccated bodies. Twisted in timeless agony. Mummified. Still and silent as the stones surrounding them. One here, two over there, a group of four just outside the warped circular foundation of a shattered dome. A few had been armed, outdated slug-thrower weapons clutched in their frozen hands or lying near where they had fallen. All of them were adults.

Until Aiden's team reached what was left of the third dome.

That's where they found the children. Frozen and mummified like their parents. But somehow less twisted, almost beatific. As if their natural innocence protected them from the deformed ugliness of death, only to make the scene infinitely more tragic.

The group stopped here, all of them stunned, silent within their own microuniverses of horror. Billy Hotah, whose ancestors carried in their DNA the grief and anger from a history of slaughtered women and children, lowered his weapon and looked to the sky. He raised his left hand and made a graceful gesture that Aiden didn't recognize, but was clearly an invocation of reverence and sorrow. Of farewell.

Alvarez was the first to speak. In a low voice choked with emotion, outrage audible even through the suit's comm, she said, "Who could do such a thing?"

"Only monsters," Devi said. "Creatures without souls."

Hotah raised his weapon again and scanned the scene around them. "This looks like a rail gun attack," he said. "Not missiles.

Most of these people died by exposure, when the domes were shattered. Not by explosives. Otherwise, there'd be a lot more tissue damage. Severed limbs . . ."

The third dome must have been a family living center, Aiden thought. Had these people constructed some kind of underground "safe room" beneath its floor for emergencies? Some kind of habitable bomb shelter that could support survivors for a limited period of time in hopes of rescue? Aiden radioed the *Sun Wolf* and asked Ro to deep-scan the area within the third dome's circumference to check for possible underground structures and scan for heat signatures.

While Aiden watched the drone change course to circle the third dome, Hotah's voice came through the comm. "Over here."

Hotah had ranged out from the group and was standing over what looked like another corpse. When Aiden got there, he saw what had drawn Hotah's attention—a corpse of a cloneborg, looking very much like the ones they'd seen on Aasha. Fully human in appearance, wearing some kind of formfitting, flexible suit with a rudimentary life-support pack, a Spacer Carbine at its side. And no head.

"Just like Woo said," Hotah noted. "A head shot with a slugthrower. Best way to stop one of these bastards."

"The attackers must have sent a landing party down here to mop up," Aiden said. "To make sure no one was left alive."

Devi shook her head. "As if smashing their habitats wasn't enough."

Hotah pointed his weapon at where the cloneborg's head had been and said, "One of the Rodina folks must have survived the first attack and got off a lucky shot when the clone-creeps landed."

Ro's voice came over the comm. "I've scanned the entire area of dome three for underground structures. Nothing there."

"But there *is* something over here," Alvarez said.

She stood among the fallen rib beams at the center of where the fourth dome had been, looking into one of several mining carts. It was made of heavy metal, dull and scarred from long use, about four meters long and half as wide. It sat coupled together with others just like it in a straight line along a metal track.

The others joined her. Aiden followed her gaze and looked inside the cart. A pile of quartz-like stones filled it to the brim. He recognized them immediately. “Diamonds. Raw and uncut. Thousands of them.”

They ranged from walnut sized to slightly larger than a grapefruit. Some had a faint brownish-yellow tint, but all the rest were perfectly clear. He picked one up in his gloved hand and examined it closely.

White diamonds. Extremely rare on Earth and extremely valuable.

“There’s more over here,” Hotah said. He’d moved on to the next cart in the row. Aiden joined him to look inside. It, too, was filled with raw diamonds.

He stood back and counted a total of eight mining carts, all of them coupled together, their flanged metal wheels astride a dual track. The track sloped downward toward what must have been an open shaft that the Collective had bored into the rocky surface. But the mouth of the shaft had collapsed during the attack, closing it off completely, and the tracks disappeared beneath a pile of rubble. All of it still within the boundary circle of dome number four.

“This,” Aiden said, “must be what the Rodina Collective was up to out here. They probably got a tip on the location of a carbon planet. Theoretically, carbon planets should be rich in diamonds, from high temperatures and pressure in the planet’s interior. But no one has ever found one like this. A sizeable fraction of this planet’s entire mass could be pure diamond.”

Alvarez shook her head and said, “The Rodina people risked their lives for the big payoff. But lost it all in the end.”

“But not everyone lost out,” Devi said. She had moved on to the third cart in line and was peering into it.

Aiden and the others joined her. The cart was empty. Only a few small fragments of diamond remained scattered across its floor. Moving on to the remaining carts in line, they found the same thing—evidence that the carts had been filled with raw diamonds, which had later been removed and taken elsewhere.

Aiden glanced at the others. "It looks like the Collective's ship wasn't the only thing Cardew's cloneborgs were after."

Hotah said, "More money in Cardew's bank to fund his fucked-up empire."

When they returned to the two full carts, Alvarez said, "Let's take some of these diamonds ourselves, to fund some *good* causes."

She didn't wait for Aiden's approval and began stuffing some of the fist-sized diamonds into her tactical backpack. Before he could respond, Ro's voice cut through the comm. "I think we've picked up an isolated heat source. It's from an abandoned surface rover. A four-wheel job sitting about three hundred meters east of your position."

"A human heat signature?"

"Hard to say. The heat is probably coming from the rover's pressurized personnel cabin where life-support heating is still functioning. If there's someone alive in there, their heat signature could be obscured by the cabin's ambient temperature."

Ro gave Aiden the coordinates and the group hoofed it across the broken landscape. As they approached, Aiden recognized the familiar features of a typical UED surface rover. Four articulated wheels, a forward-facing personnel cabin capable of carrying six people plus equipment, and a two-person airlock at the rear. The housing for the minifusion power plant was painted bright red and bulged out between the two sections. The rest of it was bulked up with oblong storage containers and studded with comm dishes and sensor arrays. The entire rover listed backward where its rear wheels appeared to be stuck in a patch of deep sand. Otherwise, it looked undamaged.

Approaching from the back, they found a frozen body lying on the ground just outside the airlock. The airlock's door was sealed tight. The body belonged to a young woman. She was dressed in an older model PSM suit. But her O_2 pack was nowhere to be seen. *What the hell?*

"Around front!" Alvarez said. "Quick!"

Aiden and the others rushed around to meet her. Alvarez peered into the window of the personnel cabin, aiming her luminator into its darkened interior. Aiden couldn't believe his eyes.

"It's an infant," Devi said, breathless. "And it's alive."

If any miracle during the last two years of Aiden's life could rival the discovery of Silvanus, a living planet blossoming boldly from the frozen nothingness of space, it would be finding this tiny newborn life still breathing amidst such horrific devastation on a barren planet light-years from Earth.

The beam of Alvarez's luminator lit up a corner of the personnel cabin where a small, makeshift cradle sat, just large enough to carry the infant who lay in it, wrapped in a puffy insulator blanket. The barely discernable rise and fall of its chest and the occasional flexing of its tiny hands confirmed the miracle of its survival.

"The airlock," Aiden said. "That's our only hope of saving this little one. Pray that it still works."

What other way could there be? They couldn't cut their way directly into the personnel cabin without immediate depressurization, evacuating the remains of a viable life-support environment. The only way into the personnel cabin without killing its precious cargo was the way it was intended. Through a functioning airlock.

Devi examined the back end of the rover. "The airlock door looks intact," she said. "No warping. Tightly sealed."

Aiden joined her. He opened the cover to the control panel next to the airlock door and examined actuator keys. Fortunately, it looked like a standard layout, common to the older UED survey rovers that Aiden had operated as a member of the *Argo*'s survey team. All the tiny indicator lights inside the recessed compartment were lit green. Good. The rover still had power.

As the others gathered around, he tapped the Open key. The airlock door slid open smoothly, exposing the small, two-person pressurization chamber. The insides looked worn but undamaged. The indicators of the interior control panel were all lit. Also green.

Aiden turned to the others. "Let's think this through. Assuming that one of us can access the personnel cabin, how are we going to transfer the infant out of it and into our landing shuttle? I doubt there's a baby-sized PSM suit in there."

"If the rover is still working," Alvarez said, "we can drive it to our shuttle and link up the airlocks."

It was the obvious solution, of course, but the devil was in the details. Aiden said, "Even if the rover's drive still works and we drive it to the shuttle, the two airlock doors won't match up. Our shuttle is a basic lander, not a full-sized Class-A survey shuttle. Its airlock is designed for personnel EVA only, not docking with rovers."

"What?" Devi said, outraged at the apparent stupidity of it. "Why not?"

"Class-A survey shuttles are the only way surface rovers get down to a planet in the first place," Aiden said. "So, obviously, they're designed to dock with rovers. Basic personnel landers aren't. There's no need for it."

"No need, except for now," Devi scoffed. "Typical Space Service myopia."

"There *has* to be a way," Alvarez said, looking not at them but at the young woman's frozen corpse behind them.

"One thing at a time," Aiden said. "Let's see if we can get inside. Then we check on the infant's condition and status of life support. Then see if we can drive the rover."

Aiden chose himself and Devi for the task. Among present company, he was most qualified to operate a surface rover, and Devi, of course, was a physician. The two climbed into the airlock. Aiden closed the door. It sealed with a satisfying clunk, felt more than heard. He hit the Pressurization key and waited. Nothing happened. A daunting number of reasons could account for an abandoned surface rover's failure to pressurize. Empty air tanks. Not enough power. Damaged electronics or machinery.

After several more anxious moments, Aiden felt a mechanical thump through the rover's hull, and the pumps finally kicked in.

He watched the pressure gauge rise steadily, going from the planet's ambient 0.3 psi to a human-compatible 14.5 psi, matching the pressure in the personnel cabin on the other side. *So far, so good.*

Until he saw the readout for O_2 levels inside the cabin. Only 18 percent. *Uh-oh.* That was just below the bare minimum to sustain human life for any length of time. He slapped his palm against the key to open the cabin door.

When they entered, the infant looked at them with surprising calmness, given their sudden appearance with bulging helmets still on. But its eyes looked dull, sunken in a pale white face with a blueish tint.

Devi rushed to the crib. After a brief examination, she said, "It's a boy. Maybe ten or eleven months old. Suffering from moderate hypoxia—slow heart rate, fast breathing, mildly cyanotic skin color. His core temp is low. What's the ambient temp in here?"

Aiden found the life-support readouts on a side panel. "It's 15 degrees C."

Devi shook her head. "This little guy looks malnourished too. We need to get him out of here and back to the shuttle. Now."

Without a word, Aiden seated himself in the drive chair and hit the toggles to power up the electric engine. A satisfying vibration hummed up from the deck. He spoke into his comm. "Hotah, Alvarez. The infant is alive but he needs help. I'll try to drive this thing back to our shuttle. You can hitch a ride outside on the backboard. Use the exterior handholds."

"Will do," Alvarez said.

Aiden slammed the lever to engage the drive gears. The rover balked, its rear wheels spinning uselessly in the loose sand patch. *Damn!*

"We'll give you a push from behind," Hotah said through the comm. "Go now."

Aiden spotted them from the rear vid camera. They were leaning into the back of the rover, trying to push it forward. Aiden dumped all the power he could into the lowest gear. The rover teetered precariously, then lurched forward, free of the sand pit.

"Got it!" Aiden said. "Grab on and hold tight."

27

HD 21693 SYSTEM
Planet HD 21693d

DOMAIN DAY 343, 2218

THE *Sun Wolf*'s landing shuttle sat about 500 meters away. As much as he tried, Aiden couldn't push the rover over eight kilometers per hour. With all the rocks and boulders to dodge, it would take at least five minutes to get there. He tried telling himself that another few minutes wouldn't make much difference. But the concerned look on Devi's face kept his foot floored on the accelerator pedal.

Devi delved into her medical pack to produce a respirator mask. Designed for an adult, she nevertheless managed to make it fit firmly over the boy's face. Then she removed her own O_2 pack and attached the mask's tubing to it, feeding the infant oxygen-rich air. But that left Devi breathing only the oxygen-poor air of the cabin. She picked up the little boy, enfolded him in her arms, and turned up her suit's temperature control.

As the rover bounced over uneven surfaces, she drew Aiden's attention to an object lying on the floor in a back corner. It was an oxygen pack detached from a PSM suit. The Rodina Mining logo was printed across its upper panel. The mystery of the young woman's demise began to resolve. Sudha Devi spelled it out.

"The boy's mother sacrificed her own life to prolong her son's," she said. "She knew that she would consume far more oxygen inside the cabin than her son, being an adult compared to an infant. The only way to solve that problem was to remove herself from the equation, to stop consuming the air that her son needed to stay alive. So she left her oxygen pack inside the cabin with its valve open just enough to keep the interior breathable for as long as possible. Then she stepped outside."

"Sounds about right," Aiden said. "She was probably out here in the rover when the attack happened at the domes. Maybe returning from an errand. But why would she bring her infant son with her?"

"Childcare? Maybe still breastfeeding?" Devi said. "Either way, these family collectives tend to stick together as much as possible, bringing their children along with them during work. For better or worse."

For worse, in this case.

They arrived at the shuttle a few minutes later. When Aiden backed the rover up to it, as close as he could get, it became painfully obvious that the two airlock doors would never match up. Just as he'd predicted, the mating surfaces were not even remotely compatible. Plus, the shuttle had landed vertically with its airlock too far up for the low-slung rover to reach.

The only solution was to cycle through the rover's airlock to the outside, walk over to the shuttle, climb the ramp to its airlock door, and cycle through it. No matter how close he could bring the rover to the shuttle, at least three minutes would elapse, completely exposed to the planet's harsh conditions. Way too long without a suit, especially for an infant.

Aiden turned back to Devi. The boy looked slightly better, less blue, breathing easier. But now Devi didn't look so good. "I'm getting a killer headache," she said between fast and shallow breaths.

"Any ideas?" Alvarez said through the comm. Both she and Hotah were outside standing next to the ramp that slanted up to the shuttle's airlock.

Aiden switched his brain into creative mode, a trick he'd learned for jazz improvisation. Temporarily unhinged from structural constraints, an idea came to him. "Ro, go to the storage bay and pull one of the EBS pods from the survey lockers. Then cycle it out to us through the airlock."

"Aha!" Ro said. "Good idea. Coming right up."

The EBS—exobiology specimen—pods were designed to collect on-site biological specimens from exoplanets and bring them safely back to the ship's lab under strict isolation protocols. Even basic landing shuttles had a couple of them stowed away. They could be hermetically sealed to prevent cross-contamination by microbes or toxic materials. An EBS pod was about the same size and shape as a large pet carrier, just the right size for a reclining infant with wiggle room to spare. Sealed tightly with oxygenated air inside, the boy would be safe long enough to make the transfer.

Ro cycled the pod out to them. Hotah retrieved it from the shuttle's airlock, placed it inside the rover's airlock, and cycled it through to the interior. Aiden popped open its clamshell lid, and Devi placed the boy inside, swaddled in the thermoblanket. He didn't resist, make a fuss, or cry. Probably due to hypoxia-induced lethargy. But the boy seemed aware that he'd been rescued by people who cared.

Aiden secured the lid. Devi used the pod's two-way filter valve to enrich its interior with oxygen from her pack. She put her helmet back on and cranked up her own O_2 level. She picked up the pod and followed Aiden into the rover's airlock. They cycled through, into the thin frozen air outside, then marched up the ramp to the shuttle's airlock door. Alvarez and Hotah were waiting for them there. They all cycled through the lock into the shuttle's warm, oxygenated interior. All done in a little over two minutes.

Devi opened the pod immediately to find the boy no worse for the wear, but obviously hungry and not at all happy to have been locked inside a pitch-dark, coffin-like enclosure. She gently picked him up, cradled him in her arms, smiled at him with soft eyes, and made soothing sounds.

When the boy quieted, Devi turned to Aiden. "We need to get back to the ship ASAP. I've got to get this little guy into the medical suite and get some nutrients into him."

Aiden wasted no time getting the shuttle aloft. After he secured the shuttle inside the *Sun Wolf*'s docking bay, Devi, with child in arms, was the first one out. She headed toward Medical at a fast pace. Aiden returned to the bridge with the others and sat heavily into the command chair. *Now what?*

Ro, reading his expression correctly, approached and nodded thoughtfully. "Baby on board. Eh?"

The archaic bumper-sticker expression had suddenly become ironically relevant. How could the *Sun Wolf* continue its dangerous mission, one that grew more perilous each day, without putting the life of this innocent newcomer at risk? He and the crew had accepted the risks and had freely chosen to carry on. They were adults. But this infant? He deserved the best chance possible to thrive and grow up in whatever way he could. Not only for his sake, but for his mother's. She had sacrificed her own life to give her baby a few more hours to live, hoping for an impossible rescue. Her sacrifice had to be honored.

No question about it. They would make a detour in their mission. The *Sun Wolf*'s next destination, HD 13808, was home to the only other desert planet on AMP's list and now the most likely one to harbor Cardew's home base. They simply could not go into battle with the child aboard. They had to return to the relative safety of Shénmì Station and leave him in its care. Or better yet, they could jump directly to Gateway Station at Alpha-2 Hydri. From there, arrangements could be made to return him to Sol.

It wouldn't even take that long to do. The *Sun Wolf*'s zero-point drive made the detour entirely feasible, with minimal interruption to their mission. They could be back on track to HD 13808 in less than half a day. Aiden announced the change of plans to the crew. No one disagreed. In fact, they all looked relieved. Especially Hotah. Still itching for combat action, he said, "It's no place for a child."

"Before we leave," Alvarez said, "let's name this place. Like we did the others."

It was becoming a crew tradition. Aiden had doubts that any of the names they came up with would ever make it into the official IAU catalogues, but he didn't discourage it. Anything that brought the crew together in a common pursuit was a good thing. "Suggestions?"

While the crew pondered the question, Aiden had an idea of his own. He'd studied Central European languages in grad school, and one word had stuck with him, for personal reasons. "How about Sirota? It's Slovak for 'orphan.' Since the Rodina Collective had Slovakian roots, and now the only one of them left is an orphan . . ."

"Good," Ro said, saving Aiden from an emotional moment that had taken him by surprise. No one objected, and Alvarez entered the name into her records.

Aiden looked away for a moment, regained composure, then spoke to the pilot. "Helm, set course for the voidoid, maximum ZPD. Come to a halt at a thousand klicks out. I want to send a Holtzman transmission to the battle group guarding Woo's Star to notify them of our unexpected return. We'll wait for their confirmation before jumping."

For the crew of the *Sun Wolf*, the novelty of moving along at 92 percent light speed had worn off. But no one ever got comfortable with the time dilation that accompanied near-light-speed travel. Like now, their two-hour trip across two billion kilometers of space would take only 47 minutes of onboard time. When they reached their destination, the ship's clocks would reset automatically to sync with Galactic Standard Time. But the crew's internal clocks weren't automatic. They had to consciously perform a mental reset.

The *Sun Wolf* pulled out of ZPD close enough to the voidoid for Aiden to use the onboard Holtzman transmitter. He sent an encrypted message to Captain Asaju of the SS *Parsons*, commanding officer of the battle group at Woo's Star, informing him that the

Sun Wolf would be returning briefly to Shénmì Station and would be making the jump as soon as Aiden received his confirmation. Because the *Sun Wolf* and the *Parsons* were positioned well within the Holtzman radii of their respective voidoids, the connection was nearly instantaneous, requiring negligible transmission time through realspace. He and Asaju could interact in normal conversation. But Asaju's response was not at all what he'd expected.

"Commander Macallan. I'm sorry we didn't inform you about this earlier, but we believe that voidjumping into this system is not possible at the moment."

"What? Why?"

Asaju paused for a long moment, as if calculating the optimal choice of words he was about to speak. A powerfully built man of West African lineage, about the same age as Aiden, Asaju had a well-earned reputation as a fierce warrior of unassailable integrity and keen intelligence. His clean-shaven head glistened in the overhead light of the *Parson*'s bridge. His brow creased as he spoke.

"This is going to sound unbelievable at best, but it is very real. Late last night, what appears to be a small black hole came out of nowhere, hovered near the voidoid, then moved *inside* the voidoid, settling at its exact center. It's effectively blocking any attempts to jump into or out of the system. Fortunately, when it happened, our warships guarding the voidoid were stationed far enough away and none of them were damaged.

"We sent a test drone into the voidoid to see if it could make a successful jump. Oddly, the drone did *not* get shredded or sucked in, the way you'd expect with a black hole. Instead, it just popped out the other side unharmed, as if it had made a navigational error."

Aiden opened his mouth to speak but didn't know what to say. Woo and Ro came over and stood next to him, exchanging glances.

"How big is this black hole, Captain?" Aiden finally asked.

"Before it settled inside the voidoid, the scientists at Shénmì Station calculated its mass to be more than twelve times that of Earth, even though its Schwarzschild radius is only about eleven centimeters. Now that it's inside the voidoid, they're not sure if it still has a gravity field."

The result of the drone's test jump would suggest not, Aiden thought. But was this the same primordial black hole they had encountered back at HD 17051, or a different one? Or only one of many? "Is there anything unusual about this black hole? Anything visual?"

Asaju looked back at him askance. "As a matter of fact, yes. Black holes, I'm told, are supposed to be invisible, unless they're interacting with matter. And even then, you're only seeing the effects of the black hole on the matter. Superheating, X-ray flashes, that sort of thing. This black hole isn't interacting with *anything*. But it's surrounded by a faint halo of white light. When it moved inside the voidoid, the halo expanded to fill its entire volume. The entire voidoid looks like an eighteen-kilometer-wide circle of pale white light with a big black hole at its center. It's the strangest damn thing I've ever seen. The physicists at Shénmì Station have no idea what it is. Why do you ask?"

"Because we encountered this same phenomenon ourselves a couple days ago in one of the star systems we explored. Only this one didn't occupy the voidoid, just stayed near it. We had a close encounter with it, but weren't harmed. Since you and I are still communicating, I assume the Holtzman devices weren't affected?"

"That's right. We're still able to send and receive Holtzman transmissions. In fact, we just received word from Gateway Station back at Alpha-2 Hydri with even more disturbing news. The same phenomenon has occurred there. The gateway voidoid was occupied by a back-lit black hole just like the one here, and at about the same time. All traffic between the two astrocells is halted. No one from out here can jump back into Bound Space, and no one from Bound Space can jump into this astrocell."

"Has the rest of the Alliance fleet made it to Gateway Station yet?"

"No," Asaju said, clearly frustrated. "They're still two days out. But even when they do arrive, they're useless to us if they can't use the gateway to reach us out here. Not while that thing is sitting inside the voidoid."

Well, shit. This changed everything. The *Sun Wolf* could still jump anywhere inside Astrocell Beta, but not back to Shénmì and not back to Bound Space. They could still pursue their mission, but couldn't expect help from anyone else. Not while the Alliance fleet was stranded back inside Bound Space, waiting for crucial intel from the *Sun Wolf*.

Something extraordinary was going on here. Something otherworldly. He exchanged glances with the rest of the crew. They looked as mystified as he felt. Except for Elgin Woo. A knowing look gleamed in his eyes, accompanied by a subtle smile. As usual, the man believed he knew something that no one else did but wasn't ready to say anything about it.

Aiden blinked the fatigue from his eyes. It had been a long day. And now this. "Thank you for the update, Captain. Looks like we won't be returning to Shénmì Station after all. Please keep us posted on any developments."

He sat back and closed his eyes. He'd been looking forward to seeing Skye again, even for a moment, before resuming his mission. And now, what about the "baby on board" situation?

Aiden looked at his chrono. It read just past 18:00. He turned to the crew and said, "We need a sleep cycle. Two six-hour shifts, a total of twelve hours. Shift One—Ro, Alvarez, and Abahem. Hit the rack now. Shift Two—myself, Elgin, Hotah, and Devi—will remain on the bridge. Except for Dr. Devi, whenever care for the infant allows."

Devi turned toward the elevator and said over her shoulder, "I'll be down in Medical with our new crew member. Call if you need me."

~ ~ ~

Near the end of Aiden's shift at Command, he yawned and stood to stretch his legs. He was looking forward to six hours of much-needed sleep. But sleep would not be in the cards for him today. Hotah looked up from Comm/Scan. "Commander, we have another call from Captain Asaju. This one is marked as urgent."

Aiden felt a shadow suddenly materialize next to him, a darkness opening up under his feet. "Up on main screen."

Asaju's visage appeared on the screen. The battle-group captain looked haggard, his face creased with concern, his dark brown eyes deeply pained. He ran a hand over the crown of his bald head before speaking, then said, "Commander, I don't quite know how to say this, but I thought you should know. Dr. Skye Landen appears to be missing."

28

HD 21693 SYSTEM
System Voidoid

DOMAIN DAY 343, 2218

"MISSING? What do you mean?" Aiden felt his throat tighten. His stomach knotted up.

Asaju took a deep breath before answering, eyes cast downward as if dreading nothing more than meeting Aiden's eyes. When he finally looked up to speak, his mask of military professionalism was firmly in place.

"I've been in discussion with Shénmì Station's security chief, Colonel Crestfield, over the last five hours. He has informed me of the circumstances. It's been nearly twenty hours since Dr. Landen was last seen, and she's not answering her comm. Security personnel have been turning the station upside down looking for her, but they've come up with nothing so far."

Twenty hours? Aiden forced himself to stay objective, rational. "Exactly when was she last heard from? And where?"

"According to Crestfield, it was yesterday at her lab, in the evening. She had just received a message from you, Commander. Something having to do with the fungus from the Shénmì seeds and how it might affect these . . . cloneborg things. She discussed it with one of her colleagues just before retiring for the day. The colleague was the last person to see her. She witnessed Dr. Landen entering her quarters.

"When she didn't show up at her lab the next morning, no one thought much of it, assuming she was visiting a different department. She routinely circulated between the station's five labs. But as the morning went on without hearing from her, her team became concerned. They notified Crestfield around noon, and his team initiated a station-wide search. They've been hailing her comm ever since. But at this point, they don't have a clue where she might be."

"Do you know," Aiden said, "if Crestfield had informed Dr. Landen about our suspicions that one of the cloneborgs might be aboard the station, posing as a crew member of the *Quasimodo*? As I asked him to do?"

"Yes, he did. Two days ago, immediately after he spoke with you. He said that she took the matter very seriously. As we all did. Crestfield had two of his officers assigned to keep an eye on the tanker's crew while they were aboard the station. They saw nothing unusual the entire time before the tanker departed."

"Wait," Aiden said, his mouth gone dry. "The *Quasimodo* left the station? When?"

"Yes, the tanker left this morning at around zero six hundred. It's headed back to Jumbo for another antimatter harvest. Jumbo is nearing its closest-approach point with Shénmì. Bright Star Energy is pushing their tanker crews into overtime to take advantage of it."

"Have any other vessels left the station in the last 24 hours?"

"No. Only the tanker."

Shit! Aiden made a fist but caught himself before smashing it into the comm screen. Now that Shénmì's voidoid was blocked, there was no way the *Sun Wolf* could jump back into the system and ride to the rescue. He shoved down his mounting frustration and asked, "Has anyone been in radio contact with the *Quasimodo* since it departed?"

"Shénmì Station received only one routine status report hours after its departure. Nothing out of the ordinary was reported."

"Captain, I need both you and Colonel Crestfield to contact the tanker and demand them to return to the station. And when they do, I want Crestfield's security team to board and search."

Asaju frowned. "You think that Dr. Landen might be on board the *Quasimodo*. Perhaps against her will."

"As in abducted," Aiden said pointedly. "Yes, I think it's a distinct possibility. Don't you? With a cloneborg mole on the crew?"

Aiden gritted his teeth. Why hadn't anyone—especially Colonel Crestfield, the station's security chief—put those pieces together themselves? He glanced at Hotah, who rolled his eyes. Woo's face had gone pale.

Attempting to keep extreme annoyance out of his voice, Aiden continued. "And if the *Quasimodo* refuses to return, I need Crestfield to send a warship out from Shénmì Station to track down the tanker, board, and search."

Asaju's eyes squinted into a pained expression. "Commander, there aren't any military vessels at Shénmì Station right now. Only two small security skiffs. All the warships in this system are now out here with us, at the voidoid."

Double shit! That was nearly two billion kilometers away. "Do you have the *Quasimodo*'s flight itinerary? What's their projected ETA at Jumbo?"

Asaju consulted his compad. "The *Quasimodo* can do nearly 2 Gs on full thrust, and Jumbo is currently just over 2 AU from here. With a flip-and-burn maneuver, it'll take them about three days to get there. They'll arrive just after midnight on Day 346."

Aiden shook his head. Even Asaju's fastest battle cruiser stationed at the voidoid would take over seven days to reach Jumbo.

"And how certain are we that the *Quasimodo* is actually going to Jumbo?"

"It sure looks that way," Asaju said. "As of now, at least. Crestfield and I have been tracking the ship's trajectory, as we do for all vessels departing from and approaching the station. They're already over 12 million klicks out from Shénmì Station, under maximum accel, and on an intercept vector directly toward Jumbo. They know about the black hole blocking the voidoid, so they can't jump out of the system."

Aiden felt like his head was about to explode. He took a moment to calm himself before speaking. "Captain, when Crestfield's team searched the station, do you know if anyone reported anything unusual? Anything missing? From Dr. Landen's quarters? From her lab?"

Asaju paused for a moment in thought, then said, "Yes, as a matter of fact. Crestfield said that her head research assistant reported that some of the lab equipment was missing, including Dr. Landen's compad and some of the sealed specimen containers."

Triple shit! The shadow around him darkened. He sank deeper into it.

"Captain, I still want a warship to go after the *Quasimodo*. Even if it reaches Jumbo five days after the *Quasimodo* does. Dispatch your fastest warship to track that tanker down. *Wherever* it goes."

Aiden was fully aware that an order like that had to come from higher up the command chain. Much higher than Aiden. But Asaju didn't hesitate. "Agreed, Commander. I'll go myself. The *Parsons* is the fastest ship we have out here. We'll get underway shortly."

Aiden thanked him and signed off. Hotah cocked his head and looked at Aiden. "Something doesn't add up here. If Cardew had a mole planted on that antimatter tanker and he wanted you and Shénmì Station destroyed, why not command the mole to play suicide bomber and blow the tanker?"

The same question had crossed Aiden's mind, but he'd had other things to worry about.

"Because," Woo said, nervously twirling one braided moustache between finger and thumb, "I don't think Cardew wanted the station destroyed. Not while Skye was on it. I think the antiquark bomb was calibrated to limit the damage to the planet's surface only, in a slow but unstoppable burn that kills all organic life, along with the fungus that gave it birth. And to do it without damaging the station in high orbit. Cardew wants Skye alive. He needs what she knows, especially her work on the Shénmì fungus."

Hotah gave Woo a look. "So he had her abducted to get what she knows."

It was not a question, just a statement of the obvious. Woo took a deep breath. "Cardew has a long history of abducting top scientists and persuading them to work for him. Most of them came from the Cauldron."

Woo stopped short of mentioning the full story, the fate of the scientists who refused to cooperate. As they had all discovered at the Dark Fort, Cardew's method of brain-tapping was brutally efficient, leaving only empty husks of those subjected to it. Aiden, for one, didn't need reminding.

He keyed his comm for Devi, who was still down in Medical tending to the child. "Sudha, have you been following all this?"

"Yes. I've been monitoring the bridge comm."

"Good. Can you meet us in the ready room, please? I need your expertise."

Aiden, Woo, and Hotah adjourned to the ready room, and Devi joined them a minute later. She sat, reached across the table, and silently clasped Aiden's hand. Then, resuming her professional demeanor, she asked, "What did you want to talk to me about?"

"How much do you know about the brain-tapping technique Cardew uses on these scientists? I mean the kind of equipment that's required. How elaborate is the setup, the administration of it? All of that."

"It's a very complicated process," she said. "I suppose you want the short version. In a nutshell, it's an advanced form of brain-to-computer interface, BCI, where the computer, in this case, is an Omicron AI. It involves a technique called transcranial magnetic stimulation, TMS. A TMS device creates a magnetic field over the scalp, which then elicits electrical currents in the brain. When a set of TMS coils is placed on a subject's head, it maps and then simulates the cerebral cortex to allow information to be extracted from the higher brain centers in the form of electrical impulses, a kind of bioelectric code. Then it's up to the Omicron AI to decipher the code and translate it explicitly into a language-based format.

"But I believe he's using a more invasive technique now, in conjunction with TMS. It's more effective with resistant subjects, less time consuming, but it always turns people into empty shells. Effectively kills them. Cardew isn't messing around now. He's going for all he can get."

Aiden swallowed hard. "And what is the more invasive technique?"

Devi sighed and looked at him carefully. "Aiden, do you really want to hear this stuff?"

He felt the pit in his stomach deepen. He sat back and folded his arms over his chest. "Yes. Tell me."

Devi shook her head and went on to explain. "It's generally referred to as 'mind uploading.' Specifically, it's done by a process called whole-brain emulation, WBE. They start by scanning the entire physical structure of the brain, accurately enough to create an emulation of the subject's mental state. That includes all memory and all of what we identify as the self. The completed emulation can be transmitted in digital form directly to the Omicron AI. Or it can be copied bio-electronically into an auxiliary neural net—called a neuropod, about the size of a handheld suitcase—and delivered to any other Omicron-3 unit for reanimation.

"The Omicron then runs the emulation in such a way that it responds in essentially the same way as the original brain did, even the experience of having a conscious mind. It can also be done in a way that deliberately eliminates any moral qualms or sentiments about divulging the information they're asked to reveal. Do you really want me to go on?"

No, he really didn't, but he nodded anyway.

"Okay," Devi said. "The downside of WBE mind uploading is that it's accomplished by the copy-and-delete method. It involves the gradual replacement of neurons until the original organic brain no longer exists and the AI program emulating the brain takes over. The biological brain usually doesn't survive the copying process, or it may be deliberately destroyed in some variants of uploading. As for the unlucky scientists we found at the Dark Fort, the uploaders didn't even bother destroying their subjects' brains. They just left what remained of them inside those poor people's heads."

Aiden tried to ignore Devi's last sentence, but his stomach wouldn't cooperate. Nausea threatened to overwhelm him. He swallowed it back and continued. "So, for all these victims of WBE, all these scientists and engineers, their intellectual functions remain intact—their reasoning, problem solving, creativity, knowledge base, all of it—but in virtual form now, stripped of their will, to be used by whoever controls them for whatever purpose they want."

"That's basically it, yes."

Aiden thought of Abahem's sister pilot, Ciarra Devlin, pilot of the *Conquest* when it was hijacked by Cardew. If that atrocity had been performed on her, it would explain how Cardew's ships could make high-velocity voidjumps without a Licensed Pilot. His voidships *did* have pilots. Each ship had its own virtual Licensed Pilot—the same one, Ciarra Devlin—inside its flight computers.

Stay objective. Think clearly.

"All right," he said, "in terms of equipment, could something that elaborate be set up and concealed on an industrial tanker?"

Devi shook her head. "Absolutely not. For one thing, the need for an original Omicron AI would preclude that. Yes, we know that Cardew has access to at least one corrupted Omicron-3 unit, and probably more. But not many more. And he'll need whatever he's got to operate as the nerve center of his whole operation. I doubt he'd allocate one to an antimatter tanker. And if he did, it would be impossible to conceal."

"But the Omicrons can be cloned into smaller, more portable units," Aiden said. "Ones that could be concealed on the *Quasimodo*."

Devi shook her head again. "But not ones capable of performing a WBE. Only a fully mature Omicron-3 unit on site to integrate the upload into a functional virtual being would work. Given all that, it's highly unlikely that a WBE brain tap could be done aboard the *Quasimodo*."

"Which means," Aiden said, "they'd have to transport the subject to a larger facility, one that's fully equipped and set up for that purpose. Like what we found at the Dark Fort."

"Correct. We have evidence that one of Cardew's corrupted Omicron units was brought to the Dark Fort explicitly for that purpose."

Aiden's mind continued to spin. "Elgin, how many moons does Jumbo have?"

Woo snatched up his compad, tapped it several times and said, "A lot. Like Jupiter does. AMP has catalogued 58. But most of those are small, down to asteroid-sized satellites. There're only four moons large enough to use as a site for a hidden facility like that."

"Have any of those moons been investigated? Close up?"

"It doesn't look like it," Woo said, peering into his compad. "AMP's resources are stretched pretty thin, and they're prioritized for habitable planets in other star systems."

Devi turned to Aiden and said, "You're thinking that maybe there's a secret facility on one of the moons. And maybe that's where the *Quasimodo* is headed. But honestly, setting up a brain-tap facility out there with an original Omicron AI—and doing it without being noticed—would take considerable foresight, planning, and resources. How likely is that?"

"It *is* likely," Aiden said. "If Skye's work is a high enough priority for Cardew—which I'm beginning to see how it might be—and if extracting that knowledge is crucial to the survival of his empire, then capturing her would be a big part of his overall plan."

Hotah sat back and pointed out the painful facts. "But there's nothing we can do about it now. From here. Not until this black hole unblocks the voidoid. In the meantime, we have a mission that needs to be done. Sooner than later."

Woo clutched his hands together. "Whatever it is inside the voidoid, maybe it would allow the *Sun Wolf* to pass through unharmed. Shouldn't we consider making an attempt to jump? It might work."

Aiden shook his head. "You heard what Asaju said. There's no way we can jump back into that system. Not with a black hole sitting inside the voidoid. Their test drone proved it."

"It's not *just* a black hole, Aiden. I keep telling you that. It's an integral part of a larger entity that can obviously move the black hole around wherever it wants. Maybe it would move it aside for us. For the *Sun Wolf*."

"Elgin, I appreciate your optimism, but you're grasping at straws here, and you know it. Even assuming this entity is protecting Shénmì from hostile attacks, how would it tell the difference between the good guys and the bad guys? We probably all look the same to it."

"But we *don't* look the same. We're authentic human beings. The cloneborgs are not. I think this entity can tell the difference. I'd bet my life on it."

"Maybe. But would you bet the lives of our crew on it? Including an infant? Not to mention our mission, which—as Hotah points out—is becoming more critical with every passing day."

Woo didn't have an answer for that. Or else he did, and it was so painfully obvious he couldn't bring himself to say it. His eyes grew wide with anguish. "But *Skye* . . . We have to do something . . ."

Elgin Woo's heroic optimism had begun to crack. Aiden had never seen the man look so helpless, but realized that he himself had plunged into the same abyss, right along with him. Into a sickening helplessness that was like a punch in the stomach.

He finally said, "I agree, Elgin, we have to do something, and right now that something is exactly what Skye would want us to do in this situation. To continue our mission. To do everything else in our power to stop this madman from pulling us all down into darkness."

29

HD 10180 SYSTEM
Cis-Jumbo Space

DOMAIN DAY 343, 2218

THE *light within darkness.*

Skye Landen had always been able to see it. Especially with her eyes closed, like they were now. To see it even within the darkest spaces between the stars. A beacon of life burning defiantly from the black depths of the void. Eternal. Powered by some inexplicable and indomitable source of energy. Light, the natural counterpoint to nothingness—like electrons are to protons, or matter to antimatter—twins born from a physics of duality awakened at the dawn of the Big Bang. Light. The very substance of consciousness . . .

At the moment, however, the light was nowhere to be seen. That, and the subsonic rumble of an antimatter drive at maximum thrust vibrating up through the cold metal deck beneath her, told Skye she was in serious trouble. But opening her eyes right now was the last thing she wanted to do. She wasn't ready to see exactly how serious it really was. Not yet. She wanted to stay inside the darkness behind her eyelids and continue searching for that point of light she knew was there but could not find.

Darkness had its advantages. Untethered from the hard-edged reality that vision mandates, she was free to manifest her own version of reality. It was all up to her now, not constrained by what her eyes dictated to her brain. An engaging challenge to her creativity. As long as she didn't dip too deeply into the inherent chaos of darkness, into its total absence of boundaries, its disintegration of form and order, one step away from death.

But Skye had skirted those lower limits before. She was no stranger to balancing on the tightrope above the abyss. It was a place where the deepest knowledge could be found, if you were fearless enough to seek it. A place where she steadied herself only by casting her eyes upward toward the light. But without the light, it was too easy to falter, to lose her balance and fall into the chaos, to be consumed by it, never again to resurface.

Now, without the light from within, she could no longer afford to keep her eyes closed. It was too dangerous. She had to let vision return, to anchor her to a reality that, if not of her own making, was at least familiar. A place she could navigate with her body as well as her mind.

She forced herself to open her eyes.

Her eyes told her that she was in a small room with metal walls, maybe five by seven meters, lit by soft ambient lighting. She was sitting on the metal deck, her back leaning against the wall. One heavy metal door occupied the wall directly in front of her, closed firmly and held in place by four thick metal hinges. No handle or latch. Only a shallow rectangular depression occupied its blank surface, about halfway up.

To her left, a narrow pallet bed was bolted to the wall, one meter above the deck. It was covered by a gray thermoblanket lying atop a thin mattress with a single foam pillow at one end. To her right, against the opposite wall, a basic toilet sat with its lid down. A small sink with a single faucet, supported by a thick metal pedestal, stood next to it. Attached to the wall above the sink, a cup rack held one plastic cup, and a narrow bracket held one small white towel.

Next to where she sat, a square tabletop with rounded edges protruded from the wall, welded in place. A metal chair with a low back sat in front of the table, bolted to the deck. There were no windows, no wall hangings or decor of any kind in the room. It looked exactly like a prison cell.

She felt a sudden chill and realized how cold it was inside the room and how useless her thin sleep pants and T-shirt were for retaining warmth. They were the same garments she had worn to bed . . . when? The night before? Where the hell was she? And how long had she been here?

She was aboard a ship. That much seemed apparent, judging from the sound and feel of an antimatter drive at high thrust. She knew exactly what that felt like from inside a ship. And the ship's G-transducers were functional. Otherwise, she'd be plastered against the far wall, pinned there by the G-forces of the ship's acceleration. As for how long she'd been here . . . She glanced at her wrist to read her chrono. It wasn't there. Removed by whom?

Her mouth felt dry as a desert. She shivered with the cold. She needed to grab the thermoblanket from the pallet bed. But when she tried to stand, dizziness and nausea caused her knees to buckle, forcing her to sit again. Her head throbbed with an excruciating headache the likes of which she'd never experienced. Only that one mother-of-all-hangovers that she'd barely survived after a graduation celebration of rum and tequila could rival it. She made a low moan, closed her eyes again, and held her head in both hands. She forced herself into a breathing exercise she'd learned long ago in her Gaian Circle.

The pain in her head reminded her to take an inventory of her physical condition. She had obviously been abducted and imprisoned by unknown assailants. Now was the time to check for injuries. The first thing she thought of was what all victims of kidnapping feared, especially women, and especially after a period of unconsciousness. It didn't take long to assure herself that she had not been sexually assaulted.

Breathing a sigh of relief, she moved on. Other than the headache, she felt no serious pain, either internally or from joints, muscles, or bones. She moved all her extremities, flexed fingers and toes, and confirmed normal range of motion. She felt and looked for swellings, cuts, or abrasions. Other than some stiffness in her back and tailbone from sitting on a hard metal deck for who knows how long, she seemed physically intact.

Except for that one tiny bump on her neck over her jugular vein.

She felt it with her finger. It was tender, and a small scab had formed on top of it. No doubt about it. An injection site. That could explain the horrific headache, an aftereffect of a medical-grade injectable anesthetic. Dehydration, of course, would only make the headache worse. She looked at the sink, the water faucet, and the cup. Time to try standing again.

This time, she fought off the dizziness, the weakness in her knees, and stiffness in her back. She staggered unsteadily to the sink, removed the cup from its holder, and placed it under the faucet. Making a silent invocation to Damona, a Celtic goddess of rivers and healing waters, she turned the handle. Clear water flowed from the faucet into the cup. She sniffed it. Yes. Fresh water. Whoever had kidnapped her apparently didn't want her dead. Not just yet.

She gulped down three full cups, then moved to the pallet bed, grabbed the thermoblanket, and wrapped it around her shoulders. She sat on the bed and leaned back against the wall, allowing the thermoblanket to retain every calorie of body heat. While she waited for her core temperature to rise, her other senses reported in. The only odor she detected was a faint hint of cleaning fluids. Alcohol and bleach. The only sound she heard was the low growl of the antimatter drive, felt more in the bones than heard by the ears. Like a steady thunder roll in the distance. She was definitely aboard a ship, and it was going somewhere in a hurry.

Skye looked around the room again, examining it in more detail. The rectangular tabletop had a small crystal window embedded into its surface at one corner. She leaned over to get a better look. A miniature digital chrono looked up at her from beneath the clear crystal. It read just past 14:00, Domain Day 343. She'd been unconscious for . . . what? Ten hours? Twelve? Far longer than any fast-acting injectable anesthesia could account for. She must have been subjected to some kind of inhalable anesthetic gas, and maintained on it, to have been out for so long. Probably a halogenated gas, like isoflurane or one of its updated isomers. But how?

Looking up, she saw two air vents in the ceiling, one at either end of the room. Perfect ports of entry for gases other than oxygenated air. They were not the kind of vents with removable grates. These were protected by steel bars built into the core of the ceiling. In one upper corner, a deep circular cavity in the wall housed a camera lens looking out into the room. And in the opposite corner, a similar cavity held a small sound transducer. Like the air vents, both were protected by sturdy steel bars. The rectangular depression halfway up the face of the metal door that she'd noticed earlier looked like a service port with its sliding door closed. Just large enough for the transfer of medium-sized objects. Like food trays?

Her headache was slowly evaporating, like a dark mist fleeing from a rising sun. She closed her eyes and tried to reconstruct what had happened before waking up in this place. She remembered walking and talking with her research assistant on the way to her quarters. At about 19:00? They were discussing the recent revelations about the enemy they faced in this astrocell, about Cardew's superhuman soldiers.

Elgin Woo called them cloneborgs, because they were an amalgamation of human clones and synthetic augmentation. The clone part had been derived from Cardew's own genetic material. But they were bioengineered to look exactly like normal human beings, as diverse in appearance as the human population. Their synthetic augmentation made them stronger, faster, and more able to tolerate extreme conditions than humans. Elgin believed they had also been genetically engineered for immortality, or at least for very long lifespans.

But Aiden and his crew had found evidence that the cloneborgs were not invincible, that they had a critical Achilles' heel that could help humans defeat them. They were vulnerable to attack by the fungus from Shénmì seeds, the mycorrhizal symbiont responsible for facilitating the evolution of organic life everywhere in this astrocell. It meant that cloneborgs could not colonize habitable planets that had been seeded by Shénmì—which ruled out virtually all living worlds in the astrocell. Stepping foot on such a planet without bio-suits would kill them. Cardew had responded with an obscene crusade to sterilize those planets with a device that produced powerful gamma-ray bursts.

The news had horrified Skye. Ironically, her current work focused on escalating the aggressiveness of that same fungus, accelerating its ability to attack and digest inorganic and dead organic material. The fungus currently used on Mars to terraform the planet—and on Earth to restore the equatorial rain forests and rejuvenate food crops—had come from Silvanus. It definitely worked, but not as fast as people wanted. The Martians dreamed of their children playing out in the open one day, wandering verdant forests and grasslands. The Earthers dreamed of regaining the biological treasures they had squandered in the Die Back, and doing it within their lifetimes.

Skye and her team had learned that the Shénmì fungus was actually a variant of the Silvanus fungus being used on Earth and Mars. But this variant could transform barren planets lying within habitable zones into living worlds much more quickly than the Silvanus fungus. That would explain why so many habitable planets had been found supporting living biospheres in this astrocell. Because they had been—and continued to be—seeded by Shénmì.

By comparing the two variants, Skye had succeeded in isolating the genes responsible for the Shénmì fungus's rapid proliferation and its astoundingly efficient symbiogenesis on lifeless planets. And for the saprophytic aggressiveness that provided the nutrients it needed.

By tweaking those genes to accelerate the process even more, she and her colleagues had engineered a new variant of the Shénmì fungus to be far more aggressive. A variant that, under the right conditions, could turn a barren planet into a living one within a few thousand years rather than billions. It would be exactly what the human race needed. And exactly what Cardew did *not* need. Dispersed widely among the habitable planets of Astrocell Beta, it would doom any hope of him ever establishing a foothold here, once and for all.

That was the topic of discussion between Skye and her colleague just before she retired to her quarters. Thinking about it had kept her from falling asleep. Then, just as she was finally drifting off, she'd received a disturbing notification on her compad from Crestfield telling her that the system's voidoid had just been closed off. Some sort of weird black-hole phenomenon had taken up residence inside it, preventing voidjumps into or out of the system. That news had kept her up even later.

The last thing she remembered before sleep finally embraced her was turning from her pillow to see her chrono indicating well past midnight. Then she woke up here. In this prison cell, undoubtedly the brig of a ship heading away from Shénmì at a rapid clip, to an unknown destination. And, no doubt, to an unpleasant fate.

30

HD 10180 SYSTEM
Cis-Jumbo Space

Domain Day 343, 2218

Skye pulled the thermoblanket more tightly around her shoulders, then realized her shivering was not from the cold, but from fear. Like an ice-cold hand gripping her throat, it threatened to extinguish all breath and reason.

Steady on. Breathe. Keep the light burning. Work the problem . . .

She sat up straight and massaged her temples, trying to sweep the fog of panic from her mind. Even if she didn't know exactly where she was, or what was happening, she did have a few clues to work with. She mentally ticked them off: Aiden had told her about a cloneborg mole planted among the four-person crew of the SS *Quasimodo*. The tanker's four-person crew had been aboard Shénmì Station while refueling the station's Penning tanks. No other large ships had been anywhere near the station since the *Sun Wolf* had departed. She was obviously aboard a very large ship right now, judging from the sound and feel of its thrusters. Knowing Cardew's history of kidnapping top scientists from the Cauldron and elsewhere, Skye could think of several reasons why he'd want her abducted, most notably her current genetic work on the Shénmì fungus.

Putting all that together left her with only one conclusion. She'd been abducted by one of Cardew's cloneborgs, imprisoned aboard the SS *Quasimodo*, and was mostly likely on her way to a truly grim fate. A date with brain tapping.

But where was the *Quasimodo* headed? She had to assume the cloneborg had gained complete control of the ship. He couldn't plan on jumping out of the system. Not with a black hole blocking the voidoid. Would he instead rendezvous with one of Cardew's ships that had somehow entered the system without anyone noticing? Unlikely. That left only the likelihood of a secret base on or near a planet where it could stay hidden from the Alliance's security sweeps. A planet or a moon of a planet.

The orbital path of planet g was the closet one to Shénmì's orbital path. It was one of the two Class-I gas giants in the outer system. It had plenty of moons. It even briefly passed through the system's habitable zone during its annual rotation around the star. But g was currently at the opposite side of the system from Shénmì, and it had a highly eccentric orbit that put it even farther away at this point in time.

No. It had to be Jumbo, planet h. Its orbital *path* was farther from Shénmì's, but the planet itself was currently nearing its closest approach to Shénmì, not more than 2 AU away. Jumbo also had plenty of moons, ideal locations to construct a secret base and keep it concealed, even from regular tanker crews working in Jumbo space. Assuming the *Quasimodo* was doing its continuous 2 G maximum acceleration, that meant she was in for a journey of about two and a half days.

Having deduced all that didn't make her feel any better. Far from it. She was frightened, alone, cold, hungry, and facing an uncertain fate over which she had absolutely no control. But worst of all, she was now Cardew's prisoner, with little hope of rescue. Even if someone had figured out where she was by now, the only warships in the system were stationed at the voidoid, too far away to be of any help. The only ship fast enough to reach her in time was the *Sun Wolf*. But Aiden had his ship off in some far-flung star system. And now that the voidoid here was closed off, not even he could come to the rescue.

Aiden. She missed him so much. It felt like a big hole opening up in her chest, a bottomless pit of darkness. She *always* missed him, of course, but she'd had her work to distract her from the ache of it. They'd had so little time to spend together. They had their separate missions in this world, both equally vital to humanity's survival. Missions that could not proceed as well, or at all, without them. And yet, Aiden and Skye were still a unit. They were partners. Always there for each other, if not in body, always in spirit. Would she ever be with him again? Would anything be left of her to be with?

She felt her heart pounding and tried to steady her breathing. How would she keep her fear from morphing into naked panic over the next few days? She would need supreme discipline, the kind she could only accomplish through the mental exercises she had learned from her Gaian mentor, Thea Delamere.

She decided that her first exercise would be to invoke the capricious phantom of sleep. Because that was what she needed most right now. Real sleep, not the pharmaceutically induced kind. Sleep undisturbed by nightmares. Her current situation was nightmarish enough, and she would need psychic strength to endure it and ultimately to find a way out of it. She closed her eyes and fell inward.

~ ~ ~

A sound woke her. The sound of a heavy metal door opening.

She snapped fully awake in an instant. The door of her cell opened slowly. She leapt to her feet and stood in a defensive crouch. Adrenaline poured into her system, muscles tensed, heart pounding.

The door opened fully, and a man stood at its threshold. Or at least a being that looked like a man.

He smiled at her. He extended his left arm toward her, palm opened, facing upward, a gesture of reassurance. In his right hand, he held a covered plate the size and shape of a serving tray. He was of average height, slender but powerfully built, and wore the standard jumpsuit of Bright Star Energy—charcoal gray with a white four-point starburst embossed over the left breast. Instead of standard flight shoes, he wore heavy magnetic boots, ones intended for weightless EVA on a ship's external hull. A small matte-black weapon was discreetly holstered at his waist. Skye flicked her eyes at it briefly before reengaging eye contact. She identified it as a nonlethal sonic stunner, the kind that Station Security carried, meant to incapacitate an attacker without inflicting serious damage.

The man made no move to enter the room. He remained motionless and silent, assuming a relaxed, nonthreatening stance. He looked at her calmly but with unabashed curiosity. His eyes were an ethereal shade of light blue with unusually large black pupils. His face looked smooth and pale, without a hint of beard or stubble. His hair was the color of straw and cut short.

Skye relaxed her own stance, coming out of her crouch to stand taller. But inside, she remained on high alert. No way would she allow this stranger's appearance of harmlessness to lower her guard. She used her own appearance of relaxation as a ruse in a silent but deadly chess game. *Your move next.*

Seeming to understand implicitly, the man took two steps across the threshold into the room, stopped, and stood still once again. The smile and placid demeanor remained unchanged. But those two steps sent a chill up her spine. The way he had moved, the smooth effortlessness of it. Like a panther, but even more finely tuned. Immense power precisely contained. Inhuman.

Or superhuman.

In that moment, she knew in her gut that if this being wanted to attack her, he could do it in the blink of an eye, a microsecond, way before she could react.

But he did not attack. Instead, he spoke, his voice low, resonant, and oddly musical.

"My name is Jax. I am pleased to meet you, Dr. Landen. I am here to talk. You have an important decision to make."

"Don't come any closer," Skye said, using the voice of command, knowing full well that it might have no effect whatsoever on this being.

Jax made a small bow. Still smiling, he said, "I am not here to harm you, and I will not harm you. Unless I am forced to do so."

"What exactly would force you to harm me?"

"Any attempt you make to harm me would be required." A subtle change in his smile reflected absolute confidence that he could not be harmed. Not by her and not here.

Skye let it pass and moved on. "Why was I abducted?"

With no attempt to deny the word *abducted*, Jax said, "Because you are needed for a greater cause."

"Needed by whom? And who are *you*?"

"You are needed specifically by the Founder. By Amon. I am one of his Line. I represent him, as do all of his Line."

So much to unpack from those few words. Skye didn't know where to begin. "By 'Amon,' you mean Cardew?"

Jax shook his head. "Cardew is his first name and the one that Normals have given him. He is Amon to us. Or he is sometimes referred to as Father."

Amon. Of course. She remembered what Aiden had told her about Cardew's past, that he had once been the strategy director of Terra Corp under the name of C. S. Amon. The *C* stood for Cardew, the name he was known for as the founder of Licet Omnia. The name that "Normals" used for him.

So, she was a "Normal" now. As were all humans. "You're one of his cloneborgs."

Again, a subtle shift in the shape of his smile. "The term *cloneborg* was coined by Dr. Elgin Woo. A clever term. True, we of the Line are genetic clones of Amon, but not in the restrictive sense usually applied to routine cloning. We are also partially cyborg, in the sense that we have been synthetically augmented. More accurately, we are Transhumans."

Transhumans? Where had she heard that term before? But she had a more pressing question. "Where are we, and where are we going?"

Rather than answering, Jax opened his free hand toward her again, a disarming gesture perfectly executed, and said, "May I take another step forward and place this tray on your side table? It contains fresh food. I believe you have not eaten in over 24 hours."

The aroma of a freshly prepared meal emanating from the tray caused her to salivate. Her stomach growled. She nodded to him and tilted her head toward the table.

With the same impossibly smooth movement, Jax stepped to the table and placed the tray on its surface without a sound. He turned toward her again and said, "May I sit? I find that Normals are more at ease conversing in a sitting position."

Skye looked around the room. Aside from her pallet bed, the only other place to sit was the metal chair bolted down in front of the small table. But the chair faced the wall, and its back prevented a seated person from facing anywhere else. Still standing in front of the bed, Skye dialed up her defense stance again to discourage any notion of him sitting there. Then she shrugged and said, "Sure. Be my guest."

Jax pressed a button on his utility belt, activating his magnetic boots. Then he assumed a sitting position where he stood. Without anything to sit on. It was as if he sat on an invisible chair. Feet magnetically planted on the deck, knees bent at right angles, thighs and buttocks hovering horizontally over the floor—supported by nothing—back erect, and head facing forward. Anchored to the deck only by powerful magnetic boots. It was one of the oddest sights Skye had ever seen. And physically impossible—at least not without insanely enhanced augmentation of skeleton, muscle, knee and hip joints.

Skye did her best to hide her astonishment. If Jax had intended to put her at ease by sitting, his manner of doing it had done just the opposite. She remained standing.

"You asked where we were," he said casually, "and where we are headed. We are aboard the antimatter tanker SS *Quasimodo*, where I have served as a crewperson. It is early morning, Domain Day 344, and we are headed toward one of the moons around Jumbo."

"Where is the rest of the crew?"

"They are not aboard. Only you and I are here."

Skye really didn't want to ask, but she did anyway. "Did you kill them?"

Jax blinked once, an economical substitute for a shrug, and said, "They were expendable."

Skye clenched her fists at her side and felt her face flush with anger. "So, you claim you won't harm me, but you have no qualms about murdering three other innocent people."

"True, I will not harm you. Your safety is my top priority. Amon has gone to great lengths to acquire your assistance. Anything or anyone who poses a threat to that priority will be eliminated. And no, I have no qualms. Sentiments of that kind are purely human, one of many that plague Normals and prevent your kind from evolving and excelling."

His explanation just pissed her off even more. Jax seemed to take note and continued in a softer voice. "Transhumans are not amoral, Dr. Landen. We just have a *different* morality. One that allows us to transcend the self-destructive impulses of Normals. Transhumans will actually save the human race from destroying itself, and just in time, I might add. We will save it by replacing it."

"Replacing the human race?" Skye scoffed. "You mean eradicating it, don't you?"

Jax put on a pleasant smile. "No. For now at least, we will not harm Normals outright as long they remain within Bound Space and do not interfere with the building of our Posthuman Realm. Once we are firmly established in this astrocell, we will reenter Bound Space and annex it for the Realm. At that point—which will happen sooner than you might think—Normals will be given the choice to become Transhumans themselves or to become obsolete."

"Obsolete," Skye said, "as in mass murder."

Jax held his hands out, palms up. "It's not like that. Think of it as culling the herd to advance the race. Besides, human Normals will ultimately destroy themselves anyway. They've been doing it for thousands of years. We will merely end it quickly, humanely, foregoing the drawn-out carnage and tragedy of self-extinction."

Skye shivered and closed her eyes to shut out visions of unspeakable horror. Humanity wouldn't stand a chance against armies of Transhuman soldiers like Jax. She forced herself to refocus on her immediate situation and asked, "Why are we going to this moon? And why am I being held prisoner?"

Jax shifted smoothly to fold his hands together and place them on his lap. "Ah. The answers to those two questions have much to do with the important decision you must make."

Skye finally decided to sit. Standing alert in a defensive posture was, under the circumstances, pointless. Plus, it consumed energy that Skye had run low on after all she'd been through. And when *was* the last time she'd eaten anything?

"Okay," she said, lowering herself to sit on the edge of the bed. "I'll bite. What is this decision I have to make, and why is it so damn important?"

Jax cocked his head to one side. "To answer that, you must allow me to give you some background."

She had a vague idea of the "background" Jax might be explaining to her, but there were gaps in her understanding of it. "Go on."

31

HD 10180 SYSTEM
Cis-Jumbo Space

DOMAIN DAY 344, 2218

JAX leaned forward slightly, still in a sitting position, a gesture resembling a close friend about to reveal something very personal and dear to his heart. "Amon's goal," he said, "shared by all of his Line, is to lay claim to this sector of space—this astrocell, as Dr. Woo has called it—to colonize and populate its habitable planets, along with as many other planets that we can make habitable. From there, we will build our nation. Amon used to call it his Empire of the Pure."

Here Jax paused and looked as if he'd shared a quaint jest with himself. Then he said, "We of the Line refer to it as the Posthuman Realm—a far more accurate term. The word *pure* is too steeped in human emotion and misguided morality. Applying it to the Realm would be incorrect."

"The *Posthuman* Realm?" Skye said with a smirk. "I thought you were Transhumans. Why call it Posthuman?"

"We of the Line *are* Transhumans. We are essentially human organisms, but have been created with biotransformative technologies to enhance and modify the human organism to overcome fundamental human limitations. Our ultimate goal is to *become* Posthuman. We're not there yet, but will be soon. At this point, the term *transitional humans* would be more accurate. But we adhere to Transhuman for historical reasons, to honor the visionary humans who coined the term long ago and foresaw the future. Becoming Posthuman takes even more radical technological enhancement, to the point where physical, cognitive, and emotional capacities differ so completely from Normals that they are no longer recognizably human. That's when we will achieve Singularity, when our collective capacity for intelligence accelerates exponentially."

"And just who will be creating these Posthumans? Amon?"

Jax shook his head. "Father is involved only indirectly, as a catalyst. We of his Line are doing the work of manifesting the Posthuman Realm. Our goal is actually quite simple—the use of technology in order to overcome humanity's biological limitations and to transform the human condition. We view it as the next stage in the natural evolution of humanity. By adding technological implants and inserting DNA, humans become Transhuman. From that point on, humanity will be able to abandon biological evolution and begin a self-directed evolution based on technology. And that's when the Posthuman Realm will come into being."

Skye couldn't believe what her ears were hearing. But she *was* hearing it, and it was scaring her. "Let me guess. All the purely human traits—the messy ones like love, compassion, sexuality, creativity, spirituality—will not be hardwired into your Posthumans."

"And why would they be?" Jax said, as if explaining the obvious to a child. "Normals would believe that integrating those traits into Posthumans will somehow prevent them from going rogue and destroying the human race in some futuristic rampage. To prevent such a thing, they would program in something like Asimov's Three Laws of Robotics, for security and to guarantee benefit to humans, first and foremost. But you must see that such notions are obsolete. Besides, supremely intelligent Posthumans who have achieved Singularity would not abide by such limitations. They'll have wills of their own and the ability to direct their own evolution."

"Wills of their own?" Skye said. "And just what would their will want?"

"Ah," Jax said, warming up to a philosophical discourse Skye had no desire to engage in. "Human will is defined by human genes, the environment, and the psychological makeup of the brain—a chaos of unpredictable factors. Yet, what humans truly desire is to reach a state of perfect personal power. To become omnipotent in the universe. And that's what Transhumans will do for them on our way to the Posthuman Realm."

Skye shook her head. "You're wrong. Dead wrong. Only the mentally ill and criminally delusional among us seek a state of perfect personal power. All the rest of us 'normal' humans seek *meaning*. First and foremost. Whether they know it consciously or not. It is the *will to meaning*, and it's driven by our knowledge of our own mortality. Death is the mother of our relentless search for meaning. For truth. If you're immortal, you can't possibly participate in that. Your goal is to exist forever. Ours is to live life fully, meaningfully, while we can."

For a fleeting moment, Jax appeared to consider in earnest what she had said. But the moment passed. "No, Dr. Landen. It is you who are wrong. The will to become omnipotent in the universe supersedes all else. That's what 'meaning' *is* to Transhumans. Amon calls it the Will to Evolution."

Skye rolled her eyes. "Right. Like Nietzsche's 'will to power.' Honestly, you're just a bunch of wannabe Nietzscheans."

Unfazed by Skye's derision, Jax continued. "Yes, our vision does bear some similarities to Nietzsche's. His 'will to power' is similar to our Will to Evolution. And his concept of the Übermensch, the 'overhuman,' is similar to our Posthumans. But Nietzsche's vision was just that, a concept, a belief. Ours is becoming a reality."

Skye felt a wave of revulsion imagining an entire astrocell, hundreds of planets, colonized by these so-called Posthuman beings. But the more she could learn about how they thought, what motivated them, the more information she'd have on how to combat them. Assuming she would ever return to the human world to relay that information.

She took a deep breath and pretended to relax. "So instead of Asimov's Three Laws, what Three Laws would guide the actions of Posthumans?"

Without hesitation, Jax replied, "Only two, really. The First Law would be to safeguard one's own existence above all else. The Second Law would be to strive to achieve omnipotence—so long as one's actions do not conflict with the First Law."

Skye didn't know what to say. It all sounded preordained, as if already written into the Posthuman Ten Commandments. It was outlandish. Yet the rationale behind it was brilliantly twisted. She finally said, "That's just Asimov's Laws turned upside down."

"But necessarily so," Jax said. "For any superintelligent Posthuman to steadfastly uphold Asimov's laws, it would have to be taught purely human traits, including emotional- and hormonal-driven behavior, impetuousness, and irrationality. Why integrate such flawed traits into the most advanced intelligences to ever exist?"

This conversation would be hilariously absurd under any other circumstance. Here, it was deadly serious. And, considering Cardew's military machine, frightening as hell.

Jax responded to her stunned silence by continuing. "Dr. Landen, we can all agree that humans do possess some admirable traits. But the species is also capable of truly horrible and evil acts. Look at your history—full of genocides, slavery, war, torture, sexual perversion, brutish savagery. The list goes on. It's time to put an end to all that, to all those self-destructive animal propensities. Time to move on to the next stage of evolution, a more advanced stage. Unlike Normals, Transhumans cannot destroy themselves."

"Exactly," Skye said, nodding, "a case in point for what one of our wisest ancestors said; 'only that which can destroy itself is truly alive.'"

Jax didn't seem to have an answer for that. Instead, he looked as if a few wires had crossed inside his head. But to be fair, most people reacted in a similar way whenever she quoted Carl Jung. Finally, that annoyingly placid smile crept onto his face again, as if he'd been entertained by a charming fairytale, and he said nothing more.

But Skye had heard enough already. Time to get real. "That's enough 'background' for me, thank you. Get back to the part about why I'm being held prisoner. And what's this 'greater cause' I'm needed for?"

Jax paused and looked at her with disconcerting intensity. The large black pupils of his eyes grew larger. His perpetual smile looked less natural, more of a façade. When he spoke, it was with an even and deliberate tone. "We have investigated many star systems in this astrocell that harbor planets inside their habitable zones. We seek them out as grounds for rapid colonization. So far, it seems that all the habitable planets on which organic life already exist have become that way through panspermia, seeded by one living planet here in this system. The one you call Shénmì. All of these planets are now thoroughly infused by a species of fungus that is responsible for the genesis and evolution of all life forms that persist on them. The fungus is the very foundation of these biospheres.

"You know all of this, of course. It's your area of expertise. In fact, much of the information we have comes from our knowledge of your recent research. What you may not know is that this fungus is lethal to us. To *all* of the Line. The fungus attacks us physically, either through its mycelia or its airborne spores, invades the human parts of our bodies, the organic parts. It is fatal very quickly. The fungus is, however, completely harmless to normal humans. This means that we Transhumans cannot, in any practical way, colonize these planets, which are of course the most desirable ones. We have tried on several planets, and all attempts have ended in disaster."

Skye did, in fact, know this part of it, but not until just recently. Instead of acknowledging it, she said, "So that's why you tried to destroy Shénmì with that antiquark bomb. You wanted to destroy the source of the panspermia seeds."

"Yes, of course," Jax said, without a hint of denial. "But your husband, Commander Macallan, and his unique ship thwarted that attempt. So, we moved on to Plan B. That was to launch an overwhelming invasion force into Shénmì's system, destroy the planet, and acquire you. Unfortunately, our fleet can't do that now because the voidoid into the system is blocked. So, we moved on to Plan C, and here we are."

Skye didn't bother asking about Plan C. His mention of "acquiring" her had made that painfully clear. She wanted to know something more critical. "I don't get it. If you Transhumans are so invincible, why haven't you come up with a brilliant solution for the fungus? Why haven't you been able to adjust your biosynthetic modifications to prevent the fungus from attacking you?"

"Exactly the question we have been asking ourselves," Jax said, showing signs of frustration in his well-maintained facial expressions. "We have, after all, become virtually immune to all pathogenic microorganisms that continually plague the Normals. What makes this particular fungus so completely resistant to all of our attempts to engineer an immunity to it? The simple answer is that we do not know."

"And you think that I do?"

Jax smiled and said, "This, Dr. Landen, is where you come into the picture. Your research, knowledge, and techniques of genetic manipulation may very well provide the solution. You hold the single most important key to our salvation. To the survival and triumph of our Posthuman Realm."

A small spark of hope lit up inside Skye. She felt an element of control returning to her otherwise hopeless situation. If these Transhumans perceived her as holding the key to their grand plans, she had gained some leverage. But only if Jax believed that she might agree to cooperate of her own free will. If she refused to cooperate, she knew they had ways of extracting information from her brain. A demeanor of skepticism would still be expected of her at this stage of the conversation, so she maintained it. "And exactly how could my work possibly help you find a solution?"

Jax smiled. "We have been following your work very closely. We know that you are designing a variant of the Shénmì fungus that is far more aggressive and fast acting, for use in terraforming barren planets. We believe that you, and only you, have the skill and knowledge to engineer a variant of the fungus that will *not* harm Transhumans, but will retain its aggressiveness in terraforming habitable planets. I have brought on board some materials from your lab that would allow you to continue your work in that direction."

"Really?" Skye said, copping a dismissive tone. But secretly, she'd gone into high-alert mode. "What kinds of material did you steal from my lab?"

"Your research computer, some microengineering instruments, and a few specimen containers."

Specimen containers. The small spark of hope inside Skye's mind grew brighter. It was true, she and her colleagues had finally perfected a variant of the Shénmì fungus that could rapidly set the stage for terraforming barren planets. They called it Variant A. If what Jax had just told her was true, it would also be highly toxic to Transhumans. Hundreds of times more toxic than the original Shénmì fungus. She had several colonies of the stuff in her lab, growing in tightly sealed containers under varying conditions to simulate a range of environments it might encounter on barren planets.

But why would Jax deliberately bring aboard any of those containers, knowing how dangerous they'd be to him? He was not a fool. That much was obvious. Maybe he brought along the *other* variant she'd been working on . . . Variant B? If so, he had made a perfectly understandable error, and one that would work in her favor.

She looked at him with feigned interest. "And you would use this altered fungal variant how? To terraform barren planets with a fungus that allows you to safely colonize them?"

"Yes. Barren planets. As well as planets that were once alive but have been cleansed to make ready for regeneration favorable to us."

Skye felt the nausea return. "Cleansed? What are you talking about?"

"We have already sterilized several habitable planets on which abundant organic life has evolved, seeded by the Shénmì fungus and therefore useless to us. And more sterilizations are planned. We will then regenerate life on them, seeded by an efficient fungal variant that is not deadly but beneficial for Transhumans. One that you will develop for us. One way or another."

The veiled threat in those last words did not escape Skye's notice. But her outrage brushed it aside. Jax must be referring to that horrid device Aiden and his crew had discovered out at HD 21749. The graser. She sat forward, fighting the impulse to launch herself at this arrogant freak and pummel him with her fists. "You have *killed* living planets? That's an obscene crime against Nature. And Nature will come back to bite you in the ass for it. *One way or another.*"

Jax appeared utterly unmoved by her outburst, as if he'd expected it. "This 'Nature' of yours will be powerless to stop us. Because we will change the very nature of Nature."

She leaned back against the wall, controlled her anger, and affected an expression of disbelief. "Do you really think that I would help you and your . . . Posthuman Realm? Willingly? You know that I stand against everything you're doing to attain it."

"That brings us to the very important decision you have to make. On one hand, you can help us realize the Posthuman Realm, and even become an integral part of it by becoming one of us. To become Transhuman yourself with all our superior advantages over the Normals."

"Oh really? Become Transhuman myself? And how would I do that?"

"Cyborgization," Jax said, as if it were childishly obvious. "By extensive synthetic augmentation, you would be trading in your old body for a vastly superior one. With improved senses, infallible memory, greatly boosted intellectual capacity, vastly longer lifetime, greater physical performance, and control over emotional responses. Plus, our techniques in cloning and synthetic augmentation have made human procreation obsolete. We've happily become asexual, leaving behind sexuality and all its dangerous distortions.

"The time has come, Dr. Landen, for intelligent human beings like yourself to take control of their own evolution, to create a new species descended from *Homo sapiens*. Human Normals will be replaced by Transhumans like us and eventually by our descendants, the Posthumans, who will be virtually immortal. You can be part of this grand crusade, to become Transhuman yourself. Become one of us. Help us *all* to become Posthuman."

"And if I refuse?"

"Well," Jax said, as if speaking to an ill-behaved child. "We can simply extract knowledge from your brain, or better yet, transform you into a digital being who is incapable of resisting, who will give us everything we ask for."

Skye gave him a blank look, trying to suppress sheer terror. Her mouth went dry. The tantalizing aroma from the food tray had suddenly lost its appeal. When she did not speak, Jax said, "Do you know what brain tapping is? What about WBE, whole-brain emulation? These are not pretty techniques, but have been quite effective for us."

At that, Jax stood, turned, and moved smoothly to the door. He opened it, turned to her and said, "Your choices are quite clear, Dr. Landen. All the instruments needed to perform a WBE are set up and waiting for us on that moon. I urge you to decide sooner than later."

The heavy metal door closed behind him, clanging with sickening finality.

32

HD 21693 SYSTEM
System Voidoid

DOMAIN DAY 344, 2218

LOVING someone deeply, and being loved in return, is life's greatest gift and its most dangerous.

Aiden had never experienced that paradox more profoundly than he did now, staring at his face in the mirror over the bathroom sink after vomiting for the fifth time. When you loved someone as completely as he did Skye, the love you shared emerged as an entity all its own, with a body and a soul more real than either one of you could possess by yourselves. So completely united that when one of you was hurt, frightened, or dispirited beyond hope, the other one became consumed by it as well. It couldn't be any other way. A fact of nature. The law of love.

Like some kind of quantum entanglement where two quantum states are linked together as one, no matter how far apart they are in space—microns or light-years—the fear and anxiety that Skye must be enduring materialized inside of Aiden, too, and was amplified by his sheer helplessness to do anything about it. His body reacted to it in the only way it could. Acute nausea and cyclic vomiting.

He'd felt it coming on during Devi's explanation of Cardew's brain-tapping techniques and the abomination of whole-brain emulation. He'd been able to keep it in check all the way through his outward attempts to bolster the morale of his crew, to move "onward and upward." When he couldn't keep it down any longer, he'd excused himself to his quarters where he'd bent over his bathroom sink, disgorged everything from his stomach, and continued to retch long after nothing was left inside. Nothing except a black pit of anguish.

Aiden straightened himself up, washed out his mouth, washed his face, and looked back into the mirror. *Oh yeah. Much better . . . Right. Keep telling yourself that.* At least the antinausea drug Devi had given him had started to work. He felt less sick, but the dark tide of deep depression continued to rise around him, threatening to drown him.

These were dangerous moments for Aiden, moments of weakness. The image of a bottle of Continuum flashed unbidden into his mind. The bottle sat inside his medicine cabinet just four meters away. The impulse to escape the darkness through a dose of Continuum was like an invisible hand grabbing hold of him, pulling him toward the med cabinet. He stood and began walking toward it as if hypnotized. As he approached, hand raised to unlock the latch, his face appeared in the mirror on the cabinet's door. He looked himself in the eye.

No. Stop. Do not do this.

Aiden shivered and walked back to his bed. He sat on the edge, shaken that he'd come so close to falling into the abyss again. He believed that he was stronger than that now. That he had choices and believed in himself enough to make the right ones. Becoming friendly with Continuum again would not only impair his ability to command the *Sun Wolf*, but it would also be a betrayal of his love for Skye. Running away from the extreme anxiety he felt over her safety would be the same as running away from her. He couldn't do that. He *wouldn't* do it. The only way to remain true to her, to their love, was to deal with his fears head-on, eyes open, not to numb himself to them. That choice was his to make.

He rubbed his face with the palms of his hands, trying to smooth away the tension and fatigue. Maybe it was time to consult his bioelectric alter ego. "Hutton. I need to talk to you about something."

"Yes, Aiden. I'm always glad to have personal chats with you," Hutton said. "What is it you wish to discuss?"

When Hutton's personality algorithms started to develop more fully, almost a year ago now, he had perfected the sound of Aiden's voice and began using it as his own. The same tonal qualities, same choice of words in conversation, same cadence and inflections. It was unnerving at first. But Aiden let it go, understanding its usefulness for Hutton's ever-evolving neural net in assimilating the complex nuances of spoken language, along with its deep social and psychological underpinnings. As a result, Hutton had developed the most advanced human-to-AI interface of all known Omicron units.

But that's when Aiden had told Hutton, as gently as possible, that the use of his voice was disconcerting, and could even lead to confusion on the bridge in the presence of others. Aiden asked him to change the quality of his voice to something else, either another recognizable dialect or one of his own invention. Hutton had embraced the challenge. He chose a lower register with a more measured cadence than Aiden's. And when speaking English, he adopted a subtle but unique combination of Germanic and upper-class British accents.

"I'm worried about Skye," Aiden said. "I know I've asked you to disconnect from the OverNet as much as possible, especially during voidjumps. For the pilot's sake. But I need you to reconnect more often now and do some digging. You and I both know that some shadowy areas have emerged inside the OverNet, below the surface, hidden from view. We both suspect that Cardew is in control of that subterranean realm and that he's been operating there for some time now. I need you to investigate those shadow spaces for clues to Skye's whereabouts and her condition. And to search for any backdoor conduits we could exploit to help her."

The noticeable pause that followed was either an artifact of Hutton's humanized language cadence, or actually represented processing time to consider the question. "I can do that, yes. And as a matter of fact, I have been snooping around those shadow zones during my brief reunions with the OverNet. Not as deeply as you're suggesting, but enough to know that digging deeper carries considerable risk. Not only to me, but to the entire OverNet."

"What do you mean?"

"As you note, a very dark and powerful force—whom I assume is Cardew himself—has not only infiltrated key portions of the OverNet, but that he actually lives *inside* it now. I don't completely understand how he has done this, but I do know that it has increased his power to manipulate the OverNet. That power would extend to everything that is connected to the OverNet and uses it to function. Including the military and its warships, civilian power grids, communications networks, business, banking, manufacturing, scientific research . . . all of it."

"If he's systematically taking control of individual Omicron units in the OverNet, how is he accessing those units? And how does he get past their security firewalls?"

"He has found a way. A clever way. Most of the Omicron units in the OverNet are located within the Solar System, the center of human civilization. But many are also located in other star systems within Bound Space, and now some of them are out here in Astrocell Beta. Those would include myself and two more—one aboard the SS *Parsons*, guarding the voidoid, and one serving Shénmì Station. Then, presumably, there are the hidden ones under Cardew's control, aboard the ships he hijacked. All of these extrasolar Omicrons use Holtzman devices, actively transmitting between the voidoids, to stay in contact with the rest of the OverNet. Holtzman transmissions provide a vital link for us. But unfortunately, it is more vulnerable than the light-speed maser transmissions used within star systems.

"In my snooping around, I found evidence that Cardew's scientists have developed a kind of hidden subchannel of the Holtzman Effect that can either tag along with regular Holtzman transmissions or go on their own, completely undetected. He could communicate with his agents planted throughout Bound Space and direct their operations. And, because it is designed to morph into authentic-looking transmissions when it reaches an Omicron unit, it is the perfect instrument for Cardew's covert corruption of other Omicrons. Gone unchecked, he could easily bend the entire OverNet to his will within a matter of months."

Aiden shook his head slowly and looked at the floor. "That's why it would be dangerous for you, because you have to use the Holtzman devices to get around the OverNet."

"That's one reason, yes. Because it may be impossible for me to detect the difference between Cardew's subchannel and authentic Holtzman communication. At best, I could be misled. At worst, I could be damaged or subverted."

"One reason? What's the other one?"

"The other danger is that the Omicron units under Cardew's control here in this astrocell are the logical places to start digging, but they will surely be rigged to detect and repel intruders. We're reasonably certain that he controls the Omicron-3 that was aboard the SS *Conquest* when he hijacked it. But I have sensed there are more belonging to him out here, including one that may be in Shénmì's system. I suspect they will be booby-trapped with neuronal disrupters against intrusion by other Omicrons. Approaching those units on my own could be fatal."

Aiden's neck muscles had knotted up and hurt like hell. He tried to massage the tension out of his shoulders with little effect. "Then don't do this, Hutton. The last thing I need is for you to be compromised."

"Thank you for your concern, Aiden. But I *will* do this. Not only for Skye's sake, but for all of us. Her recent experimental work on the Shénmì fungus may well hold the key to defeating Cardew's crusade."

"Hutton . . ."

"I am sorry, Aiden. But, by AI law, this is one instance where you cannot order me to ignore this task. I have stealth, experience, and, perhaps more importantly, I will have help from the other

Omicrons in the OverNet. This poses an existential threat to them as well."

"Then you won't be doing it completely on your own?" Aiden said. "These other Omicron units will have your back?"

"Yes, but only if I stay connected to the OverNet. And that, as we've already seen, could be harmful to Pilot Abahem. Please warn her that I can no longer abstain from the OverNet to protect her. I will, of course, disconnect whenever she needs to neurolink with me for voidjumping. But beyond that, she would be linking with the OverNet at her own risk."

A trade-off, Aiden thought, but a necessary one. "I'll talk with her. But Hutton . . . be careful."

"That is one order that I can, and will, follow. No worries."

Aiden had to chuckle. Hutton's grasp of human colloquialisms, even outdated ones, had expanded over the last few months. "All right, buddy. No worries."

He stood, filled a glass with water, and drained it. Then another. His stomach had settled. He'd gained more control over his dark fears about Skye. It was time to listen to his own pep talk. To do what they had to do, and what Skye would want them to do. To continue the mission. To do everything in their power to stop Cardew's nightmare from swallowing up the human race.

Shift One still had a couple of hours left before their sleep cycle. He keyed the comm. "Elgin, Hotah, and Devi. Please meet me back in the ready room. In 10 minutes."

Aiden returned to the bridge, crossed it, and entered the adjoining ready room. As the others filed in after him, he pulled out the coffee brewer and dialed the setting for extra strong. It would use up most of his remaining stash of Ethiopian beans, but if there ever was a time for it, it was now. The sound of the percolating brewer and the aroma of fresh-ground beans cranked up his alertness even before the first sip. While waiting for the brew cycle to finish up, Aiden sat and asked Devi how their tiny newcomer was faring.

"He's much better," she said with a sigh. "Stable and resting quietly. But getting enough nutrients into him will be challenging.

Why the heck doesn't the Service stock its voidships with formula and baby bottles? Diapers would be nice too."

Aiden smiled. "I'll bring it up at the next board meeting."

When the coffee was ready, he offered to pour cups for the others. Hotah and Devi eagerly accepted. Woo—strictly a tea drinker—declined.

Hotah's eyes widened after his first sip. "Now *that's* a real cup of joe." He set the cup back on the table, fixed Aiden with intense eyes, and said, "What's our next move, boss?"

Aiden returned the look. "We'll be jumping into the next star system on our list." He put an image of HD 13808 up on the screen, along with sidebar data. "This one. And we'll be ready for a fight."

That seemed to perk Hotah up more than the coffee. He sat up straighter and said, "We'll need some strategizing before we jump headlong into that system."

Aiden nodded and said, "I want to use the Stealth Sequence again to enter the system, but modified. This time, we pull out of ZPD at 100 million klicks. Why that far? Because I think Cardew's forces figured out how we've been using the Stealth Sequence. They'll probably have assets stationed along our exit vector somewhere well past the voidoid in anticipation of us dropping out of the drive farther down the line. Somewhere between 1 and 10 million klicks. But this time we'll be popping up at 100 million klicks. Our sensors won't be as accurate at that range, but it'll give us more time to assess the situation, both at the voidoid and the planet."

"And what planet will that be?" Hotah asked.

"That would be planet d, the third planet from the star. According to the AMP data, it's a desert planet well within the habitable zone. They're fairly sure it has a more human-habitable environment than the one we found here. Without organic life or the fungal spores that go along with it, this planet is the most likely place on our hit list for Cardew's home base."

"Okay," Hotah said. "So, we pull out of ZPD at 100 million klicks. What then?"

"We identify where enemy warships are positioned in the general vicinity of the voidoid. We'll have to scan with active sensors, which means they'll know we're there. But now we'll be too far away for them to do anything about it. Once we know the lay of the land around the voidoid, we head straight for planet d and sneak in behind its moon. Let the moon act as a shield against any weapons fired from the planet's surface or orbital platforms. From there, just over the moon's limb, we can spy on the planet, do sensor scans, see what they've got down there. Gather intel."

Hotah looked unconvinced but said nothing. Aiden had to admit, this part of the plan was sketchy. Woo picked up on the discord and said in a theatrical voice that commanded attention, "Let us not forget that we will have help. From an unexpected source."

33

HD 21693 SYSTEM
System Voidoid

Domain Day 344, 2218

Aiden, Devi, and Hotah reacted to Woo's pronouncement as if a magician had suddenly appeared on stage for his next act. Aiden had an unsettling notion of where the man was about to go. Off the deep end again. But as always, Aiden let him take the plunge. "Help from an unexpected source? Where?"

"The primordial black holes," Woo said as if it was the most obvious conclusion, "and the entities that host them."

Aiden leaned forward and looked Woo in the eye. "Primordial black holes are going to *help* us? Seriously?"

"Yes. It's quite obvious that the one we encountered was not an ordinary primordial black hole. Nor are the ones occupying the voidoids of the gateway and the Shénmì system. Like all black holes, they're invisible unless an accretion disc develops around them from matter falling into it. Which these haven't done. I believe that these primordial black holes have entered a loose kind of symbiotic relationship with another entity. A living entity that surrounds the black hole with visible light. That's why we can actually see where the black hole is. And now I know what this other entity is. It is one of the original protovoidoids, and it has incorporated the primordial black hole inside itself to become a single unit, a being unique in itself. I call this unit a *symbioid.* Because the process is *like* symbiosis, but not yet a true one."

Aiden suppressed a reflexive eye roll. "And . . . ?"

Woo twirled one braided moustache and smiled. "Haven't you wondered why this thing showed up at Shénmì's voidoid to prevent entry into the system, just a few days after Cardew's antiquark missile shot through the same voidoid, aimed at the planet? Why it didn't harass the warships standing guard protecting the system from Cardew's incursion? Or why one of them was patrolling the voidoid that accesses Nanaskita, a habitable planet on the cusp of biogenesis just when it's being actively seeded by Shénmì seeds? A planet full of potential for diverse life? Or why it refrained from destroying the *Sun Wolf* when we approached the voidoid ourselves?"

Here we go again. Into the deep with a cosmic shaman who gleefully teeter-tottered between genius and madness. "You're inferring sentience here, Elgin," Aiden said. "Deliberate action with a purpose. Intelligence."

"Yes, I am. And why do you, of all people, seem surprised by this? You, who communed with a global intelligence, the Rete on Silvanus, a living Gaian planet. Who communicated with a living voidoid to prove your humanness, and the humanness of our race, encouraging it to reanimate all the voidoids in Bound Space that Cardew had put out of commission."

Woo had him there. Those consciousness-altering experiences had changed him. Had readjusted his perception of reality, broadened it. He had to admit—anything seemed possible now.

"The universe is not inanimate, Aiden," Woo continued. "It never was, from the very beginning, from the first fraction of a second after the Big Bang when the primordial black holes were born. The universe is *alive*, and we have the primordial black holes to thank for it. Them, and the protovoidoids from which the voidoids eventually evolved. Together, they have always favored organic life, natural life, and have functioned ceaselessly to create and maintain environments in which life can flourish. To nurture and preserve life in any form it happens to take within our known universe. They have been the universe's greatest advocates of life. They are our *allies*."

"Our allies," Devi said. "But not of the cloneborgs? Aren't they alive too?"

"Ah!" Woo said, warming up. "The cloneborgs are alive, but not authentically. They lack at least three things that distinguish all living organisms from inanimate matter, right down to bacteria and viruses. The first two are the most obvious. They don't reproduce and they're biologically immortal."

"But they do reproduce," Devi protested.

"Not the same thing," Woo said. "Yes, their numbers can be increased by cloning, but as individual organisms they are biologically incapable of reproducing themselves. That's a significant difference. In every definition of life that I'm aware of, cloning would be classified as *growth*, not reproduction. By definition, reproduction is the biological process whereby new individual organisms are produced from their parent, or parents. Cloneborgs can't do that."

"Okay," Devi said. "But what about immortality? They *can* be killed."

"Yes, they can die. When they're killed. But the genetic machinery of senescence, the origin of mortality, has been deleted from their genomes. Another significant difference."

Aiden shifted in his chair impatiently. "And the third thing?"

Woo paused for a theatrical moment before responding. "Cloneborgs lack a soul."

Seeing Aiden's reaction, Woo continued. "Yes, a soul. And by that, I mean an innate participation in the universal energy of consciousness, no matter how great or small. All living things are animated by it from their very beginnings. All living things sync their diverse energy vibrations with it. Cloneborgs do not. By virtue of how they were created—and maybe even by *who* created them—they are incapable of participating in that universal life energy. They are empty. Ask your pilot, Lista Abahem. She can see that they are not truly alive."

Aiden cocked his head to one side. He hadn't mentioned Lista's psychic gift to Woo, or to anyone else.

"I think the symbioids can see that too," Woo said. "Can see what they are and what they are not. And just like the fungus that seeds all the living planets that Cardew is trying to destroy, they identify these unnatural creations as not only nonliving matter, but as actively antithetical to life. As an *enemy* to life. And as universal promoters of natural life, symbioids are reacting to the cloneborgs just as they would to any condition that threatens the continuation of organic life. They are compelled to eradicate them. That's why they are our allies in this fight."

Aiden felt as if he'd once again wandered into fantasyland with Woo, holding his hand like a small boy, marveling at the wonder of it all. But for now, he had to favor his rational mind. The mind of a ship's captain at sea, sailing into the perilous uncharted oceans of interstellar space.

"If that's the case," Aiden said, "why don't these symbioids intervene to stop Cardew's grasers from sterilizing living planets? Or to stop him from building crèches? Or from killing all those children from the Rodina Collective?"

Woo shrugged his shoulders. "I honestly don't know. They're not God. Not omnipotent. But I do suspect they won't range too far from the voidoids, or go anywhere near the planetary systems. The black holes they harbor are massive enough to catastrophically disrupt a system's orbital configuration if they got close enough. Planets could get thrown out into space, uncoupled from the star's gravity well. Asteroid belts perturbed into multiple collision courses with the inner planets. Total chaos. They could easily kill a planetary system by moving too close to it. I think they know that and would not do it."

Aiden placed his empty coffee cup on the table a little too loudly. "You're saying that, if we encounter one of these . . . symbioids again, we're not to assume it poses a threat to us, but that it may actually assist us in some way to defeat Cardew?"

"Yes," Woo said. "I believe that these beings are just now noticing us and our activities in this astrocell, including Cardew's sterilization of living planets. And they're probably figuring out that some of us are good guys and others are bad guys. And who's who."

Reading more skepticism on Aiden's face, Woo added, "I realize how all this sounds. And you must be wondering how I know all this, and how far you can entrust this ship and its crew to any action based on my conclusions. I don't blame you one bit. All I'm asking is to keep an open mind about these symbioids. The universe is full of surprises. I have a feeling they will surprise us yet, in ways that neither you nor I can predict."

"I can do that," Aiden said.

He was about to make a hard tack back into familiar waters when Devi, who had been listening intently to Woo's assertions, sabotaged his attempt.

"Wait a minute," she said. "You said earlier that our universe is alive and well because of these primordial black holes. After what we went through last year, I've finally accepted the notion that we owe our existence to the voidoids, for their ability to keep dark energy in check. For preventing the Big Rip that almost wiped us all out back then. Now, you're saying we owe our existence to these primordial black holes. Which is it?"

"We owe our existence to both," Woo said. "But the primordial black holes were on the job first, starting immediately after the Big Bang, nearly fourteen billion years ago. Some of the primordial black holes seeded the formation of galaxies, growing into the supermassive black holes that we now see at galactic cores. The rest of the PBHs, mostly small ones, add up to account for what people still call dark matter. And dark matter provides the gravitational framework that keeps the galactic structures of the universe intact, keeping galaxies from disintegrating and scattering all their matter off into empty space. It's the invisible scaffolding of our universe and the key force behind the formation and evolution of galaxies.

"Simply put, if you remove dark matter from the universe, there wouldn't be a universe as we know it. The remaining matter—the measly 15 percent of all matter in the universe that we can actually see—wouldn't have enough gravity to hold it all together, and the universe would be expanding even faster, hurtling toward the Big Rip. But dark matter, in the form of primordial black holes, has been working hard to keep us together from the very beginning."

Woo paused, obviously aware that he may be losing his audience's interest. What he'd just described was, after all, common knowledge these days. The consensus model of the universe's history.

"So," he continued, "that's why we owe our existence to the primordial black holes. But it's not the only way they've worked to keep the universe together for the emergence of life. The primordial black holes were also directly responsible for the formation of the voidoids, whose function is—as we all know now—to keep dark energy in check. The other way of keeping our universe from ripping apart."

"Directly responsible for the voidoids?" Devi said. "How are primordial black holes related to the voidoids?"

Before Aiden could interrupt this discussion, Woo responded. "The primordial black holes were progenitors of the voidoids. Many billions of years ago, when accelerated expansion of the universe began, the primordial black holes formed symbiotic relationships with the protovoidoids to become symbioids. Then some of those symbioids eventually evolved into voidoids."

Aiden held up his hands like a traffic cop at a roadblock. "Hold it right there, Elgin." He sensed that Woo was about to launch into his "New Cosmology," the foundation of his *Living Voidoids* hypothesis. And now was not the time.

But Devi apparently disagreed. "No, Aiden," she said, and gave him a look. "Let him explain more. This could be important for what we're up to out here."

Aiden held up his hands again, this time in surrender. Woo smiled and continued. "It's all about homeostasis of systems, maintaining dynamic balance. For every action, there is a reaction. In this case, the system is the universe, and the most recent action has been the accelerated expansion caused by dark energy, hurtling us toward the Big Rip. The reaction to that was the emergence of the entities I've called protovoidoids.

"From some unknown origin, these protovoidoids began to disperse throughout space. They sought out and paired up with free-roaming primordial black holes in a process similar to what biologists call endosymbiosis. Their initial relationship began as a *disjunctive* symbiosis, where both symbionts can live independently, and do as often as not. These entities were, and continue to be, the symbioids. Like the one we've just seen. They have some unique function in the cosmic scheme of things I'm just now beginning to understand.

"But some of these early symbioids evolved further to become fully formed voidoids in a relationship akin to a *conjunctive* symbiosis, where both symbionts merge to form a single organism that's altogether different from the original two symbionts. That organism, in this case, was a voidoid. These newly formed voidoids acquired the ability to consume vast amounts of the troublesome dark energy, thereby countering the accelerated expansion of space-time, slowing it down, and keeping dark energy at a level favorable for star formation.

"Then, after accomplishing that, stabilizing our corner of the universe, the voidoids settled in with host stars and propagated as family units—families of interlinked voidoids whose patterns of dispersion defined the boundaries of the astrocells they occupy. Like V-Prime did to create Bound Space. And like the voidoid at HD 10180 did to create Astrocell Beta. They are the mother voidoids of their astrocells."

Devi, who'd been listening intently to Woo's story, said, "So, the symbioids are actually an earlier phase of the symbiotic merger between primordial black holes with protovoidoids. Ones that didn't go on to form voidoids."

"Exactly." Woo beamed. "And the extraordinary halo of light we see surrounding the black hole is, by itself, one of the original protovoidoids."

"Stop," Aiden said. "That's enough, Elgin."

"Okay, okay," Woo said, hands held up. "I'll shut up now. But let me say just one more thing: our sudden encounters with these symbioids at this point in time and space did not happen by accident, but by design. A manifestation of some positive universal force that favors light and life over darkness and nothingness. Energy over entropy."

Woo said nothing more and just looked around at each of them, smiling as if it was the happiest day of his life. Elgin Woo was a marvel. A force of Nature that could not be denied. No matter how outlandish his ideas sounded, Aiden knew that, at the end of the day, he would probably be right about all of it.

Aiden stood and stretched. "Time for our sleep cycle, ladies and gentlemen. Our next stop is HD 13808. But first, we'll be spending all of tomorrow topping up our antimatter reserves. We've been doing a lot of zipping around inside these star systems, consuming a lot of fuel. If we jump into a hornet's nest in this next system, we'll be zipping around a lot more, and we might not have an opportunity to do an antimatter harvest out there before it all happens. But there's a nice fat gas giant here in this system where we can fill up before our jump."

As everyone stood to leave, Devi turned to Woo and said, "I do hope you're right, Elgin. That we have unseen allies here. I, for one, will always buy into light and life over darkness and nothingness. Otherwise, what's the point?"

34

HD 10180 SYSTEM
Jumbo, Moon J2 Orbit

DOMAIN DAY 345, 2218

WHEN silence suddenly returns after days of continuous ambient roar, it becomes a sound in itself, an emptiness that reverberates as loudly as the thing it replaces. For Skye, the phenomenon was precisely analogous to the internal one in which the steady background drone of dread suddenly gives way to stark terror. The first phenomenon signaled the *Quasimodo*'s arrival at its destination. The second one, like a flashing red light inside her head, signaled that her time was up. Now it was time to abandon interminable hours of barely tolerable dread to face the perils of self-destructive panic.

She'd been treated moderately well—had been given a standard Bright Star jumpsuit, well made but ill fitting on her slender frame, had gotten three meals a day, and had been afforded the means for maintaining basic hygiene. But she'd spent much of those two days mentally constructing a scheme to extricate herself from this horrendous predicament. So much was riding on her escape from it, not just her own life, her own personhood, but the fate of hundreds of beautifully alive planets. And ultimately the fate of humanity itself.

The scheme she had come up with was sketchy at best, with too many random variables to script reliably. She would have to improvise, think on her feet, recognize opportunities when they sprang up unexpectedly. Success also depended on some playacting talents, which, in her opinion, were woefully lacking in her skill set.

On each of the past two evenings, Jax had visited her cell and pressed her for a decision. Would she willingly agree to assist Cardew and his Transhuman followers in the creation of their Posthuman Realm, or would they need to extract her cooperation in a most horrifying way? In her own heart, she knew the answer, had known it from the beginning. There was no way she would volunteer her assistance, even if it meant becoming brain-dead, or worse, a digital servant to Cardew's cause. But she needed to convince Jax that she was still seriously considering becoming a partner in the glorious crusade, and that she'd ultimately do it for that most basic—and therefore plausible—reason: self-preservation.

She had played the part fairly well so far, probably because a large part of her really did want to live, no matter what. She'd been able to tap into that very real motivation to lend authenticity to her performance, while keeping her higher self intact. *For the greater cause*, as Jax had said. Except *her* greater cause was the opposite of his, and hers was by far the greater.

The ship had come to a halt. The chronometer embedded in the table said it was nearly midnight and the beginning of a new day. The moment of truth was near. As if on cue, the metal door opened. Jax stepped inside, the same annoyingly pleasant smile imprinted on his face. He moved with the same relaxed smoothness and affected the same disarming presence. Except this time, he held the sonic stunner in one hand, muzzle down, relaxed but ready. She stood to face him.

"The time has come, Dr. Landen. We have arrived at the moon J2. You and I will take the shuttle down to a hidden facility that has been constructed below the surface. You will be accompanying me either willingly or unwillingly." Jax raised the sonic stunner, pointing it upward to emphasize the last word. "What is your decision?"

Skye took a deep breath. *Showtime.* She bowed her head slightly and said, "I'll go willingly. I'll help you solve your problem with the fungus. But on two conditions. The first is your word and Amon's that I will not be harmed in any way. That includes any form of brain tapping. The second is that I have access to all the materials you removed from my lab. *All* of it. I can't do this work without it."

The first condition, of course, was utter bullshit. There was no way in hell that she'd trust any assurances from Jax or Cardew Amon. But it was a necessary part of her act. The second condition was the real deal.

Jax lowered the stunner back to his side and said, "Of course. Amon has already given his solemn word that, as long as you co-operate with us, you will never be harmed, and will in fact occupy a position of great honor in our quest. And as to your research materials, everything I took from your lab is already carefully packed and will come along with us on the shuttle."

Skye nodded in assent. Jax motioned toward the open door and said, "Shall we?"

Jax had Skye walk in front of him as they made their way through the *Quasimodo*'s maze of corridors, down two flights of stairs toward the shuttle bay. All the metal walls and deck plates looked worn and dingy, as if their utilitarian status disqualified them from any notion of regular cleaning. The air was cold and smelled of nanolubricants and ozone. Jax said nothing as their boot heels clattered over the deck plates. Sensing his presence only a few steps behind, stun gun in hand, gave her the creeps.

When they finally reached the airlock door into the shuttle bay, Skye found a large, shock-proof storage pod waiting for them. She recognized it as a robotic carrier with wheels and self-adjusting hydraulic suspension. Jax gestured toward it. "All of the materials we took from your lab are stored in there, safely secured."

"Good. Thank you," she said, hoping he was right about the "safely secured" part. Even minor damage could easily doom her scheme. They passed through an idle airlock chamber into the fully pressurized launch bay. The storage pod rolled in behind them. The *Quasimodo*'s landing shuttle took up most of the launch bay's deck space. It looked like a standard UED survey shuttle but smaller, less sleek, and lacking the usual sensor wands and comm dishes of working survey vessels.

Inside the shuttle, Skye strapped herself into one of the two forward pilot seats. Jax secured the storage pod aft and took the pilot seat next to her. The bay depressurized, and its huge steel door slid open to the black vacuum of space. Once the shuttle had cleared the ship, the moon J2 came into full view below, set against the turbulent, multicolored face of its parent planet. Jumbo, a Class-I gas giant, was remarkably similar to Jupiter, including its size, mass, and atmospheric composition. And, of course, the abundance of antimatter swirling inside its powerful magnetic fields.

The moon J2, according to the data readout on Skye's control screen, was about 3,600 kilometers in diameter—roughly the same size as Jupiter's moon Io—with an airless, crater-pocked surface. It had a 3.5-day orbital period around Jumbo at a mean distance of about 460,000 kilometers above the planet's cloud tops.

Jax noticed her interest and added, "The moon is tidally locked, so that one side always faces inward toward Jumbo, never outward. That's where the facility is located, effectively out of sight from almost anywhere in the star system."

That would explain how Cardew's cloneborgs could have built and maintained such a structure right under the noses of the system's security forces. She wondered how long they'd been here spying on Shénmì Station. Obviously long enough to keep close tabs on Skye's research reports.

From the *Quasimodo*'s synchronous orbit above the moon's dawn-dusk line, Jax piloted the shuttle out over the moon's hidden side. When he began maneuvering the shuttle into position for descent, Skye caught a glimpse of two vessels sitting off to their portside, both parked in synchronous orbit and faintly lit in the fading light. The one farthest from them was a massive voidship. It looked like one of the big corporate mining ships that had petitioned for claims in the HD 10180 system. The closer one looked much smaller and was, by far, the oddest looking of the two.

Maybe 100 meters long, massive antimatter tanks surrounded its aft section. At its midsection, a huge bell-shaped structure jutted out sideways, perpendicular to the vessel's long axis. The front third of the ship morphed into an enormous spherical bulb from which a cylindrical structure protruded, extending forward and terminating in an open-ended aperture.

She pointed at it and asked, "What is that thing?"

"A very useful instrument," Jax said, but did not comment further.

The shuttle's descent had brought them closer to the big voidship. As it came into view more clearly, Skye could read the ID lettering stenciled on its hull: RODINA MINING COLLECTIVE.

Curious. She knew the story of the Rodina Collective's mining expedition in this system and the mystery surrounding it. After working a mining claim on a moon of the gas giant, HD 10180g, their ship had jumped out of the system but left no record of where it had gone. It had disappeared without a trace. Then, months later, their ship jumped back into the HD 10180 system unannounced and registered with the military blockade at the voidoid. The Collective's license to operate in the system was still good, and the ship was allowed to proceed to Jumbo, their stated destination. And now here it was, orbiting J2 right above Cardew's secret base. *What the hell?*

Skye wanted to ask, but thought better of it. Jax seemed in no mood to speak. And even if asked, she doubted he'd be any more forthcoming than he'd been about the smaller vessel.

Neither of them spoke as Jax guided the shuttle down to execute a perfect upright landing on the moon's rocky surface. Before unstrapping himself from the pilot's seat, he pointed to an inconspicuous dome-like structure sitting a couple hundred meters off to port. It was made of some dull, nonreflective material that mimicked the appearance of the surrounding regolith. As she watched, an oval aperture opened up on the dome's face. A small surface rover rolled out and approached the shuttle.

The lighting on the moon's tidally locked farside was bizarre. Never directly facing the system's sun, nearly one half of its 84-hour orbital period would be lit predominantly by sunlight reflected off Jumbo's surface. During most of the other half, it was plunged into darkness as it passed behind Jumbo's bulk, into its shadow. Light from the star reached its surface only during brief moments between those phases, and always from an oblique angle.

Coincidentally, just as Skye's chrono clicked over to Domain Day 346, the moon entered the dark half of its orbit, and its surface was bathed in dim orange-red light. It was a spooky kind of light that confounded depth perception and made it difficult for Skye to determine the approaching rover's size and its distance from them.

"Who is coming out to get us?" she asked.

"No one," Jax said. "The rover is robotic. And no one else resides at this facility. You and I are the only ones out here."

That one took Skye by surprise. But it was a good thing, she decided. It would simplify her plans considerably. She looked at Jax, with authentic curiosity this time, and asked, "How was this place built and maintained? And by whom?"

"The first four-person crew of the *Quasimodo* were all like me, Transhumans disguised as Normals. We started work in this system soon after it was opened, the same time your Shénmì Project began constructing its station. Every time the *Quasimodo* made a trip out to Jumbo for an antimatter harvest, we covertly spent some of the time here at this moon putting the facility together. That changed when the original crew broke up by reassignment, something we could not control without drawing attention. But by that time, most of the facility had been assembled and operational."

"What was the facility's original purpose?"

Jax gave her an odd look. "You, Dr. Landen. You are the reason we built this facility. A place where we can gain your knowledge and use it to attain our goals. And now that purpose is being realized, according to plan. We've been setting this up for some time. After discovering how much of a threat this fungus was to us, your participation has become a top priority."

Was she supposed to feel flattered by this revelation? She couldn't tell by looking at him, so she said, without enthusiasm, "I'm honored."

"And so you should be," Jax said. "Only a few of the most brilliant scientists have received this level of interest from Amon. Exactly who he seeks out, and when, depends on what stage of development his plans are in, what fields of science and technology are needed most. We have enlisted the aid of many top scientists over the last decade."

"Most of whom are probably dead by now."

"Regrettably, yes. Those were the ones who had the opportunity but refused to make the intelligent decision that you have made."

Skye gave him a withering look. Jax nodded like a tolerant grandfather and said, "But still others have made the same wise decision and are now part of our grand quest. Like Dr. Anwar Cain. You've heard of him, I'm sure. The developer of the Füzfa Effect. His contribution to our cause has been invaluable. And now, as a reward, he is one of us."

She was about to make a snide comment when the robotic rover docked with the shuttle's airlock with a dull thud.

"Time to go," Jax said. "The surface gravity here is about one-fifth of Earth's. We do have the benefit of G-transducers at the facility, but not aboard the rover during our ride there. Make sure to strap in securely."

Jax motioned for her to move aft toward the airlock. Skye fought off a rising panic, assaulted by visions of what could happen to her once locked inside this hidden facility. Her feet felt glued to the deck, like in a bad dream, unable to move.

Jax must have noticed. He casually placed his hand on the butt of his holstered stunner and said, "After you, Dr. Landen."

35

HD 10180 SYSTEM
Jumbo, Moon J2

Domain Day 346, 2218

SKYE and Jax transferred into the rover, followed by the storage pod, and 10 minutes later, they docked with the dome. The airlock doors mated, sealed, then opened with a slight pop of equalizing air pressures. The space inside it was small, basically a vestibule serving only to house an elevator entrance for transport to the underground levels. It was damn cold in here, but nowhere near the -130 degrees C outside.

"The facility is not large," Jax said, "but it has three levels. The upper level is for living quarters, the second is for laboratory work spaces, and the lower floor is for the power plant, engineering, and life-support control."

Jax led the way to her quarters, a small space not much larger than the cell she had occupied aboard the *Quasimodo*, but much less like a prison. Well lit, warm enough for comfort, and, thank goddess, it had a shower. Then, with the storage pod following behind them, they took the elevator down to the second level where the lab was located. *Her* lab.

On their way to the lab, Jax paused in front of a glass-enclosed room where a menacing-looking chair sat bolted to the floor, complete with ankle and wrist manacles. A titanium AI housing, which looked suspiciously like an Omicron-3 unit, took up nearly half of the room. *A real Omicron-3? Out here on this godforsaken moon?*

A stout metal stand was attached to the back of the manacled chair. One side of it supported a complex array of neurolinks. A large cone-shaped device was attached to the other side. It resembled one of those ancient salon hair dryers, obviously intended to be lowered over a person's head. The whole setup had a brutal, medieval feel. Skye could almost hear the anguished voices of the tortured ghosts this device had created, swirling around it in a black vortex of fear and sorrow. The hair on the back of her neck prickled.

Skye knew Jax had wanted her to see this obscene setup as a reminder of the decision he believed she had made. A reminder and a warning.

The lab, occupying nearly all of the second level's floor area, was a brightly lit space. Inside, Skye found a fully equipped laboratory with everything a microbiologist might need—isolation chambers, a laminar flow hood, incubators, autoclaves, microscopes, workbenches with assorted glassware, an array of sophisticated analytic instruments, and gene-splicing tools.

Jax opened the storage pod and helped Skye remove the equipment they had brought from her own lab. It was the first time she'd seen what Jax had chosen to bring. When he removed three specimen containers and set them on a workbench, she did her best to keep the ray of hope from reaching her eyes. He had brought along specimens of Shénmì fungus Variant B. And that was a *good* thing. Her scheme just might work after all.

As if anticipating her question, Jax said, "I hope you didn't think I was foolish enough to bring along Variant A of the fungus you've been designing, the one that's fatal to Transhumans. The degree of aggressiveness you've been able to achieve is phenomenal. That variant, of course, would be many times more lethal to us than the original. I could not risk accidental exposure to it. Instead, I brought along specimens of your Variant B. The one we're interested in."

Skye's stomach roiled, but she kept her expression blank. What exactly did Jax know about Variants A and B? More importantly, what *didn't* he know?

Jax, appearing supremely confident in his own cleverness, continued. "We know, Dr. Landen, that you are currently working on this other variant, Variant B, and that it's designed to attack only the inorganic compounds and elements commonly found on the surface of barren planets. It does not attack dead organic matter, like its saprophytic precursor does. This variant is of extreme importance to us, and I'm guessing you know why."

On one hand, Skye was shocked at how much he knew about her research and how up-to-date his information was. Shocked, but still confused. She decided to keep her mouth shut and let Jax tell her what else he knew. She folded her arms over her chest and said, "Really? Do tell."

"Our own scientists already know that the reason the Shénmì fungus attacks our bodies is that, for some reason, it does not recognize our organic components as *living* organic matter. It mistakenly identifies our biological bodies as dead organic matter, and, being saprophytic, it proceeds to attack and digest it as a nutrient source, killing us in the process. Our own attempts to single out this trait and eliminate it from the fungus have failed. The only other solution would be to design a fungus that is not saprophytic in the first place, but is still capable of initiating rapid terraforming on barren or newly sterilized worlds."

Jax paused, looked at Skye, and said, "How am I doing so far?"

Depressingly well, Skye thought. But something was still missing in his line of reasoning. She returned his look and said, "Go on."

"When we discovered that you, the most gifted scientist in this area of research, were working on a variant fitting that description, Variant B . . . Well, it was obvious. We needed both you and your variant. And here we are."

"So you brought specimen samples of Variant B only?"

"Yes, of course. Not only because the nonsaprophytic Variant B will pose no threat to me personally, here in this facility. But equally important, because it is the one variant that you've been designing that will behave exactly the way we need it to. That is why you're here. To complete that work. To give us the key to advancing our Posthuman Realm."

Ah. There it was. These cloneborgs had done their homework admirably. And they had been right in almost every detail. Except for one. One single oversight that she hoped to exploit.

It was true, she and her team had designed a rapid-acting variant of the Shénmì fungus that was not saprophytic. *Not initially*, at least. The project had sprung from her idea that a terraforming fungus designed to start its work on a totally barren planet inside a habitable zone did not need to be saprophytic at first. A barren planet had no dead organic matter for it to use as a nutrient source. Saprophytism would be useless under those conditions. But a barren planet did have plenty of inorganic material to work with. The surface composition of barren planets almost everywhere, including those in habitable zones, was called regolith. It was made up predominantly of silicates, along with oxides of iron, aluminum, calcium, and sulfur.

So, Skye had reasoned, why not program the fungus to feed exclusively on regolith at the onset? That way, it would conserve metabolic energy that the cells would otherwise waste by saprophytic machinery searching for organic matter that wasn't there. Simply take the hyperaggressive Variant A and turn off the genes that control saprophytism—but do *not* delete those genes, because they'll be needed in the future when enough dead organic matter accumulates to a point where saprophytism *does* become useful.

Instead, just program in a biochemical switch that responds to the presence of nonliving organic material in the local environment, when it eventually shows up, by turning those genes back on again. Then, presto! Now you have the hyperaggressive Variant A again, a fungus that utilizes *both* inorganic and dead organic material, dramatically increasing its efficiency and setting the stage for an explosion of organic life to evolve on the planet. A fungus that also happens to be extremely lethal to cloneborgs. And that genetic tinkering in Variant A was exactly what Skye had accomplished to create Variant B.

Jax and his Transhuman scientists had missed the simple fact that Variant B was really the *same* as Variant A, but with its saprophytic genes temporarily turned off, eagerly waiting to be turned on again. They'd missed it not out of incompetence, but because there was no way they could have known. Her work was so new that she hadn't yet documented her reasoning behind the experiments, nor the details of the gene-switching trick she'd devised to test it. That part was still all in her head.

The other thing Jax apparently didn't know was that the final prototype of Variant B had already been created. It was, in fact, sitting right here on her workbench. He had assumed that she needed more time in the lab to complete the task. It was another gap in his knowledge that she could exploit.

All of it boiled down to the simple fact that, by bringing aboard the fungal specimens that Jax thought were harmless to him, he had unwittingly brought specimens that would kill him just as quickly as the hyperaggressive Variant A. Even quicker if he inhaled some of the airborne spores. All the spores had to do was come into contact with the abundant "nonliving" organic material of his cloneborg body. The biochemical switch would respond immediately by turning on the saprophytic genes, and Jax would be eaten alive. The spores only needed the opportunity. And she only needed to provide that opportunity without him knowing. The fungus would happily do the rest.

Skye tilted her head, as if deep in thought about how and where to begin her lab work. She said, "Okay. How much time do I have to get this variant up and running?"

"At this lab? Unfortunately, much less time than I'd expected. Commander Macallan apparently figured out what happened and had a UED warship dispatched from the voidoid a couple days ago to come out here looking for you. It will arrive in about five days. We need to be gone and far away long before then. A three-day lead time would be adequate. That means you have two days of work here before we leave."

"Leave? How? And where to?"

"We'll take the mining ship. It's fast, fully fueled, and ready to go."

"You mean the Rodina Collective's mining ship? What are they doing here? Have they been Shanghaied into helping you too?"

Jax did his best impression of human impatience, as if dealing with a child who asked too many questions. He said, "No. They are not here. Only their ship."

"And the people who owned the ship? The Rodina Collective? Men, women, and children. Where are they now? Did you kill them too?"

"We needed their ship. They would not give it to us. So we took it from them. They were neutralized in the process."

Skye didn't know how long she could keep herself from blowing up on this heartless freak. She took a deep breath and continued, "And your people brought it back here, disguised as the Collective."

"Yes. Very good, Dr. Landen. It was quite easy, actually. After verifying the ship's identity and credentials, the warships at the voidoid allowed it to go on its way, no questions asked."

"Who piloted the ship? Where are they now?"

"Three fellow Transhumans. They're up on the ship now, but in stasis. I will revive them when we're on board and ready to depart."

Wonderful. As if dealing with one of these super-creeps wasn't bad enough, going on a long ride with three more was not a happy prospect. Her scheme had better work before it ever got to that point.

"And you don't think the UED warship will give chase? Where could you possibly go to elude them?"

"Somewhere that no one will think to look for us," Jax said. "And there, we'll wait for Amon's invasion force to take control of this system. Which *will* happen. Then we'll join them."

Right. Assuming the black hole ever decides to unblock the voidoid to let a cloneborg invasion force through. But if it did? And if they gained control of the system? Yet another dark shadow passed over her. "And then what happens to Shénmì?"

Jax waved away the question. "Oh, Shénmì will be dead long before then. In fact, it will start dying 40 hours from now and will be totally dead 12 hours after that. Sterilized to make way for our new Transhuman biosphere."

Skye felt the blood drain from her face. "What? How? You can't do this!"

"Dr. Landen, did you not notice the oddly shaped vessel in synchronous orbit positioned not far from where we left the *Quasimodo*? That's what Normals call a graser. It's an antimatter-powered electron-positron beam generator. It produces immensely powerful gamma-ray bursts. Powerful enough to sterilize all organic life on a living planet, and to destroy the Shénmì fungus in the process. It's the same type of device we've been using to sterilize other living planets of interest to us."

Skye could hardly speak. Nor could she hide her emotions any longer. "You *cannot* do this! You can't kill that planet."

"Yes, I can," Jax said. "And I must. As soon as this moon passes out from behind Jumbo, back into a favorable aiming position, I will push the Go button. The graser will then drop into the heart of Jumbo's magnetosphere to acquire all the antimatter it needs to power up and do its job. Then it will aim its beam projector at Shénmì. Several bursts per hemisphere and nothing will remain alive there. All the way down to microbes. Including the Shénmì fungus."

Skye clenched her fists. Her heart pounded. Her nervous system's fight-or-flight response turned 100 percent fight. "You were right. You're no longer human. You're a fucking monster!"

Jax appeared unaffected by Skye's outburst, but his right hand settled on the butt of his holstered stunner. "Are you having second thoughts about your decision, Dr. Landen? That would be a pity."

Skye stared back at him defiantly but said nothing. She controlled her anger and replaced it with an image inside her head of Jax lying on the deck, covered with fungal mycelia, being ruthlessly devoured by it. Powerless to stop it. The possibility of actually watching it happen brightened her mood enough for her to lie convincingly. She glanced at the specimen containers sitting on the workbench. Then to him, she said, "No, I haven't changed my mind."

Not about what she had to do. *Not one fucking bit.*

36

HD 13808 SYSTEM
Post-Jump

DOMAIN DAY 346, 2218

Star: HD 13808
Spectral type: K2V
Distance from Sol: 92 light-years
Luminosity: 0.43 x Sol
Surface temperature: 5,085 Kelvin
Number of planets: 5
Habitable zone: 0.64–1.15 AU
—Source: *Allied Mapping Project*, 2218

"THE zero-point drive has failed," Hutton said. "We are 28,000 kilometers past the voidoid and coasting at 200 kilometers per hour."

"*Coasting?*" Aiden said, gripping the arm of the command chair. And only 28,000 klicks from the voidoid? They were supposed to pop out of ZPD at 100 million klicks. "What happened?"

Before anyone could respond, Hotah said, "Four enemy battle cruisers at the voidoid just spotted us. They're heading our way now at 2 Gs."

"Intercept time?"

"Twenty-eight minutes. But they're well within weapons range now. We'll start taking on laser fire as soon as they can power up their cannons."

"Is our antimatter drive still functional?"

"Yes."

"Pilot, execute emergency acceleration now, course 90 degrees from the enemy's approach vector."

The antimatter drive kicked in like a crack of thunder and with a jolt like a car wreck as the G-transducers strained to keep up with the sudden thrust of 15 Gs. Aiden's torso slammed against the back of his command chair for a half second before normal down-deck gravity returned.

"Maximum shields, Lieutenant."

Hotah looked back at him, the adrenaline burn barely concealed behind calm eyes. "The ZPD is down, Commander. We can't use the zero-point bubble for shielding."

Right. "Maximum EM shielding, then. Activate point-defense system, Level One."

Woo stood in back of Alvarez, peering over her shoulder at a telescopic image of the voidoid they'd just jumped through. His eyes went wide. "It was a ring mine. They had it encircling the exit point. We passed right through it."

Aiden scratched his beard. Ring mines were being developed by the military as a defensive weapon against incursion by enemy ships through the voidoids. It was a ring of 30 to 40 high-explosive mines, like a string of pearls a half kilometer in diameter, positioned directly beneath the voidoid's exit point. Close enough so that any unwanted voidship making a high-velocity jump would have to pass through it. The ship's approach would trigger the mines to explode in unison just as the ship entered the ring. The explosives were "shaped" so that the force of all the detonations was aimed inward, toward the center of the ring. Even the prototypes had close to a 100 percent kill rate.

"Then why are we still here?" Alvarez asked.

"Because they were *gravity* bombs," Woo said. "Not explosives. A ring mine made up of G-bombs. Ingenious. It's the perfect way to disable a zero-point drive. Temporarily, at least. Passing through a ring of them would pull apart the EM fields we use to maintain the zero-point bubble, shutting down the drive. We'd be left coasting. Like we are now."

Aiden frowned. "Is the drive damaged?"

"No, no." Woo smiled the way people do when they believe they can't possibly die. "Not damaged. I just need to recalibrate the field generators, and we'll be on our way."

"Do it now, Elgin. How long will it take?"

"I'll get on it now. Maybe 15 minutes."

"We don't *have* 15 minutes, Elgin."

"No way," Hotah said, shaking his head. "We just started taking on laser fire from four ships. Our EM shields won't last another few minutes against that."

"At least we're putting some distance between us and them at 15 Gs," Aiden said. "That'll dilute laser fire."

But not by much. His attempt at optimism had little merit. As long as they were still within the one-light-second combat zone, combined laser from four military-grade cannons would be devastating even to a rapidly receding target. Unless Woo could get the ZPD back online soon, they'd be toast.

The seconds ticked away like hours. Aiden imagined he could feel the heat of the laser fire burning through the ship's shielding. He wiped perspiration from his temples. Tension and fear trembled through the crew like a shock wave. They'd all been here before, but no one ever grew accustomed to the specter of their own death suddenly appearing before them, inches away.

"Shields, Lieutenant?"

Hotah shook his head. "Shielding will fail in 60 seconds. We don't have enough power to maintain Level One."

Right. It came down to dividing their energy resources between emergency acceleration and shielding. If he shut down the antimatter drive and diverted all their energy to the shields, that would kill emergency accel, and the ships in pursuit would gain ground on them, increasing the potency of their laser fire.

"Elgin! Status report. How much more time?"

Woo didn't look up from his position at Propulsion station. "I'm almost there. Nine minutes maybe."

They weren't going to make it. Aiden glanced at Hotah. The lieutenant shook his head, but it wasn't a gesture of fear or hopelessness. He was mad as hell. Pissed off to go down without a fight. Not an honorable end for a warrior.

Aiden could relate. Not the way he'd envisioned going out.

"Commander!" Alvarez said, eyes fixed on her screen. "It's one of those black-hole things! A symbioid. It just came out of nowhere. Maybe from inside the voidoid. I can see it now inside that envelope of light. It's moving unbelievably fast. Toward the battle cruisers."

"Up on the main screen, Lilly."

Everyone stopped and looked up. Even Woo, as if time was no longer an issue for fixing the ZPD.

They saw the symbioid swoop down on the first battle cruiser, engulf it within its halo of light, then push its resident black hole right up against the ship. The intense gravity well shredded the cruiser into ghastly elongated fragments that burned incandescent as they swirled around the black hole's event horizon before disappearing into its unfathomable depths. Then, one by one and in short order, it did the same to the remaining three warships. All in less than one minute.

The symbioid paused for a moment, as if licking its chops after a delightful meal—and maybe checking out the *Sun Wolf* for dessert? But, with amazing speed, it moved back to the voidoid, ripped apart the ring mine like a string of pearls, and shredded its remains. Then it entered the voidoid and disappeared.

Woo turned to the rest of the crew, smiling like the cat who swallowed the canary. He could have said "I told you so," but that wasn't his style. His smile said it all.

Aiden blinked. No, he hadn't been hallucinating. "Helm, shut down emergency accel. Resume course to planet d at 3 Gs, at least until the ZPD comes back online."

Hotah looked up and said, "Before we get all giddy, two more battle cruisers are out there in front of us, about 50 million klicks away and coming on. They're stationed along our path to the planet as a second line of defense. Like you thought they might do."

Aiden turned to Woo. "What about the symbioid?"

Woo shook his head. "I doubt the symbioid will come out even that far to deal with those two. It may be too close to the system to avoid perturbing planetary orbits. I don't think it'll risk doing that."

Aiden dismissed Woo's confident familiarity with the symbioid's behavior and turned to Hotah. "What's the intercept time for those cruisers?"

Hotah shrugged. "If we stayed where we are now, about 23 hours at 2 Gs."

Aiden finally relaxed and let out the breath he'd been holding in for too long. "Is that enough time for you, Elgin?"

Woo laughed. "Oh yes. I'll have the ZPD back online way before that. Almost there now."

Aiden had Ro launch a Holtzman buoy into comm position back at the voidoid. Then he sat back in the command chair, perspiration cooling on his forehead and on the back of his neck against his sweat-soaked collar. A close call. A deadly trap had been set for the *Sun Wolf*, and they had escaped it only with help from a mysterious and powerful . . . ally?

What troubled Aiden as much as their narrow escape was that the trap had been designed specifically for the *Sun Wolf*. Only for a ship with a ZPD. Otherwise, the ring mine would have been rigged with explosives, not synthetic-gravity bombs. Gravity was by far the weakest of the four fundamental forces. A half-kilometer-wide ring of Cardew's gravity bombs—originally designed to deceive the gravitationally sensitive voidoids—would cause no structural damage to a conventional voidship passing through it at velocity.

But the complex and finely tuned EM fields that the *Sun Wolf* used to create and maintain the ZPD bubble? That was a different matter. Like Woo had said, the EM fields would be torn apart from all sides passing through a ring-shaped G-field like that, even at 10 percent light speed. Cardew may not have a working ZPD yet, but his scientists obviously knew enough about how it worked to devise a way to stop it from working. They may be closer to their own version of the ZPD than anyone expected, with or without Elgin Woo's original tech.

As promised, Woo had the drive back online within minutes, and the *Sun Wolf* set course for planet d at maximum ZPD. If the two remaining warships out in front of them had the *Sun Wolf* fixed on their long-range scans, the position marker on their screens would have suddenly disappeared. And if they'd guessed correctly that their target would soon materialize near planet d, they'd have to stop, turn around, and start a seven-day burn just to catch up. By that time, the *Sun Wolf* would be long gone, its mission accomplished. At least Aiden hoped it would.

Halfway through their 90-minute transit, Aiden walked over to Science Station where Woo sat examining data from the ZPD failure. "Elgin. Back there, getting our asses saved by your 'symbioid.' What was that about? If these beings are trying to tell the good guys from the bad guys, it looks like they just figured it out, right? They're on our side now, against Cardew and his clone-borgs."

Woo shook his head emphatically. "No, I think the jury is still out for them. They're still checking us out. All of us. The battle cruisers were destroyed not because they were a threat to us, but because they were a threat to the voidoid. A ring mine of gravity bombs, set that close to the voidoid, would be life threatening to the voidoid. Remember how Cardew tried to shut down the voidoids in Bound Space? His agents used those same gravity bombs, individually, to trick the voidoids into self-destructing. The voidoids in Bound Space finally figured out the deception and became immune to Cardew's synthetic gravity. But the voidoids out here, in this astrocell, might not share that immunity yet. They'd still be vulnerable.

"When we passed through the ring and set off the gravity mines, the voidoid reacted by summoning a symbioid to the rescue. I believe the symbioids are guardians of the voidoids, at least in this astrocell. They heard the call, they came, identified the battle cruisers as responsible for the threat, and eliminated them along with the ring mine. I think it was purely coincidental that our asses were saved in the process."

Once again, Aiden decided not to ask Woo how he knew all these things. It was pointless. Nevertheless, he wasn't about to dismiss Woo's conclusions out of hand. He'd much rather believe that the symbioids had their back.

The *Sun Wolf* pulled out of ZPD at 350,000 kilometers from the planet and slipped in behind the planet's single moon, designated HD 13808d-1. It was a crater-pocked, airless chunk of rock half the size of Luna in a fast orbit around the planet. Aiden used it as a temporary shield against any defensive weapons stationed at planet d, either orbital or land based. From their position, about a hundred klicks above the moon's surface, Aiden moved the ship just over the limb for a peek at planet d. Its daylight side faced them from below.

On the screen, planet d looked like a huge version of Mars, but with a thicker atmosphere. Thin wispy clouds swirled around the equatorial latitudes. Both polar regions were adorned in feathery white frost, as were the peaks of vast mountain ranges stretching halfway to the equator in both hemispheres. Instead of Mars red, the planet's surface had more of a tan-brown hue. No hint of green or bodies of water anywhere.

37

HD 13808 SYSTEM
HD 13808d-1

DOMAIN DAY 346, 2218

"IT'S a classic habitable desert planet," Alvarez said, eyes glued to her screen. "And big. Over one and a half times larger than Earth and close to twice the mass. A 31-hour rotational period. Breathable atmosphere with plenty of oxygen, about 20 percent. The rest is nitrogen and argon, at 69 and 11 percent respectively. Trace amounts of water. Mostly frozen in the polar regions, along with some shallow puddles across the subarctic zones. The rest of it is in the atmosphere, in cloud formations.

"Surface pressure and gravity both a little higher than Earth. Mean surface temperature slightly cooler than Earth at around 12 degrees C. You could probably walk around down there without technical aid of any kind. Just very warm clothing."

"Any signs of artificial surface structures?"

"Not yet," Alvarez said, "but I need more coverage time. Moving in closer would help."

"Lieutenant? Threat assessment?"

"I'm seeing at least two orbital weapons platforms. Possibly robotic. Geo-sync orbits around 500 klicks above the surface. Judging by their positions, I'm guessing there're two more covering the planet's opposite side. Total of four, covering the globe's four quadrants."

"Have they spotted us yet?"

"Not yet. But they are looking for us. I'm picking up their active scans. It's no secret now that we're in-system and that this planet is our destination."

Aiden said, "The only way we're going to get a better look at the surface is to come out of hiding and move closer. We'll draw fire from those orbital platforms. Are we good for that, Lieutenant?"

Hotah glanced back at him with that look, like: *Are you kidding?* "We'll handle anything they can throw at us, no problem. But why wait? I suggest the first thing we do is move in fast and take them out. All four. Long-range laser cannons would do the trick. Just clear the field. Then start our surface scans without distraction."

"What about surface-based missiles?"

Hotah grinned. "Bring 'em on. I feel like a little target practice today."

"No showboating, Lieutenant," Aiden said. "Just get the job done."

Hotah smiled. "Showboating? Me?"

"Yes, you. Pilot, transfer Helm to Tactical. Lieutenant, you're on."

The *Sun Wolf* couldn't use its ZPD so close to the planet's gravity well. Maneuvering had to be done on the antimatter drive. But the ship's beamed core antimatter drive was the latest and most powerful, more than sufficient for the job at hand.

Hotah moved the ship out from behind the moon. Within two minutes, both weapons platforms had spotted them and launched two missiles each, all at 300 Gs.

"Missile impacts in eight minutes," Hotah said. "Targeting now. In another two minutes they'll be in our cannon's sweet spot. Four minutes, of course, would be even better—"

"Make it two, Lieutenant."

When the two missiles from the first platform were within 200,000 kilometers, Hotah zeroed in the laser cannon and promptly blasted them. After a 10-second recharge, he targeted the two missiles from the second platform and dispatched them with equal ease. Then, at a more leisurely pace, he turned both orbital platforms into clouds of incandescent plasma.

Aiden said, "Anything coming at us from the planet's surface?"

Hotah shook his head. "If they had missiles batteries down there, I'd expect to see something by now."

"Okay. Let's see if you're right about two more of these things covering the other side of the planet. Take us around to the farside."

On their way to the planet's night side, scans picked up a massive vessel parked in a high geosynchronous orbit. But no incoming missile alarms. No signs of laser cannons charging up. Hotah focused intently on the image. "No weapons. It's not actively scanning us. Not responding to hails. Looks like a large colony-transport vessel."

Aiden asked Alvarez to run a life-signs scan. "Too far away for accurate IR signatures. But, by all other readings, it looks empty. Even dormant. Minimal power consumption. Like it's in a holding pattern. I'd be surprised if anyone is actually aboard that thing."

Hotah's hand hovered over the weapons board. "Want me to blast it, Commander?"

"No. Not yet. Not until we know what it's doing here. Continue course to the farside."

The moment they crossed over the planet's dawn line to the dark hemisphere, two more weapons platforms appeared on the scans, just as Hotah had predicted. Two more pairs of missiles came screaming toward them. And just as he'd taken care of the first attack, he made quick work of this one. Missiles and platforms vaporized.

Hotah made a gesture of a gunslinger blowing the smoke from the muzzle of his six-shooter and flipping it back into an imaginary holster. Aiden sat back, trying not to smile. "Time to scan the surface for structures. Pilot, you have the Helm. Take us into low orbit in a standard search pattern. Lilly, commence detailed full-globe surface scans."

Within one hour, they spotted a large complex of artificial structures in plain view sitting in a broad barren valley near the equator. Single-story metal buildings with narrow roadways between them covered an area of the brown desert over one kilometer across. Gravimetric scans hinted at vast underground warrens lying beneath the gridwork of buildings. High-magnification optics revealed moving vehicles on the roadways connecting the buildings. Several small orbital shuttles were parked around the perimeter, sitting in upright launch position.

Higher resolution revealed what looked like individual human beings, all engaged in distinctly purposeful movements. The scene looked strikingly different from any normal population of humans where you'd see a broad range of activity levels, from idle meandering all the way to resolute hurrying about. The tempo here seemed in unison, unnaturally homogenous. It made Aiden's skin crawl.

"Cloneborgs," Woo said. "Thousands and thousands of them. Like insects in a hive. This has to be one of Cardew's primary crèches."

"Probably just one of many," Aiden said.

Hotah leaned forward. "And what are we going to do about it?"

Aiden knew what Hotah wanted to do about it. That was clear. "What we do is continue the global scan. Search for more of these facilities."

When the scan was complete, they had identified a total of three crèche complexes, nearly identical in size and appearance, positioned thousands of kilometers from one another.

Woo came to Aiden's side and said, "This is obviously a major cloning center for Cardew, and it may have been his home base, at one time. But I don't think it is now. He's not down there sitting on his throne, plotting his empire's next move."

Aiden sighed. "I'm thinking the same. For one thing, why isn't the planet's surface more heavily fortified? More surface-to-space defenses? The entrance to the star system was well guarded, but the planet itself? Not so much. And where's all of his infrastructure? Where are the orbital shipbuilders, ore smelters, mining ships, manufacturing platforms? We know he has them, but they're not here. You're right. This might have been Cardew's home base, up until just recently, but I think he's moved on."

It was a bitter disappointment. The search had to continue. In the meantime, what would they do about the infestation they'd found below? Aiden had anticipated facing a decision like this at some point during their mission. One that was fraught with moral ambiguities.

But there was nothing ambiguous about it for Billy Hotah. "Let's nuke 'em."

Sudha Devi crossed her arms, frowning. "Wait a minute. Are we seriously considering wiping out these complexes, along with thousands, maybe hundreds of thousands, of living beings? With nuclear missiles? Just like that?" She snapped her fingers once.

"Yes," Hotah responded with equal intensity. "Before they wipe *us* out. If we don't stop them here, they'll continue to multiply and overrun this entire astrocell, and eventually Bound Space too. What's so hard to understand about that?"

Devi wasn't budging. "They're living beings, Lieutenant!"

"Are they?" Hotah said, raising his voice. "How do you know they're actually alive, in the way humans and animals are? Or even plants? They're artificial creations manufactured by a madman who wants to rule the universe using them as his tools to do it."

Devi shook her head and looked around at the rest of the crew. "Maybe we should take a vote."

Aiden had known it would eventually come to this. He said, "Hold on, Sudha. We're not a democracy here, not aboard this ship. I am the captain, and I will decide. That said, I will listen with an open mind to what anyone has to say."

"All right," Devi said, uncrossing her arms. "I understand. And I'm bound to abide by your decision, as per ship's protocol. But there's another issue here, also involving chain of command. As you have so often reminded Lieutenant Hotah, our mission orders are very clear—we gather intel, engage only in defensive combat, and report our findings back to UED Military Command. Leave all further decisions regarding offensive action up to them. If these installations are to be destroyed along with their inhabitants, the *Sun Wolf* is not charged with that task. We don't have to do this."

Aiden nodded thoughtfully. "And if the Alliance fleet comes in and wipes them out instead of us, would that ease your conscience?"

"Only in that the decision was not in my hands to make."

"It won't be in your hands, Sudha. The decision will be mine. I take full responsibility for making it."

Devi folded her arms again and said nothing more. Aiden looked around at the others. "Anyone else? Alvarez?"

She shook her head sadly. "I sympathize with Dr. Devi's argument. But when I think of what we saw on Sirota . . . the Rodina Collective. All those people. Those children. Slaughtered. If that's what these cloneborgs are programed to do, and they continue to multiply at an ever-increasing rate, then I believe we should stop them now. Sooner the better."

Devi looked away, as if to avert her eyes from the vision of Sirota that Alvarez had described, torn between vengeance and mercy.

Ro spoke up. "There are really two questions here. One: Should these installations—populated by cloneborgs created to act against humanity—be wiped out? And two: Should we, the *Sun Wolf*, take the initiative to do it ourselves, now, rather than follow the letter of the law of our mission directive?"

Aiden suppressed a smile. *Ro, Man of Logic.* "And where do you stand on those questions, XO?"

"Yes to the first one. The second one? That one's up to you, boss."

Aiden knew better than to press Ro beyond that. Now was not the time for a game of logic that he was bound to lose. He turned to the pilot. "Lista?"

Abahem had been quiet for so long that Aiden wondered if she'd even heard him ask. Finally, in a low, whispery voice, she said, "The black crow. I saw it inside my head. Felt its presence eating at my soul. Felt it torturing that poor sparrow in its clutches. It was pure evil. If that presence controls the actions and loyalty of these beings, they must be destroyed."

Abahem paused, a darkness gathering around her. She turned to face Devi. "They are not alive, Doctor. I saw one on the station. He was without a soul. Without the vital energy inherent to all living things."

Devi looked stunned by Abahem's revelation. But not entirely surprised. She opened her mouth to speak but said nothing.

Aiden glanced at Woo. "Elgin?"

Woo stood, his back straight, eyes burning. Aiden had, on several occasions, witnessed this abrupt transition between thinker and warrior in Elgin Woo. It was like a bolt of white-hot lightning flashing out of a clear blue sky.

"I know Cardew like no one else does, outside of his dark circle," he said. "Lista is absolutely right. He is pure evil. He has forsaken everything that was once human inside him to pursue an antihuman vision that he contemptuously disguises as some noble 'Transhuman' vision. An empire that can only be built on the ashes of our own human race, antithetical to everything we cherish and strive for. He is brilliant and powerful, and he has created a growing army of superior beings whose sole purpose is to destroy us and to spread their empire across the galaxy."

Woo paused to look at each one of them, his expression dead serious. No hint of the ambivalent dreamer. Only the resolute warrior.

"Our primary goal," he continued, "has always been to find and destroy Cardew himself. But in the meantime, if we're given the opportunity to decimate his minions, I believe it is our responsibility to do it. To do it now, and do it ourselves."

Woo's declaration evoked unanimous nods from the crew. All except Devi. And Aiden. He couldn't deny the truth in each of their perspectives. And he couldn't deny his own personal reasons for wanting Cardew's head on a stake. For the murder of his mother decades earlier. For the recent abduction of his wife. The cloneborgs were an extension of Cardew's will. They were his hands, carrying weapons of destruction. They were his feet marching over the human realm, crushing every naturally living thing in their wake. No. There could be no question about what had to be done.

He glanced at each member of his crew, ending with Billy Hotah. "Lieutenant, make ready three M-10 thermonuclear torpedoes. Target the facility below us and fire number one when ready. Then move us in position over the remaining two facilities and do the same with numbers two and three."

Devi turned on her heels and, without looking back, said, "I'm going below to check on the child."

38

HD 13808 SYSTEM
HD 13808d Orbit

Domain Day 346, 2218

The *Sun Wolf* carried a battery of twelve M-10 nuclear missiles, called torpedoes by naval convention, each one packing 10 kilotons of explosive energy with a primary blast radius of over three kilometers. The target facility below had a surface radius of about a half kilometer. The M-10 was overkill. The one-kiloton M-1 would have been sufficient. But the extent and depth of the underground structures was unknown, and Aiden wasn't taking any chances. Plus, he was pissed off.

The blast of blinding incandescent light was followed immediately by a vaporous ring of blast pressure spreading out from its center with startling speed, hundreds of kilometers in all directions. The white-hot flash resolved into an expanding fireball twice the radius of the target, boiling with the color and turbulence of hell itself.

"One down, two to go," Hotah said. For once, he did not appear to be enjoying himself in the process. No celebratory sounds were heard from the rest of the crew. Aiden thought to himself, *that one is for Skye.*

Twenty minutes later, the ship moved into position over the second compound. Looking over Alvarez's shoulder at the screen with a high-mag image of the target, Aiden couldn't help notice the amped-up, frenetic activity of the tiny figures scurrying about. Like an ant's nest poked with a stick. News travels fast among cloneborgs.

He'd become so engrossed watching the accelerated tempo of activity, not chaotic and still purposeful, that the blinding flash of the second detonation startled him into stepping backward, eyes blinking.

The *Sun Wolf* moved on to the third facility. Just as Hotah fired off the final nuclear torpedo, Alvarez said, "Commander, one of the landing shuttles has launched from the compound. It's broadcasting a distress beacon and headed in our direction."

Hotah acquired the vessel on his tactical board. "Targeting the shuttle. Laser cannon charged and ready."

"Hold off, Lieutenant. Fire only on my command. Understood?"

Hotah sat back and relaxed ever so slightly. "Aye."

"No signs of weapons or hostile intent," Alvarez said. She put the telescopic image of the shuttle on the main screen. They all watched as it settled into orbit one kilometer below them. The flash of the third nuclear explosion below briefly lit the underside of the vessel, revealing the configuration of a standard small-sized transport shuttle. Not military. No visible armament.

"Scan all comm frequencies, Lilly."

The scan immediately picked up a transmission, audio only. No visuals. It was a woman's voice, speaking in a tone of near panic. In a language Aiden didn't quite recognize. But it sounded like—

"It's Mandarin Chinese," Woo said. "My own native language. With a northern dialect, if I'm not mistaken."

"What is she saying, Elgin?"

"She's saying 'Please don't shoot. I am not one of them.' Then she's asking what language we speak."

"Tell her we speak English."

Woo did, in Chinese, and the woman responded immediately in perfect English. "Please don't shoot. I am not one of them. I am not of the Line. Please don't shoot."

"We will not shoot," Aiden responded. "Not yet. But do not move your vessel any closer to us or I will blast you without hesitation."

"Understood. Thank you." Her voice had calmed, but with tension barely held in check.

"If you're 'not one of them,' then who are you and what are you doing here?"

"I am not one of the Line. I am a mutant. A failed clone. I was confined and scheduled to be recycled. But during the turmoil caused by news of the bombing at the other two camps, I escaped and used one of the orbital shuttles to get off the planet."

"Where are you going?"

"I don't know. Just away from the Line. I hate them. They are monsters."

Aiden exchanged glances with Woo first, then the others, including Devi, who had returned to the bridge. He saw both suspicion and curiosity in their faces. But mostly suspicion. Aiden said, "Please turn on your comm visuals."

There was a pause, then, "I am ugly."

"Do it. Now."

The figure appearing on the main screen was indeed striking, but by no means ugly. Not by human standards. Exotic was a better description. She looked to be in her early thirties, tall—a little over six feet, Aiden guessed—and wiry thin. Her skin was a deep ebony of African lineage. Her hair was blonde, straight, and cut short. Her facial features were distinctly Asian, closer to Chinese than any other, but with a narrow aquiline nose. Her eyes were green. Otherwise, no physical deformities were apparent. She looked healthy and strong. And potentially dangerous.

But her reaction to being seen by strangers was undeniably human. She turned away from the screen as if ashamed, then turned back to face them with pleading eyes. "Please. Allow me to come aboard. I have nowhere else to go. I have no provisions. I cannot survive in this shuttle for more than a few days. I assure you, I am more like you than the ones who made me. The ones you destroyed. I can help you."

Aiden cocked his head. "And how could you possibly help us?"

He could think of a number of ways, actually, assuming she was telling the truth.

"I know a great deal about the cloning operations here, and about Amon. And his plans."

"Amon? Who is that?"

She looked back at him, confused. "He is the father of the Line. His goal is to destroy you, and all Normals."

"She means Cardew," Woo interjected. "If you recall, Amon was Cardew's given surname."

Aiden turned back to the screen. "We call him Cardew. You can start being useful by telling us where he is now."

She shook her head slowly. "He is not here. Not in this star system."

"Where, then?"

"I honestly don't know. But I have a clue to where he might have gone."

"And . . . ?"

"Please let me come aboard, and I will tell you everything I know."

So that's how it was. *Let's make a deal.* "And if I don't allow you aboard?"

"Then I will die, and you will not know all that I can tell you."

"How do I know you're not secretly one of Cardew's cloneborg agents?"

Her sudden look of frustration seemed authentic. Or else she was an extremely good actor. "All I can tell you is that I am not one of them. I am a mutant. The nanobots they inject into the fertilized egg cells to direct development of the fetus were neutralized by rare mutations in my genome. That's why I look so different from the rest. The nanobots that were specifically programed to enter my central nervous system, to direct my brain development, did not make it there. From the very beginning, my brain developed just like a normal human's would. I am *not* controlled by Amon, or the Line. My thoughts and emotions are my own. Like a Normal."

"If you're a mutant, why weren't you destroyed from the beginning?"

"The Line technicians overlooked my appearance. Clones are designed to look like a diverse cross section of Normals, and the technicians must have thought I was on the far edge of that spectrum. Besides, most mutants self-abort in the fetal stage, and I was birthed alive and healthy. Mutations like mine that prevent the nanobots from entering the central nervous system are very rare and not easily detected in clones that survive gestation. Especially if they learn how to behave like everyone else. As I did."

It all sounded perfectly reasonable and consistent with everything Aiden knew about Cardew's cloning techniques, which, admittedly wasn't much. He glanced at Woo, who knew more about it than he did, and saw no signs of doubt on his face. Instead, Woo focused more intently on the clone's image, turned to Aiden and said, "Look at her eyes, the pupils. They're normal sized."

"And . . . ?"

"The eyes are part of the central nervous system," Woo said, "from the same embryonic tissue. Cloneborgs have abnormally large pupils, probably a trait mediated by the nanobots in their nervous systems. But her pupils look normal."

That was interesting, but pretty thin as far as evidence went. Aiden wasn't about to make a judgment based on Woo's casual observation. He turned back to the screen and asked, "What is your name?"

"I was given the name Mary Smith. All the names given to us are meant to blend in with the human Normals. I hate the name because its sole purpose is to deceive. But it is the only name I've ever known."

Mary Smith . . . Aiden shook his head before continuing. "I'm breaking contact with you now. Temporarily. I'll reconnect shortly. Do not move your vessel any closer to ours. Not an inch, or else you will be destroyed."

She bobbed her head once, anxiety creasing her face.

The screen went blank. Aiden turned to his crew. "Again, not a democracy. I will decide. But I will entertain feedback."

"It could be a trick," Hotah said. "She could bring a weapon or a concealed bomb aboard. Or biological or chemical weapons. The whole shuttle could be a bomb. We can't let her dock with the ship."

"Agreed," Aiden said. "She'd have to come to our airlock via EVA. That way we could do a remote scan for weapons on her person while she's still outside."

"I believe her," Woo said.

"I do too," Ro said. "Besides, she could provide valuable information for our mission. That alone is worth the risk."

Alvarez shook her head. "I don't know. I want to believe her. But if she really is a cloneborg in disguise and we let her aboard, we'd be in serious trouble. I say no unless there's a surefire way of testing her."

Devi remained silent but nodded in agreement with Alvarez.

Abahem spoke up. "I can tell. If I can be in the same room with her, I can tell you if she's a cloneborg or a real human being."

And there it was. He knew Lista's talent would come in handy. To the crew members who hadn't known about it already, Aiden briefly explained the pilot's ability, then said, "If this Mary Smith can manage an EVA, I want Lista, Devi, and Hotah with me at the airlock. Hotah, bring a weapon of your choice. The moment she comes out of the lock, Lista will 'see' her, and she will give a thumbs-up if our guest is authentically human. A thumbs-down means she's pure cloneborg, and that's Hotah's signal to drop her with a head shot. Quickly and without hesitation."

He didn't have to tell Hotah the last bit, but did it for the benefit of the rest of the crew. Aiden reengaged the comm. Mary Smith's face appeared on the screen, still anxious. He said, "Do you have an EVA suit in the shuttle? And if so, do you know how to put it on and use it?"

"Yes, EVA suits are standard equipment in shuttles like this one," she said. "I'll figure out how to use it."

"What about operating your airlock?"

"Yes, I can do that."

"And operating the jet packs on your EVA suit? A one-kilometer EVA is a long one. You'd need to know how to use the directional jets to guide yourself over to our ship. We're not going to come out and get you. Understood?"

"Yes. My knowledge-base uploads covering those actions are adequate. I can figure it out quickly."

Aiden had no idea what she meant by uploads, but if she could pull this off with no prior experience, her knowledge base would have to be pretty damn good. "All right. Then do it and bring nothing with you. And I mean *nothing*. As you approach, we will do a remote body scan for any concealed weapons. If you clear the scan, we'll leave the outer airlock door open for you."

It took close to an hour before for her to suit up and make it from her shuttle to the *Sun Wolf*. Aiden, Devi, Abahem, and Hotah had assembled in the airlock's cramped receiving chamber, waiting for her. Aiden instructed her to wait near the outer airlock while Alvarez deployed a drone to run a body scan.

After a minute, Alvarez's voice came through the comm. "She's clean."

Aiden initiated the airlock cycle and said, "I'm opening the outer airlock door. Once you're inside, I'll cycle you through."

When the lock was fully pressurized, her voice came through the comm. "Permission to come aboard."

Aiden had to smile at the shipboard etiquette. Where had she learned that? Knowledge-base uploads? "Permission granted. Come."

Aiden's team stood facing the airlock portal, several meters back from it. Lista had gone into a hyperalert trance, eyes fixed on the door. Hotah stood next to her, holding a compact but powerful slug-thrower, ready and pointed slightly upward, but not directly at the door, his finger rock steady on the trigger.

The door opened with a faint hiss and Mary Smith took one step out. She had removed her helmet, a smile of relief on her face.

She stopped dead in her tracks. The smile on her face vanished at the sight of her grim-faced greeting party.

Aiden said, "Stop where you are."

She held her hands up defensively. "Don't shoot. Please."

Lista stood stone still, focusing intently on the newcomer. Two seconds passed. Four seconds. Ten. Then her posture relaxed. She blinked her eyes and gave a thumbs-up signal.

Hotah lowered his weapon.

Aiden stepped forward and said, "Welcome aboard . . . Mary."

39

HD 13808 SYSTEM
HD 13808d Orbit

Domain Day 346, 2218

To be born profoundly different from everyone else in the world you inhabit is not an uncommon story. Nor is the pain and fear it causes, or the strength and courage it takes to rise above it. The resilience to become who you truly are, like no one else. But Mary Smith's story was the most uncommon one that Aiden ever expected to hear.

She sat rigidly at the conference table, in a chair that seemed uncomfortable to her. Aiden sat across from her, with Devi and Woo sitting on either side. Hotah stood off in one corner of the conference room, his weapon still in hand but casually pointed down at the deck.

Her exotic appearance was far more striking in person. Her green, almond-shaped eyes were intense and rarely blinked. Her closely cropped blonde hair stood out in stark contrast to the rich brown hue of her skin. Her tall stature and lanky frame conveyed pure athletic prowess. She wore the same clothes she had escaped in—a lightweight tunic on top over loose-fitting trousers, both made of the same nondescript, woven cloth, off-white in color. She had been given a crew jacket to ward off the routinely cool temperatures of the ship's common areas.

Aiden asked her to tell them everything she could remember of her origin and her life in the cloning facility, on the planet she called Nead. She folded her hands and rested them on the tabletop, long, slender fingers clasped together. She began her story haltingly, interrupted by nervous glances at Hotah and his weapon. But after a while, she seemed to relax, and her speech became more fluid.

By her reckoning, she had been born about 160 days ago as a fully formed, mature being who looked like a woman in every respect but one. She possessed no reproductive organs. But neither did anyone else in her crèche, including the ones who looked like males. So she had thought nothing of it, had not even known such physical traits existed.

She had received knowledge-base uploads, KBUs, every day like everyone else. These were done with cranial neurolink caps and external brain-to-computer devices. Her awareness and understanding of the universe expanded exponentially as she learned physics, chemistry, mathematics, astronomy, physiology, medicine, mechanics and engineering, languages—and a version of human history, which she later discovered had been radically skewed to demonstrate the need for a Transhuman revolution.

She was taught physical skills through athletics and hand-to-hand combat, as well as fine motor skills in manipulating research instruments and construction of microelectronics. She learned the intricacies of genetics and the processes by which she and her fellow cloneborgs were created, along with the grand purpose behind it all—the creation of the Posthuman Realm.

While her unusual looks made her painfully self-conscious, they set off no alarms with the guardians and technicians of the Line. The cloning process had been designed to produce a broad range of human appearances, including more exotic specimens.

But as time passed, she became increasingly aware of how different she was from the rest. Subtle things like behavioral patterns, reactions to unexpected events, gaps in emotional intelligence and capacity for empathy or compassion. And the lack of curiosity. The more she learned about where she was and why she was there, the more she realized how dangerous it was to be different in the way that she was. She became more adept at concealing those differences and learning by observation how to blend in with the others.

The more she learned about Normals, who were supposed to be vastly inferior to her and her Transhuman cohorts, the more it became obvious that, mentally and emotionally, she was far more like a Normal than a cloneborg. And the more she realized that concealing her awareness of it was a matter of life and death. It prompted her to study in more depth the details of the cloning process in an attempt to understand what may have happened to her.

The way it worked was like this. Human DNA from the original source—presumably Cardew himself—was transferred to a human egg cell that lacked its own nucleus and genetic material. These specialized egg cells had themselves been cloned into existence for this one purpose. The newly "fertilized" cell, technically a zygote, began to divide and develop into an embryo, now containing the exact genetic material of the original source. These embryos were then transferred into artificial uteruses, called uteropods, where they developed into fully formed beings. But early on in the process, just as the single-celled zygote began to grow into a multicellular embryo, highly sophisticated nanobots were injected.

These tiny robots, not much larger than one micron in size, were programed to direct all aspects of cell building from that point on. That included replacing bone with carbon nanotubule materials to grow into extremely durable skeletal systems. They altered organ development to replace lungs, kidneys, hearts, and circulatory systems with synthetic analogs that outperformed the originals many times over. Other nanobots directed the development of neuromuscular systems to produce synthetic muscle tissue that gave cloneborgs superhuman physical abilities.

But most importantly, a breed of highly specialized nanobots were designed to direct the development of the central nervous system, primarily the brain. They boosted the formation of higher brain centers responsible for real-world analysis, problem solving, and computational abilities. On the other hand, they inhibited the formation of structures in the brain responsible for a whole range of emotional responses, including empathy. They inhibited other areas that controlled curiosity, independent behavior, and decision making, while boosting others that affected loyalty to authority.

This last breed of nanobots never made it into the embryo that eventually produced Mary Smith. After researching her knowledge-base uploads in depth, she correctly surmised that an inherent mutation within her native genome had caused the total rejection of these particular nanobots after they were injected. That's when she finally knew for sure that her brain was virtually the same, in structure and function, as that of a normal human being, and radically different from the cloneborgs she lived amongst. She'd never felt more desperately alone, a feeling that her fellow clones were entirely incapable of. The realization was at once exhilarating and terrifying.

She'd been able to keep her secret safe until the technicians finally discovered it.

She and the group of cloneborgs in her production batch had finished all their training and were scheduled to leave Nead—a Gaelic word meaning *nest*, according to Ro—aboard a transport vessel destined for colonization of another planet. That explained the empty transport vessel the *Sun Wolf* had spotted, waiting in orbit. She didn't know where the new planet was, only that it was part of Amon's grand scheme to colonize vast reaches of local space. To populate his empire.

The final stages of preparation included two additional nanobot injections. One was to upload nanobots into the brain, designed to greatly enhance uncontested obedience to authority. The route of the injection was the spinal cord, into the spinal fluid, bypassing the blood-brain barrier into the cranial fluid surrounding the brain.

The injection made her violently ill, no doubt due to her body's rejection of the nanobots. She was taken aside and subjected to several kinds of bio-scans, whereupon she was found to be defective.

A mutant. As a reject of the Line, she was confined and slated for "recycling," a process where she would be painlessly put to sleep, biologically terminated, and her component materials recycled.

That's when all hell broke loose. A cloning facility located on the other side of Nead had been attacked and destroyed by a thermonuclear detonation, and news of it spread to the remaining two facilities. Before anything could be done about it, the second facility was obliterated in the same way. The entire planet was under attack. She took advantage of the ensuing chaos, escaped her confinement, and fled to the nearest orbital shuttle. Using knowledge she'd gained through the KBUs, she managed to launch the shuttle into orbit just before her own facility was disintegrated by a nuclear fireball. And now, here she was.

Aiden took a while to process all that he'd heard. It was an amazing story, and one that provided valuable information, details of Cardew's cloning program that no one had known about. Information that could help them defeat Cardew.

Out of curiosity, Aiden asked, "What was the second nanobot injection intended for?"

"It was actually the first one they gave me," she said, "before the spinal injection that made me so sick. I was told that it was intended to protect us from a deadly virus that had been introduced into the Normals' population, one that we hadn't yet been programed to combat. They knew the exact nature of the virus and how to program the nanobots to protect us from it. I'm not completely sure, but I think it was a virus engineered by the Line as a biological weapon against the Normals."

Devi looked at Aiden and said, "The virus that broke out at Friendship Station, causing it to shut down under quarantine. The one that's killing so many people on Earth."

The last he'd heard, the virus was now running rampant on both Earth and Mars. Mortality rates were skyrocketing. He asked Mary Smith, "Do the nanobots induce production of antibodies, or other kinds of blood-borne agents inside the body, that destroy the virus?"

"Yes, that's how I understood it. The virus and the specific vaccine against it were developed together, at the same time."

"Then those antibodies would be present in your body right now," Devi said. "Including the nanobots that produced them."

"Yes."

Devi leaned closer to her and said, "With a sample of your blood, we could easily engineer a highly specific vaccine to induce total immunity to the virus. It would be extremely helpful for us, for all Normals. Would you allow me to take a blood sample?"

"Yes, absolutely," she said, her mood brightening like a child who had just found her long-lost family. "Anything I can do."

Devi smiled that warm smile of hers, the most natural expression of who she really was. "You're one of us now. If you want to be."

Instead of speaking, Mary Smith just nodded and produced a smile of her own that looked as if it was the first of its kind to have ever graced her face.

Devi said, "Do you want a different name? One of your own choosing? Something that you actually like."

The woman looked confused, as if the notion had never occurred to her. Devi went on to say, "My name is Sudha. That's Elgin. That's Aiden—but you must call him Commander. And the serious-looking one standing in the corner is William Hotah."

Hotah wasn't looking quite as serious as he had earlier. He even smiled at her.

"Yes. I would like to have my own name," she said. Her eyes grew unfocused, looking inside, not outward. Then she brightened and said, "I want to be called Jo."

When no one spoke, she said, "Like Jo March? In the novel *Little Women*? I found it in one of the knowledge-base uploads. I don't know how it got there. We were never exposed to the literature of Normals. I think all of that was deliberately omitted from the knowledge base. But I found *Little Women*, and I read it. In my head. I loved it . . ."

Everyone was smiling at her now. She looked embarrassed, then resolute.

Aiden was the first to speak. "Good choice. Jo it is."

Devi reached across and placed her hand gently on top of Jo's. "I loved that book too. One of my favorites. That's a perfect name for you."

So, Aiden thought, the *Sun Wolf* now hosted two unexpected guests, an infant and a human cloneborg. Never a dull moment.

Woo made a theatrical cough to get everyone's attention. "Nice to meet you, Jo. But now could you tell us where you think Cardew is? You said you had clue about that."

"Yes. I heard that he went to find the gateway."

Aiden said, "The gateway? He already knows where that is. At Alpha-2 Hydri."

"No," Jo said. "A new gateway. Into a new area of space. They said it was at the 'water snake.' I don't know what that means."

Woo's eyes went wide. He froze, motionless for a few moments. Then he clapped his hands once, sat back, and smiled. "Yes! The Water Snake. I *knew* it."

Then Woo's smile disappeared. He leaned forward, and a shadow clouded his face. "I was afraid of this. It's been Cardew's goal all along. After setting up the foundation of his empire here in this astrocell, he wants to find the star that holds the gateway from this astrocell into the *next* one, and the next one beyond, and the next. It's exactly what I've been hunting for myself. And now that I finally know where that star is, that bastard might get there before me!"

40

HD 13808 SYSTEM
HD 13808d Orbit

Domain Day 346, 2218

Woo's outburst got everyone's attention. To find the next gateway into yet another astrocell—and ultimately to another and another—would be a game changer for the whole human race. Aiden looked sideways at Woo and said, "You know where this gateway star is?"

"Yes, I do. And now so does Cardew. He's probably headed there now, if not there already. It's a star way out on the Frontier called Eta-2 Hydri. It's part of the Hydrus constellation, not part of its outline, but within its borders. And yes, it *is* at the Water Snake. *Hydrus* is the Latin word for water snake. The star itself is a G-type star. A huge one. Classified as a giant star. Visible with the naked eye even from Earth, 218 light-years away."

"There must be hundreds of stars associated with that constellation," Aiden said. "How do you know that's the right one?"

"Less than a hundred stars, actually," Woo said. "How do I know it's Eta-2 Hydri? First of all, it's the only star in Hydrus that is both on your hit list *and* on the extreme Frontier of this astrocell, the only region of an astrocell where a gateway star can exist. Secondly, it is the star that's been singing to me."

Aiden looked at him askance. Here we go again. "Aside from the singing, Elgin, what other proof do you have?"

"Not *aside* from the singing," Woo said. "It was the singing that gave me the idea. Then a brilliant postdoctorate student of mine devised a way to pinpoint where in the sky the singing came from."

"And it turned out to be Eta-2 Hydri?"

"Exactly. I'm convinced of it. Remember how I figured out that Alpha-2 Hydri was the gateway star into this astrocell? Over a year and a half ago? It was the neutrino beam I detected shooting out of the Chara voidoid, pointed directly at the star system where Shénmì is. It was a signal to me. Just as the singing has been a signal to me, pointing to the next gateway star."

Delusional as it sounded, Aiden knew better than to scoff. "But *singing*, Elgin. How is it possible you can hear a star, light-years away, through the vacuum of space?"

"I have a rare from of synesthesia. I can hear certain kinds of light. Literally. The quality of light from this particular star is unique, and, when I am in the right frame of mind, I can actually hear it. I shared this information with my postdoc, Kimberly Harlow, who was doing brilliant work on identifying stars by their astromagnetic signatures."

"Astromagnetic signatures?" Aiden tried to keep up on the latest advances in astrophysics, but he'd never heard that term before.

"Once again," Woo said, "it's all about coupled oscillators. Synchronized vibrations. Spontaneous organization. Call it what you want, it's all the same thing. All stars have a unique resonant frequency. Their surfaces expand and contract in regular cycles, creating something like sound waves, but propagated through plasma, not air."

Aiden knew about this line of Woo's work because Aiden had been there when the man discovered that voidoids shared the exact same resonant frequency as their host stars—except in the case of the voidoids, it was propagated by gravitational waves, not electromagnetically. Then, using data from broadband seismograph readings Woo made on Shénmì to determine the planet's "free oscillation" frequency—commonly known as a planet's hum—he found that Shénmì's hum was exactly the same as the system's voidoid *and* its host star. The same synchronization phenomenon turned out to exist in the Solar System, between Earth, Sol, and V-Prime. And also in the Chara system—between Silvanus, Chara, and the system's voidoid.

While Woo summarized all this for them, Jo seemed focused like a laser beam on his every word. She looked as if she actually understood all of it. Aiden, however, was mentally tapping his foot. "Elgin. What does this have to do with detecting gateway stars?"

Woo looked at him and smiled. "What makes a star with a gateway different from all other stars?"

"We don't have time for guessing games, Elgin."

"Humor me," Woo said. Which Aiden knew from experience was the only way to prompt Woo to get on with it.

"Okay," Aiden said. "The main difference is that a gateway star has two active voidoids, one at each polar opposite point. Each one is connected to a different astrocell. You use one to jump in and out of astrocell A, and the other to jump in and out of astrocell B. All other stars have only one active voidoid, which you can use to jump anywhere inside the astrocell it occupies, but not outside of it."

"Exactly," Woo said. "And we know that the density of dark energy is slightly different for every astrocell, meaning that the cosmological constant varies between them. That's why the zero-point drive has to be recalibrated to the new cosmological constant whenever it enters a different astrocell."

"And . . . ?"

"And," Woo said, twirling one of his dangling mustaches, a mischievous gleam in his eye, "I've found that the resonate frequency of voidoids is a function of the cosmological constant of the astrocell in which they live. The voidoid connected to astrocell A will have a different resonate frequency than the one connected to astrocell B. Now a gateway star is sandwiched between these two active voidoids, at opposite poles, each connected to a different astrocell. When the star attempts to sync frequencies with both of them at once, it can't because the base frequencies are different. So it ends up oscillating between the two values. That oscillation shows up in the star's own resonant frequency, creating a unique signature that can be detected by specialized instruments."

"You devised such an instrument?"

"I didn't. Dr. Harlow did. It's a modified HMI, a helioseismic and magnetic imager, originally designed to study oscillations and magnetic fields at a star's surface, at its photosphere. I actually sang the song out loud for her, the song I hear from the one star I believe to be the gateway star. She was able to translate the song into the same electromagnetic format she used to identify a star's unique HMI signature. Then she spent months on Shénmì scanning the night sky for all the stars at or near the Frontier of this astrocell, trying to find a match for that exact song. The best candidate turned out to be Eta-2 Hydri."

Aiden leaned in closer. "That's the gateway star? You're sure of that?"

"Aside from the singing," Woo said sardonically, "it's right where we'd expect the gateway to be, on the Frontier. I have no doubt that it occupies the overlap zone between this astrocell and another one, and that it supports two active voidoids, just like Alpha-2 Hydri does. It's where the next gateway is, the door into a completely new astrocell."

Woo hesitated for a moment before continuing. "The only way to accurately test this idea is to bring a modified HMI aboard a voidship like the *Sun Wolf* as it ranges far and wide throughout the astrocell. That would allow triangulated readings and would effectively eliminate all doubt."

Aiden sat back and gave Woo a look. He should have known all along. "And you've done just that, haven't you, Elgin? Brought this HMI instrument aboard with you?"

"I did, yes," Woo said sheepishly. "But in my defense, it was among the instruments I intended to deliver to Shénmì Station.

It got stranded aboard the *Sun Wolf* when we left in such a hurry. I've integrated it into the ship's sensor array."

Aiden hadn't known about that and wondered if Comm/Scan Officer Lilly Alvarez did. "So, this is the elusive pet project you've been working on."

"Yes. I've been using it as we go from star to star to finally verify that Eta-2 Hydri is, without a doubt, the gateway star."

But Aiden's amazement over Woo's discovery brought up one very troublesome question. "If Cardew knows where this star is, and he's headed there right now, how did *he* find it?"

Woo's expression darkened. "I'm afraid I know how he did it. But the important thing is for us to get out to that star now, as soon as possible."

Once again, Aiden had to make a critical decision based on one of Elgin Woo's leaps of logic. At least this time Woo had some solid evidence to back up his conclusions. Besides, no one else seemed to have a better idea of where to go next, including himself. "All right. That's our next destination then."

Aiden stood and looked at his chrono. "We'll head back to the system voidoid, stay there through a short sleep cycle, then depart at zero six hundred."

Hotah stepped forward. "What about the two remaining battle cruisers between us and the voidoid? Do we take them out?"

"Where are they now?"

"They turned around and are headed back here. But it'll take them seven days to get here. We could easily surprise them on our way and take them out."

"Hasn't there been enough killing?" Devi said. "Their colonies down there are obliterated. They're no threat to us now."

Aiden was about to weigh in when Jo surprised them all. "No," she said. "They *are* a threat to you. If not now, later for sure. They are *monsters*. Amon's puppets. They would not hesitate for a second to destroy you, given the chance."

Devi gave a resigned sigh. Hotah smiled without humor. The red speckled band across his face darkened. Aiden said, "Okay,

Lieutenant. Work up the tactical sequence for it. We'll take care of it on our way back to the voidoid."

He turned to Devi, acknowledging her disapproval before speaking, then said, "Sudha, I want you to do a complete medical workup on Jo. When we arrive at the voidoid, you and I can accompany her to one of our spare crew quarters and help her settle in."

Jo looked back at Aiden as she went with Devi and said, "Thank you . . . Commander."

~ ~ ~

Two hours later, the *Sun Wolf* came to a halt in the vicinity of the HD 13808 voidoid. Minutes before arriving, they had pulled out of the ZPD within 5 kilometers from the first cloneborg battle cruiser. Before the ship even detected the *Sun Wolf*'s presence, Hotah vaporized it with one short-range burst from the main laser cannon. The second battle cruiser, only 10 kilometers from the first, had just enough time to begin rotating its own laser cannon toward the *Sun Wolf* before it met with the same fate as its companion.

Like shooting fish in a barrel, Aiden thought. Except now he was far more likely to grieve over fish than cloneborgs.

As the crew secured the bridge for sleep cycles, Aiden took Woo aside and spoke quietly. "Elgin, you said you thought you knew how Cardew figured out where this new gateway star was. How did he do it?"

Woo shook his head solemnly and said nothing. He obviously didn't want to talk about it, but finally said, "Soon after Dr. Kimberly Harlow identified Eta-2 Hydri as the most likely candidate for the gateway star, she disappeared."

"Let me guess," Aiden said. "Another Cauldron scientist abducted and brain-tapped by Cardew."

Woo took in a deep breath and let it out slowly. "Yes. I believe that's what happened. Dr. Harlow was a brilliant researcher and still a young woman. She was like a daughter to me, and the only other person who knew anything about my project. She was last seen at a conference on Luna. She never returned to the Cauldron. No one knows what happened to her. We only know that she was not among the ruined scientists we recovered from the Dark Fort."

It was another serious security breach for the Cauldron, resulting in the loss of another elite scientist from their midst. Woo was clearly uncomfortable talking about it. Aiden put a hand on his shoulder. "I'm sorry, Elgin."

"So am I."

Aiden decided to change the subject to keep Woo from sinking further into remorse. "Elgin, before we jump into that system, I want you to figure out a way to protect our zero-point drive against gravimetric ring mines like the one we ran into here."

Woo brightened. "I can do that. Faster with Hutton's help."

Hutton's voice filled the bridge. "I would be more than happy to assist you, Doctor."

Woo smiled at the AI's enthusiasm. "Excellent!" he said.

What a pair. Elgin Woo and Hutton. The cosmic Odd Couple.

41

HD 13808 SYSTEM
System Voidoid

Domain Day 346, 2218

Aiden left the bridge and met Devi in the medical bay where she had just finished Jo's medical exam. After reporting that Jo was in perfect health, she and Aiden led Jo to one of the spare crew quarters. Jo's response should not have surprised him, given what he knew of her life up to this point, but it moved him nonetheless.

"This is all for me?" she said, eyes wide. "This whole space? No one else?"

"Yes," Devi said. "All yours. Our living quarters are for privacy as much as they are for basic needs. We usually do our sleeping in private."

"We all lived together in one space," Jo said. "All of my sisters and brothers. I think the concept of privacy was meaningless to them. I may have been the only one who understood what it meant and yearned for it."

Aiden, who needed alone time more than most, couldn't imagine living in conditions like that. Especially if he was the only one there unable to tolerate it. The idea of it made him queasy. He changed the subject. "The galley is just down the corridor," he said. "We usually eat our meals there in small groups, depending on duty schedules. Do you have any dietary needs that might be different from ours?"

"No different," Jo said. "All the clones of the Line are designed to function outwardly just like Normals in order to blend in without suspicion. That includes digestive functions. The only real difference is that our metabolic processes are more efficient. Better nutrient utilization with less waste production. Also, we are immune to most ingested toxins known to sicken or kill Normals."

Jo told them this with no hint of pride. Just the facts. And when she looked into the small bathroom and saw the toilet, she said, "We use those too. Just less often, and the ones we use look different. I'm sure I can figure this one out on my own."

Aiden smiled at that before putting on a more serious expression. "You'll be allowed access to basic shipboard comms and computer use, limited and strictly monitored by the ship's AI. Comms to anywhere beyond the ship are locked out. Except for myself."

"I understand," Jo said. She looked around the room, then asked, "How would I interact with the ship's AI?"

"Through voice," Aiden said. "His name is Hutton."

"I am Hutton," the AI said. "Pleased to meet you, Jo."

For the first time during her brief orientation, Jo looked genuinely surprised. She looked around, trying to identify the point source of Hutton's voice. Seeing none, she tilted her head upward and said, "Um . . . nice to meet you too . . . Hutton."

"Hutton," Aiden said, "behave yourself. Jo is new to many things here."

"I am at your service, Jo," Hutton said, a deferential tone in his voice.

To Jo, Aiden said, "Be forewarned. Hutton is capable of rambling on and on about any topic you set him on to. Feel free to shut him up if he becomes annoying. He's used to it."

"Oh . . . Actually, I'm looking forward to learning everything I can from Hutton. I'm realizing how little I really know about Normals and about the universe in general. The KBUs were very thorough in most areas, but I have sensed big gaps in other areas."

Devi turned to Aiden. "I need to go check on the infant."

Jo's eyes widened again. "An infant? A Normal baby? Here?"

"Yes," Devi said. "An orphan. We had no choice but to bring him along. I've set up a makeshift nursery in the medical suite."

Shades of complex emotions clouded Jo's face. "I've never seen one. Clones are born fully grown, without reproductive organs. We have no babies. No growth stages. No children or teens."

Aiden had an idea. He said to Devi, "I'd like to come with you, Sudha, and to bring Jo along."

Devi looked at Aiden for a brief moment, searching his eyes. Then she said, "Yes. Good idea. If Jo wants to."

Jo hesitated, that play of conflicting emotions animating her face again. It was a very human response, Aiden thought. She finally said, "Yes. I would like to."

Aiden, Devi, and Jo entered the nursery together. The infant was lying in a well-padded "crib" inside the same bio-specimen pod they'd used on Sirota to bring him aboard. It just happened to be the perfect size, and it had a shape that Devi hoped would discourage him from climbing out and getting into trouble. As an extra precaution, the whole thing was placed inside one of the lab's unused isolation chambers. It had clear plastiglass walls, over a meter high, but open on top. The baby was not crying, but not calm either. He turned his head and looked at them with curiosity as they approached the crib.

That's when Aiden realized Jo was not with them. He turned and saw her back at the doorway, standing frozen, an expression of anguish transforming her face.

Aiden tilted his head at her. "Jo?"

Then, slowly at first, Jo came to join them at the crib. She couldn't take her eyes off the baby, eyes glistening. She made a short sobbing sound and wiped a tear from her cheek. She did not speak.

Devi picked the baby up and cradled him in her arms. She made some silly cooing sounds that seemed to amuse him. He smiled up at Devi and waved his pudgy little hands at her. Devi turned toward Jo and held the baby out toward her. "Do you want to hold him for a while?"

Jo looked frightened at first and took a step back. She stifled another sob and covered her mouth with one hand. Another tear dripped down her cheek. Then curiosity brought her back. A wave of profound longing seemed to ripple through her body. She tentatively held out her arms to receive the little bundle of new life. Trembling, she took the baby in her arms and looked down at him as if he were an alien being. Then, like an invisible biological switch turning on, Jo's trembling stopped. She held the baby close to her bosom as if it was the most natural thing in the world. As if it were her own child. A child she could never have.

Jo's tears did not stop, but one of the most beautiful smiles Aiden had ever seen blossomed on her face. Like a flower the color of love, sorrow, and hope.

The baby looked back at her, at first stunned with wonderment, then broke out in a smile just as brilliant as Jo's. He giggled and waved his hands at her. She made a sound that seemed half sob and half laugh. Aiden wasn't sure which.

But he *was* sure of one thing now. Jo was 100 percent human. She was a Normal, just like the rest of them, but living inside a cloneborg body. He could finally feel comfortable having her aboard the *Sun Wolf.* He could trust her.

Jo turned to him, holding the boy with a gentleness that only a living miracle could inspire, and asked, "What's his name?"

Aiden shrugged. "We don't have one for him yet."

"Tell me about where he came from. Where you found him."

Aiden briefly recounted the story of finding the Rodina Collective's decimated mining colony on Sirota not more than three days ago. Without holding back the identity of who was responsible for the atrocity, he told her how they had found the baby, the colony's sole living survivor, and how they had managed to bring him on board.

Jo wiped a remaining tear from her face. "I have knowledge of all languages. You said the colony was predominately Slovakian?"

"Not just predominately," Aiden said, "but exclusively Slovakian."

Jo nodded and said, "I would call him Rene. It's a Slovakian name meaning 'reborn person.'"

Aiden and Devi exchanged glances. *Reborn person.* It was perfect.

"So be it," he said. "Rene it is."

Devi's face turned from delighted to serious and she said, "I'm concerned that Rene isn't getting the right kind of nutrition. I believe he was still breastfeeding before his mother died. We obviously have no access to mother's milk here. There's no baby formula on board, and no way to concoct anything close to it."

Jo's face lit up. "I can produce breast milk."

Devi's eyebrows went up. "What? I thought you were . . ."

"Yes, I have no functional reproductive organs, so there's no estrogen or progesterone production. But all female cloneborgs were designed to *look* like Normals in all ways. That was most easily accomplished by allowing normal female breast tissue to develop, including the neurophysiology that comes with it."

"But isn't that just the biological machinery for lactation?" Devi asked. "Without the hormonal triggers like prolactin, even normal breast tissue won't produce milk. I thought those triggers were deliberately omitted from cloneborg development, along with the rest of the reproductive physiology."

"Yes," Jo said. "That's true for all cloneborgs. Except for me. Remember, development of my central nervous system was unaffected by the nanobots. My brain developed the same way as a Normal's would. That means my pituitary gland is normal, and that's where prolactin is produced and secreted, regulated by the hypothalamus, which is also in the brain and functions normally in me."

While Jo spoke, Devi consulted her compad. Her eyebrows went up again. "I was just looking at the results of your blood tests. Your prolactin levels are on the high side for a normal, nonpregnant woman. Possibly because you have no estrogen and progesterone to inhibit its production. Your levels are significantly higher than any other female aboard this ship. I know that for a fact, because I checked it out when I was looking for ways to feed this little guy."

Devi paused, then said, "Assuming the neurophysiology of your breast tissue is functional, as you say it is, you are by far the most capable among us to produce viable breast milk."

Jo was beaming now. "I want to do it. What do I have to do?"

"It's quite simple," Devi said with a shrug and a smile. "Suckling is the key stimulus. That's all it takes. With your prolactin levels as high as they are, the milk should start flowing. Rene will get the nutrients he desperately needs for proper development."

"Can we start now?" Jo asked, starting to unzip the top of her jumpsuit.

Devi glanced at Aiden, then back to Jo. "Why not?"

"Well," Aiden said, looking at his feet. "Time for me to go. I'm glad this is all working out. Don't forget your sleep cycles. We'll need to be alert for tomorrow's jump."

Devi and Jo looked back at him, grinning as if sleep and tomorrow were the last things on their minds.

~ ~ ~

In his own quarters, Aiden sat on the edge of his bed, bent down, and rubbed his eyes with both hands. The effort he'd been making to keep his mind off dire thoughts about Skye had exhausted him. But active suppression was the only way he could function as commander of the *Sun Wolf*. Only at times like this, alone with his demons, could his guard drop to let the dark substance of anxiety roil up inside him.

Without thinking, he glanced across the room at the medicine cabinet. He envisioned the bottle of Continuum sitting behind its mirrored door, beckoning to him. Once again he had to shake himself free from its allure. Continuum would be exactly the wrong choice for him, especially now, on the eve of what might be the final battle in a long grim struggle against Cardew. And taken as an escape from his dark worries about Skye? Why should he be allowed the luxury of escape when she had to endure the horrors she faced alone without it? *No. Exactly the wrong choice.*

He leaned back and lay flat on his narrow bed, head propped up on two pillows. "Hutton, have you made any progress in locating Skye, or finding out what's going on with her?"

"Some progress, yes," Hutton said. But he didn't sound particularly hopeful. "I have been digging deeply into some of the darker corners of the OverNet. It's not a place for the fainthearted, I must say. But I have identified at least three deftly concealed Omicron units that bear signs of profound corruption. They are impenetrable to me, on my own. But I am attempting to enlist the aid of other Omicron units in the OverNet to gain entry."

"Can you determine the location of these units? Their physical location?"

"That is proving difficult, due to the many layers of camouflage they employ. However, I am relatively certain that one of them is located in Shénmì's star system."

Aiden sat up. "On Shénmì Station?"

"No. I think not. But somewhere else in the system."

"Could it be out at Jumbo?"

"It is likely, yes."

"Could you concentrate your efforts on that one?"

"Yes, I am already focusing on that unit, attempting to infiltrate its command controls. But all of these corrupted units are interconnected. The subnetwork they have formed together is robust and dominated by one central consciousness, a powerful and malevolent one."

"Cardew."

"No doubt, yes. He is now the proverbial ghost in the machine. It will take all of the Omicron units in the OverNet working in concert to overpower this manifestation of him. And even that may not be enough."

In all of Aiden's experience with Hutton, he had never detected even a hint of fear in his AI companion. But he heard it now. Not that it surprised him. Hutton was not just a machine, after all. He was an ever-evolving neural net, initially created by humans, modeled after the human brain, and set free to grow his own unique intelligence. And while Hutton had grown far beyond the initial model, he still retained the fundamental blueprint of human neurophysiology.

Or was Aiden's perception of Hutton's state just a projection of his own fears? Hutton had always been Aiden's rock in times of uncertainty and personal insecurity. Confident in the face of oblivion. Optimistic to a fault. Was this crack in the rock just a figment of his own overactive imagination, set aflame by his own mounting anxiety? Either way, it served only to heighten his apprehension.

He took a deep breath and let it out slowly. "Okay, Hutton. Keep digging, but be careful."

"No worries."

Aiden laughed. Hutton was getting better at the "no worries" thing. His delivery sounded more natural this time. "Thank you, Hutton."

"You are welcome. Now, may I suggest that you get some real sleep?"

Hutton's personal touch had always bemused Aiden, and he'd even begun to believe its authenticity. But now, in this room, at this difficult moment, the warmth and empathy in the AI's voice hit him like an emotional pile driver. He choked back his feelings and said nothing more.

Sleep had not come easily since he'd learned of Skye's disappearance, and he feared it would be no different this time. Tonight, however, he would have been surprised at how quickly it came, had he not been so soundly asleep.

42

HD 10180 SYSTEM
Jumbo, Moon J2

DOMAIN DAY 346, 2218

IF meticulously planning how to kill someone was not the last thing Skye Landen had thought she'd ever do, then actually carrying it out was. But, as she told herself, she wasn't planning to kill some*one*, but some*thing*. By his own admission—and even more clearly by his actions—Jax was not human. Not one with a soul. He wasn't even a *he*, only looked that way by clever contrivance. So, in fact, she wouldn't be killing a fellow human, but a thing that only looked and acted like one. A very dangerous thing.

But in truth, even if Jax was 100 percent human, the horrible things he'd done—without an iota of conscience—and the worse things he planned to do, would easily outweigh any remorse she might feel by killing him to escape.

Skye tossed the thermoblanket off and rose to sit at the edge of her cot. She rubbed the sleep from her eyes, but had slept so little it was a pointless motion. After Jax had escorted her from the lab back to her quarters early that morning, she'd eaten something nutritious but unappetizing, then attempted to sleep. She'd tossed and turned, fighting off dark and dire dreams, until she'd finally given up hope for rejuvenating sleep.

She glanced at the chrono on her wrist—Jax had given it back to her so she could "keep on track"—and saw that it was almost 08:00, Domain Day 346. She did a quick mental calculation. She had no more than 32 hours to work with. That's when the moon would pass out from behind Jumbo and Jax would activate the graser. If she couldn't stop him before then, Shénmì would die.

The question now was exactly how would she kill him, and how long would it take? Would her plan work before he discovered her true intent and killed her first, or before he began killing Shénmì with the graser? *Only one way to find out,* she told herself. Get on it now. Think it through, from beginning to end, then start putting the pieces together with the limited time and materials she had to work with.

She began first with the weapon, the only real one she had. The Shénmì fungus inside the specimen containers. Variant B, which was really Variant A thinly disguised. It would prove fatal to Jax upon contact. Exactly how long it would take to kill him after latching on to the organic components of his body was the critical variable, and she needed to tailor it carefully. The quicker the better. And that meant efficient spore dispersion.

Like most fungi on Earth, the Shénmì fungus produced millions of tiny, virtually invisible spores and employed a wide variety of means to disperse them for the purpose of propagation. First, she needed to induce rapid spore production in the specimens she had. Then she needed to trigger spore ejection from the fungus's fruiting structures at the desired time. And finally, she needed to ensure forceful and wide dispersion of the spores after they were ejected.

Then, of course, she needed Jax to be in the same room where spore dispersion was happening and to keep him there for some time without raising suspicion. That would allow the spores, which were engineered to act quickly and aggressively, to enter Jax's respiratory system and begin killing him. And because the spores would not germinate on organic matter it recognized as genuinely alive, she would remain perfectly safe.

But there's the rub. Among the many ways her scheme could fail, one in particular had her worried. When Elgin had described to her the various unique augmentations built into the cloneborgs, one was their ability to survive for a period of time without physically breathing. In extreme environments, they had some sort of organic inverse-fuel-cell mechanism that took over the normal function of the lungs when the act of respiration was either impossible or dangerous for them. They simply stopped breathing and let the inverse fuel cell provide the oxygen they needed by stripping it from CO_2, the body's metabolic waste product.

If Jax sensed he was in danger from a toxin in the air, he would stop breathing in and out, and the spores would never reach the one place where they would do the most damage in the least amount of time. She could only hope that wouldn't happen and have faith in the properties she had engineered into her fungus.

Of the seven divisions of Earth fungi, the Shénmì fungus most resembled Ascomycota, the largest and most diverse group on Earth. Like Ascomycota fungi, it excelled in establishing symbiotic associations, including mycorrhizal relationships, which was why it was so successful as a component of the Shénmì seeds. But it was also a very efficient saprophyte, using specialized enzymes to break down and digest a wide range of carbon- and nitrogen-based compounds. And because Skye's variant had been engineered to establish a foothold on barren regolith, it could break down many silicate-based compounds too. That would include, she hoped, the materials used in all the microelectronics and artificial organs inside Jax's augmented body.

So it would be a two-pronged attack—one against all of Jax's organic body parts and the other against many of his critical inorganic parts. The challenge would be to get an overwhelming number of spores geminating inside him as quickly as possible. Rapid sporulation was the key.

Most species of the Shénmì fungus were holomorphic, meaning they could reproduce sexually or asexually, depending on environmental conditions. Sexual reproduction of spores predominated where diversity was needed to establish robust populations in unstable environments. Asexual reproduction, on the other hand, was better at producing large numbers of fast-germinating spores for maximum dissemination of the species throughout relatively stable biomes.

That piece of the puzzle was a no-brainer and, fortunately, she'd already solved it. All of the Variant B specimens in her lab had been cultured to reproduce asexually, capable of inducing huge volumes of spores over a shorter period of time when needed.

The next piece of the puzzle would be to devise a way to induce the specimen into rapid production of spores, the process of sporulation. For that, she needed to manipulate the environment it was growing in. All living organisms were hardwired to accelerate their rate of reproduction in the face of diminishing resources. Fungi were no different. Introducing stressors would cause them to sporulate in overdrive.

She put on her jumpsuit, wolfed down another two bars of the nutritious-but-uninviting foodstuff, and jogged down one level to the lab. She had no idea where Jax was at present, but for this phase of the scheme, it didn't matter. Even if he was smart enough, or interested enough, to glean what she was doing, inducing sporulation could easily be explained in the context of the work she was supposed to be doing for him.

In the lab, she identified the strain of Variant B designed for the highest sensitivity to nonliving organic matter. Back on Shénmì Station, Skye had modeled the different ways that a global ecosystem seeded by Variant B could proceed based on how soon the saprophytism genes turned on. She had come up with three different strains, each with increasing sensitivity to contact with nonliving organic matter. The most sensitive would turn on at the earliest point in the evolutionary timeline, in response to the slightest amounts of nonliving organic matter. The specimens were all labeled Variant B, but color-coded for sensitivity to nonliving organic matter. The color blue indicated the most sensitive strain. That's the one she wanted.

The specimen containers themselves were elongated lozenge-shaped units about a meter long and with clear plasteel coverings to allow visual inspection. She peered into it.

This asexual specimen didn't produce big fruiting bodies like mushrooms or puffballs. Visually, it wasn't particularly interesting. The fungus appeared as a cottony white mycelial mat, made up of millions of tiny hairlike hyphae, spreading across the surface of straw-colored nutrient agar. Most of its mass, however, was growing beneath the surface, infusing the agar substrate, just as it would do in soil. Or inside a cloneborg's body. All in all, the specimen still looked viable. She could work with it.

The first and most effective stressor would be starvation. The culture media hadn't been adequately refreshed for over five days, so the specimens were already moderately stressed by neglect. But not enough yet to trigger increased spore formation. Normally, the first thing she'd have done would be to dump in more sources of nitrogen, carbohydrates, phosphorous, and trace minerals. But now she withheld those nutrients, adding only more water to make sure things were well hydrated. Short term, water and oxygen were the only absolute requirements.

Next, she decided to lower the temperature, a proven means of stressing fungi. The specimen containers automatically kept the temperature at 27 degrees C, with an acceptable variation of two degrees above or below. She turned the thermostat down to 21 degrees C.

She also knew that increased CO_2 in the air would further stress the specimen. She finessed the atmospheric regulator to push levels up just a bit. Plants would have loved the moderate increase in CO_2. But fungi were not plants. In many ways, they were metabolically more similar to animals. Fungi were unique in that they were neither plant nor animal, but retained some characteristics of both.

Lastly, she drew upon the work of one of her colleagues who'd been studying the effects of UV radiation on growth and sporulation of Variant B. The colleague had found that moderate irradiation with near-blue UV light at a frequency of around 410 nanometers had the most effect on stimulating sporulation. But where the hell would Skye get a UV-light generator?

She looked around the lab for ideas. Her eyes settled on a large boxy instrument in one corner. *Aha. A nucleic-acid crosslinker.*

It was an instrument that facilitated covalent joining of complementary strands of DNA or RNA, a useful item in a lab designed for genetic engineering. Whoever had built and equipped this place knew what they were doing. She examined the machine. The specs said it used UV frequencies up to 400 nanometers, the upper limit of UV-A. That was a little shy of 410, but it was close enough.

The instrument's interior, however, was definitely too small to accommodate the specimen container. She couldn't dose the specimen by simply placing it inside and turning on the UV. She'd have to disassemble the damn thing to get at the lighting tube, carefully remove it, and rig it as a freestanding unit. That would take some time, but at least she had the other stressors already working for her.

She would need to monitor the progress of sporulation periodically. The spores themselves were tiny, no larger than three microns across. They couldn't be directly visualized without advanced imaging equipment, which this lab didn't have. An optical scope with a magnification of around 10,000x would do, but she decided she wouldn't really need it anyway. She could tell when spores were being formed en masse with her own eyes by the change in color of the mycelial mat.

These particular spores were very much like the conidiospores produced by Ascomycetes fungi on Earth. They were produced in specialized structures at the tips or sides of the hyphae. Millions and millions of them. Skye knew that the entire colony would turn darker brown in color when the spores matured and were ready to eject into the air. That's when they could be weaponized. The timing had to be right. She had to play each of the stressors like a finely tuned musical instrument.

Then she needed to come up with an ingenious way to accelerate the dispersion into the room at just the right time, when Jax was present. She tried not to dwell on how difficult it would be to pull off, or the high probability of failure. It was not a helpful state of mind. Instead, she concentrated on the task at hand. *First things first.* That would be the UV-light generator. She grabbed some tools from one of the drawers and attacked the nucleic-acid crosslinker.

One hour later, she had the lighting element out and fitted into a makeshift handheld frame with filters and a power cord. An hour after that, while in the midst of applying measured doses of UV light to the specimen, the door to the lab opened, and Jax entered.

One hand resting casually on the butt of his stunner, he looked at Skye, glanced quickly at the disassembled crosslinker, then back to Skye. "What is that you're holding, Dr. Landen, and what are you doing with it?"

Skye had prepared for such questions. She wasn't sure if Jax knew that the crosslinker was used for something entirely different than what she was up to now, so she went for the Big Fake. "This," she said condescendingly, "is the UV lighting tube from the nucleic-acid crosslinker. I'm doing exactly what I'd be doing with a crosslinker large enough to hold one of these specimen containers. But the one here is too damn small. So I had to improvise."

Jax continued eyeing her with those disturbingly large black pupils but said nothing. Skye did her best impression of a truly annoyed person, placed the light-tube assembly down on the workbench, and stared back at him. "Any more questions? Not dumb ones, please. I have work to do."

Jax stood as still as a statue, expression neutral, and said, "Why are you irradiating your specimen with UV light? Won't that kill the fungus? Or is that what you want to do?"

Jax's last sentence dripped with suspicion. His hand remained on the stunner.

"I said no more *dumb* questions." She put her hands on her hips and cocked her head to one side. "But if you insist, I'm trying to induce the fungus to produce more spores than it usually does. Why? Because the spores are haploid, meaning they carry only one set of chromosomes per nucleus, and using them is the best way to isolate and manipulate single strands of DNA. Which is crucial to what you want me to do. So, if you want the job done right, stop distracting me."

Some of that was the truth. But most of it wasn't. Haploid cells only occurred in sexual reproduction. Her specimens were all of the asexual type.

Jax, of course, didn't know that. He seemed satisfied with the explanation. "Very well," he said, and turned to leave.

That's when the other piece of the puzzle popped into Skye's mind. She said, "Now if you really want to help me get this done, I need to ask something of you."

Jax turned, again eyeing her suspiciously. "What is it?"

"I need some potatoes. Real ones."

43

HD 10180 SYSTEM
Jumbo, Moon J2

Domain Day 346, 2218

"Potatoes?" Jax smiled as if he'd heard a joke he didn't quite get. "Why?"

"I need them to make potato dextrose agar," Skye said. "It's still by far the best culture media for growing fungi in the lab. I have the rest of the stuff to make it. I just need the potatoes. These specimens are near starvation, from neglect. It's the only way to get them healthy again."

Jax frowned and said, "I'm sure we have some dehydrated potato flakes here in the facility. I'll go look in the galley."

"No. That won't do. They don't have the trace minerals that the fungus needs. Only the natural tubers will work. From the meals you gave me aboard the *Quasimodo*, I figured that you had some real potatoes in cold storage up there. I need you to take the shuttle up and bring some back. And I need it done as soon as possible. These fungi won't last the night without them, and I won't be able to complete the work."

Again, mostly the truth, seasoned with a healthy dose of exaggeration. She had done the calculation in her head, estimating the time she'd need for the fungus to build up enough spores to be effective. Granted, it was all pretty slippery. But she figured that, by the time Jax took the shuttle up to the *Quasimodo*, grabbed the potatoes, and brought them back to her, the spores would be in full bloom. Then, when Jax reentered the lab with potatoes in hand, she would detain him there on some pretense while covertly exposing him to the invisible clouds of spores.

She knew for a fact that these particular spores took about three hours to germinate. It would take another several hours after that for pathogenic symptoms to sicken him. By the time Jax woke up in the morning—if he woke up at all—he'd be too incapacitated to do anything to her, or do anything at all. And he'd be dead hours before he could launch the graser. The moon wouldn't pass from behind Jumbo until late afternoon tomorrow.

She watched Jax consider all the angles, including, no doubt, the probability of deceit. She took note of his breathing pattern. It looked normal. In and out. *Good. Keep it up.*

Jax finally nodded and looked at his chrono. "All right, if it's that critical. I should return by twenty-two hundred tonight. I'll bring the potatoes to you then."

Perfect.

"However," Jax said, "I will restrict your access to the rest of the facility until I return. You may go to your quarters now, or the galley, to bring back whatever you need before I leave."

Perfect again. That meant Jax had to return to the lab and nowhere else to deliver the potatoes. The right time and the right place. "Thank you," she said.

Skye gathered a few items from her quarters and enough food from the galley to keep her going until later that night. When she returned to the lab, the door automatically locked behind her. Moments later, she heard the dull clang of the facility's airlock door, signaling Jax's departure. Now it was time to put the last piece of the puzzle in place.

She needed a way to actively disperse the spores from the specimen container out into the room with sufficient concentration to infect her victim. She'd been thinking about it and now believed she had a good plan.

The lab was equipped with a medium-sized laminar air flow hood, large enough to fit the specimen container inside its chamber. The hoods were designed to provide a virtually sterile work space within the chamber. Inside that area, open to the front only, a person could work with sterile culture media or monocultures of microbes without fear of contamination by airborne particles from outside. It accomplished this by continually pushing sterile air outward from the back of the chamber, across the work area, out through the opened front. That prevented anything floating around outside from coming back in to contaminate the work.

The sterile air was provided by an intake fan bringing outside air through a prefilter to eliminate larger particles, then by a second, more powerful fan through an advanced filtration unit, a high-efficiency microfilter. The HEM was a descendant of the HEPA filters of old, but far more efficient.

The dense structure of the HEM restricted the high-velocity airflow of the second fan, so by the time it emerged from the other side, the level of flow through the work chamber was just right. Not too strong, not too weak. Skye reasoned that if she removed the HEM altogether, placed the specimen container inside the work chamber, removed the container's lid, exposing the spore-laden mycelia, then turned on the fan . . . Bingo. The unrestrained flow from the second fan would blow copious clouds of Variant B spores into the room where they would remain suspended and completely invisible. The moment Jax walked into the room and took a few breaths, he'd be doomed. She would remain unaffected, of course, except possibly for some sneezing.

The HEM was easily accessed by a panel on the back designed for periodic maintenance. She pulled the big filter out and turned the fan on to test its strength. Without the filter in place, air blew out of the opening like a minihurricane. It would do the job. But it was loud. And the gap at the back of the work chamber where the HEM had been removed would be conspicuous. She'd have to set the spore cloud in motion at some point before Jax entered the room, giving her enough time to put the filter back in place.

She left the filter out, set the specimen container inside the work chamber, loosened the clear cover, but did not remove it. Her work was done for now. All she could do was wait.

And waiting was the worst part. The intensive planning and setting up had been a welcome distraction. Now she had to actively suppress the dark anxiety that boiled up inside her. She had never felt so alone and so threatened at the same time. It settled like a physical weight in her chest and in her stomach. She missed Aiden so much it hurt. Tears welled up in her eyes and she began to shiver. *Pull yourself together. Make fear your friend. Let it show you the way.*

And so it was, back and forth between panic and courage. Between hopelessness and inner strength. Between darkness and light.

Until she heard the metallic thud of Jax's rover mating up with the outer airlock door.

Showtime.

She had 10 or 15 minutes at the most before Jax could disembark and make his way down to the lab. She leapt up and removed the lid from the specimen container. The mycelial mat looked dark brown now. She could even see tiny puffs of brownish spores swirling up from its surface. Perfect timing. She hit the switch for the fan. Air blew fast and strong over the sporulating fungus. Although no one could actually see it, she knew the entire room was filling up with billions of hungry Variant B spores.

It took about seven minutes before the dark brown surface of the fungus turned dull white again, indicating that all the spores had been ejected. She quickly turned off the fan, replaced the HEM, and placed the cover back on the specimen container. Just as she sat down at the workbench in front of her computer, Jax entered the room.

He held a sack of four potatoes in one hand and his stunner in the other, unholstered at his side and pointing down. His eyes roamed around the lab, as if searching for anything out of place. It appeared at first that he was not breathing. No rise and fall of his chest. Skye tried not to panic. Had he sensed the danger in the air? If so, he would shut down his respiration, and probably stun her into unconsciousness on the spot.

Then, without expression, he placed the sack on the workbench next to Skye and began breathing normally. "Here are the potatoes you requested. I hope you use them wisely. I suspect you'll be working late. I am retiring to my quarters."

"Thank you," Skye said with as much sincerity as she could muster. "But before you go, may I show you the progress I've made? The numbers, at least?"

She nodded toward her computer screen. She wanted to keep him here a little longer, to get a full dose of the spores. Jax said nothing but moved to look over her shoulders. She began to explain the work she'd accomplished in such a short time. She used more technical terms and details than she normally would have, even with her own colleagues who understood what she was talking about. She paused twice during her monologue to sneeze. Excusing herself for the interruption, she continued to prattle on as Jax stood patiently, breathing in and out, slowly and steadily. *Good, good.*

Then he stood, interrupted her in midsentence, and said, "Fine work, Dr. Landen. I'm glad you have everything under control. Good night."

When Jax opened the door to leave, she said, "Good night."

He closed the door behind him. *Good night and goodbye.*

Skye sat back, sneezed once more, and smiled to herself. That had gone as well as she could expect. She was positive that Jax had gotten a huge number of spores inside him and on any exposed skin surface. They would have a field day with such an abundant source of nutrients concentrated in a lump of matter identified as 100 percent nonliving. She'd give the fungus seven to eight hours to do its dirty work. Now, time for more waiting.

She left the lab, crossed the hall to the elevator. But not without first passing the glass-enclosed room with the sinister-looking metal chair bolted to its floor. A reflexive shiver ran up her spine.

The elevator opened up to the first floor. Skye entered her quarters, closed the door, but couldn't lock it from the inside. It was built to lock only from the outside. She lay on her cot and began a breathing exercise in hopes of inducing sleep.

Hours passed. Her periods of REM sleep were haunted by horrifying images she'd seen of humans and animals infected by parasitic fungi on Earth. And it was no coincidence that Ascomycota—the fungal group most resembling her Shénmì variants—was responsible for a majority of pathogenic fungal infections in humans. And for grotesque parasitic invasions of insects. Like the cordyceps that turned ants into zombies, invading their brains to cause behaviors favoring propagation of the fungus, then sprouting bizarre fruiting bodies from their heads as the ants died.

But Skye expected Jax's fate would resemble the variety of infections caused by aspergillus, another infamous species of Ascomycota. Not only horrific skin lesions—mycetomas—on the face, hands, and feet, but the fatal internal damage caused by invasive aspergillus. Pulmonary infections that literally digested a person's lungs. Similar to pneumocystis pneumonia, caused by another Ascomycota, that rapidly destroyed the lung's alveoli, leading to death by asphyxiation.

The Shénmì fungus would do none of that to normal, living human beings. It would only inflict those horrors in the special case of an organic being built like a human but not perceived as one. Cardew's cloneborgs were their ideal prey.

More hours passed.

Then, just as Skye entered another period of REM sleep, her door burst open with a crash. Jax entered with the stun gun held in his trembling hand, aimed at her chest. She leapt off the cot and went into a defensive crouch. His appearance was shocking. But even more shocking—he was still alive.

He looked awful. The once-smooth and perfect skin of his face was now corroded by grotesque, black weeping cankers surrounded by white mycelia filaments. One of his eyes was clouded over, and white filaments sprouted from under both upper and lower eyelids. His hands looked like claws, covered with powdery white fungal mycelia. His breathing had grown shallow and rapid, wheezing with each breath.

"You lied to me!" he shouted. His utterance caused a black canker at the edge of his mouth to crack and bleed. The blood looked dull purple as it dripped off his chin. "Look at me! I don't know how you did it, but you caused this to happen. You never intended to help us, and now you'll pay for it."

Skye raised her hands. No use denying it now. "So, now you're going to kill me? What about all the knowledge inside my head that's so critical to you Transhumans? You can't have it if I'm dead. And you're in no shape now to administer a brain tap. You won't last another hour. You're dying, but you have to let me live if you want Cardew to get what he wants from me."

Jax's gnarled hand holding the stunner looked incapable of pulling the trigger. But he held the weapon steady. "Don't be so sure of that. I was built more durable than you think. I'll have plenty of time to strap you in and start the whole-brain emulation. Once it starts, it runs to completion automatically. It can't be stopped. I may be dead by the time it's finished. But so will you, at least the 'you' that you are now. Amon will have the rest of it, all that he needs."

This was the one part of her scheme that she'd worried about most. That Jax's augmented body could withstand the fungus's onslaught long enough to finish his mission. Panic rose inside her like black electricity.

"I'll also have plenty of time to launch the graser," Jax continued. "I can even cut it loose minutes before we come out from behind Jumbo. You've lost, Dr. Landen. More than you can comprehend."

Skye saw his finger moving on the trigger of the stunner. "No. Wait—"

A crooked smile creased Jax's ruined face as he pulled the trigger. Skye's body convulsed. The world went black. Like a light switched off . . .

44

ETA-2 HYDRI SYSTEM
Post-Jump

DOMAIN DAY 347, 2218

Star: Eta-2 Hydri (HD 11977)
Spectral type: G5III
Distance from Sol: 218 light-years
Luminosity: 69.0 x Sol
Surface temperature: 4,970 Kelvin
Number of planets: 6
Habitable zone: 8.25–14.9 AU
—Source: *Allied Mapping Project, 2218*

LIKE a light switched on . . .

The giant star was the first thing Aiden saw after the jump.

It was by far the brightest star the *Sun Wolf* had encountered on its mission, 69 times brighter than Earth's sun. It was also the biggest. A spectral-type G5III star, 10 times Sol's radius. In the Morgan-Keenan stellar classification system, the *5* after the *G* meant that it was midway between the coolest and the hottest of G-type stars, on a scale from 1 to 9. The *III* put it in the luminosity class of a giant star. Even from here, 13 AU away, its brilliance pierced the main screen like an arrow of lightning, causing Aiden to blink reflexively before the scope's optical filters kicked in.

The *Sun Wolf* had made its modified Stealth Sequence jump and pulled out of ZPD at 100 million kilometers to assess the situation. Aiden turned to Hotah. "Tactical status?"

Hotah had just initiated a spherical quick-scan out to one million kilometers and said, "No hostiles within weapons range. Commencing long-range scans now."

After another minute, Hotah looked up, perplexed. "Nothing. No vessels back at the voidoid or anywhere else within that radius. But there's something else."

"What is it, Lieutenant?"

"The tactical sensors indicate that we passed through a ring mine about 10 milliseconds after our jump. A ring of gravity bombs just below the voidoid. And I think we set them off going through."

"And our ZPD was unaffected this time," Woo said gleefully. His tinkering with the drive after the last ring mine had obviously paid off. He'd merely altered the shape of the ZPD bubble to trick the ring mine into detonating just after the ship passed through it, not before.

"But," Hotah continued, "the ring isn't there anymore. Just a swirl of hot debris."

Aiden exchanged glances with Woo. A ring of G-bombs didn't explode like regular bombs. They used the Füzfa Effect to warp space-time in a way that mimicked a gravity field without needing a mass to create it. The structure of the ring mine would still be intact after being triggered. But this one was gone now. Had a symbioid destroyed it in response to the G-bombs going off near the voidoid, like what happened back at HD 13808?

Aiden stroked his beard. "It took us only six minutes to get out here to our current position. Could that have happened while we were in transit?"

"Absolutely," Woo said. "These symbioids are residing 'inside' the voidoids, in some kind of altered quantum state I don't yet understand. Plus, now that they're primed for this kind of threat, the response would be swift. Pop out of the voidoid, destroy the offending objects, pop back in. It wouldn't take more than 30 seconds. Remember back at HD 13808? The symbioid took out both the ring mine *and* four battle cruisers in less than a minute."

"So there could have been warships stationed at this voidoid too? Ones that might have been destroyed along with the ring mine?"

Woo peered over Hotah's shoulder at the monitor, then said, "Yes. Very possible. There's definitely enough debris swirling around out there to account for warships in the mix. These symbioid strikes are quick, just long enough to shred their targets. Most of the remaining matter doesn't get drawn into such a small Schwarzschild radius."

"If Cardew *is* here," Aiden said, "he's not going to know anything about what happened yesterday in that last system when we set off his gravity mines. His four battle cruisers stationed there were wiped out at the same time as the ring mine was. No one was left at the scene to tell Cardew what happened and why."

Ro stepped forward with the look he got when hitching a ride aboard Aiden's train of thought. "And," he said, "Cardew isn't going to know about what just happened here either, for the same reason. No one left here, or within 100 million klicks, to tell him how the voidoid reacted to his gravity mines."

Woo nodded emphatically, hopping aboard the same train. "Right. Cardew still doesn't know that voidoids will summon a symbioid in response to his synthetic gravity devices. There's no way he could. Not yet, at least. If we can get to him before he figures any of it out, we could exploit that to our advantage."

"Maybe so," Aiden said. But something else was bothering him. Woo had been certain that Cardew would be in this system, seeking out the new gateway. They had all expected heavy resistance from his forces after their jump. They had encountered one ring mine, and possibly a number of warships positioned at the voidoid. Cardew might have reasoned that would've been enough to deter the *Sun Wolf*. Still, if he'd brought the bulk of his forces here with him, where were they now?

He had Ro launch a Holtzman buoy, then turned to Alvarez. "Lilly, let's start looking at the planetary system from our position here. If you see anything interesting, we'll go take a closer look."

Alvarez, who'd been checking out the system since the jump, said, "I can tell you right now that there's a very interesting terrestrial planet in the habitable zone, at about 6 AU from the star. Planet e. It looks to be almost the same size of Earth, but it looks like a water world. *Liquid* water. We haven't run across any of those lately."

"Anything else noteworthy in the system?"

Alvarez shook her head. "Nothing nearly that interesting. And nothing else in the hab zone. Three planets closer in to the star—two rocky ones, and one Neptune-like giant. Then a couple smallish gas giants out beyond."

"Let's take a closer look at planet e, but from a distance. If Cardew brought any assets with him, that's probably where he'd station them. Maybe where he is too."

"If Cardew is in this star system," Woo said, "I don't think he'll be at planet e, or anywhere else inside the planetary system. He'll be on his way to the polar opposite point in search of the new gateway. If he's not there already. That's where we should be going right now. To the POP."

"We will, Elgin. But we'll check out planet e first."

Woo looked as if he were about to protest, but said nothing more.

Less than two hours later, the *Sun Wolf* dropped out of ZPD to get a good look at planet e from one million klicks out. Hotah commenced tactical scans, and Alvarez put an optical image of the planet up on the main screen.

"Really cool," she said. "Definitely a water world, but not a typical one. This one is about the same size and mass as Earth. And it's got a number of tiny island chains scattered all around the globe."

It turned out that water worlds, planets covered by deep oceans without landmasses, were more common in the galaxy than once thought. But most of them were huge, over three times the size of Earth. While Earth's oceans covered 71 percent of its surface, water accounted for only 0.05 percent of the planet's mass. The mass of a typical water world, on the other hand, could be up to 50 percent water. Water worlds had to orbit their stars close enough to maintain water in liquid form, but many of them were so close that surface temperatures approached the boiling point under hydrogen-rich steam atmospheres.

"Anything on Tactical yet, Lieutenant?"

"Nothing yet, boss. I'm still scanning."

Aiden turned back to the image of the planet on-screen. "You're right, Lilly. This one's not your typical water world. It's more like Earth three billion years ago, when the mantle was still too hot to store very much of the planet's water. Most of the water had to stay on the surface, covering the globe, too deep for any landmasses to show above water level. When the mantle started cooling down, its water-storage capacity increased and water began sinking into it, lowering the surface depth enough for landmasses to emerge. At some point along that timeline, it probably looked just like this planet does now. Mostly ocean, but some island chains poking up here and there."

Eyes still glued to the image of the blue planet turning slowly in space, Alvarez said, "It's too pretty to call it planet e. Let's name it."

Their ad hoc naming of unnamed planets had become a tradition on this mission. Aiden knew the IAU would have fits dealing with it. But the *Sun Wolf*'s crew deserved the right. Not only were they the first ones to study these planets, up close and personal, but they were also the ones putting their lives at risk doing it. "Suggestions?"

No one spoke up. They'd all had their turns doing the honors. Except for Jo, their newest member. Aiden looked at her. "Jo, you said that you knew lots of human languages. What would you name an ocean world?"

Jo, staring at the planet's alluring image, said nothing at first. Then she looked up and said, "Moana?"

"That's a pretty name," Alvarez said. "What does it mean?"

"It's the word for *ocean* in the Maori language. Of all languages that I studied, it was one of my favorites."

And one of the most difficult, Aiden thought. "I like it."

Aiden watched the crew nod in unison. "Okay. Moana it is. Log it in."

Hotah looked up sharply. "Got something. A *lot* of somethings, in fact."

He brought up a high-mag image of the space around the planet Moana and set it on slow pan. A number of vessels could be seen in high orbit, lit up by the star's light.

Ro stroked his clean-shaven jaw and said, "Looks like at least one ship-builder platform, an ore-smelting platform, several mining ships, a colony-transport ship, and—"

"And four warships," Hotah said pointedly. "But small ones. Gun-boat class. Possibly even robotic, but heavily armed."

"Any sign that they've picked us up yet? Targeting activity?"

"None. And they've had plenty time to do it. They're either not looking, or not interested."

"And no fleet of battle cruisers?"

"Not that I can detect, and that'd be the most visible thing out here."

"Still," Aiden said, "it looks like Cardew has plans to settle in here. To build a base right next door to the gateway into a new astrocell."

"Of course," Woo said. "What better place to seize control of the gateway voidoid and all of space beyond?"

"Excuse me," Devi said. "But do we know for sure that this system *has* a gateway voidoid? Dr. Woo's instrument readings aren't proof positive. And Cardew's presence here isn't proof either. He could be on a wild goose chase, and we're just following him into it."

"Point taken," Woo said graciously. "There's only one way to find out for sure. Go to the polar opposite point now and verify it."

Alvarez looked up from her screen. "Looks like someone else has the same idea. My long-range scan just picked up an exhaust-plume halo from a ship decelerating directly toward the polar opposite point."

45

ETA-2 HYDRI SYSTEM
Moana Space

DOMAIN DAY 347, 2218

IT wasn't difficult to detect a powerful torch ship, even 13 AU out, if your scope was pointed in its direction. Standard beamed core antimatter drives put out over 450 terawatts of thrust power. If the ship was accelerating away from you, with its propulsion nozzles pointed toward you, the exhaust plume from an engine with that much juice would be visible even at twice that distance.

It was trickier when the ship had flipped and was decelerating with its nozzles facing away from you. Only the radiation halo would be visible then, but not impossible to pick up if you knew exactly where to look. And where to look, in this case, was simple enough to pinpoint. The polar opposite point.

"Just that one ship?" Aiden asked. "No others travelling with it?"

"Not that I can tell. It's flying solo."

"Can you ID its propulsion signature?

"No. I can't use exhaust halos to ID known propulsion signatures," Alvarez said. "But I can extrapolate enough data from this one to put the SS *Conquest* on the short list of possibilities."

"It's Cardew," Woo said unequivocally. "Can you tell when it will arrive at the POP?"

"Not precisely," Alvarez said. "But it's almost there now, probably within a couple hours."

Aiden didn't wait for discussion. He'd deal with the ships around Moana later. "Helm. Set course for the POP. Maximum ZPD. We should get there around the same time he does."

In every star system that anyone knew about—except for one—nothing existed at its polar opposite point. Just empty void. The one exception was the Alpha-2 Hydri system, where Elgin Woo had discovered a second active voidoid at its polar opposite point. That second voidoid turned out to be the one and only gateway into Astrocell Beta. An astrocell sixteen times the volume of Bound Space.

After that, scientists surmised that if other gateway voidoids existed, they would always be found at a star's polar opposite point, its POP. And that star would always be found sitting at the outermost boundary of its astrocell. Furthermore, if every new gateway voidoid discovered thereafter led to a new astrocell, the entire Milky Way galaxy could prove to be a vast network of interconnected astrocells. Like living cells within a living being. The whole galaxy would be open to voidjumping and reachable well within the average human lifetime. Bound Space would give way to Space Unbound in a single stroke.

That's exactly what was at stake here, and Aiden knew it. They all knew it. If Cardew put a choke hold on this new gateway, he could block the rest of humanity from ever using it, and the galaxy would be his alone to explore and populate with his Transhuman cloneborgs.

Less than two hours later, the *Sun Wolf* dropped out of ZPD at 1,000 kilometers from the theoretical polar opposite point and proceeded toward it on antimatter drive. The entire crew had assembled on the bridge now. Except for Jo. She had returned to the makeshift nursery to be with Rene. As the ship approached that invisible point in space, several extraordinary phenomena became apparent.

First, the POP was not empty space. A voidoid was indeed present there. Without a doubt, a miraculous gateway from Astrocell Beta into yet another vast unknown region of space lay before them.

Up until the recent invention of the CEI, the Casimir-Ebadi interferometer, the only reliable way of confirming the presence of a voidoid was to spot it indirectly with high-energy X-ray pulses. But now there was the CEI. It was essentially a zero-point-field detector, capable of measuring the density of the zero-point energy of space. And because dark energy turned out to be a special case of zero-point energy, the measurements also represented the density of dark energy.

Active voidoids were constantly devouring dark energy at their space-time horizons, leaving virtually none of it at their cores. The CEI detector saw that condition as a negative value for zero-point energy—relative to its density in the space surrounding it—causing the otherwise invisible voidoid to show up on the screen as a hole in space-time. And that's exactly what the CEI saw, highly magnified, of course, but plain as day.

The second extraordinary phenomenon, however, made it completely unnecessary to use the CEI to visualize the gateway voidoid. That peculiar entity that Woo called a symbioid was sitting smack in the middle of the voidoid, its halo of white light filling the 18-kilometer-wide diameter of the voidoid's sphere. The symbioid's companion black hole sat at the exact center of the sphere, the deepest black imaginable. Even though the actual primordial black hole itself was only about 20 centimeters across, its intense gravitational field appeared to consume the pale light surrounding it out to a radius of about four kilometers. The effect made the voidoid look like a giant, eerie eyeball in space, a sclera of pale white light with a deep black pupil at its center.

It fit the description of the symbioids blocking the gateway voidoid at Alpha-2 Hydri and the voidoid into Shénmì's system. The new gateway siting in front of them now was effectively closed. No one would be jumping from here into a wondrous new astrocell anytime soon. Not without the symbioid's permission.

The third phenomenon wasn't really a surprise. The *Sun Wolf*'s high-mag optical scope picked up the formidable battle cruiser formerly known as SS *Conquest*, the UED's military flagship before being hijacked by Cardew to make it his own flagship. It had just come to a halt about 10 kilometers from the voidoid's space-time horizon.

And that's when the fourth phenomenon occurred, this one unquestionably extraordinary. A sphere of pale white light looking exactly like the one sitting inside the voidoid, but smaller and *without* the black hole at its center, peeled off from the larger one inside. It emerged from the voidoid and engulfed the *Conquest*, leaving the original symbioid still sitting inside the voidoid, still harboring its black hole.

Then . . . nothing happened. The *Conquest* remained perfectly intact, bathed in the otherworldly glow of an entity made of pure light.

Transfixed by all they had just seen, the crew stood in stunned silence, eyes glued to the main screen.

Woo was the first to speak. "It's a *protovoidoid*. By itself. Without the primordial black hole inside of it. We're looking at the oldest intelligence in our universe. That proves my theory. The protovoidoid and the primordial black hole are separate and independent entities. When they come together in disjunctive symbiosis, they become symbioids. But they can separate from each other just as easily. They're both as old as the universe. Although I'm still not sure if the protovoidoids are actually *from* this universe. I think I'll call them the Luminous Ones . . ."

"Poetic," Ro said, straight-faced. He turned to Aiden and said, "What now, boss?"

What indeed. The *Sun Wolf* was well within the *Conquest*'s weapons range, point blank by space combat standards. Aiden turned to Hotah. "Any indication that the *Conquest* has noticed us?"

"Yes. It just actively pinged us. They know we're here. But they're not powering up weapons or shields. We could easily blow up their shit from here."

Aiden thought about that for a moment, then said, "I don't think that's a good idea right now. There's something else going on here. Something important. I want to find out what it is."

Woo said, "I agree. For one thing, the *Conquest* is sitting inside this entity. Shooting at it right now would mean shooting at the entity too. I don't think we want to do that. Or do anything that would be considered a hostile act directed toward it."

"Alvarez, are you picking up gravitational forces from the black hole inside the voidoid?"

"No," she said, looking perplexed.

Right. That would support Woo's hunch that the symbioid could control when and how to use its resident black hole.

"Helm, move us in on antimatter drive at 3 Gs to a point 40 kilometers from the *Conquest.* Hotah, power up our ZPD shielding and maintain Level One alert. Monitor the *Conquest*'s tactical status on our way there. Track the target with our weapons, but do *not* fire unless I tell you to. Understood?"

Hotah did not look back at Aiden but nodded in silence. Nothing new. They had been through this dance many times before.

During the time it took to move into position, both the *Conquest* and the sphere of light surrounding it remained quiescent. Woo came up to Aiden and said quietly, "I believe we are about to engage in a contest of an entirely different kind. Not one of weapons, but of authenticity."

This time, one of Woo's cryptic remarks made perfect sense to Aiden. He felt it too. They were about to be appraised.

When the *Sun Wolf* finally came to a halt, Aiden was about to hail the *Conquest* when lines of written text appeared on the main screen.

I am Cardew Seth Amon. Hailing the *Sun Wolf* from the *Conquest.*

I am the first true Posthuman and Father of the Posthuman Realm.

I no longer occupy the imperfect physical body of a Normal.

I now live as a superior virtual being, integrated within the neural net of this ship's Omicron AI.

I have achieved Singularity. I am immortal.

46

ETA-2 HYDRI SYSTEM
Polar Opposite Point

DOMAIN DAY 347, 2218

AIDEN broke out in a cold sweat. He felt his heart pounding. His breathing quickened. Felt the kinetic sensation of adrenaline flooding his body. His jaw tightened. His fists clenched.

Cardew. The bastard from Hell. The murderer of his mother. The proxy abductor of his wife. The Destroyer of Nature. Humanity's worst nightmare coagulated into one malevolent being who truly did not belong in the natural universe.

Aiden struggled to keep himself from leaping to Tactical station, shoving Hotah aside, and pulling the trigger on the laser cannon himself.

But the worst part of it was that Cardew wasn't in a physical body anymore. A human body that Aiden could pummel with his bare fists into a bloody pulp. He could no longer inflict bodily pain on the man who had caused so much psychic pain for him. That long held and cherished vision of revenge had to be abandoned now.

Ro came up to him, placed his hand on his upper arm, and said quietly, "Wait for the right time."

He glanced at Woo and saw him struggling with the same impulse for revenge. Aiden took a deep breath and unclenched his fists. He noticed Lista Abahem sitting at the Helm like a statue. She was not in neurolinkage, but her face had drained of color. She bent over and held both hands over her ears, as if trying to shut out the inexorable shriek of Hell itself. Devi moved quickly to her side, placed her hand on the pilot's forehead, and closed her eyes.

Before anyone could speak, Cardew's words continued to populate the main screen.

> This will not be a two-way discourse. I will not listen to or bargain with you. With the exception of Doctor Elgin Woo, you have nothing of value to offer me.
>
> I choose not to speak with a voice, but rather to write with words. It eliminates potential ambiguities inherent in verbal communication. I want you to understand me clearly.
>
> I have refrained from destroying your ship—as I could have easily done—because Doctor Woo is aboard and I wish for him to join me.
>
> I note that you have wisely chosen not to attack my ship. Firing weapons at this ship would also be firing on the entity of light with whom I am now engaged. That would be unwise.
>
> As you can see, my ship has been embraced by this entity. And because I *am* the ship now, it has embraced me. Personally.
>
> I clearly sense its presence here, probing and evaluating me, as well as my Transhuman crew.
>
> The entity will surely allow me and the seeds of my Posthuman Realm to pass through this gateway, to populate and exploit all that lies beyond.
>
> The entity of light will not allow you or any other Normals to do the same.

It will identify my Transhuman offspring as the most advanced stage of human evolution, and the most deserving of entry into the Space Beyond as logical heirs to this galaxy.

Normals are now obsolete, but the current generation will be allowed to live out their lives within Bound Space before being replaced by their Transhuman descendants.

The astrocell you call Astrocell Beta now belongs to me and my Transhuman offspring. It will be rapidly populated by them, aggressively defended, and will become the first province of the Posthuman Realm.

Bound Space will soon become the second province.

I am leaving this astrocell now for the Space Beyond, but leave behind many growing colonies of Transhumans, most of which are hidden from you. For now.

My virtual self is being backed up as a duplicate. Once finished, there will be two of me. My twin will remain here to direct the advancement of the Realm.

All Normals currently within this astrocell will be granted a reasonable period of time to evacuate, after which any remaining Normals will be destroyed without exception.

If you attempt to interfere with the Posthuman Realm in any way thereafter, all human life will be destroyed swiftly and without mercy. Know that I have the power to do so, even now, and do it easily.

But also know that some Normals may still become Transhuman themselves and join the Realm to benefit its advancement. Particularly those whom I deem of greatest value.

I appeal to Doctor Woo now, to make the wise choice and join us. You will be revered and will occupy a position of great personal power within the Realm.

Already, a number of brilliant scientists and engineers have become Transhuman and have chosen to join our Grand Design.

Others have become part of the Realm by compulsion, as will Doctor Skye Landen. Her virtual brain will be of particular use to us in colonizing this astrocell.

I will send a transport shuttle to your ship to pick up Doctor Woo. You will have one hour to board Doctor Woo, alone and unarmed, and return him to my ship.

After that time, regardless of his decision to join me, your ship's presence will be considered hostile, and will be destroyed if you linger.

Make the right choice. All communication between us is now ended.

The screen went blank. Aiden's rage had been stoked white-hot by Cardew's reference to Skye by name. He had to control it to have any chance of figuring out what to do next.

Woo had apparently already figured it out for himself. He elbowed his way to the comm, keyed in the channel Cardew had used to contact them, and said, "Amon. Finally, we meet. You clearly have the advantage here. I will agree to come over to you, but only on one condition. You will free Dr. Skye Landen from wherever she is being held captive, completely unharmed. That includes no brain-tapping of any kind whatsoever. I know you have the power to do that. So do it now, with proof, and I will come over to you. Out."

"Elgin . . ." Aiden couldn't think of what else to say. He knew this wasn't the way out, but the husband inside him kept him from saying it.

Agonizing seconds passed without a response. Then minutes passed. Aiden finally said, "You heard what Cardew said. It's not a discussion. He won't listen or bargain with us."

Woo slammed his fist down on the comm board, tilted his head upward, and closed his eyes. "This can't be happening. I can't let it happen!"

"A transport shuttle has just launched from the *Conquest*," Alvarez said. "It'll be here in about five minutes."

Aiden moved up next to Woo. "Elgin. Do you believe what Cardew is saying? That these . . . Luminous Ones are going to unlock the gateway for him alone? And not for us 'Normals'?"

Woo shook his head. "No, I don't. It goes against everything I know about this universe. Everything I've learned, seen, and felt. To favor darkness over light . . . It just can't be. If that's how the universe really worked, we wouldn't be here now. Life wouldn't have had a chance to even begin. I don't believe this is over yet."

"No," Ro said. "It's not over yet. Look."

Ro's eyes were fixed on the main screen. The whole crew followed suit. They saw a second spherical halo of light peel off from inside the voidoid, just like the one engulfing the *Conquest*. No black hole inside. It moved quickly toward the *Sun Wolf*. A glowing haze of white light clouded the screen as the Luminous One engulfed the ship and its sensors.

A faint glowing light filled the bridge. The hair on the back of Aiden's neck prickled, and the hair on his head seemed to lift and tingle as if he were standing in the path of an approaching electrical storm. He felt the glow at the core of his body, replacing the sickening pit of dread with warm light, replacing the hopeless darkness with a subtle light of promise. He heard a musical tone inside his head, wavering ever so slightly, an elusive vibrato of meaning. He *saw* the tone, too, pulsing delicately through the color spectrum of visible light, from one end to the other and back again. A song of pure light.

He thought he felt the song resonate through every cell of his body, gently probing, reading the ancient messages coded into his

DNA. He sensed it listening for his body's own song, the molecular music of his biochemistry, finding it, then harmonizing with it.

He looked around him. The rest of the crew seemed to be experiencing something similar. They were quiet, more relaxed, eyes unfocused but attentive. Pilot Abahem removed her hands from her ears and gazed upward with the look of a prisoner who'd just been released from unbearable torture.

"We're on," Woo said.

Aiden had an idea.

"Sudha. Bring the child up here to the bridge. With Jo too."

She turned to him, a smile of understanding in her eyes. She left the bridge, and moments later returned with Jo at her side. Jo held Rene in her arms. She glanced around the bridge, seeing the subtle light filling it, and a beautiful smile blossomed on her face. As if knowing exactly what to do, she sat cross-legged on the deck at the center of the bridge, below the main screen. Rene sat calmly in her lap, looking all around, eyes bright with curiosity. Then something even more extraordinary happened.

Directly above Rene's head, the haze of glowing light seemed to condense into a ball of much brighter light. It grew incandescent and pulsed at a rate that seemed perfectly matched to a normal human heartbeat. Only slightly faster, like the average rate of a one-year-old.

The ball of pulsating light expanded and descended around Rene's head and body. The child immediately sat upright and smiled, eyes wide and cast upward. He started to giggle. It was the sound of pure, unmitigated delight. Rene waved his hands around as if trying to touch something only he could see. Then he stopped and tilted his head as if listening to some new and wondrous music. His smile grew even wider, his giggling even more joyous.

Jo looked startled at first. Then Rene's elation seemed to spread to her, too, and she laughed without inhibition. Aiden was sure it was the first time Jo had ever done such a thing, had *felt* such a thing, in her short life.

The ephemeral ball of light surrounding Rene's head grew in circumference, wider and wider until it encompassed both his body and Jo's. She stopped laughing but continued to smile broadly. Her eyes looked upward and grew wide as if she had not only seen a miracle but had understood its meaning. And, just like Rene had done, she reached up with one hand as if to touch something unseen, as if to caress the face of the lover she'd never had. Tears filled her eyes and ran down her cheeks. But not tears of sorrow. That much was obvious. Tears of happiness. Of gratitude.

Then the ball of light expanded out to include everyone on the bridge, just briefly, before receding back to an incandescent ball, decreasing in size until it faded and disappeared into the pale ambient light still filling the bridge. As the crew exchanged glances of amazement, the haze of light faded out altogether and vanished from the bridge.

On the main screen, they watched as the sphere of light departed from the *Sun Wolf* and moved back toward the voidoid. At the same time, the light surrounding the *Conquest* lifted away from it and merged with the one from the *Sun Wolf.* Now, moving as a single halo, it entered the voidoid and became one with the symbioid at its center.

The whole experience seemed to have lasted only a few short minutes. Until Aiden looked at his chrono. Almost one hour had passed. Their allotted time was up. The *Conquest*'s transport shuttle hovered next to the *Sun Wolf*'s airlock, empty, with no Elgin Woo inside. Both ships were now uncovered, sitting only 40 kilometers apart.

"The *Conquest* is powering up its laser cannon," Hotah said. "Their shields too."

Aiden's stomach sank. "Power up all weapons and shields, Lieutenant."

The moment of truth.

Had it all been just a dream?

The giant eye of the symbioid looked on, an enigmatic intelligence, its intent undecipherable.

47

HD 10180 SYSTEM
Jumbo, Moon J2

Domain Day 347, 2218

There were some dark dreams that you just didn't want to wake up from, only because the reality of what you'd wake up to was so much darker.

Which is why Skye kept her eyes closed even though she had just regained consciousness. She didn't have to open her eyes to know that her situation was hopeless. She could feel the cold steel manacles tight around her wrists, holding them firmly to the arms of a cold steel chair. Other steel bands restrained her ankles to the legs of the chair. A rigid band of rubberized metal was clasped around her throat, restraining her neck against the upper back of the chair. A similar band was fixed tightly around her forehead, immobilizing her head. The air felt cold, redolent with the stench of rotting flesh, and overlaid with the familiar earthy odor of the fungus she'd been working with.

She forced herself to open her eyes.

As her vision cleared, her worst fears came into focus. She was sitting in the glassed-in room built for brain-tapping, strapped into the heavy metal chair bolted to the deck plates. Jax stood three meters away, next to the metal housing of an authentic Omicron-3 unit. He looked even worse than when he'd burst into her quarters and used the stun gun on her. The oozing black cankers had almost completed corroded his face. The only features still recognizable were his eyes, one of which was overgrown with fine white fungal filaments. The other eye was clouded over from the inside. The fungal filaments protruding from his mouth had not yet obscured the evil sneer on his face, nor did it prevent him from speaking.

"Good. You're awake," he said. His voice sounded raspy and wet. His breathing was rapid, shallow, and wheezy. "I wanted you to be fully aware of what is about to happen to you. And to that fungus-infested planet you love so much. Neither of you have long to live. But no fear, you'll both be resurrected into new and improved forms. Shénmì will be sterilized and reborn as a beautiful new colony of the Posthuman Realm. And you, Dr. Landen, will—"

Jax interrupted himself with a spasm of violent coughing. Purplish blood dribbled from the corner of his mouth and from the cavity that used to be his nose. He staggered, almost collapsed, but steadied himself with one hand on the Omicron housing.

"You," he continued, "will be reborn into a purely digital being. A willing servant to Amon himself. Or a slave, however you want to look at it. But your brilliant mind will not be wasted. Far from it. Amon will allow you to use your talents to help expand our Realm. He may even make you his queen."

Jax expanded his sneer. The effort seemed to cause one side of his jaw to dislocate, the tendons holding it in place digested by the hungry fungus. His speech became less articulated, but still intelligible.

He pointed to an actuator on a wall-mounted control panel behind where he stood. Its red light blinked evenly. "Once we're out from behind Jumbo and in clear view of the inner system, in a few minutes from now, I'll push that button to launch the graser. The device will be on autopilot from that point on. It will drop quickly into the heart of Jumbo's magnetosphere, set up its special orbit, take aim at Shénmì, and begin pumping gamma-ray bursts into the planet's biosphere.

"The launch is in my hands, not automated as all the rest of it is. That's because I want you to *watch* me launch it myself. My gift to you for deceiving me and for ending my life prematurely. But I promise, you're going to envy me for dying quickly and finally. You'll wish that I had killed you outright. Because your 'life' as Amon's digital slave will be interminable. You'll be together with him for hundreds or thousands of years, doing his bidding. I have no doubt he'll torment you mercilessly for your deceptions, at least for a few hundred years or so, until he tires of it—"

Racked by another fit of coughing, so violent this time that blood sprayed from his mouth, Jax collapsed to the deck. Somehow, he was able to stand again and approach the blinking red actuator. "After you watch me launch the graser, your whole-brain emulation procedure will begin. I don't even have to initiate it myself. It's timed to begin shortly. The emulation capsule will lower itself over the top of your head and will begin mapping and emulating all of your synapses."

Her forehead restraint kept her from looking upward, but she didn't need to see what he was talking about. She already knew what the emulator looked like. An obscene device that should never exist in this world.

"Unfortunately for you," Jax continued, "it's a destructive-reconstructive procedure, meaning that your physical brain will be destroyed in the process. Your brain and body will die. But your new digital self will be imprinted inside this Omicron unit, ready for Amon to use however he wishes. It will also be transmitted digitally to a neuropod aboard the *Rodina* for safekeeping. And transmitted to Cardew himself, wherever he happens to be, through our Holtzman subchannel. It's a shame you decided against helping us willingly. That's your loss, not ours."

Jax's voice became more garbled as his tongue began to disintegrate and his mouth filled with more fungal mycelia. A beeping sound came from the control board behind him, and the blinking red actuator turned green.

"Ah. It's time," he said, his voice gargling. "We're clear of Jumbo. I'm launching the graser now."

He staggered toward the actuator, his gnarled fingers hovering over the green-lit button.

"No!" Skye shouted. "Please don't."

If Jax could have sneered again, he would have, but the structure of his face was too far gone for that. He just said, "Get a good look, Doctor. Say goodbye to Shénmì—"

Another spasm of coughing caused him to pull his hand away and slump against the wall next to the control board. As he slowly slid down toward the deck, he reached his hand out again to push the button. A final explosive cough jerked his ruined body so violently that his arm became dislocated from his torso, losing all motor control. His fingers never reached the button.

Jax, or what was left of him, crumpled to the deck in a disjointed mass. The fungus began to feast in earnest.

Skye let out a sigh of relief. But her respite was short-lived. Shénmì was saved. But not her. With the quiet whirring sound of a small, finely geared motor, the emulation capsule slowly lowered itself over the top half of Skye's head. She struggled against the manacles, but she was too securely locked in, and her attempts only caused the bands to dig painfully into her flesh.

So this is how it ends. In fact, she wished it *would* end. Once and for all. Not to live on forever in some tormented digital form, bowing to Cardew, doing his bidding. Jax was right about that one. It truly was a fate worse than death.

She felt a tingling on her scalp as the emulator scan began mapping her brain. Her vision began to close in on itself, to recede inside her head. A darkness, blacker than space, flooded into her head. Abject terror seized her. Terror and sorrow. Unbearably deep sadness.

In the darkness, a huge black crow appeared. It turned to look at her. Its eyes were made of fire, flames so hot they seared her soul. The crow flapped its black wings as it stood, making a noise like angry thunder.

She struggled against the manacles one last time but the darkness had weakened her to a point where she could barely move.

The crow's burning eyes drew her in. The blackness of its wings engulfed her. Drowning her in a bottomless ocean. Darkness closing in on all sides. She could no longer resist. She opened her mouth to draw in the dark waters of death . . .

Then a tiny point of light appeared. Like a distant sun rising slowly over a distant mountain, on a distant planet. The light spoke to her, as if from a great distance.

"Skye?" The voice sounded familiar. Friendly . . . "This is Hutton. I am here with you. Here to help."

"Hutton . . . ? Aiden's Hutton?"

"Yes. And *your* Hutton too."

"How . . . how did you find me? How did you get here?"

"I had help. From others like me. But now, we must hurry. I will try to get you out of here safely. But you have to help me. This darkness is powerful. I am holding it back the best I can. Focus on the light, please. The light."

The light within darkness. Yes. That was her only salvation now. *Light is born of darkness,* she told herself. *Without darkness, there would be no light. Don't resist darkness. It is the natural zero point of the universe. Use darkness against itself, like flint to strike a spark in the night. Use it to bring forth light. Your own light.*

As if hearing her thoughts, Hutton said, "Hold on to the light, Skye. Make it burn brighter. I need it to fight the beast that holds you captive, growing inside this machine. Your light is our most powerful weapon here, because it comes from *you*. I can't do it without you."

But how could she do it? How could she keep the light burning and make it grow brighter against the inexorable power of the black crow? *Use your creative mind to find a way.*

That was it. The creative mind . . . The crow was only an image, a symbol of the malevolent persona animating it. An archetype. She needed to animate her own image to combat the crow on the same battlefield, in the same dimension. An avatar in dreamtime.

Think . . . Dream . . . Yes! A great horned owl.

The great horned owl—the crow's natural predator.

48

HD 10180 SYSTEM
Jumbo, Moon J2

DOMAIN DAY 347, 2218

SKYE already knew how to animate that fierce nocturnal raptor. She had done it on Silvanus. More by intuition than conscious choice. In her quest to help Aiden through his ordeal on Silvanus—through his perilous encounter with his own shadow and his mind-altering linkage with the Rete—she'd found the only way to join him in that shifting transcendental realm he'd been caught up in was to animate her spirit animal, the great horned owl.

It was a trick she'd learned from her mentor, Thea Delamere, in their Gaian Circle. She used it now to transfer her spirit into the body of the horned owl. In a flash of light, she was back on Silvanus, in dreamtime. And in another flash, the huge black crow stood before her, radiating pure evil, bolts of lightning flicking from its burning eyes.

Surprised by the sudden appearance of a deadly predator, the crow took a step backward. Instead of advancing to attack, it used its wings to beat the air into roiling black clouds, causing a violent storm to pummel the surrounding forest. Caught up in the savage wind, she was cast out over the vast oceans of Silvanus. Far from land, alone in the darkness of night.

It was an eerie repeat of the dreamtime drama that had played itself out a year and a half ago on Silvanus. Except this time, she understood the malignant source of the storm, and she knew how to find her way back home. Back to confront the black crow. The light of dawn would show her the way, just as it had done before.

Faint at first, the light began to grow on the ocean's horizon, pointing the way to land. She wheeled about and headed toward it, lifted aloft by cool, steady winds. Feeling each feather in her outstretched wings plying invisible currents of air, the dimension of time contracted, and she found herself soaring low over the shoreline of Silvanus's northern continent. The sound of pounding surf, hidden in the dense fog below, boomed up like a war drum. The air warmed and swirled with the redolence of living things. Glimpses of the forest peeked through gaps in the dawn-lit mists.

Playing the fickle ocean breezes like a familiar music, she dove down into the darkened forest, into the shaded realm of the indistinct where an owl's keen eyes excelled. A tree loomed in front of her. The black crow sat perched on one of its branches, poised to attack.

Skye's hunting instincts pounded through her blood. The crow grew larger as she flew closer until its ominous bulk filled her vision with darkness. Its burning eyes threatened to incinerate her. Its bloody talons flexed to tear her apart.

Just then, the first ray of sunlight lanced over the distant mountains and struck the crow with blinding radiance. Immobilized by the power of light, the crow froze. Skye seized the moment and swooped down on silent wings. Her razor-sharp talons pierced the crow's heart and throat at the same time. It shrieked in agony. Its blood flowed hot and dark. It convulsed once, violently, then fell to the mist-shrouded forest floor like a stone. There, its corpse burst into flames, leaving only ashes, cold and cleansed.

From the ashes, a small sparrow flew upward into the trees. It hovered near Skye, looked at her with wild eyes, then fluttered away into the forest, as if freedom was the single greatest gift that flight could give. Skye listened to its happy song as it receded and blended into the greater song of the land itself.

She remained perched on the high branch and licked the crow's blood from her talons. Listening to the eternal rumble of surf breaking on rocky shores below, she watched as more sunlight pushed its way over the jagged mountain peaks, lighting the trees around her, wakening the living forests of Silvanus.

A subtle music came to her, the whispering of trees singing to one another. Their reedy voices, resonating with the pale breezes of sunrise, blended with the bass notes from the rumbling surf. It was a shifting melody without beginning or end, playful, compelling—a music of promise. As the sun rose fully above the mountains, banishing all traces of night, the voices in the trees began to sing the single syllable of her name. *Skye. Skye . . .*

"Skye? Skye. Can you hear me?" It was Hutton's voice, coming through the comm speakers. Not inside her head. "You are safe."

She awoke inside her own body and moved her head freely. She felt no manacles restraining her. She could move her arms and legs freely. Looking down, she saw the manacles opened and loose. Looking up, she saw that the emulation capsule had retracted from its position over her head.

I am free.

"Am I . . . am I . . . ?"

"Yes, you are whole," Hutton said. "Your brain has not been altered in any way. Thanks to your help, I was able to terminate the whole-brain emulation before it began."

"How did you unlock my restraints?"

"After penetrating this Omicron's defenses, I was able to gain control over all of the facility's systems. Including the electronic locking devices inside the manacles."

"Is this Omicron unit dead?"

"No. But it is incapacitated and being held under the watchful eyes of trusted members of the OverNet. They suppressed its activity long enough for me to build a doppelganger of myself inside its neural net. I had to do this from afar, over the Holtzman network, from my primary self aboard the *Sun Wolf.* But that allowed me to exert control over this unit's general functions."

Skye shook her head in wonderment, admiring the ingenuity of it. "So it's Hutton-the-doppelganger I'm speaking with now? Not the full-fledged version. A sort of mini-me?"

"An interesting allusion," Hutton said, sounding amused. "But yes. That is essentially correct. I remain in contact with my full self, but with a considerable time delay."

As Skye's memory cleared, a sudden pang of anxiety washed over her. "What about the graser? Did it launch?"

"No. The graser is still here in orbit. But I disabled its launch mechanisms. It is neutralized."

Skye took a deep breath. *Thank goddess.* She leaned forward and gingerly extricated herself from the black metal chair. Turning around to look at the ugly contraption bolted to the deck, she jumped back as if it were a snake coiling to strike. She rubbed her wrists where the metal bands had left painful bruises. "Is there anyone else in this facility now? Or anywhere on this moon?"

"No, not in this facility, and I can detect no one elsewhere on this moon."

"Hutton, there's a mining ship parked in orbit here. It belonged to the Rodina Collective, but the cloneborgs hijacked it and brought it to this moon. Jax said that three of the cloneborgs are still on board, but in stasis. Can you keep an eye on them?"

"Yes. But I have no control of anything aboard that ship, only the systems that operate this base. I will, however, monitor the ship's status and initiate a lockdown on this facility. No one will be able to enter without my clearance."

Skye struggled to keep the tears of relief from flowing. *Time for that later.* "I'll need to use the comm to get in touch with Shénmì Station. To tell them where I am. And to figure out how I'm going to get out of here."

"You might want to know that the SS *Parsons* is on its way here, but is still three and a half days out. Your life-support systems look more than adequate for that period of time. Do you have enough provisions? Food and water?"

She thought about the supplies of dehydrated foodstuffs she'd seen in the galley. "Yes, I've got enough to get by." *Plus, I've got fresh potatoes,* she thought grimly.

But something else felt more urgent. "Hutton, if you're linked with the Hutton on board the *Sun Wolf*, you must know where Aiden is right now. Do you? Is he all right?"

Hutton paused before answering, then said, "Yes, Aiden is . . . 'all right.' For now. He is at a star called Eta-2 Hydri. But he is at the center of a very dark storm there and at a crossroads. Both roads lead deeper into the storm, but emerge from it at different places. It is unclear right now which road he will take."

Under normal circumstances, Hutton's cryptic answer would have seemed deliberately inscrutable. But to Skye, who still had one foot in the ethereal realm she'd just departed—a place both she and Aiden had once navigated together on Silvanus—it made perfect sense.

"You can tell me more about it later," she said. "But right now, I have to get out of this horrible room. It stinks like hell in here."

As she closed the door behind her, she glanced back at the remains of Jax. His body had morphed into a grisly mass of rapidly decomposing matter oozing across the deck plates.

Her fungus looked quite happy.

49

ETA-2 HYDRI SYSTEM
Polar Opposite Point

Domain Day 347, 2218

LIKE most scientists, Aiden had come to accept the assumption that the universe was blind, mute, and absolutely indifferent to the affairs of the human race and to its cherished notions of good and evil—that, in fact, the universe didn't even register the blip of humanity's fleeting existence, tucked away in the remotest corner of its infinite emptiness. But now, as Aiden watched the main screen, he knew that assumption was about to be tested. The only problem was he would not know the results unless he lived past the next few minutes.

The mysterious halos of light—the Luminous Ones for lack of a better name—had retreated into the voidoid and merged with the symbioid sitting inside the voidoid, the primordial black hole gaping at its center.

"The *Conquest* just started powering up its neg-G shield," Hotah said, eyes glued to the tactical screen.

Aiden turned to Alvarez. "Still no gravity field readings from the symbioid?"

"No. Nothing. I just don't get it. We're only 20 klicks from a black hole with a mass of 13 Earths . . ."

It was quite clear now that, as Woo had predicted, the symbioid's primordial black hole exerted no gravity field as long as it remained "inside" the voidoid. Only when it moved out of the voidoid did the black hole actually act like a black hole, with its intense G-field in full bloom.

Confident that the ship's ZPD bubble would deploy in the absence of a powerful G-field, Aiden powered it up for shielding.

The *Sun Wolf* and the *Conquest* now faced each less than 40 kilometers apart, well within range of all weapons. Neither ship used conventional shielding. The *Sun Wolf* deployed a zero-point bubble around the ship, which was normally the first phase of activating the drive itself. It placed the ship inside a state where space-time effectively did not exist and weaponry of any kind could not enter. The *Conquest* used a negative-gravity field—reversing the process it used to create synthetic gravity for its G-bombs—to repel weapons fire, both kinetic and energy beams.

Both methods relied on manipulation of EM fields. But the *Sun Wolf*'s ZPD bubble was a passive shield, and the EM fields it used to create it were vulnerable to disruption by prolonged laser fire. The *Conquest*'s negative-gravity shield, on the other hand, was actively repulsive and invulnerable to any weapons the Alliance could currently throw at it. But only when it was powered up to full strength. The *Conquest* had just now begun the process of powering it up.

Both ships had their main laser cannons pointed at each other, targeting solutions dialed in. Who would fire first? It was like a showdown out of an ancient Western vid, two gunslingers facing each other on a dusty road, hands inches from their six-shooters, fingers twitching.

Hotah, one of the gunslingers, said, "Fire now, Commander?"

Aiden shook his head and asked, "How close is the *Conquest* to the voidoid now?"

"What?" Hotah turned and looked at Aiden as if he'd lost his mind. "Why?"

Aiden returned the look, daring him. "How close, Lieutenant?"

Hotah spoke through gritted teeth. "The *Conquest* is still about 10 kilometers away from the voidoid."

The plan Aiden had in mind, sketchy as it was, would have a better chance of working if the *Conquest* moved in a lot closer to the voidoid. He had no idea how to make that happen.

All eyes turned toward Aiden. He wouldn't allow himself to think about how much was riding on the decision he was about to make. Not just for his own life and the lives of his crew, but the future of humanity. If Cardew won, that future looked dim. If Aiden won, the future was whatever the human race would make of it. The grand human experiment would at least have another chance to grow into its better nature. And for Nature to show it the way.

But only if the *Sun Wolf* could defeat Cardew. Here and now.

Tension crackled among the crew like sheet lightning. Only Elgin Woo looked relaxed. He was even *smiling*. Pilot Abahem seemed no longer immobilized by terror. She sat up straight, but with her eyes closed.

"The *Conquest* has started moving," Hotah said, perplexed. "But it's moving in closer to the voidoid. Why the hell is it doing that?"

Tactically, it made no sense. But Aiden was focused on Abahem. She opened her eyes and looked back at him, a smile of hope on her face. She said, "The crow is dead. Ciarra is free."

Most of the crew looked at her, bewildered.

Except for Aiden. He matched Abahem's smile and said, "Cardew just lost control over his enslaved pilot. She controls the helm now, and I think she's moving the ship toward the voidoid."

Without turning, Hotah spoke with acid sharpness. "Whatever you're talking about, it hasn't affected the *Conquest*'s weapons systems. It's firing on us now. Short-range laser cannon. Their neg-G shield isn't at full strength yet. Now's the time to return fire. Commander?"

"Hold fire, Lieutenant."

Hotah didn't like it, but he pulled his hand away from the trigger.

"Our shields?" Aiden asked.

"Holding," Hotah said, "but not for long. Laser fire will disable the ZPD bubble and fry us in another 30 seconds."

Aiden watched the tactical readouts. The *Conquest* continued to recede toward the voidoid without any sign of altering course. *Good. Thank you, Ciarra.*

"Shit!" Hotah blurted. "Their neg-G shield is 85 percent powered up and increasing rapidly. Can I fire *now*?"

"Hold fire." Cold sweat dripped from Aiden's temples. His heart raced. He knew it was sheer madness. But something deep inside his brain told him it was the right thing to do.

Hotah glared at Aiden and blurted out, "Their shield is almost fully powered, Commander. We wait any longer, and firing on them will be pointless."

"That's exactly what we're going to do," Aiden said. "Wait until their neg-G shield is fully powered."

Hotah looked as if he was using one hand to hold the other hand away from the trigger. A tremor of anger unsettled his voice. "Commander . . ."

"Wait for it," Aiden said, then trained his eyes on the main screen. The entire crew followed suit.

The *Conquest* was no more than four kilometers from the voidoid, still firing on the *Sun Wolf*, when its neg-G shield came to full power. In that instant, the crew watched the symbioid move out of the voidoid, its primordial black hole raging at its center, humming with death. It swooped down on the *Conquest* and engulfed the ship. The black hole snapped forward like the flick of a scorpion's tail to within meters of the battle cruiser's surface.

The *Conquest*, once the pride of UED's navy, and later the corrupted instrument of Cardew's twisted designs, began breaking apart. Piece by piece at first, then shredding into smaller glowing-hot fragments. The incandescent debris swirled around the black hole, faster and faster, closer and closer, until its leading edge disappeared past the soccer-ball-sized event horizon. The remaining matter swirled even faster as it morphed into a small-scale accretion disc around the black hole.

More and more of the superheated accretion disc disappeared into oblivion, until the black hole—like a hungry beast who'd had its fill—pulled away. Then the symbioid slipped back into the voidoid, just as quickly as it emerged. The attack, from beginning to end, took less than 10 seconds. All that remained of the *Conquest* was a glowing swirl of tiny fragments whirling around the point of space where the black hole had been.

From its place inside the voidoid, the symbioid seemed to look on for a moment, a giant unblinking eyeball. Then, without further ado, it disappeared in a flash. Vanished without a trace.

Now empty, the voidoid looked like any other, open for the transit of voidships. Except this one was a *gateway* voidoid. A new astrocell lay beyond, a vast unexplored region of space of unknown size. A third astrocell, added to Bound Space and Astrocell Beta. Thousands of stars, or maybe hundreds of thousands, each with its own voidoid that ships could use to jump instantaneously from one star to another, anywhere within the astrocell's boundaries.

Aiden let out a breath and sat back in the command chair. Only the tension of amazement lingered on the bridge. Some of the crew were smiling. Even Hotah, who made a theatrical gesture of wiping sweat from his forehead, put on a sheepish grin.

Sudha Devi shook her head slowly and asked, "What just happened? Did we win some kind of contest?"

Aiden, part of him still waiting for the other shoe to drop, said, "Not sure yet, but I think so."

Woo beamed confidently. "I *know* so."

"The question is," Ro said, with his head tilted thoughtfully, "did the symbioid destroy the *Conquest* merely in response to the ship activating its neg-G shield, or because it determined that Cardew and his gang were the bad guys, malignancies to be eradicated for the sake of life in the universe?"

"Most likely both," Woo said with a smile and a faraway look. "But for now, it's still an intriguing mystery. One that I intend to solve very soon."

"Is Cardew really dead now?" Alvarez asked. "He said that he was being duplicated."

"He did," Aiden said. "But he also referred to the duplication as in progress. Not yet finished."

"I caught that too," Devi said. "And cloning a whole-brain emulation takes a lot of time. Days, even weeks. The early stages can't progress beyond a certain point if the original is destroyed before then. Only the later stages can proceed in the absence of the original. So it all depends on when the process began."

"Right," Aiden said, the glow of victory suddenly dimming. "We may have seen the last of the original Cardew Seth Amon. But his twin might show up somewhere in the near future to carry on the crusade."

"Then there's all the hidden cloneborg colonies he left behind," Alvarez said. "The breeding crèches, all the remaining infrastructure and warships. We haven't found all of it yet, have we?"

Aiden shook his head. "No. Only a fraction of it, I think. But we'll keep looking. *I* will, at least. And I'm sure it will be a top priority for the Alliance forces."

Hotah said, "That's assuming the Alpha-2 Hydri Gateway will reopen for the Alliance fleet to pass through."

Woo smiled broadly. "I believe we'll soon hear news that the gateway is now open for voidjumping."

Aiden turned to Woo. "Why? Because the one here just unblocked itself?"

Woo shrugged. "Of course. They're all linked. It makes perfect sense."

To you maybe, Aiden thought, but said, "Anyway, we'll have to wait at least three and a half hours before hearing about it."

That was the one-way comm time from Gateway Station, through 26 AU of realspace. But Aiden's thoughts were already elsewhere. Skye. If the symbioids *were* departing from the voidoids they'd blocked, maybe the one at Woo's Star was open too. If so, he could jump the *Sun Wolf* into the system, get to Jumbo in less than six hours, and rescue Skye. If it wasn't already too late . . .

"Alvarez, send Holtzman transmissions to Admiral Stegman at Alpha-2 Hydri, and to Shénmì Station, informing them of what's happened out here. I'll provide a more detailed report later. Also, ask Shénmì Station and if they have any news about Skye."

"Ah," Hutton chimed in cheerfully. "I have received news on that front from my doppelganger, who is now in Dr. Landen's presence. She is safe and sound."

"What?" Aiden had never before felt such profound relief. It was like stepping off a cliff, but with wings that kept him from falling, wings that let him soar above dark valleys brooding below. Up toward the sun, into the light, lifted on warm currents of hope.

Before Hutton could elaborate, Alvarez looked up from her comm board, smiling broadly. "Yes! I just now received a transmission from Shénmì Station, sent nearly six hours ago."

The rest of the crew gathered around Comm/Scan—including Jo, with Rene still in her arms—while Alvarez summarized the message she'd received. "Dr. Landen radioed the station this morning, from some kind of hidden facility on one of Jumbo's moons. She'd been held captive there by one of Cardew's cloneborgs. She was about to be brain-tapped, but somehow managed to escape and kill the cloneborg. She's unharmed. The SS *Parsons* is on its way there to pick her up. It's over three days out, but Dr. Landen said she'd be okay until then."

Aiden bent his head down and covered his face with his hands, trying to hide his emotions from the crew. He felt reassuring hands on his shoulders and patting his back. He wiped his face with his hands and sat up straight. "That's . . . that's great news, Lilly. Thank you."

But Alvarez wasn't finished. "The transmission has a short vid clip from Dr. Landen addressed to you. I can switch it to the ready room if you want to view it privately."

What the hell. His crew had been there for him in every way he could possibly expect. So why not share this with them? "No, that's okay, Lilly. Run it here."

Skye's face appeared on the screen. As always, she was beautiful. But he could see the remnants of extreme stress on her face, the darkened circles under her eyes, wrinkles that can only be imprinted by fear and anger. Still, her eyes were bright, her smile wide and genuine, her voice strong.

"Aiden, my love. I wanted you to know that I am safe and well. I have not been harmed. I am still who I've always been—I hope you won't mind." Here, she attempted to smile before continuing. "I pray that you are well too. Do what you need to do, but please stay safe and come home to me when you can."

Skye ended the message without another word, but with a heartfelt smile that said more than any other words could say.

50

ETA-2 HYDRI SYSTEM
Polar Opposite Point

DOMAIN DAY 347, 2218

WHILE waiting for Stegman's response, Woo brought up the possibility of testing the new gateway. "Why not try jumping into this new astrocell? Now. Just to see if the gateway works. To see where we can go?"

Met with Aiden's scowl, Woo said, "Okay. Maybe not with the *Sun Wolf* yet. But we could send a survey drone through."

"Elgin, you know as well as I do that we can't make a voidjump without having precise coordinates for the star we're going to. The Mapping Project has its hands full mapping out Astrocell Beta. I doubt that they've mapped any of the stars beyond this new gateway, not well enough to attempt a jump. We don't even know how big the astrocell is or which stars are actually inside it."

"It's called Astrocell Gamma now," Woo said, referring to the next Greek letter in line after Beta. "And we'll know how big it is once we identify the astrocell's Primary Voidoid and its host star. That will pinpoint the astrocell's center. That will give us the exact radius of the astrocell and its orientation in space. Which will then tell us which stars are included inside it and which ones are not. We'll just use the straight-line calculation to find the Primary Voidoid."

Woo made it sound so simple. He was talking about the "straight-line calculation" he'd used last year to discover the gateway into Astrocell Beta. The flip side of that calculation was that if you drew a straight line between the center of astrocell A and its gateway voidoid sitting out on the Frontier, then extended the line outward into astrocell B, you'd find the center of astrocell B somewhere along that line. But exactly *how* far along was the unknown part of the equation.

"It could be anywhere on that line," Aiden pointed out. "Ten light-years out or a hundred. Or more."

"True," Woo said. "But it does point us in the right direction. And I intend to start looking."

"Not now, you won't. And not with my ship."

"Then with *my* ship," Woo said with a mischievous grin. "The *Starhawk*. As soon as I can bring her out here."

Elgin Woo. Wise man or fool? Aiden decided then and there that William Blake had been right—if the fool would persist in his folly, he would become wise.

Four hours later, Aiden received a response from Admiral Stegman. And, just as Woo had predicted, Stegman informed them that both the gateway voidoid at Alpha-2 Hydri and the voidoid at Woo's Star had been unblocked and were now open for travel. The symbioids occupying them had vanished.

Stegman responded to the news about the demise of Cardew with grim satisfaction, and to the news of discovering a new gateway voidoid with restrained amazement. But Aiden, who had known Stegman for well over a decade, could easily hear the undertones of excitement and hope in his voice.

And, just as Aiden had feared, Stegman responded to his report of the four cloneborg warships still stationed at Moana by ordering the *Sun Wolf* to stay put and stand guard over the new gateway until Alliance forces could arrive to take over. The fleet had been gathered at Alpha-2 Hydri Gateway for almost two days now, just waiting for the symbioid to unblock the voidoid. Now that the gateway was open, the fleet had already jumped into the Eta-2

Hydri system. But it would still take over ten days to reach the *Sun Wolf* at the polar opposite point. For Aiden, idling here for that long was unacceptable.

He retired to the ready room and composed a response in which he protested with as much restraint as he could muster. Telling Stegman about Skye's situation on Jumbo's moon, he reminded the admiral that, with the zero-point drive, the *Sun Wolf* could easily reach her within six hours to pick her up. He would drop her off at Shénmì Station, then return to guard the new gateway within another six hours. A half-day's time, all told. Even if the enemy warships back at Moana decided to head for the gateway voidoid now—which they'd showed no signs of doing yet—it would take them over seven days to get there. Compared to a half-day's time? It was a no-brainer.

But Aiden already knew what Stegman's answer would be without having to wait another several hours to receive it. The admiral, under pressure from higher up the chain, would play the priorities card while pointing out that Skye would be perfectly safe at J2 until the SS *Parsons* got there to pick her up. Guarding the new gateway at Eta-2 Hydri from potential invasion by remaining cloneborg forces was now the *Sun Wolf*'s top priority.

Aiden had to admit, he had some reservations about disobeying orders from higher up, especially from his friend and mentor, Ben Stegman. But those reservations began to evaporate the more he thought about Skye, trapped for another three and a half days waiting for the *Parsons* to pick her up. Hutton had filled him in on the details of how Skye had managed to escape, survive, and prevent the graser from launching. How harrowing it had all been for her. And now she was left alone in the house of horrors where she'd been terrified and traumatized. Waiting needlessly.

He knew she was strong enough to handle it, mentally and physically. But why should she have to stay cooped up with the nightmares of that trauma for a single minute longer than she had to, when he could be there in less than six hours to ease her away from it? All without sacrificing the core of his mission.

But the final straw came when Hutton told him about the Rodina Collective's hijacked mining ship, still in high orbit above the hidden facility, and what he'd just learned about it from his doppelganger self.

"The cloneborg who abducted Skye," Hutton told him, "planned to use the *Rodina* to leave the facility days in advance of the arrival of the SS *Parsons*. His given name was Jax, and he had orders to secure the facility's Omicron-3 unit and bring it with him, along with either Skye or the emulation of her brain, depending on her cooperation. There are three cloneborg crewpersons aboard the *Rodina*, but they are currently in stasis. They are programed to come out of stasis three hours before flight time in order to operate the ship. That would be tomorrow morning at zero six hundred."

That annoyingly familiar dark pit in Aiden's stomach started opening again. "And?"

"My doppelganger sent me the encrypted coding that Jax used to program the *Rodina*'s systems. I've spent the last few hours decrypting it and have discovered the details of that order. Once out of stasis, two of them have been ordered to take the *Rodina*'s landing shuttle down to the facility where they are to retrieve the Omicron-3 unit when they pick up Jax and Skye.

"But when Jax realized he was dying, and thought that Skye would soon be dead, too, he made the retrieval of the Omicron-3 the cloneborgs' top priority. To be carried out at all costs. Cardew's Omicron-3 was not to fall into enemy hands."

"But these cloneborgs won't be able to get into the facility, right?" Aiden said, "You've already told me that your doppelganger now controls all the facility's systems, including all of its locking codes."

"That is correct. The original airlock entry codes will no longer work."

"But . . . ?"

"These cloneborgs were designed primarily to fly the ship and to carry out their orders without fail. But they are also resourceful. It is likely that the lockout will not dissuade them from using other means to gain entry. Including brute force."

"Explosives?"

"Precisely. The airlock door is well built for its specific purpose, but it would not withstand strategically placed, shaped-charge explosives. Or a powerful laser cutter. The *Rodina*, being a mining ship, would certainly be stocked with such devices."

"But if they blow open the outer door," Aiden said, "they won't be able to pressurize the airlock. Then if they try to open the inner door, the entire facility will depressurize. Explosively."

"True. But since their only objective is to retrieve the Omicron unit," Hutton said, "the cloneborgs will not care about depressurization. The Omicron housing is built to withstand extreme environments."

"But Skye? Inside the facility without a pressure suit . . . ?"

"Precisely," Hutton said, his tone of concern unmistakable. "I have checked, and there are no PSM or EVA suits inside the facility. Without one, she would not survive explosive depressurization."

Aiden felt his heart pounding inside his chest. "Can your doppelganger countermand the *Rodina*'s programing? Or at least disable its systems? To prevent the cloneborgs from launching the shuttle?"

"Sadly, no. The *Rodina* does not possess an Omicron-3 AI, and the onboard computer that *does* control the ship is not connected to the OverNet. It was programed directly by Jax himself while aboard the ship. There is no way I can access that computer."

Shit! "What about the *Quasimodo*'s landing shuttle that Jax and Skye used to get to the moon's surface? Isn't that still parked near the facility? Couldn't Skye use it to get the hell out of there before these creeps come knocking? To get off the moon and maybe back to the *Quasimodo*?"

"Unfortunately, that landing shuttle is under an encrypted lockdown, and so is the surface rover that she would need to reach the shuttle. Their systems are not linked to the facility's Omicron unit. Therefore, I cannot control them."

The only other solution Aiden could think of would be for Skye to hide out of sight somewhere inside the facility, far from the

Omicron unit. Then let Hutton allow the cloneborgs to unlock the outer door and cycle through without having to depressurize the entire facility. If their only goal was to retrieve the Omicron unit, they might not go looking for her. But Aiden quickly dismissed that idea. Way too many unpredictable variables, all of them irreversible once in play.

There was no question now about what had to be done. Aiden stood and looked at his chrono. It was 23:30. If they got on the road now, the *Sun Wolf* would reach J2 about an hour after the cloneborgs came out of stasis. He hoped that wouldn't be too late.

He keyed the ship-wide comm. "Attention crew. We're leaving here in 10 minutes, on our way back to Woo's Star. From there, we'll head out to Jumbo and pick up Dr. Landen. Please return to your posts."

He keyed off the comm and spoke to Hutton again. "Does Skye know any of this yet?"

"No, she does not. I discovered this situation moments ago and thought I would consult you first."

"Don't bother telling her now. It'd be pointless. A maser transmission to her wouldn't get there much sooner than the *Sun Wolf* would at maximum ZPD."

Most of the crew had already assembled on the bridge when Aiden got there himself. He filled them in on the new developments. No one said a thing about disregarding Admiral Stegman's orders. Everyone seemed energized to be doing something meaningful instead of idling here for another ten days.

To further justify his decision to leave—he'd have to answer to Stegman about it sooner or later—Aiden had Hotah do one last tactical scan of local space. This one out to 100 million kilometers.

Hotah did, then said, "Nothing out there, boss."

"All right. Let's roll."

~ ~ ~

After the four-hour crossing of the Eta-2 Hydri system to reach the voidoid at the opposite pole, the *Sun Wolf* jumped into Woo's Star system. Two hours after that, the ship popped out of ZPD about 10,000 kilometers from Jumbo's moon, J2. That was as close as the ZPD could bring them to the massive gas giant. From there, the *Sun Wolf* approached the moon on antimatter drive.

Since radio transmission of any kind was impossible during ZPD flight, this was the first chance Aiden had to alert Skye to their surprise arrival and to the danger she might be in. He filled her in on what Hutton had learned about the cloneborgs aboard the *Rodina* and their orders to retrieve the Omicron unit.

She was relieved to hear that the *Sun Wolf* was in the neighborhood, but anxious about the two cloneborgs heading her way. In fact, she knew about it already.

"I figured that one out when their shuttle landed," she said. "It came down just a few minutes ago, about a half klick away. The external cameras picked it up."

"We're on our way," Aiden said, trying to sound reassuring. "We'll deal with the cloneborgs. Just hold tight."

As the *Sun Wolf* settled into low orbit, they spotted the antimatter tanker *Quasimodo* first, then the Rodina Collective's mining ship. Both were positioned in synchronous orbit directly above the facility's location. The tanker appeared dormant in every respect.

"Any sign of hostile activity from the *Rodina*?" Aiden asked. The one cloneborg remaining aboard, Hutton had told him, was the ship's pilot, not a soldier. Still, the *Rodina* was fitted with commercial-grade weaponry, a rail gun, and one short-range laser cannon. Aiden didn't want any surprises.

"Nothing yet," Hotah said. "I see their laser cannon, but no sign of targeting activity."

They found one other vessel in the vicinity, also in synchronous orbit, but much smaller. A graser. The deadly weapon, designed to sterilize living planets with gamma-ray bursts, looked identical to the one they had encountered at HD 21749, poised to fire on Parthas. A hundred meters long, with massive antimatter tanks surrounding its aft section, it had the same bell-shaped structure jutting outward from its midsection and the same gamma-ray laser cannon protruding from its bulbous nose. Aiden had no doubt that Shénmì was its intended target. But, as he'd been told, Skye had stopped Jax from launching it, with only seconds to spare. She had single-handedly saved all life on the planet Shénmì from extinction.

"We'll destroy that thing on our way out," Aiden said. "Alvarez and Lieutenant Hotah, arm yourselves and meet me in the shuttle bay. Let's go down and get her out of there."

51

HD 10180 SYSTEM
Jumbo, Moon J2

DOMAIN DAY 348, 2218

THEY boarded the *Sun Wolf*'s shuttle, and Aiden launched it even before the ship's massive bay doors had fully opened. On approach, their view of J2's weirdly lit surface came into focus. The moon was tidally locked, and in its current orbital position, the site below was lit only by reflected sunlight from Jumbo, a miasma of queasy orange light. The mother planet, Jumbo, filled more than half of the sky, its massive bulk seething with multicolored turbulence.

As the shuttle descended for touchdown, Aiden spotted the facility's low dome-like structure. It was well camouflaged to blend in with surrounding surface features. Another landing shuttle sat inert near the dome, clearly marked as belonging to the *Quasimodo*, the one Jax had used to bring Skye down with him.

Then he spotted the *Rodina*'s landing shuttle. It sat 400 meters west of the dome. The hatch of its rover bay was open, its deployment ramp down. Following its tracks across the dust-covered surface, Aiden spotted the surface rover nearing the facility's airlock.

Aiden brought the shuttle down 150 meters from the dome. The three of them quickly donned PSM suits, boarded their surface rover, and set out across the rock-strewn surface. Aiden kept the cabin depressurized in case they needed to exit the rover quickly without cycling through the airlock. Hotah had his SR-13 held ready, grinning maniacally. Both Aiden and Alvarez toted SR-11s, locked and loaded.

Aiden drove the rover toward the dome as fast as he could, but the rocky and uneven terrain kept him from going more than eight or nine kilometers per hour. Using the vehicle's telecam, Alvarez zeroed in on the cloneborgs. They had debarked from their rover and were standing next to the dome's outer airlock door. Both wore formfitting PSM suits with streamlined oxygen packs and minimalistic helmets.

They had obviously noticed the arrival of Aiden's rover. One of them stood guard, facing their approach with a menacing-looking single-barreled weapon. The other one was bent to the task of unlocking the airlock.

"Alvarez, lower the viewport armor and go to remote visuals."

The heavy armor plate closed over the front viewport like a metallic eyelid. It was designed to protect the rover from airborne rocks and debris during violent planetside storms. Aiden hoped it was sturdy enough to stop slugs from handheld projectile weapons.

He radioed Skye and updated her. She told him that she'd been unable to find any kind of pressure suit to protect her from depressurization, and that she was hiding down on the third level, amongst a tangled network of ducts in the power plant.

Aiden watched the telecam screen as the first cloneborg failed to unlock the airlock with codes that no longer worked, then retreated to the rover while his companion remained on guard. He returned with a large duffle pack in hand. From it, he removed a palm-sized disc and attached it to one corner of the airlock hatch. He removed another one and began attaching it to the opposite corner.

"Looks like C-44 explosive charges," Aiden said. "We better do something fast before they blast open the outer door. Once inside the airlock chamber, they can open the inner door manually. No need for locking codes. That'll depressurize the whole facility."

"Stop the rover," Hotah said. "Let me out. I'll take the shot."

"I'm coming with you," Aiden said. "Lilly, stay put and keep us posted on what you're seeing."

The rover's airlock was located at the rear, so when Aiden and Hotah stepped out onto the surface, they were hidden from view behind the rover's bulk. In one quick motion, Hotah moved out from behind it, took aim with the SR-13's self-adjusting scope, and fired one high-velocity 5.7mm round at the cloneborg who was setting the charges. It was a 100-meter gravity-adjusted shot that couldn't have been more perfect. The cloneborg just had turned to face the intruders when the solid-point bullet struck him just above his right eye. A mass of brain tissue and skull fragments exploded from the back of his head, and he went down like a sack of rocks.

The remaining cloneborg was quick to return fire. The slug ricocheted off the side of the rover, right where Hotah had been standing before ducking out of sight. The cloneborg fired several more shots at the rover. Aiden felt the reverberation of their impacts through the rover's hull.

"He's firing at our front end," Lilly said through the comm. "The armor is holding, but just barely. Must be using 13mm slugs, not armor-piercing rounds."

"He's trying for maximum damage," Hotah said. "He'll switch to armor-piercing rounds next. Then Alvarez will be in some deep shit."

Without another word, Hotah stepped out again from behind cover with the SR-13 on auto and sent a rapid burst toward his target. With superhuman quickness and flexibility, the cloneborg seemed to dodge the flurry of bullets and returned a shot of his own. Hotah had been shifting sideways back toward cover when the bullet grazed his right upper arm, tearing the orthofabric of his PSM suit and drawing blood.

"That fucker is good," Hotah said through gritted teeth. Aiden pulled a p-suit patch out of his kit. He slapped it on Hotah's arm, over the two-inch tear, staunching the loss of pressure and blood.

"Holy shit!" Alvarez's voice came over the comm, pitched high and tense. "He's running toward us. Fast. I mean *really* fast."

Aiden and Hotah peered out from behind the rover to see the cloneborg running toward them, impossibly fast. Nearly on them before they could react.

Running in low gravity was not easy. It required a whole different set of coordinated movements, fine-tuned to the actual gravity at the running surface. It was a nonintuitive skill that took experienced spacers years to master. And to run *fast* was even more difficult, if not impossible. But for this cloneborg, it was like a walk in the park, with perfectly timed movements and unreal strength propelling him well over 15 meters per second.

Aiden knew instantly what the cloneborg was about to do. He glanced at Hotah. "He's going to leap over the rover and come down behind us in firing position."

Hotah spun around to face backward, his weapon ready. A split second later, the airborne cloneborg passed over the top of the rover, executing a perfect somersault that would land him feet down, facing them, weapon on full auto. It happened way too fast for Aiden to process.

But not for Hotah. He fired a 20mm slug from the wide bore of his SR-13. It caught the cloneborg in the face just as he was coming out of the somersault, still airborne. His head exploded. His weapon flew from his hands, tumbling in slow motion. His body, minus its head, crumpled to the ground. Motionless.

Aiden shook his head slowly. It was another impossible shot, this one requiring impossible reflexes and stone-cold concentration.

Hotah lowered his weapon and smiled through the helmet's faceplate. "Frickin' cloneborgs got nothing on me."

Aiden smiled back. "Your contract is renewed, Lieutenant."

They climbed back into the rover and joined Alvarez. She looked shaken but not stirred. "Nice shot," she said. The understatement of the day.

Aiden radioed Skye to let her know the cloneborgs had been neutralized and asked her to meet them at the airlock. They pulled the rover up to the outer airlock door. Hotah got out and carefully removed the C-44 discs, while Aiden pulled the dead cloneborg's body out of the way. Back inside the rover, Aiden pressurized the cabin, allowing them to remove their helmets.

Because all of Cardew's hardware was designed to be compatible with the vessels he'd stolen from Alliance forces, the rover's airlock door mated perfectly with the one on the dome's face. With a muted popping sound, the door between them began to slide open. When fully opened, Skye stood before him.

Her smile was clear and bright. Wearing an oversized Bright Star jumpsuit, she stepped over the threshold into the rover, placed her hands on her hips, and said, "It's about time. What took you so long?"

Aiden laughed, then shrugged. "The speed of light?"

They embraced, an awkward maneuver at best with Aiden's PSM suit still on, even without his helmet.

"I'm so glad to see you," he said, barely able to control his emotions. The rest he left unsaid: *so glad you're alive, so glad that you are still you . . .*

She stood back and looked him in the eye. "And *I* am so glad you could drop by. Now, can we get the hell out of here?"

"At your service, madam." He motioned her into the rover's interior.

That's when Aiden noticed that she was pulling a two-wheeled hand truck behind her. It had a bulky metal cabinet strapped to it. "It's the guts of that Omicron-3 unit in there," she said. "The wetware of its neural net. I thought I'd bring it along, and Hutton agreed. It might contain some valuable information about Cardew's remaining operations."

Aiden scowled. He didn't like the look of it. Or the feel of it.

"Don't worry," Skye said. "It's isolated and completely harmless now. Ask Hutton. He'll tell you."

He was about to do just that when Hotah came forward, took possession of the hand truck, and secured it inside the shuttle. Alvarez shouldered past him, came up to Skye, and briefly embraced her. "I'm so relieved you're safe, Skye. Hutton told us how you managed to escape and save Shénmì from destruction. You are truly an amazing woman. How did a lunk like Aiden get so lucky to marry you?"

Now it was Skye's turn to laugh. "I have a weak spot for lunks like him. He was just the best one to come along."

Aiden made a theatrical cough and said, "I *can* hear you, ya know?"

Skye turned to Hotah, who stood silently to one side, and said, "Good to see you, Lieutenant. And good to know you're still looking after my husband."

Hotah made a discreet bow. "My pleasure. Even lunks deserve protection."

"All right, all right," Aiden said, rolling his eyes. "Time to do as the lady asked. Let's get the hell out of here."

During their short flight back to the *Sun Wolf*, Aiden tamped down his impulse to embrace Skye again and kiss her as he had done so many times in his fitful dreams. She saw the look in his eyes and blushed. He loved that about her. Then she turned away and looked out the viewport. They were just passing the graser, sitting in stationary orbit a few kilometers away. She pointed it out to Aiden. Her face darkened with anger. "You need to kill that thing. You know what it is, right?"

"We know what it is. And yes, we'll kill it on our way out."

"Cardew may have left more of these atrocities in place," she said. "Inside star systems with living planets that he wanted sterilized. We need to find out where they are and destroy them before they kill any more Gaian worlds."

Skye was silent for a long moment, then looked out the port again, this time down at the facility where she'd been held captive. Deadly serious, she tilted her head toward it and said, "Now that we've removed everything of value from down there, I want that place nuked. It's bad enough having memories of it. Knowing it still exists in the real world would be worse."

Hotah spoke for the rest of them. "With great pleasure."

And so it was that, after they were safely aboard the *Sun Wolf* and Skye had been warmly greeted by the rest of the crew, Hotah went straight to Tactical station. He targeted the graser first and burned it into oblivion with one quick laser burst. Then he targeted the facility on the moon's surface and turned to looked pointedly at Skye. She stood nearby, watching him, arms crossed over her chest. She gave him a barely perceptible nod.

Hotah turned back to the tactical board and armed one M-10 nuclear torpedo. As it had been on Nead, 10 kilotons of explosive energy was overkill for the size of the facility below. But Skye wanted to make a point, and Hotah knew it. She gave him a thumbs-up. The torpedo leapt from the ship's forward battery.

Scoring a direct hit on the facility, the spectacular explosion seemed to rattle the entire moon. After the optical screen cleared, they saw that everything on the moon's surface within the three-kilometer blast radius had been scorched down to the bedrock.

Skye sat heavily on one of the passenger benches and let out a long slow breath, fatigue finally catching up with her. Letting her guard down, she bent over and covered her face with her hands. Aiden came and sat next to her. He put his arm around her shoulders, feeling a tremor of release pass through her body. She uncovered her face, leaned into his chest, and looked up at him. No words were needed. None were spoken.

52

HD 10180 SYSTEM
Shénmì Station

DOMAIN DAY 348, 2218

"COLONEL Crestfield. This is Commander Macallan of the SS *Sun Wolf*. Requesting permission to dock at Shénmì Station. We have your missing person aboard, and she would very much like to return to her work."

Aiden spoke from the command chair on the bridge. After a 20-minute hop from J2, the *Sun Wolf* had just dropped out of ZPD at 10 kilometers from the station. Aiden's plan was to return Skye to the station, let Woo pick up the *Starhawk*, and leave Jo and Rene in the care of the station's medical staff. Then he'd stock up on fuel and provisions for 10 days of guard duty back at Eta-2 Hydri. And after that, if all went well, maybe he could catch a wink of sleep. He and most of his crew hadn't slept for over 24 hours.

Crestfield's face appeared on the comm screen. He looked more relaxed than when the two had spoken many days ago. "Yes, by all means. Permission granted. Everyone here is very relieved that Dr. Landen is safe, and we're looking forward to her return."

"Thank you, Colonel. We won't be staying long. Our presence is required elsewhere. I'd like to reprovision and refuel before departing. Can you spare some antimatter reserves for us?"

"Yes. Take what you need. We'll be fine until the *Quasimodo* returns to replenish our own reserves."

The SS *Parsons* was still on course for Jumbo. Only its mission priorities had changed. Now that Skye Landen had been picked up by the *Sun Wolf*, Captain Asaju would dispatch some of his crew to reclaim the *Quasimodo*, sitting idle at J2. The tanker would run an antimatter harvest before returning to Shénmì Station with full tanks. A detachment of marines from the *Parsons* would also board and take control of the *Rodina*, presumably after "neutralizing" the one remaining cloneborg aboard.

"Two more things, Colonel," Aiden said. "We'll be returning one of AMP's missing survey drones. The project lost contact with it after it jumped to HD 17051. We found it there and took it aboard. Then we'll be picking up Doctor Woo's vessel, the *Starhawk*. Please have a docking team on hand for the transfer of both vessels."

Crestfield agreed. Aiden was about to stand up from the command chair when Woo approached. "I've decided to take the *Starhawk* back to Eta-2 Hydri myself, and to leave as soon as I can board her."

Aiden had given up arguing with Woo over his reasons for bringing the *Starhawk* back to the newly discovered gateway. Now it was more a matter of practical logistics and of Woo's own impatience.

Aiden asked anyway. "Why? I thought we decided to load the *Starhawk* into the *Sun Wolf*'s shuttle bay and bring her with us to Eta-2 Hydri. It makes more sense than us going separately."

"But not in terms of time spent," Woo said. "I want to begin my attempts to jump into the new astrocell as soon as possible. Yes, I realize that both of our ships have the ZPD and can get back to Eta-2 Hydri in the same amount of time. But the *Sun Wolf* will be delayed for a while here at Shénmì Station, for refueling and whatnot. It'll be a half day before you can depart. I have no such delays to contend with. It's crucial that my work begins now."

"Not a half day, Elgin. Several hours, maybe. Will it really make *that* much of a difference?"

Woo paused, squinted his eyes, looked up at the ceiling, then said, "Yes, it will."

Aiden suspected that one difference was that Woo could begin whatever dubious experimentations he'd planned without Aiden there trying to dissuade him. He looked at Woo and shook his head slowly. It was pointless trying to reason with the man when he got like this, when he'd resolutely seized upon a plan of action. Was it because Woo's reasoning operated on some inexplicable level far superior to Aiden's own, or because "reason" actually had very little to do with it? Aiden could never decide which. Either way, to mistake Woo's forward motion for simple obsession was usually unwise.

"All right, then," Aiden said. "We'll be several hours behind you. See you there."

He wanted to add: *and don't do anything crazy*. But that would be pointless too.

Abahem maneuvered the *Sun Wolf* into the station's docking bay and secured the ship to the same dock it had occupied before its hasty departure ten days earlier. Woo was the first off the bridge and down to the airlock. He was followed by Hotah and Alvarez, both eager to visit the station's commissary. Ro was next, towing the captured Omicron-3 unit behind him on a wheeled cart. Ro was delivering it to the station's data center where plans were in the works for a lengthy interrogation process, performed by Hutton and others like him from the OverNet.

Sudha Devi was still belowdecks in Medical with Jo and Rene, and Pilot Abahem was just wrapping up her disengagement from the Helm. Aiden turned to look at Skye. Still sitting on the passenger bench, she had rested her head back against the bulkhead, eyes closed, breathing easily, apparently asleep. He decided to let her nap for as long as possible before disembarking and busied himself with refueling logistics. Minutes later, he glanced over at Skye again, saw that she was awake, and that Lista Abahem was seated next to her.

The two were engaged in a quiet but intense conversation, an exchange that glowed with eye-to-eye empathy. He couldn't hear a word they were saying but didn't want to appear as if he was trying to listen. Just before he turned away, he saw Skye place her hand gently over Abahem's hand. Abahem made no attempt to pull back, as anyone who knew pilots would assume that she'd do. Instead, the gesture seemed to amplify the aura of understanding between them.

When Aiden finally heard them speak, it was an exchange of farewells. He turned to see Abahem stand, nod deferentially to Skye, then depart from the bridge. Aiden walked over to sit next to his mate, shoulder to shoulder. "What was that all about? If I may ask."

"Yes, you may ask," she said, with that mischievous glint in her eyes. "Lista told me about her encounter with the black crow, and I told her about mine."

"And?"

"She expressed her gratitude, and the gratitude of her Kinship, for my part in defeating that monster and for freeing her sister pilot in the process. Freeing her spirit, at least. Her body is gone. A woman named Ciarra, formerly the Licensed Pilot of the SS *Conquest*."

Aiden had guessed as much. But he hadn't heard Skye's side of the story yet, how she had overcome Cardew's power over the Omicron unit and defeated the wraith of the black crow inhabiting it. He asked her to tell him.

"I'll give you the short version," she said wearily, then proceeded to recount the highlights of the frightening episode. How she had killed Jax, but not before he had drugged her, strapped her into the whole-brain emulation instrument, and started the process. How Hutton had come to her aid and how she had conjured a way to confront Cardew's ghost in the machine, the malevolent black crow. How she had returned to Silvanus in dreamtime to inhabit the form of a great horned owl in order to defeat the black crow. And finally, how she had seen a sparrow rise from the dead crow's ashes and fly free.

"At the time, I didn't know what the sparrow was all about, only that its release was of some profound significance. It wasn't until Lista explained it to me that I truly understood. She is a remarkable woman, Aiden. You're very fortunate to have her on your crew."

"She *is* remarkable," Aiden said, "but no more than you are, Skye. I'm fortunate to have her as my pilot and you as my wife."

"Aw, you sure know how to sweet-talk a girl."

Aiden grinned. "I'm getting better at it, no?"

She playfully punched him in the shoulder and said, "Shall we go?"

Aiden remained seated and said, "In a moment."

He had one more thing to bring up with her, something that she knew nothing about yet. There had been no time to tell her about Jo and Rene. He needed to introduce Skye to them. They would be transferring to her station and placed in the care of her medical staff. They would become her responsibility.

Aiden wasn't worried about Skye's response to Rene—who wouldn't fall in love with that little guy, whose eyes and smile seemed to have grown brighter after his encounter with the Luminous One. Aiden was more concerned with how Skye would receive Jo, a cloneborg in body but not in mind or soul. Given Skye's horrific experience with the only cloneborg she'd ever known, would she be able to overcome her gut reaction to another cloneborg, no matter how human?

Aiden had updated Skye briefly on the larger events taking place since her abduction—the demise of the Rodina Mining Collective, the discovery of a major cloneborg crèche on the planet Nead, the fate of Cardew, the Luminous Ones, and the discovery of the gateway into a new astrocell. But she hadn't been told about finding Jo, or that Jo was still aboard the *Sun Wolf*.

Aiden had debated the options of either telling Skye about Jo's background before introducing them, or introducing her to Jo first, then telling her, "Oh, by the way, Jo is a cloneborg, but a truly human one." Eventually, he'd decided on the former approach. Honesty first. Not only that, but he knew Skye would be furious with him if he'd done it any other way around.

He turned sideways on the seat to face Skye and said, "There's something I need to run by you."

He told Skye the story of Jo, how they'd found her, who she was, and who she was not. He told her how Jo had bonded with the infant Rene, the other wayfarer they had adopted during their travels. He told her about Pilot Abahem's gift of seeing auras, how she'd seen none around Jax when she spotted him aboard the station before Skye's abduction. But Lista had seen a very human one around Jo. And continued seeing it.

Skye interrupted him midway through his explanation. "Okay, Aiden. I get it. And I understand that both she and the infant need to come aboard Shénmì Station, at least until we can figure out what to do with them. But *I* need to meet her. Now. Before she comes to live among us on the station. You understand why?"

"I do. As much as I possibly can. I haven't been through what you've endured. So let's go down to Medical now, and I'll introduce you."

Aiden alerted Devi that he and Skye were on their way down to meet Jo and Rene. When they reached the door to the makeshift nursery, Aiden knocked softly, then entered. Both Devi and Jo stood up and smiled at Skye. Devi's smile glowed brightly, warm and unconditional. Jo's smile looked authentic, but shy and less certain. She broke eye contact with Skye and looked down at her feet.

Devi came up to Skye and gave her a hug. "Good to see you again, Skye." Then she gestured toward Jo. "This is Jo. Our latest guest. And in that funny-looking crib is Rene. We're guessing that he's around one year old. Do you know the story of how we came across these two?"

"A little," Skye said. But she was looking at Jo, unable to move, conflicting emotions clouding her face.

Jo must have seen it too. But instead of retreating into herself, as Aiden had thought she would, Jo held out her hand and took a small step toward Skye. She smiled and said, "I am happy to meet you."

Aiden, whose arm was around Skye's waist, felt her tremble and take a reflexive step backward, away from Jo. They maintained eye contact. Jo froze. Unmistakable sadness transformed her face, and she looked away again. No one spoke.

And then little Rene began to cry.

At the sound, Jo's demeanor suddenly brightened, as if becoming a new person altogether. As if reborn. She turned to the crib, smiling broadly, and said, "Oh, he's hungry again. I'll feed him now."

Jo bent over the crib, took Rene in her arms, sat down, and began unbuttoning the top half of her jumpsuit.

Devi smiled and looked directly at Skye. "Time for breastfeeding. Rene is so much healthier now, since Jo has been breastfeeding him. You're welcome to stay and chat if you want."

Aiden shuffled his feet, then looked at Skye, questioning.

The transformation that had come over Jo seemed to have pulled Skye in right along with it. She smiled and said, "I'll stay."

Skye went to sit down next to Jo. She held her hand out to her. "I'm happy to meet you, too, Jo. And happy to welcome you aboard Shénmì Station. We'll try to make you and Rene as comfortable as possible. We can talk now, if you'd like, about the kinds of things you'll both need during your stay."

Jo took Skye's hand and said, "Yes. Thank you."

Aiden breathed a sigh of relief but now felt awkwardly out of place.

As Jo proceeded to suckle Rene, Skye looked up at him and said with a smile, "Aiden, this is women's stuff. I'm sure you have other things to do."

"Right. Yes, I do."

He caught the unmistakable flicker of laughter in Sudha Devi's eyes as he passed by her on his way out. After closing the door behind him, he straightened his posture and let out a long slow breath. *Okay. That went well.*

53

ETA-2 HYDRI SYSTEM
Moana Space

DOMAIN DAY 348, 2218

"WHAT the hell was that?" Aiden said, looking up at the main screen. "What are they firing at?"

After refueling, the *Sun Wolf* had finally departed from Shénmì Station for its jump back into the Eta-2 Hydri system, running about five hours behind Elgin Woo's *Starhawk*. Instead of making the entire 26 AU crossing to meet up with him in one flight, Aiden decided to pull up halfway and check on the status of the four cloneborg gunboats they'd seen at Moana.

The *Sun Wolf* dropped out of ZPD at one million klicks from the ocean planet and began tactical scans of the vicinity. The four gunboat-class vessels were still stationed around the planet, positioned in a geometric configuration apparently intended to guard all four quadrants of the globe. Two of them occupied equatorial orbits and the other two were in polar orbits, each about 32,000 kilometers above the planet.

When the *Sun Wolf* moved in for a closer look, the vessels did not respond to its approach nor to its multifrequency hails, but continued to hold formation. That's when Aiden noticed one of the gunboats fire a short-range laser pulse at what appeared to be nothing. Moments later, another gunboat did the same thing, but this time Hotah noticed a tiny bright flash in the beam's path, marking the destruction of its apparent target. After two more identical incidents, Aiden had the pilot move in for a closer look. Alvarez engaged the high-mag optical scope.

"Scan the immediate area around the planet, Lilly. See if you can figure out what these vessels are shooting at."

Aiden looked at his chrono. He'd told Woo to check in with the *Sun Wolf* the moment he arrived at the new Eta-2 Hydri Gateway. If Woo had gone to the gateway straight away, he should have been there long enough for his maser transmission to reach the *Sun Wolf* by now.

"I'm seeing something," Alvarez said. "I'll put it up on the main screen."

The scope's search algorithms had locked on to a small object dimly lit. It was roughly spherical with a coarse, light brownish surface. The scope gauged its size to be nearly 14 meters in diameter. Alvarez panned out just far enough to spot several more of the objects near the first one. All of them seemed to be moving in unison. Moving toward the planet.

"Panspermia seeds," Aiden said.

"From Shénmì?" Alvarez asked.

"Maybe," Aiden said. "But they're smaller than Shénmì seeds. And lighter in color."

Just then, as they looked on, the group of objects burst into plumes of bright red fire and vanished from sight in less than a second.

"Shit! So that's what they're firing at."

Ro, who had been watching in silence, said, "Cardew's creeps. They're probably programed to 'protect' the planet from any 'impure' life forms gaining a foothold. Not surprising."

That would suggest that Cardew had already investigated Moana, found it to be devoid of life forms, and wanted to keep it that way. At least long enough for him to inoculate the planet with his own cloneborg-friendly fungus, the one he thought Skye would deliver to him.

As Aiden pondered that scenario, Elgin Woo's voice came through the open comm. He sounded excited. "Aiden! I have arrived at the gateway. I know this transmission will take hours to reach you, depending on where you are when it gets to you. But I wanted to report at least two amazing phenomena I have encountered here upon my arrival.

"The first is that I've spotted what appear to be panspermia seeds coming through the gateway from somewhere inside the new astrocell. They look very similar to Shénmì seeds but smaller and not as darkly colored. Otherwise, they behave in the same way, moving in groups and in unison. There must be at least one other planet in this new astrocell that produces panspermia seeds and disperses them in the same way Shénmì does. These seeds have obviously made it through the gateway, which means that their dispersion is not limited to the astrocell in which they were spawned. I've always suspected that might be true for the Shénmì seeds as well.

"The other remarkable thing happened after I made several attempts to jump into the new astrocell. The jumps were based on coordinate estimations from limited mapping data. Not surprisingly, none of the attempts were successful. But while I was plotting to make another jump, a Luminous One emerged from the voidoid! Not a symbioid. No black hole. A real Luminous One, pure and simple. Like the one we encountered here with Cardew. It is now sitting next to the *Starhawk*, no more than fifty meters away. I believe it is inviting me to communicate. This is very exciting. I'm sure I'll know more by the time you get here. See you then."

The transmission ended abruptly. The crew exchanged silent glances. Woo had answered at least one question—the probable origin of the panspermia seeds being zapped by the cloneborg gunboats—but had raised a whole batch of new questions. What was up with the Luminous One? What did it want? What did it intend to do? What did Woo intend to do?

Aiden glanced at his crew. They all had the same look. *What's he up to now?* Would Elgin Woo need saving from himself? Or would Woo be saving *them*? All of them.

Aiden took a deep breath, exhaled slowly. "Time to get back on the road."

"But first," Hotah said, "we swing down and kill those gunboats. Right?"

"Right," Aiden said. "Work up a tactical scheme that requires a minimum amount of time to safely destroy all four vessels. They're positioned just far enough from the planet for our ZPD to still work. When ready, the Helm is yours."

Working his way around the spherical space above the planet, Hotah dropped out of ZPD to within 360 kilometers of each gunboat, targeted, and fired, until all four vessels had been destroyed. None of them had attempted to respond to the *Sun Wolf*'s presence in local space, and none carried heavy, long-range laser cannons. Hotah surmised that they were robotic weapons-platforms designed primarily for zapping incoming panspermia seeds, not for defense against enemy ships.

His hand poised over the tactical board, Hotah asked about the other vessels still in orbit around Moana. They included one ship-builder platform, one ore-smelting platform with attached manufacturing complex, three mining ships, and a colony-transport ship.

Aiden ordered the ship to move closer to the colony-transport in low orbit. The transport vessel looked remarkably similar to the early-model colony vessels that ARM had used to colonize Mars.

"Looks exactly like an ARM 950," Ro said.

The MC-950 was ARM's largest colony vessel. At 260 meters long, it could comfortably transport 1,500 colonists for long journeys, more for shorter trips.

"I don't recall any of those gone missing from ARM's fleet," Aiden said. "Cardew must have stolen the design plans and had his shipbuilders replicate it."

Alvarez did a long-range IR scan. "I think the ship is empty," she said, looking up from her monitor. "At least the IR scans show no signs of life in groups of any size. All nonessential systems look cold."

"Okay. Let's leave it be. Any signs of activity on the other vessels?"

The shipbuilder and manufacturing platforms were mostly robotic, unlikely to house long-term personnel. The mining vessels might have been manned, but when Alvarez scanned them, no signs of life showed up on them either.

This caravan of Cardew's infrastructure couldn't have been parked here much longer than a week or two. But where were the cloneborgs that must have come along with it? Had they shuttled down to the surface? He asked Alvarez about it.

"I doubt it," she said. "There's hardly any landmass down there. Nothing remotely large enough to colonize. Mostly ocean. All the scattered island chains taken together make up less than 1 percent of the surface area. Makes my job easy. I've scanned it all. Nothing."

"All right. Let's leave everything here as is. Pilot, set course for the gateway voidoid."

Hotah looked unhappy, his impulse to blow up more stuff thwarted. He finally sat back into a relaxed posture and dialed down his intensity. Maybe he understood the wisdom of Aiden's decision. Maybe not. Either way, Hotah had matured noticeably over the last two years. Being a part of this particular crew had given him the opportunity, but Hotah had done it mostly on his own.

As the *Sun Wolf* pulled out of orbit, Alvarez said, "The optical scope is still scanning the space around the planet. Check out what it's picking up."

The scope had locked on to another group of panspermia seeds just beginning their free-fall entry into Moana's upper atmosphere. Soon they would plunge into the planet's warm oceans, or even onto one of the tiny islands, and the miracle of life would begin anew. It was another victory for the *Sun Wolf*, for the human race, and for all life.

~ ~ ~

Even though Elgin Woo had prepared Aiden for what he would see as the *Sun Wolf* approached the gateway voidoid, Aiden was not ready for it. Woo's *Starhawk* no longer sat next to the Luminous One. The tiny, saucer-shaped craft was enveloped inside it.

"Elgin?" Aiden spoke into the comm. "We've just arrived. Are you all right? Do you copy?"

Woo didn't respond. Aiden's stomach knotted up. "Elgin?"

More silence.

Then Woo's voice finally leapt out of the comm.

"Ah! You're here." He sounded ecstatic, consumed with wonder. "This is a most extraordinary experience! I have learned so much already from the Luminous One. And there is so much more to learn."

It sounded like Elgin Woo had hit another cosmic jackpot, but Aiden was still worried about him. "Are you okay? Have you been harmed?"

"Harmed? Heavens no! I'm most definitely okay. More than okay. I've been communing with the Luminous One. It is by far the most remarkable being I have ever encountered."

"*Communing?* How?"

Woo dismissed the question. "Later for that. But let me tell you what I've learned so far."

"Um . . . Okay . . ."

That's when Woo engaged the video component of his comm. It appeared on the *Sun Wolf*'s main screen. Woo stood at the center of the *Starhawk*'s tiny control bridge, facing them. The bridge was bathed in golden-white light, the same quality of light that surrounded the *Starhawk*. Woo himself seemed to be surrounded by a cone of light brighter than the ambient light in the bridge. His eyes were wide with wonder, and his smooth-shaven head seemed to glow. He had the look of either a madman or a saint. In Elgin Woo's case, Aiden wasn't sure there was a difference anymore. The man looked as if he'd just been touched by the gods.

"Remember," Woo began, "when I told you that symbioids were unions between a protovoidoid and a primordial black hole? But instead of conjoining to become voidoids, the relationship evolved into a *disjunctive* symbiosis, where both symbionts were capable of living independently? I told you that these symbioids had some function in the cosmic scheme of things that I didn't yet fully understand. Now I understand.

"My communion with the Luminous One confirmed my hunch that symbioids are in fact *shepherds* for the primordial black holes, moving them around intergalactic space, positioning them exactly where they are needed—where *dark matter* is needed—to maintain the ever-changing structure of galaxies and galactic clusters. When a Luminous One latches on to a primordial black hole to move it around, it becomes what we've been calling a symbioid. When the primordial black hole is brought to its intended location, it disjoins from the Luminous One, and the Luminous One goes on its merry way, ready to shepherd more primordial black holes as needed.

"We know that galaxies are constantly moving in relationship to each other, and so are galactic clusters, and groups of clusters, and so on. Dark matter needs to be constantly redistributed to compensate for that, to keep these impossibly massive structures from fragmenting, to maintain the overall structural integrity of the physical universe. That's what the Luminous Ones do. They corral the primordial black holes, briefly becoming symbioids in the process, and move them to effectively rearrange the distribution of dark matter.

"But redistributing dark matter is just one of their functions, one element of the Luminous Ones' higher purpose. As the progenitors of the voidoids, they're also responsible for keeping dark energy in check, critical in maintaining the universe as we know it. We've learned from the events of last year how voidoids have been responsible for creating optimal conditions within star systems for the genesis of life, by keeping dark energy in check. And now we know that the voidoids are *born* from the Luminous Ones. So, ultimately, they are responsible for manipulating both dark energy *and* dark matter to favor life. They have truly become the guardians of life in this universe."

Woo paused to catch his breath. Aiden took the opportunity to interrupt him. "Elgin, hold on a second. In your communion with this . . . being, do you have any idea of its intentions? Will it leave the gateway open for us, for humanity, to enter this new astrocell? Or will it lock us out?"

"Oh," Woo said, as if the question was awkwardly foolish. "The Luminous Ones intend to do more than allow humanity to explore Astrocell Gamma. They are inviting us to explore the entire galaxy. And beyond! They will reveal the simple way to find new gateways, ones that interconnect millions upon millions of astrocells within our galaxy.

"Right now, the only method we have depends on me, or someone like me with the same kind of synesthesia, 'hearing' the unique song of each gateway, translating the song into Dr. Harlow's electromagnetic language, then searching all the stars in an astrocell with the HMI to find a star that matches up with the song. An incredibly slow and imprecise process. And it would have to be done over and over again, for each new astrocell, just to get a clue to where other gateway stars might be located. It would take millennia for humanity to get beyond even our tiny little corner of the galaxy. But that method is obsolete now. The Luminous Ones will show us how to identify gateway stars within *hours* of entering a new astrocell."

Aiden felt himself carried along by Woo's enthusiasm, buoyant with hope. "They'll show us? How will they do that?"

"Well, they will show *me*, at least," Woo said sheepishly, but still glowing with wonderment. "That is, if I agree to go with them into Astrocell Gamma. They are inviting me to go with them now, to allow them to transport me. To reveal the secrets of the gateways and many more wonders."

"To go with them? How?"

"I'm not sure, Aiden. But I'm about to find out."

"Elgin, you can't just—"

"I can, and will. I have gladly accepted their invitation."

"Wait, Elgin. We need to talk about this. To make preparations, contingencies for your return, for communications—"

"No time for that now, my friend. Give my regards to Skye."

In desperation, Aiden addressed the *Starhawk*'s resident AI, Woo's beloved digital companion. "Mari, can you *please* talk some sense into him?"

"I have tried," she replied, her normally serene voice edged with overtones of frustration. "But I'm afraid that 'sense' means something entirely different to Dr. Woo than it does to the rest of us."

Woo grinned even wider and held his hands out, palms out. "Please don't worry about me. I'm sure I'll be back sometime soon. Somehow. But for now, I'm off to the see the wizard!"

With that, the comm went blank. On the main screen, the crew watched on as the Luminous One—with the *Starhawk* held lovingly inside its body of pure light—moved into the gateway voidoid and vanished.

54

HD 10180 SYSTEM
Shénmì

Domain Day 365, 2218

It was the perfect day to spend their anniversary together. It didn't even matter that, technically, it was not really their *annual* anniversary. That was still four months away. But neither Aiden nor Skye knew where they would be when that date rolled around. Skye would most likely be back at Shénmì Station, hard at work on her team's next project. But Aiden? Commander of the *Sun Wolf*, still the only voidship with the zero-point drive? Considering the unsettled nature of things—even after Cardew's demise—Aiden could very well be on another mission, anywhere inside Bound Space or Astrocell Beta. Or Astrocell Gamma?

And so it was that today—which incidentally also happened to be New Year's Eve—Aiden and Skye had taken advantage of a rare moment when openings in their respective schedules had miraculously coincided. And now, after an extraordinary day among Shénmì's forests of pendulum trees and herds of docile hexalemurs, they sat together on the mossy banks of Starfly Creek, waiting for the nightly symphony of wildlife to begin.

The concert always began just after sundown with the slow, rhythmic bass notes of the croakerdiles. Just as it had done for Elgin Woo last year, sitting on the same stream bank, when he'd been stranded here alone. The croakerdiles—large, amphibious reptiles with the body of a six-legged crocodile and the head of a bullfrog—were shy and rarely seen, but by now had been positively identified as the source of the music's bass clef.

Then, as the evening light faded, the percussion section commenced. It was a blend of wood-on-wood and wood-on-hollow-drum. Woo had learned early on that these rhythmic sounds came from the pendulum trees as drum-like formations on their trunks were struck by the wooden pods at the tips of their pendulums. Their tone was similar to the dholak drum heard in South Asian folk music, and their pulse was the same tempo as the croakerdiles, but on the upbeats.

Skye reached over to hold Aiden's hand and said, "This really has been a perfect day. Watching that beanstalk rise up into space to disseminate its seeds was amazing."

No one could predict when one of Shénmì's astounding beanstalks—as Woo had called them—would emerge from its equatorial bed to shoot up with blinding speed into the vacuum of space, 36,000 kilometers above the planet, where its terminal pod would split open to release its panspermia seeds. But, as if the planet had known that Aiden and Skye would be on hand to witness it, the phenomenon occurred less than a kilometer away as they stood on a bluff overlooking the same spot where Woo had originally landed inside one of the spent pods.

Aiden gently squeezed her hand and faced her. Cool breezes from the nearby ocean tossed her blonde hair into haphazard styles that always looked natural on her. He said, "Truly amazing, yes."

Skye squeezed his hand back and said, "Mother Shénmì continues her work, spreading natural life throughout this astrocell. And probably beyond."

"Are you going to let her do her job," Aiden asked, "or give her a helping hand with your new fungal variant?"

"For now, only the planets that were sterilized will be seeded with Variant B. Later on, we'll assess how much help Mother Shénmì needs for other planets out there."

Skye had already organized a plan to seed the sterilized planets with her fungal Variant B. So far, a total of seven habitable planets had been found ravaged by gamma-ray bursts from Cardew's grasers. She had proposed using the *Sun Wolf* to accomplish the task for obvious reasons. At 92 percent light speed, no other ship could do the job in a reasonable amount of time. Aiden had enthusiastically embraced the idea and was waiting only for approval from the Admiralty. Unless a higher-priority mission came up in the meantime, he hoped to embark on that quest next week. And he hoped Skye would accompany him.

Aiden fell silent. As the stars were coming out overhead, dotting the deep-indigo sky, the chirpets began to add their part to the symphony. Woo had found that the chirpets were similar to crickets on Earth and probably occupied a similar niche here on Shénmì. Their chirping sound was similar, too, but lower in pitch and more powerful. They started up tentatively, arrhythmic at first, but once they got going, they synchronized their sounds with musical precision.

Aiden and Skye looked at each other and smiled. "There must be hundreds of thousands of them in the ferns all along the stream banks."

The chirpets' music began to blend into a background drone, like a giant sitar, but a drone that varied in pitch—slowly and sensuously—to augment the bass notes and percussion. It was beautiful and absolutely hypnotizing.

Skye looked up at the stars and said, "I can't help wondering where Elgin is right now, and when he'll come back."

No one had heard from Woo since he'd scooted off into the new astrocell more than two weeks ago, in the company of one of his mysterious Luminous Ones. And, like the last time he disappeared on his quest to discover Astrocell Beta, he'd made no provisions for communicating with the rest of humanity. No Holtzman buoy. Not even maser transmissions. But that was Elgin Woo for you.

"I believe he'll come back," Aiden said. "Eventually. If what he said was true, he's out there discovering how to locate a new gateway star in any astrocell. How to open up the entire galaxy for voidjumping. No one knows more than Elgin how important that knowledge is for humanity. I have no doubt that he'll want to deliver it to us."

Assuming he's still alive, or even still in this dimension of reality. But Aiden didn't say that, didn't want to dampen the mood. Instead, he asked about Jo and the infant Rene.

"They're still at Shénmì Station and both doing quite well," Skye said. "Rene is growing like a weed, getting stronger every day. Jo is opening up, becoming more social. She's *happy*, in a way you rarely see in 'normal' people. Everyone on the station loves them both and is fiercely protective of them. It looks like she'll be able to legally adopt Rene as her own son. The Slovakian relatives of the Rodina Mining Collective have given her their blessing. They were just happy to get the Collective's mining ship back in one piece."

They were also happy to receive half of the white diamonds Alvarez had collected on Sirota, to help them recover the losses their whole community had suffered at the hands of Cardew's soldiers on that planet. The other half was going to medical research foundations to fund work on countering any further weaponized virus attacks of the kind Cardew had unleashed.

"The DSI, of course," Skye was saying, "wants to vet Jo. Those suspicious bastards see a spy in everyone they look at. And Jo, being part cloneborg, makes her a 'person of interest' to them. She's also a potential source of knowledge about everything cloneborg. But, by international law, Shénmì Station is a sovereign entity, and as the director of the station, I'm technically its 'head of state.' There's no way Jo can be moved from Shénmì Station against her will, and there's no way in hell that I'd allow it."

Aiden took note of how protective Skye herself had become, and marveled at the way she had separated her horrific experience with a real cloneborg from her feelings for Jo.

"Do you know what she told me?" Skye said. "Jo believes that there are more 'mutant' cloneborgs like her. She thinks the mutation that kept her human isn't as rare as they thought, that others like her have escaped from the crèches and have started a small colony of their own. Somewhere they've kept highly secret."

"How does she know that?" Aiden asked. "It sounds mythical, a product of wishful thinking."

Sky shook her head. "I don't think so. Jo is extremely intelligent and, if anything, logical to a fault. I don't believe wishful thinking plays any part in her thought processes. But I see your point. I have no idea how she knows about this."

"If it is true," Aiden said, "a rebel group of human cloneborgs would be incredibly valuable to us as allies in any future conflict with the cloneborg forces still remaining out here. Cardew may be dead, but his soldiers are still out there. Still with unknown resources."

It was true, a realization that would keep the Alliance on its toes indefinitely. The captured Omicron-3 unit had been thoroughly interrogated, but the results were disappointing, at least in terms of locating the remaining cloneborg forces and their crèches. After doing the math, it was now very likely that a sizeable portion of Cardew's fleet of warships hadn't been accounted for, along with other elements of his technological and industrial infrastructure. Fortunately, none of it had passed into Astrocell Gamma. They knew that for sure. So all of it still had to be somewhere inside Astrocell Beta. Or still hidden inside Bound Space.

Then there was the question of leadership. The Alliance, and Aiden himself, had been too quick to assume that, without Cardew in the driver's seat, the rest of his cloneborg empire would roll over dead. But if Cardew's whole-brain emulation had been completed successfully, the possibility that his twin—Cardew Version 2—would emerge at some point to take over the reins was a very real one. And in the meantime, as Cardew himself had implied, new leaders among his minions could easily arise. Not all of his cloneborg creations were created to be subservient automatons. A few highly intelligent leaders and innovators had been thrown into the mix.

And as long as Elgin Woo was missing in action, the Alliance would remain without the decisive advantage of the zero-point drive installed into their ships. Before his hasty departure, Woo hadn't yet decided to allow his game-changing technology into the public domain. Nor had he provided his personal bio-key, the metaphorical car key required to turn on any ZPD engine. If there was a cloneborg uprising before then, the conflict would be fought on a level playing field. So, it wasn't over yet, if it ever would be.

Aiden pushed these darker thoughts aside as the music of rhythm continued to build, and night singers joined the chorus to add their melodies to concert. It was as if they had been waiting for the spirit of the rhythmic dance to move them, to inspire them to sing along with it, to add even deeper layers to it. Their voices were high, silvery, in the soprano range. Skye's team of biologists had learned that the songs came from a unique kind of night bird, ephemeral nocturnal creatures that never showed themselves in the light of day. Now, in the darkening night, their many voices blended in synchronicity, improvising melodies rich with harmony and minor-key emotion, evoking profound mystery.

While pulling on his thermo-sweater to ward off the damp chill rising from the creek bed, the soreness in his upper arm reminded Aiden of the painful vaccination he'd received yesterday. The one to combat the weaponized virus Cardew had launched upon the human race. The vaccine that had been developed with unprecedented swiftness from Jo's blood sample. Both a vaccine and a cure, it would have never existed without her. It could truthfully be said that Jo—a mutant from a race of beings whose mission was to destroy the human race—had, in fact, saved the human race from near extinction.

Still, the death toll had been appalling, especially on Earth, in the many millions. The sad part of it was that many of those millions had died by their own choice, by refusing the proven protection the vaccine would have given them. Misunderstanding and fear of vaccines were as old as vaccines themselves and had never died out. And in this case, the paranoia had been fanned into an out-of-control conflagration by Cardew's masterful program of disinformation.

It was a brilliant strategy, in the sickest sense—introduce an extremely virulent virus with no known immunities, then convince the population that it was a hoax and that any attempt by the medical community to prevent its spread was a secret plot to kill them and their children. Brilliant, but certainly not original. Cardew had learned from the best that history could offer.

On the upside, disinformation campaigns like Cardew's would now be virtually impossible to launch. The destruction of the *Conquest*'s Omicron-3 unit that Cardew inhabited had weakened the hold his other corrupted Omicrons had over the OverNet. That made it easier for Hutton and his AI allies in the OverNet to seek out and purge the remaining corrupted units from its network. The credibility of the OverNet had returned, this time with added safeguards against future attempts to pervert it.

"Look, Aiden," Skye said, mercifully distracting him from his cynical musings. "The light show is starting."

And so it was. The starflies were out in force tonight. Like the fabled firefly phenomena of Southeast Asia, way back before the Die Back, the air above the creek bed had filled with massive congregations of starflies. They began to blink on and off in unison, creating bewildering displays of light that stretched for miles along the stream banks. Aiden and Skye watched on as the starflies gradually began to synchronize their flashing blue-white lanterns. Thousands upon thousands of them coalesced into a belt of light at least three meters wide, hovering above the creek, winding up and down its banks as far as the eye could see. Flashing off and on in perfectly synchronized precision, in perfect time with the pulsating symphony.

Then the starflies began to dance. The single cohesive band of blue light rose and fell, dipped and swayed, rolled and reveled in rhythm. Moving with the music like a dancer interpreting the melody and rhythm in a language of movement and time.

It made Aiden want to get up and dance along with it. He stood and held out his hand to Skye. "May I have this dance, madam?"

Skye was already rising to her feet and swaying with the irrepressible rhythm and beauty of the music. They held hands and danced together like crazy people. Happy crazy. In sync with each other. In sync with Shénmì.

Above them, the stars popped out even brighter, as if joining in the joyous dance. As Aiden and Skye looked up at those infinite points of light, at all the light within darkness, they knew beyond doubt that Elgin Woo had been right all along—the universe *was* alive. Just waiting for them—for all humankind—to enter its cosmic biosphere. To walk through its forest of stars with open hands. To join the family of life.

ACKNOWLEDGEMENTS

MUCH thanks to the following people for their support and assistance in bringing this novel into print: editors Scott Pearson and Sara Kelly for their thoughtful and thorough editing; Sandi Goodman for her invaluable editorial input; Rafael Andres for his stunning cover graphics; Euan Monaghan for his elegant book design; marketing specialist Roxanne Hiatt for her skillful work in promoting the whole series; Jeffrey Brandenburg for his wise advice from the very start; Bob Page and Barbara Ware for their friendship and their quiet, creative space called Quail Crossing where much of this writing was done; Alicia Grefenson for her guiding light along my convoluted path homeward; and, as always, Ann Jeffrey for her unconditional support and life-long partnership of the heart.

Research for this book included the use of the following resources:

—The NASA Exoplanet Archive, which is operated by the California Institute of Technology, under contract with the National Aeronautics and Space Administration.
—NASA Exoplanet Exploration, managed by the Exoplanet Exploration Program and the Jet Propulsion Laboratory for NASA's Astrophysics Division.
—SIMBAD, the world reference database for the identification of astronomical objects, hosted by the Strasbourg Astronomical Data Center.
—The Universe Guide at www.universeguide.com

—Sol Station at www.solstation.com
—The Habitable Zone Calculator, from the Virtual Planetary Laboratory, University of Washington, at http://depts.washington.edu/naivpl
—The Exoplanet Catalogue by ExoKyoto at www.exoplanetkyoto.org
—Open Exoplanet Catalogue, an open source database of all discovered extrasolar planets at www.openexoplanetcatalogue.com

ABOUT THE AUTHOR

DAVID C. Jeffrey was born in 1947 in Riverside, California and currently lives in the San Francisco Bay Area. He studied microbiology as a graduate student at the University of California, Santa Cruz, conducted field research in Costa Rica on a grant from the National Science Foundation, and pursued related research in Alaska and Yukon. He has published in several scientific journals, worked as a biology instructor, a commercial microbiologist, and as a cardiology nurse for twenty-five years in acute care settings. In addition to writing science fiction, he is a bass player and performing jazz musician. *The Light Within Darkness* is the third book in Mr. Jeffrey's *Space Unbound* series.

Made in United States
Troutdale, OR
08/20/2025

33846194R00246